FOR JUAN CARLOS,
ENJOY YOUR TRIP TO KARAWALA.
KEEP YER HOOKS SHARP

PIRATE

FINDING
KARAWALA

PIRATE LANFORD

D1567991

This is a novel – a work of fiction. It is entirely the product of the imagination of the author. Any similarities to the names of actual people and places are entirely coincidental and not related in any way to the real world. If you think you are in this book, then your ego has spun completely out of control.

ISBN 978-0-9856359-1-6

Printed in the U.S.A.

Sharp Hook Press
P. O. Box 151244
Arlington, TX 76015

For Sheryl

The Real Byrdie

And for Glenda, my editor, who thinks it's profound.

The Army sent me to Karawala during World War Two. My duty was coast watch, looking for enemy ships and submarines. When they told me where I was going, I thought I was being punished. I thought it was an ungodly horrible assignment for an officer.

But I took some fishing tackle and a shotgun, and it didn't take long to fall in love with it. The fishing was like nothing you have ever imagined, and I haven't seen anything like it since. There is something else there. You should find it.

Go to Bluefields. Someone there can take you to Karawala.

Col. Silas Johnson, in his last letter to his grandson, McBeth Johnson

BLUEFIELDS

Chapter One

Kum

March, 1972

"You looking Karawala?"

I looked up and saw two black men on the walk. One was tall, lank and sinewy, with a nasty scar across his face. The other was short, but massive.

"Yes, I am," I answered and stood.

They came cautiously up the steps to the hotel veranda, as if it might be a forbidden place. I could not read anything but nervousness on their faces. By answering my call and making contact, they seemed to be stepping into unfamiliar territory, as had I.

"My name is McBeth Johnson," I said, extending my hand. The tall one was Lyman; the heavy one Hendry. Both had huge, strong hands, and both shook mine gently, as if they were embarrassed by the contact.

We sat down and began to talk. They could not imagine that anyone, let alone an American on his own, would want to hazard the trip to Karawala. In Caribbean English, they informed me that Lyman had a boat with a motor and Hendry knew the way to Karawala. If I was set on going, they would take me.

"Why Karawala?" Hendry asked.

"I hear the fishing is good."

"Got fish here. Got Corn Island. Karawala got nothing."

"Maybe, but that's why I came, and that's where I'm going."

We talked about price and how long did it take and how long would we stay and what had I seen in Bluefields, and all the while they seemed to be looking over their shoulders.

"You guys look like you're expecting trouble. What's up?"

"They say some fellas on Managua side making revolution. They say plenty Guardia coming here today. Any place have Guardia have trouble."

It was obvious that they wanted to be off the streets when the Guardia arrived. I didn't know enough to be worried.

"Could leave off now, you know."

"No, Hendry. If it takes a full day to get there, we'd be on the water all night. I'd rather wait until the morning."

They were reluctant, but agreed.

I gave them some money to buy fuel and supplies and agreed to meet them before sunrise at the market wharf. I watched them walk off with my money, knowing I might not see them again, and if I did, I would be getting into their boat in the dark of night. Would I see the sun come up?

"So let's go fishing," I muttered.

My destination was a little Indian village about eighty miles north. I was going through a part of the map that was white and marked "Unexplored". I had nothing but an old letter and an older map that showed the location of Karawala. Now I had guides.

It had taken three days to find Hendry and Lyman – three days of visiting the wharf, the shops and the bars of a decaying, rusting seaport that smelled of salt, fuel spills and old fish. I was ready to give up and go home when they appeared.

One shot from a large caliber pistol in the enclosed space of a hotel is enough to cause permanent tinnitus or burst eardrums. Even through walls, the first shot was loud enough that I was on my feet before I was fully awake. Someone, perhaps a soldier, had fired a gun at something, or someone, inside the hotel. I heard shots outside, near and far.

My only thought was to get the hell out of that hotel. I had to get out and get to the wharf and hope to find Hendry and Lyman. I pushed my saddlebags and rod tube out the window, dove out after them and took off full speed down a muddy alley toward the street. I hadn't gone twenty feet when I heard the door to my room come crashing down. I ran as fast as my load would allow, but as I rounded the corner onto Avenida Comercial, I saw that I was not escaping. They were behind me and ahead of me. No choice. I ran.

I heard shouting behind me, people yelling at each other, and then I heard screams of terror. A bullet slammed into the building next to me an instant before I heard the shot. It shattered concrete and mortar, and something stung my cheek. Another shot, and the screaming stopped. People were running for cover everywhere in random confusion. A few lay twisted on the ground. Who were they shooting at, and why?

"Mr. Bet?"

The voice was almost in my ear. Someone grabbed my arm, and I swung around with fists clenched. It was Hendry, and I just missed his jaw. I saw the white of his teeth flash and hoped it was a smile.

He didn't have time for a greeting. He pushed me violently to the edge of the wharf, picked me up and dropped me into the dori. In the next instant, he was in the bow, pushing us away from the dock. Lyman gunned the engine, and we were off.

I had to laugh. It was a dugout canoe with an ancient twenty horse Johnson clamped to its transom. We were not roaring off into the concealing darkness of the bay. We were putt-putting away from the dock so slowly I was sure we would have bullets in our backs before we were out of sight.

I heard a few stray bullets whispering overhead, then nothing from the town. I looked ahead, into the black of a moonless night. I could hardly see Hendry in the bow, just ten feet away. Those on shore, the ones with the guns, could not have seen us.

As much as I wanted to ask questions, talk was impossible. The old outboard was too noisy. Lyman couldn't listen, and Hendry sat hunched over in the bow. We slipped through the darkness with our thoughts, our relief, and the fear of pursuit.

Dead ahead, perhaps on the far side of the bay, I could see

the faint glow of one light. It seemed that it was our first mark. Our wake glowed faintly from bioluminescence, giving a ghostly tail. Looking up, I could see a few stars between the scuds. Looking down, I saw nothing. My heart and breathing slowly returned to normal.

It was so calm and dark that it felt as if we were suspended in space. I couldn't find the horizon. The force of gravity was the only orientation there was, and it wasn't enough. The onset of vertigo must have come to each of us at the same time. It was a dizzy, floating sensation. Almost in unison, we shifted our weight and moved a hand to the gunnel. The boat rocked with the movement and the feeling vanished.

I became aware again of the stinging in my cheek. It was beginning to throb. I touched the place with my finger and felt something sharp. I felt it on my fingertips and I felt it scrape my cheekbone. It was a long, thin sliver of something sharp. I tried to grasp it to pull it out. I had the stuff of murder inside me, and I couldn't get it out. My fingers kept slipping on the blood. I put my hand in the water to wash it away, and when I tried to wash the blood off my face, I felt the sliver rub against bone.

By feel, I found the tweezers in the first-aid kit in my saddlebags. I could grasp it with the tweezers, but with the first tug, I found that one edge of the thing was sharp and jagged. It wasn't coming out without a fight. My only choice was to get as good a hold on it as I could and rip it out. The increased bleeding might help disinfect it. Out it came, with a wincing acknowledgement of an intense sensation. I dropped it into my shirt pocket. I would have to wait until the sun came up to see what it was.

I opened a bottle of Mercurochrome, knowing I wasn't going to like what came next. The hole had to be disinfected, all the way to the bone, and going back to Bluefields to see a doctor was not an option. I pushed the glass applicator into the wound until it bottomed out against the bone, pulled it out, dipped it into the tincture and applied it again. It stung, but the stinging was better than the alternative.

As the third application found the bone, the boat bounced over something. It might have been a wake or a little log, but it was just enough to make me snap the little glass applicator off in my cheek. I laughed again. Not laughing meant frustration or anger or both, and I didn't need it.

The glass rod was harder to get out than the sliver. I had to push the tweezers up into the wound, get hold of the glass and try to ease it out. The tweezers kept slipping off the glass, and my fingers slipped in the blood on the tweezers. Every time I got it started, the sharp end dug into flesh, and I had to push it back in and start over. I was about to give up when the damn thing fell out.

*

The rising sun revealed a world so vastly different from ours it might as well have been a different planet. The clouds that had darkened the night were gone; the dawn poured gold into the tops of the trees. We turned into the creek that runs north to Pearl Lagoon, and the jungle closed in on us. The trees and vines rose straight up from the water's edge like the walls of a green canyon. In places it closed over the creek like a tunnel. And it seethed with life.

I had the feeling that if I stepped into it, I could be assimilated, or devoured, with total indifference. Contempt of nature, or even disinterest in it, could be a fatal attitude here. My life is no more significant than that of a gnat. If I am not important, what is?

The bow struck an unseen log, and Lyman killed the engine. Hendry turned to look. Lyman shrugged his shoulders and pulled the lower unit out of the water to inspect it, hoping not to put the paddles to use.

In this brief moment of silence, I felt an inherent sense of place. I felt strength in the connection, and I laughed for the sheer joy of being. I could hear the calls of birds and the movements of life. I could also hear the silence behind it. We who live in the civilized world are accustomed to a background roar that never goes away. It is the pounding of our machinery in the chest of the city, and it is the incessant blood of traffic rushing through the streets.

Here the silence never goes away. It is the foundation of all sound. One can hear into the jungle through the silence much farther than one can see into it through the trees.

The harbor of civilization no longer existed for me, and I felt changed. As quickly and as simply as the snap of a twig, I had changed.

When Hendry turned to look at Lyman, his gaze fell on me, and there was an honest look of surprise on his face. "What happen to you?"

I looked down. There was blood all over my shirt, and my face was caked with dried blood. I reached into my shirt pocket and held up the little sliver. "This," I said. "On my way to the wharf."

It was a half-inch piece of copper shrapnel from a bullet. I dropped it back in my pocket, dipped my hand in the water and began washing blood away.

"What was that about?" I asked. "Who was doing the shooting, and why?"

"That the Guardia. You lucky fella, you know."

It always amazes me when people call bad luck good.

"Who were they shooting at?"

"Must be they think Sandinistas in Bluefields. Maybe Sandinistas shoot back."

"Why did you wait for me? You could have been shot."

"Got job."

*

We slid along on glassy water through an emerald world. My

6

fascination never dimmed. Hendry and Lyman pointed out the things they saw, most of which I would not have seen otherwise. They were enjoying their role as tour guides.

Too soon we were out of the creek and into Pearl Lagoon. The jungle fell away and we were out in open, choppy, brown water. Suddenly I felt stiff and cramped. There was no way to stand and stretch; an attempt would surely capsize us. So I sat, with the shores on the horizon, thankful for the salt spray that relieved the blistering heat of the sun.

At the first sign of feeding fish, I asked Lyman to stop and let me catch a few. He laughed, shook his head and wagged his finger. "Not if you want reach Karawala."
I couldn't stand it. We had all day to get to Karawala. Even if we spent half our time fishing, we should make it before dark. Yelling over the outboard, I said as much.

Lyman's scarred eye rolled back in its socket and he and Hendry laughed. There was something I didn't know about this trip, and they weren't telling. Something lay ahead, I guessed, that was going to slow us down or bring us to a halt.

With my legs half folded under the thwart, I watched Pearl Lagoon slip by. Occasionally a tarpon rolled its back out of the water, and I got excited again. Some of them were huge, but my guides could not be deterred. We held our course.

At about noon, Hendry pointed ahead. "Toplock. You soon see tapom." It wasn't the same word, but I knew it must be the same fish. We had been seeing tarpon all along the way. In the distance, a few miles ahead, I could see what appeared to be the end of the lagoon.

As we got closer, I could see the mouth of a river feeding the lagoon. It was the Kurinwas, and it fed more than the lagoon. At the mouth and up the river as far as I could see were the backs of tarpon. There were thousands of them - some as small as twenty pounds, some pushing hard at three hundred. It was a thrilling sight.

No one will believe this, I thought. No one will believe I saw

7

even half this many tarpon, let alone tarpon of this size. I watched the explosions they made as they fed, and I heard their music as they swam. I gave no thought to catching one, but sat and watched as we motored through.

Not far into the Kurinwas, another mouth opened to the north, and we took it, into Laguna Top Lock. We soon crossed the small lagoon and arrived at the northern shore, but there was no land there. The lagoon became a swamp, and we were heading right into it.

The water was different here. Out in open water, it had been brown and opaque with the silt stirred up by the waves. Here, under the trees, it was dark and clear. We were in a mangrove forest, where aerial roots hang from the branches and prop roots spread out from the trunk, forming an impenetrable barrier for anything but snakes. Tannic acid leached from the roots to give the water the color of tea. It was blackwater.

Our passage was easy to see once we were under the canopy. There was a channel deep enough that trees did not grow in it. We motored slowly through this eerie place. Though the tops of the trees stirred with the breeze, the air and water below were still. There was no understory. There were only the tall, sleek trunks of the red mangroves and the tangle of roots. And there were hoards of mosquitoes. Other than a kingfisher, I saw no other wildlife.

We soon came to higher ground and left the mangroves behind. We were in a creek, but how wide and deep I could not tell. At times it seemed we were in a tunnel of vegetation. Hyacinths, lotus and water cabbage concealed the water. Vines, branches and leaves concealed the sky. We pulled and paddled for long stretches, using the motor only occasionally to hurry across what little unclogged water there was. This was why they wouldn't stop. We had not far to go, but would be a long time getting there.

Unlike the mangrove swamp, we were now surrounded by wildlife, some of which hurried to the sounds we made to get a look at us. A troupe of white-faced monkeys came to scold us for invading their territory. Only partially visible, they screamed and shook the branches.

Hendry and Lyman were doing all the work. I sat entranced, not caring whether we moved on or sat where we were forever. Never had I imagined such an abundance of life. The predominant color is green, but there is a profusion of life concealed by it. It was moving, as if I was hallucinating. I did not see it at first, and when I did, I thought my eyes were playing tricks on me. I tried to stop it. I shut my eyes and shook my head, but when I looked again, it still moved.

I tried to look closer, but I could not see exactly what was moving. It just did, and it was entirely unsettling. It was an image of life on life so perfectly concealed it could parade before my very eyes unseen. And so it did, to my profound amazement.

I was shaken out of my trance by Hendry's startled yell as he fell backward, out of the boat, into the hyacinths and into the water, grasping a large, heavy-bodied snake with both hands. His eyes showed terror, and as he went under, I saw the white of the snake's open mouth as it struck home at Hendry's thick wrist. Thinking it was a branch, he had grasped it to pull us along.

The mat of plants on the water quickly swallowed the splash. We looked, but there was no trace of Hendry and the snake. "His panic might drown him," I said. Lyman was nearly panicked himself. "But the worst the snake can do is scratch his wrist." I hadn't seen the snake too well, but I knew there were no fangs in its mouth. If Hendry could turn loose, the snake would swim to the surface and escape the monster that had yanked him from his tree.

Lyman looked at me as if I was crazy. "He dead!" Was all he could say. "He dead!" He was up on his feet, holding on to the gunnels, trying to get to the bow, where he might reach his friend. He was more likely to turn the boat over than to save anyone.

"Lyman! Sit down!"

9

But he kept coming. "He dead!"

I didn't know whether to go in after Hendry or try to keep Lyman from dumping us. If we lost the motor, we would be in deep trouble. I decided that getting Hendry out was the most immediate problem, and was poised for a jump when Hendry's hand shot up out of the water, followed by his gasping face, still lit up with terror, hyacinths and water cabbage draped over his head.

I couldn't see the snake. I reached out for Hendry's hand. He took mine and jerked me right out of the boat. Now we were both tangled up in vegetation in water over our heads, and Lyman was still going wild in the boat.

In his panic, Hendry latched on to the first thing he could reach that was above water. I was it. His weight pushed me under, without so much as a breath of air in my lungs, and his grip was far too strong for me to escape. My only chance was to pull him under and hope he would let go and swim for the surface.

The vegetation closed over us as I pulled him down. There was no light down there, and with my chest in spasms, I knew that if Hendry didn't break my neck or drown me, some unknown monster would rise up out of this black jungle river and have me for lunch. I could become so entangled in the vegetation that I couldn't reach the surface. If this was the end, the only thing anyone would ever know is that I never returned. Lyman would see a few bubbles, and I would be gone.

But Hendry let go and we both broke the surface gasping for air. I got behind him and pushed him to the boat. The energy of his panic spent, he hung to the side, breathing heavily. I tried to pull myself into the boat, but I was too tangled. I hung on to the boat and began cutting Hendry loose, then myself. Lyman held Hendry at the shoulders, pulling him against the boat. His fear gone, he said, "You got to stop playin wit dem snakes, Hendry."

*

Hendry and Lyman didn't talk much - not to each other or to me. When I asked questions, I got simple, brief answers, but never an elaboration. Never did they paint pictures for me that I could see their world in the same colors as they. Never did they play music that I could know their harmony.

What they said was what they needed each other to know. There were brief exchanges, sometimes not requiring an answer or acknowledgement. They had to do with the sphere we moved in and whatever reached our senses. It was as if nothing else existed. There was this place and this moment and nothing else to complicate things.

I began to feel comfortable with it. We were going to Karawala, but it wasn't part of here and now, and so had no importance, no urgency, no place in our thoughts. It would not matter until we got there. It would not even exist until we got there. The only thing that existed was here and now, and part of it was constantly disappearing as something else appeared. And if nothing else existed, there was nothing else to talk about.

Commanding all attention and in brilliant focus was the flood of input from the senses, insisting that awareness was the only key to survival.

I could hope that a man's mind might mirror his environment, and that in this clean air and clear silence, the mind could be equally clear. If it could be for them, then it could be for me. Thought is impertinent; the absence of thought is pure being.

The going got tougher the deeper we went. The bush closed in around us and made us hack and cut our way through thorny vines and branches and ants that rained on us when we touched a tree and hornets that drove us into the water. There were great caiman that came much too close for comfort, and there were heavy-bodied, yellow-chinned fer-de-lance snakes that stood their ground and dared us to come within reach of their fangs and poison.

And there was the heat. The humidity hovered oppressively at one hundred percent; the afternoon heat and the exertion of movement burned as if we were in a steam oven. Our clothes were plastered to our bodies and sweat dripped from everything.

Hell couldn't be more miserable. I made a mental note to stay out of the bush in the heat of the day. But there were no complaints. Each inconvenience was dealt with as it arose, sometimes with curses and sometimes with comic relief, but there could be no resentment from uninvited pilgrims.

I was both uninitiated and vulnerable. I knew that this place would be no camp-out on a fishing trip. A night here would be a confrontation of the primeval both within and without, and though my guides were in their place, their vulnerability was equal to mine. This was no place to spend the night.

There were no stops to rest. Foot by foot we pulled and pushed and hacked our way along. As we inched along, I felt wholeness, and it occurred to me that the more densely packed humanity becomes, the more diluted the wholeness feels, until it disappears altogether at the top of the steel and glass.

The dense trees gave way to grasses over our heads. I turned to look where we'd been and saw a wall of forest behind us. Ahead, I saw nothing but grass. It grew from the clay walls of a canal just barely wide enough for our boat.

"No one pass here of late." Lyman said.

Hendry was busy in the bow fending off the cutting blades of grass and clearing our way. "Not of late." He repeated. "Watch for the shrimps, them," he said as he flipped a large freshwater prawn into the boat.

There were fist-sized holes at the water line, and in the holes I could see the antennae, and sometimes the eyes, of the oddest looking crustaceans I have ever seen. They were larger than crawdads, smaller than lobsters, and long, thin and delicate. Hendry and Lyman stuck their hands into each hole, hoping to catch its inhabitant before it jerked itself out of reach. I had greater respect for my hands and much less confidence in the occupants of the holes. I sat and watched.

It was obvious that we were in a canal. It was a long, straight ditch that left the forest and crossed what seemed to be a savannah.

"Where are we?" I asked.

"In the canal." Lyman answered. "Soon reach the river." He was poling the boat along with his paddle. We were making good time.

"Who dug the canal?" I asked.

"The Indians," he answered. "The missionary make them dig it. He make them come from all about and dig with shovels and buckets until the dori go from Top Lock to the river at low tide."

Where we were, the cut was about eight feet deep to the water. We had gone about a mile in it.

"How long is it?" I asked.

"Two, maybe three miles. Can't tell."

"This missionary still around?" I asked.

"Nah. He gone long time. Maybe twenty years."

I wondered about what kind of man would have come so deep into the unexplored to save souls and dig canals.

"How long did it take?"

Hendry and Lyman looked at each other. "More'n a year, I guess," Lyman said. "I wasn't here."

"Me neither," Hendry said.

There was a sizeable pile of prawns in the bottom of the boat when we broke out of the canal into the Rio Grande de Matagalpa. The sun had less than an hour to go to the horizon. It had taken the better part of the afternoon to go just a few miles. But we were home free now. There was nothing but open river between us and Karawala.

Looking at the prawns, it occurred to me that we had taken no food or water with us when we left Bluefields, yet we had not gone for one moment without food and drink. We had eaten when hungry and drank when thirsty without having to do more than reach out and pick something.

And there, crawling around in the bottom of the boat, were a few dozen of what looked to be the makings of a delectable dinner. I reached down and picked one up. Two hard flicks of its tail freed it from my grasp, but it lost a claw in the process.

The shell was soft; almost paper thin. I rinsed it off in the river and took a bite. It was delicious. I could imagine sitting down with some butter and garlic, a bottle of wine and a comely companion, all in the midst of tropical flowers and brightly colored birds.

We passed a village and the banks were lined with brown-skinned children cheering and waving. We waved back, but did not slow down.

"Kara," Lyman said. I was becoming accustomed to his brevity. I filed it away, along with the picture, assuming it was the name of the village.

Just beyond the village, the river narrowed and doubled back on itself to the west. The width at the bend was two hundred yards or so. At the next bend, where it turned back to the east, it widened out to more than a mile, and with each bend, there was a new landscape with its own flora and fauna. We were winding in and out of different soil types and chemistries, each one the parent of a different world. Here along this strip of land was the greatest diversity of life on earth. One lifetime could not be enough to explore it all.

We turned into the Rio Karawala and the temperature dropped as if we'd crossed a line into an air-conditioned room. There was a visible line where the deep green of the Karawala met the lighter green of the Rio Grande.

The big river was salty, mixed by the tides with warm water from the sea. I dipped my hand into the Karawala. It was cool. I tasted. It was sweet; runoff from rain, I guessed.

The cool air felt clean and fresh. The water was so perfectly still it was like a mirror, reflecting the trees and the darkening sky. The Karawala is not a wide river. But for its depth, it might have been called a creek. I guessed it was seventy-five feet at the widest points.

The trees were close by on both sides and laden with flowers of all descriptions. In places the air was heavy with their perfume. Vines grew up the trunks of the trees; orchids and bromeliads clung to the branches, and all of them stretched out toward the river to catch the light where the canopy broke. The trees, too, bore flowers high up where the leaves touched the sky.

Fishing bats flew alongside us, and now and then one did a little flip and came up with a minnow in its feet. There were skimmers, too, flying along with their beaks just barely breaking the surface, leaving a perfect little vee of a wake behind them.

KARAWALA

Chapter Two

Wal

They say that long ago, when the people first came to this coast to find a new home, they were looking for a plant we call kara, like agave. They used it as a sweetener, a fermented drink, medicine, needles and thread and fiber for clothes. When they found it, they called the place Kara. It's the village up the river past Sani Warban.

Then they found another place with kara. Wala is the Miskito word for other, or second. Karawala is the other Kara, or the second Kara.

I have never seen kara. No one here has ever seen kara. They used the last of it long ago.

As told by Eddie Wilson

The sound of the outboard announced our coming long before we arrived. We rounded a bend and there was the Karawala wharf, rickety and weathered. The planks jutted this way and that, showing the effects of neglect and age. Every square inch of it supported children – brown-skinned, cheering children. They crowded onto the dock and spilled out onto the turf behind. Every face was bright and happy and excited.

Behind them stood adults, watching our progress and waiting to give the command that would scatter children like a school of minnows fleeing the sudden appearance of a predator. As Hendry leaned from the bow and laid his hand on the dock, it was said, and in a flash they were gone, and the dock was empty.

It was comic to me. I laughed out loud as gleefully as the children, and their laughter increased. Just as suddenly it was gone when the man I took to be a leader took the first step. He and five or six other men came to the dock to meet us with hands outstretched and smiles on their faces.

The handshakes were weak and some of the smiles tentative. "Good night," said the first. "I am Leopoldo Palmiston. Glad to make your acquaintance." He spoke carefully and seemed genuinely pleased to see us.

His salutation was a bit odd, I thought. It was not night, and we were saying hello.

"I'm McBeth Johnson," I said. I hardened my hand and tightened my grip, but he did not respond.

To each one I spoke my name very clearly and with enough volume that it could not be mistaken. Leopoldo and a black man named Eddie Wilson were the only ones in the greeting party to impress me.

Eddie was absolutely bashful. When I introduced myself, he averted his eyes and his hand was completely limp. All he said was, "Eddie Wilson."

But there was something about him that made me think he was just the opposite of what he appeared. In spite of what I saw, I could tell he was a man who could handle himself very well, and knew so. Here I saw one thing and faced another.

We left the wharf. As we walked the first few steps, I realized that it had suddenly become night. The sun went down, there was a brief sunset, and then it was night, almost as if someone had flipped a switch. A newly waxing moon shone from the west enough to flood the landscape with a light that was easily bright enough to walk by. Only in the shadows could I not see clearly. Without one watt of electricity, I could see.

The children fell in behind us. As we walked, Leopoldo asked, "How was the pass?"

"The passage? Aside from a little trouble at the start, it was fine. Very fine. As a matter of fact, it was wonderful."

"Where you going?" he asked. Leopoldo was very short - not over five feet tall - and every time he asked a question, he stepped aside and looked up at me, then fell in beside me while I answered.

"This is it," I said. "I came to find Karawala, and I have done it. I am here." I stopped as I talked and held out my arms to everything around us. I saw thatched roof houses with the yellow glow of kerosene lamps inside. I saw people coming and going without the aid of a flashlight. I heard them talking in their own language, in their singsong voices. Behind us there was a parade of children.

Ahead were two large buildings: a church and a house. "Where are we going?" I asked.

"Right here." Leopoldo jutted his jaw in the direction of one of the buildings and puckered his lips. "To the Reverend house, him."

"Oh, God," I muttered.

"Amen," Leopoldo answered. His retort was reverent, if automatic.

"Why the Reverend's house?" I asked.

"For you to eat and sleep," he said.

We got to the gate at the Reverend's fence, and our entourage bid us good night. They turned and walked off slowly, talking in low voices, toward a cluster of houses, one of which was much more brightly lit than those around it. They hadn't walked but a few steps until they were part of a different night.

I turned and followed Leopoldo up the walk. In front of the porch he stopped and called, "Oh, Reverend," and not waiting for an answer, he climbed the steps. As his foot hit the landing, the door opened.

"Good night," said a voice within. There was no light inside, so I could not see who spoke. The voice conveyed confidence.

"Good night, Reverend," Leopoldo answered. "I bring the visitor to you."

"Yes?" he replied.

18

"My name is McBeth Johnson," I said, and held out my hand. His shake was like the others. I made sure my hand felt like a rock in his.

"And I am Reverend John Hooker. It is a pleasure to meet you, Mr. Johnson. Please come in." He backed away from the door to make way for us. I still hadn't seen his face. He was a slight man, not much taller than Leopoldo.

"Make I light the lamp," Leopoldo said. With a series of quick, sharp strokes, he tried to light a match, then another. "Caught cold."

"What?" I asked.

"Caught cold," he repeated. With a jut of the jaw and a pucker of the lips at the matches, he said, "The match, them."

The fourth match caught fire. With the lamp in his hand, the Reverend led us to the sitting room, only a few steps away. There was an old couch and two wooden chairs in a small room. He offered the couch to me.

It was an old wooden house, with perhaps five or six rooms and that many times larger than anything else I'd seen since Bluefields. The paint was long since gone from every surface with any wear. The floor was worn by the abrasion of generations of sandy feet.

"Please sit down and tell us why God has brought you here to our poor little village." He spoke carefully and slowly with all the gentleness and holiness his years of practice could give him.

I glanced at Leopoldo. He sat in his chair with his feet dangling above the floor, an old, dirty ball cap in his lap, watching the Reverend with true reverence.

I felt uneasy, but I was his guest. It looked to me like I was going to spend the night in his house and have breakfast with him in the morning, and there was nothing I could do about it - without risking offense.

"I came here to fish," I said. "I heard the fishing here was very good."

Leopoldo and Reverend John Hooker looked at each other

with great delight. "God did sent him!" Leopoldo exclaimed.

"Yes!" The Reverend agreed. "It must be!"

They broke into the Miskito language, wringing their hands in pleasant anticipation, and chattering excitedly about what I'd said. I had no idea a fishing trip could generate so much excitement.

Suddenly Leopoldo jumped up, said, "Good night, sar," and bounded out the door.

"Well, I guess the fishing must indeed be good here," I said.

"Oh, yes, it is," he answered. He was very excited. "It is good. Now I am sure you must be tired. You will sleep here tonight," he added, motioning at the couch. "I will bring you water and bed clothes."

His manner had changed. His calm had gone when I mentioned fishing. He was anxious now to get out into the village, I guessed to talk about the fishing, and perhaps take credit for its discovery.

I was causing quite a stir. I had no idea how big or why, but at the moment, fatigue was taking its hold and the offer of a place to sleep was welcome. At the least, I was safe.

*

I stepped out onto the porch just as it was getting light enough to see. Standing in front of the porch, waiting for me, were at least fifty men from the village. Many of them leaned against long paddles. Others carried nets and hand lines. All were smiling.

I surveyed the crowd for a moment and said, "Good morning!" in a loud, friendly voice. In that early morning silence, it was probably heard for miles around. I would have cringed and laughed at myself had not their response been fifty times my greeting.

Eddie Wilson stepped forward and said, "We are ready." He, too, was smiling with great delight.

"Ready for what?" I asked. I hoped I looked genuinely perplexed, because I really was. Why were they here?

"For fishinin," he replied. He, too, was perplexed. Wasn't it obvious?

"For fishing?" I repeated.

"Yes, Mr. Bet. For fishinin. Ain't that what you here for?"

"Yes, it is, Eddie, but why do all these people want to go with me?"

"They not going with you," he said, thinking he understood my confusion. "They going for you!"

"Oh," I said. Now I was genuinely confused. I dared not laugh. I might have offended them. But it was all I could do to keep from doubling over. Never before in my entire life had so many people been so sincerely delighted at the prospect of going out and having fun for me. It was overwhelming.

Leopoldo stepped forward. "Tell us what fish you want buy. We catch and salt for you." His eyes were bright. The light was growing, and I was beginning to see.

They were here to work. When I said fishing, they thought buy. I was going to have to tell them I was not there to buy, but to enjoy their river and the fish it held. I was going to disappoint them, and I did not like that prospect at all. To be disappointed can be unhappy; to be disappointing can be unhealthy.

"Eddie," I said. "Leopoldo." I stepped down off the porch to stand next to them. "I don't think I made myself clear last night. I didn't come here to buy fish. I wouldn't know what to do with them once I had them. I just came here to catch a few for sport." That seemed plain enough to me. No more confusion.

They didn't say anything. They looked at me, at each other and at the gathered crowd. They didn't understand. "What you mean, 'For sport?'" Eddie finally asked.

"I mean the only reason I have for catching them is the enjoyment of finding them and catching them. And eating them later, of course. But I'm not going to buy them or sell them."

Leopoldo turned to the crowd and said something in

Miskito. I didn't understand a word of it, but I couldn't have been wrong about the effect. I had introduced an entirely foreign concept. Not one of them understood what I was talking about.

After registering the reaction, he turned to me and asked, "Then what you going do?"

The way they looked at me, I felt like I'd been caught trying to cheat someone. It was an unsettling feeling. Somewhere in the back of my mind a voice echoed, 'Don't piss off the Indians.'

"I was just going to rig up my tackle and go out and catch a few fish," I answered.

"What you going do with them?" He asked.

"Except for something to eat, I'll put them back."

They chuckled. They told the crowd and everyone laughed, some uncertainly and some riotously. Some of them must have passed me off as crazy. They began to walk off. Some stayed, still confused.

Eddie spoke. "You alone going fishinin?" He asked.

"Well, not just me," I said. "I'll need a guide to go with me, and Hendry and Lyman, I guess."

"And you not going buy and you not going sell." He said.

"Correct."

"Why?" He asked.

I was not going to get out of this easily, if ever. There was an impasse here; a cultural gulf that could not be crossed. I would not be understood.

"What are you doing today?" I asked Eddie.

"Me? Well, nothing, sir." He fidgeted a bit.

"Do you know the river?"

"Yes, sir." He said proudly. "I am the captain of Mundo Poop Poop."

I figured that was another story that could wait for another day. Whatever was a 'Poop Poop', and who was Mundo?

"You want to take me fishing?" I asked.

He was pleased with the invitation. "I guess so, Mr. Bet. Haps to I going to."

I asked him to get my rod tube from the house. If I couldn't explain what it meant to fish for fun, perhaps I could demonstrate.

As he walked away, I added, "And Eddie, find Hendry and Lyman and tell them we'll be going out soon."

The remainder of the crowd began to disperse.

When Eddie returned, I was sitting in a rocking chair on the porch with my reels and lures laid out in front of me. He slowed, then stopped, at the top of the steps. He looked at the array on the porch with wonder.

After looking over each item without speaking, he asked, "What kind of hook this is?" He picked up a Creek Chub Pikie and examined it. It was a large wooden plug with a red head and white body. Three large treble hooks swung from belly to tail. He held it like it was a treasure.

"That's a tarpon plug, Eddie," I answered.

"I never see these things before." He said. He picked up a trolling reel, a Penn International 30, and turned it over and over.

"You make this from gold?" He asked.

"No, Eddie. It's just gold colored."

"What it do?" He pulled some line off and inspected it.

"I think it would be easier to show you," I answered.

"This line too small," he announced. "You never catch with this. Break it right off."

"We'll see," I said. "Open up that tube."

He did as I asked and pulled four rods from it. I asked for the heaviest, and when he gave it to me, I began seating the reel to it. He watched intently, never missing a move. When I had the line pulled through the guides, I handed it to him to hold while I got a leader ready.

"What this thing for?" He asked.

"To catch a fish," I answered. "You will see soon enough, and then you will know much better than I could explain."

As I was rigging, Hendry and Lyman ambled up. One look

23

was enough to tell the rum bug had bitten them the night before. If they felt as bad as they looked, they would not be able to take me out on the river.

A boy was tagging along with them. He bounced up on the porch and began jabbering in Miskito and picking up every item I had. Within seconds he had handled everything and was starting through again. Eddie grabbed him by the scruff of the neck and picked him up, lures dangling from his pants where the hooks had stuck.

"Yeowww!" He wailed, waving his arms and kicking his feet. "Put me down, Eddie!"

"Make I send you home, Ferlan?"

"No!"

"Then be still." He set the boy down away from the tackle.

I laughed and turned back to Hendry and Lyman. "You ready to go out?" I asked.

"You mean leave off?" Hendry asked. There was pain in his eyes.

I didn't know for sure what 'leave off' meant. Nothing seemed to mean what I thought it meant. The language was the same, but it was different.

"I mean go out on the river and catch some fish."

Lyman looked at Hendry and back at me. "We got 'nough gas to make the pass to Bluefields. Not more."

The events of the morning raced through my mind. I had fallen into a culture gap. No one I had talked to, from the time I arrived in Bluefields to now, had known why I was here. I couldn't be mad at Hendry and Lyman for not bringing enough fuel for a few days of fishing. I wanted to be angry at something, but I had no target - not even myself.

So there I sat. I looked around. I saw green upon green upon green. Even the sliver of river I could see was green. It was broken only by the brown of raw wood on the houses and the boles of the trees. The smoke of wood-burning fires flowed from the eaves and through the leaves of the thatched roofs and converged above the houses in straight plumes in the dead-calm air. The clouds were a low, perfectly uniform gray ceiling.

People were going about their business, which to some was sitting in a rocking chair on a porch. The sounds of the village came to me from what I could see and the sounds of the jungle came from a wide circle around the village. I couldn't guess the distance of the farthest. The morning was still cool. If this was all I could have here, it was enough.

Eddie said something to Ferlan and the boy scampered off.

"Boss?" I looked up at Lyman. The scar looked worse today, perhaps aggravated by rum. "We going leave off?" He asked.

"Not yet, Lyman," I answered. "You need some sleep. I'll send for you if I need you."

Both of them looked relieved. They thanked me and walked off to find a place to sleep. I watched them for a moment and wondered how much sleep it would take.

So. No boat. I looked at my tackle and picked up a stiff popping rod. If I had to stand on the bank and cast at the same spot all day, I was going fishing. I put an Ambassadeur 6500C on the rod and rigged some leaders and lures.

Eddie fingered the twenty pound test line. It was even lighter than the first. He shook his head. "This sure not going catch."

I stood up with the rod and a box of lures and said, "Let's go to the river and see." We walked toward the wharf.

The grass felt good on my bare feet. I looked down. Bermuda grass! I hadn't noticed before, but everywhere the brush was cleared, Bermuda grass was growing, and it all looked manicured, like a lawn.

By the time we got to the wharf, there was a small crowd with us. A large gold Hot Spot hung from the rod tip. I looked at Eddie and asked, "How deep is the water here?"

He looked at me and shrugged his shoulders. "Can't say."

"Well, is it deep or shallow?"

"I never see the bottom. Must be deep," he concluded.

I turned to face the opposite bank, about fifty feet away, checked my footing, and cast the plug up under the mangroves. A spontaneous cheer exploded behind me and excited voices proclaimed a miracle. I chuckled and began the retrieve.

Nothing. No strikes. But the miracle grew with each turn of the reel as they realized the bait was swimming back to me.

I put the second cast in the same spot, with the same result. The third cast went into a little pocket to the left. I had hardly started the retrieve when it was jolted to a stop. The water boiled up around it and another cheer went up.

I set the hook and felt the solid weight of a large fish. The rod bent double, but the fish didn't budge. She just shook her head slowly side to side. If I couldn't get her out of the roots, she would cut my line. I stuck my thumb between the bar and the spool and pulled back with both hands.

That did it. She came out of the mangroves and lunged down the river, stripping line as she went. I could neither stop her nor turn her. About fifty yards away, she jumped. It was a huge snook - thirty pounds or better - and I knew that if this fish went back into the mangroves, I didn't stand a chance. There was nothing I could do about it.

My body was shaking and my heart was thumping like it hadn't done since I was a kid, fishing on another river far away and long ago. As calm as I had thought my experience had made me, I was excited.

The volume of the cheering grew rapidly. I could tell the crowd was growing behind me, but I could not look.

The fight didn't last long. She took another fifty yards of line as if there was no resistance, started around a bend and cut me off on a mangrove root.

I went limp. My arms hung at my sides and I breathed heavily, in spite of my attempt to look normal. The crowd jabbered noisily behind me and I heard these words repeated: "Mupi tara!"

"Son of a bitch!" I muttered. "That was one hell of a snook."

"Sandy Bay man!" Eddie said. "That one mupi tara, that." He looked at my line again. "You hear what I say? That line not going catch."

I reeled in my limp line. It was cut just above the leader. Most of the double line remained. I traced it with my fingers, feeling for nicks, from well above the Bimini to the tag ends. I cut off a foot or so, tied on another plug and tightened the drag on the reel.

Another cheer went up as the plug splatted into the water again right under the mangroves. A few casts later, I was beginning to relax again. My breathing and heartbeat slowed and my hands quit shaking. What a fish.

Another strike bent the rod over hard, but this fish wasn't half as big as the first. I managed to pull it clear of the mangroves. It jumped and thrashed its head over and over to the pleasure of the gallery. It was nothing but luck that kept it out of the roots and in clear water. It could have gone wherever it wanted and I couldn't have done anything about it. If they were all like these first two, I had found a honey hole full of one of the greatest of the sport fishes.

It was beginning to tire and I thought I had it when it made one more lunge and pulled free. I reeled the bait in to find both treble hooks straightened out like frog gigs.

I held the lure in my hand and looked at it, wondering how I was going to catch a snook. Eddie snorted. He was proud of his river's fish and he was proud of himself. He crossed his arms, leaned back and grinned.

"I'll catch them, Eddie. It might take me a day or two to figure them out, but I'll catch them, and I'll do it with this." I held the rod up and waved it.

"Nah!" He returned. "How that thing work?"

I showed him how to disengage the gears for freespool casting, how the level wind kept the line from bunching up on the spool during the retrieve, and how the drag slipped when the fish pulled hard enough.

It was magic to him. And his wonderment was a wonder to me. I watched him as intently as he looked at the reel. His comprehension could not have been less if I'd come from another planet with things never before seen in this world. The real wonder, the real miracle, was that we spoke the same language.

He looked from the reel into my eyes. At once bewildered and sad, his eyes demanded, 'Who are you?'

This was no longer just a fishing trip.

*

The boy named Ferlan came bounding down the path, jabbering as he went. He walked up to Eddie and handed him a large coil of heavy monofilament with a big homemade spoon tied to it.

Eddie looked long at the coil and sighed. "You want go, we go," he said.

"Huh?"

"You want go fishinin, we go fishinin now," he explained. He didn't look too happy, but I let it go.

"How?" I asked.

He turned toward the canoes, all pulled out of the water, looking like a logjam. Still in the water, with her bow resting on bamboo rollers, was an old plank boat, about thirty-five feet long, with a cabin of sorts amidships to stern. Eddie pointed at it and said, "Mundo Poop-Poop," and smiled.

She was a round-bottomed river trader, made to carry a hold full of rice, beans, flour, salt and sugar. Her old turquoise paint was worn through in places to bare wood. If she wasn't "The African Queen", she could have been.

As we walked to her, I asked, "Why do they call her the Poop-Poop?"

They all laughed. "You soon see."

Remembering the rest of my tackle laid out on Reverend

John Hooker's veranda, I stopped. "I'll be back in a minute, Eddie. I might need another rod."

Several voices barked in unison at Ferlan and off he scampered. "You not to back notin' notin'," a voice behind me said. I turned to look.

He had a baseball cap on his head, cocked off at an angle, and an impish look on his face. "I is Mudi," he said, extending his hand. His left hand held a harpoon and a coil of rope.

I shook his hand. It was weak. "My name is McBeth Johnson," I said. "And it is my pleasure."

"Yessir, Mr. Bet. How is it?"

"It is fine," I answered. "And you?"

"Right here, boss."

"Where are you going with the harpoon?"

Mudi smiled. "I going strike you tapom."

My fishing trip was changing, perhaps in engaging ways.

As we approached the boat, a tall lanky man rose to greet us. His cheeks were sunken and he looked like there was nothing under his skin but bones. His eyes were so bloodshot he must have thought the universe was red.

He wobbled as he extended his hand, then withdrew it. "I is Larry," he mumbled. "I is the engineer." He put a hand on the bow to steady himself.

"And you drunk," Eddie said. "You not my engineer when you drunk. Go home."

Larry was dirty, and he stank. He fumbled for a cigarette, but couldn't find one. He was bent forward and off balance. He would have fallen but for the boat to lean on.

He looked at me and asked, "Mr. Bet? I is hungry. I need a few Cordoba to get me some rice. You give me a few Cordoba now and I will do a little work for you."

Eddie didn't like that. He stepped between us and hit Larry with a stinging verbal barrage. I couldn't understand it, but like a caustic chemical, you don't have to read the label to be burned. Larry cringed and wobbled off.

I hadn't liked it either. Never have and never will. I was glad Eddie intervened.

My entire body jerked violently as a deer fly bit into my calf. I swatted involuntarily and looked, expecting to see a plug of meat missing. It felt like someone jabbed a sharp stick into my leg.

Everyone laughed, and the laughter was so clear I had to laugh with them.

"That fly sure make you jump, Mr. Bet," Mudi said. He laughed again and slapped his hat against his leg.

"Yes, Mudi, it sure made me jump," I agreed, still laughing. "Now, let's go fishing."

We rolled the Poop-Poop into the water and hopped on. We drifted slowly out into the Karawala as Mudi scampered below. I looked down into the hold where he had disappeared and saw him leaning over an old one-lung Lister diesel that easily dated back to World War Two, if not earlier.

"Okay Eddie?" he asked.

"Okay Mudi," Eddie answered.

Mudi started turning the hand crank, slowly at first, and when the flywheel was turning as fast as he could make it go, he pulled the crank out with one hand and pulled the compression lever with the other.

Poop.......poop......poop.....poop....poop...poop..poop-poop-poop-poop-poop. I laughed. Mudi pointed at the engine and said, "Poop-Poop!"

She was called the Poop-Poop because she was the Poop-Poop, and there could not have been another name for her.

"Ahead slow," Eddie commanded.

The only way to fish from the Poop-Poop was to climb up on the roof and sit with your legs dangling off the stern. The cabin was open aft of the wheel house, but the "head" blocked the stern below the roof.

Built above the transom was what could only be described as a nautical outhouse. It offered privacy, but emptied directly through the seat into the water below. It was ingenious, practical and amusing, but there was no way to fish around it.

So up I went. I sat down, tied a plug to the trolling rod and began letting out line. I looked back at the wharf and saw it packed with a crowd. I waved and they broke out in a cheer and waved back.

Through the roof, I felt every "poop" the Lister made. I knew the fish felt it, too, and wondered how jolting it must be to their nervous systems. Would they take a bait trolled from this boat? Or would they spook?

We started around a bend and I very nearly rolled off into the water. With little ballast in the hold, the round bottom rolled away from the turn, listing enough to dump the unwary.

Someone yelled, "Hold on, Mr. Bet!" But it was a bit too late. I managed to hold on to the rod and stay on the roof, but it couldn't have looked very graceful.

I had no sooner regained my balance than someone yelled, "Drop down, Mr. Bet!"

Now what? The answer came quickly enough. Whap! An overhanging branch caught me square in the back. As it scraped by, ants and spiders rained from the tree above. Holding the rod down and away with one hand, I swatted and swept with the other.

There was great mirth below. Mudi thought I was absolutely hilarious. "You to drop down like a deer," he said. "Dodge the stick."

With all sorts of arthropods crawling over me, I got a strike. "Fish on!" I yelled. "Fish on!"

Mudi stuck his head out and looked up at me, curious as to what I was yelling about.

"Fish on," I repeated, a little irritated. "That means stop the boat and let me fight it."

Mudi jerked his head back under and jabbered at Eddie. Eddie jabbered back and I heard the Lister go into neutral.

I turned my attention to the fish. "This one I can catch", I

31

said to myself. The tackle was strong and the leader long enough to keep the line out of the mangrove roots. I played it easy in the open, hard in close. Above the waterline, up to the high tide line, I could see the barnacles that covered the roots.

Each time she tried to get back into the roots, I stopped her, at the risk of straightening the hooks. Each time I stopped her, she jumped, trying to shake loose the thing that stuck in her mouth.

We were drifting in a wide stretch of the river. Tarpon were rolling around us. I could hear howler monkeys in the distance. I could smell the sweet perfume of flowers. And I was being eaten alive by everything that lived in trees.

A few minutes after the strike, I had a twenty-plus pound snook at the boat. And we didn't have a gaff. Before I could scream, "No!", Mudi wrapped the leader and lifted the fish, trying to swing it over the gunnel onto the deck. The hooks pulled out and the snook splashed into the water and disappeared.

"Hoopah!" was all he said. He looked at the water where the fish had been.

"And I so hongry," Eddie said. "How you can do so?" He chided Mudi. He stuck his head out and looked up at me. "Didn't I told you? You never catch with that." He disappeared into the Poop-Poop, laughing.

Again I let a lure out behind the boat and had barely put the reel in gear when the rod bent double and line began peeling off. I thought I was snagged and opened my mouth to tell Eddie when a six foot tarpon shot out of the water like a missile, shaking and rattling, almost reaching the branches.

One jump was all I got. The plug went sailing through the air to plop into the water at the end of a limp line. I began to reel in line to check the hooks, but another strike nearly yanked the rod out of my hands. Another tarpon shot ten feet into the air, shook the hook loose and crashed into the water.

"Mother of God!" I said to myself. I could do no more than

stare at the water, shaking my head. I had neither seen nor heard anything from my guides indicating this was out of the ordinary, but it surpassed everything I had ever seen or heard about. I imagined waters full of ravaging fish concealed by the mirror on the surface. I shuddered to think of falling in.

Again and again I hooked and fought fish as the Poop-Poop rolled along the river. Occasionally a smaller snook took the bait and we managed to get it into the boat, but not until we were out in the open water of the Rio Grande did I land a big one.

I never thought about thirst or hunger. Occasionally someone handed me a coconut to drink or a piece of fruit. Not until afternoon did I think about returning to the village, and then only because exhaustion set in.

As if they had never left, a crowd greeted us when we returned. The laughter and cheering were infectious. I laughed involuntarily and felt muscles in my belly contracting eerily of their own volition. And then I saw the Reverend's house.

"Eddie," I asked, "Is there anywhere else for me to sleep?"

I had intended to get that out of the way first thing. Now it was urgent. No matter how good the fishing was, I might not be able to take much of the Reverend. I preferred other accommodations.

Eddie thought for a moment, his brow wrinkled, with no results. Mudi jabbered at him and he shook his head as if shocked. I heard the name, "Billy Rose".

"What?" I demanded. "What is it?"

"Nothing," Eddie answered. "Just an old house out by the field. No one live there. Too much danger."

"You mean there is no place here to stay but the Reverend's house?"

"No, sar," Mudi answered. "We is poor people here. If you hap family here, sure. But no family, you stay to de Reverend house."

"Why you can't stay there?" Eddie asked.

"The Reverend and I might not agree on everything," I

answered. I hoped they wouldn't be offended.

There was a brief silence before Mudi laughed and slapped his thigh with his hat. "Hya! More better to sleep with tigers, Mr. Bet?"

I grinned and said, "Something like that, Mudi."

"Didn't I told you, Eddie? He not like them."

They seemed pleased with the revelation. We were cut short by the necessity of docking. Mudi ducked below, and suddenly everyone was busy but me.

BILLY ROSE HOUSE

Chapter Three

Yumhpa

They speak four languages here. Miskito, Ulwa, Spanish and English.

They learned English from the pirates, for which this coast was a haven. Legend has it Bluefields was named for a Dutch pirate named Blaufelds. Then Her Majesty's Navy came along and ruined their fun. The coast became a British protectorate from the Mexican border down into Costa Rica. When the coast was secure, the British traders came.

Until 1894, this coast was called Mosquitia. Nicaragua was just a small strip on the Pacific coast west of the mountains between Honduras and Costa Rica. The British presence here ended when the Queen ceded everything from the Rio Coco to the Rio San Juan to Nicaragua in 1860. It took the Nicaraguans thirty-four years to realize their territory had expanded.

While the British were here, everyone learned English, and we kept it fresh when we came to harvest the mahogany and plant bananas. It's more the second language than Spanish.

As told by Sunshine Down

The evening sun cast gold into the pines behind the house, if you could call it a house. It was round, about fifteen feet in diameter and up on stilts. It had split bamboo sides and a conical thatched roof. It was in disrepair, but in that setting, I could have accepted less.

I could not see the village from there, but a fifty yard walk to the edge of the trees would put me where I could see the last houses, about one quarter of a mile away.

Eddie had sent help ahead of us. Several men chopped with machetes at weeds and brush around the house. Women cleaned inside the house while others brought a table, a chair and an old canvas cot they called a tijera. Mudi and Ferlan brought my things from the Reverend's. They worked at a feverish pitch. I was amazed that they would be so anxious to help.

Eddie pulled me off to the side. "Mr. Bet, you sure you want this so?"

"Yes, Eddie," I smiled. "This is perfect."

He looked at the ground nervously. "Mr. Bet, the last man sleep here get eat up by tiger."

I felt a sudden flight of uncertainty. What was it Mudi said about sleeping with tigers?

"Maybe he wasn't very careful, Eddie," I offered.

With tropical suddenness, it was almost dark, and as quickly as darkness comes, they all dropped what they were doing and left for the village. All of them; all at once. Eddie, Ferlan, Mudi. All gone. Vanished. I turned around, looking to see if maybe there was a jaguar standing behind me, ready to pounce.

But I saw nothing. I stopped breathing to listen, but heard nothing. They left in fear, but I had no notion of what.

I climbed the steps and sat down. I felt the silence all the way through my bones. It was at once comforting and fearful. It was peace and harmony. This is the time of day when the world breathes a sigh of relief and relaxes. It is also the time of day when tensions build against the cloak of night, when the prey sense the breath of the predator and quicken their pace to their lairs.

I looked around. The little house was in a clearing, with tall pines standing like a half-circle of guards around me. To the west, across the Karawala, I could see the hardwood canopy of the rain forest. The gold was gone now; the light dim. Green was almost black. I wondered what might be moving now before me, unseen and unheard. I stood up and stepped inside.

By feel I found my saddlebags and retrieved a flashlight and a Browning Hi-Power. The old leather holster felt good to the touch; the steel of the pistol better. It was my only hedge against the night. The walls of this rondel stopped neither wind nor sound, let alone man and beast, but they were the physical boundary of my territory, and having a territory is power and comfort.

With the exception of a mosquito bar, the tijera was bare. I made a pillow with a pair of rolled up jeans, slipped off my moccasins and slid in under the bar with the Browning, cocked and locked, and the flashlight.

The realization began to sink in that I was utterly and totally alone. The nearest road had to be more than one hundred miles away, and the village might as well have been on the other side of the earth for all the help it could have been.

I was weary, but my mind would not relax. My hearing sharpened with every new sound, testing them for hints of danger. I reminded myself not to worry about a threat until it actually showed itself, but my breathing and heartbeat felt loud enough to ring a bell for every hungry beast around.

Sleep would come when it was time. Until then, I relaxed and absorbed whatever my senses brought. The night was full of the sounds of insects, tree frogs and birds, all piled one on the other, but all crisp and clear, sharpened by the foundation of silence.

I listened with great intensity. I found that with my hearing I could extend myself beyond the hut and explore each creature. I went to each source of song in turn and held it until I was familiar with it. Holding one, I found like sounds scattered in the trees or in the grass. I could not know their form or size or color this night, but I came to know the sound.

I have no idea how long it took to fall asleep. I awoke

instantly with my hair standing on end and the Browning pointed at the sound inside the house. It was a violent clawing, beating, scraping sound on the other side of the room, on the floor. I flipped on the flashlight and began to squeeze the trigger even before the light fell on the target.

And then I didn't know what to do. Against the wall I saw a scorpion, jet black and as big as a beer can, locked in deadly combat with a roach as big as he. It was obvious I'd have to kill the thing, but I wasn't anxious to move until I'd checked to see if he had company.

As big as he was, his relatives would be easy to see. A quick look around showed him to be alone. I swung out of bed and looked for something to smash it with. Failing that, I pulled a knife from my bags and stabbed it through his back, into the floor, where I left it.

The claws on his feet scraped at the floor and his stinger clacked at the blade as he tried to sting it. The roach, his dinner, lay dead on its back.

Now I was awake. Fuck the tigers! I sat on the edge of the tijera, looking around the room, searching every square inch of floor, chair, table, bed, bar, wall and roof for deadly monster scorpions. What if one of those things got a stinger into you? How long would you live?

I remembered a bottle of Flor de Caña, retrieved it and drank. The rum was hot and did nothing at first to soothe my nervousness. I put the light on the floor, between my feet, rum and pistol by my side, and watched the scorpion.

After a few swallows of rum, I became accustomed to the scorpion's presence. Nervousness changed to curiosity. I wondered how common they were, and what else was going to surprise me in the night. I watched and thought, and the scorpion's movements became steady; robotic. He felt no pain, I thought, even with a knife through his back. Though going nowhere, he was continuing his hunt, and would go on until a stimulus prompted a response.

Millions of years of successes had programmed it so completely it had no options. It was nothing but a perfect biological expression of its niche, lacking awareness of itself and its environment.

But I am more. I slid back under the bar and went to sleep. In my dreams I saw myself being eaten, and I was indifferent to it, as was the rest of the world. I saw other creatures being eaten, and they were taking as much pleasure in it as were the predators. They danced a waltz that had no beginning and has no end. We fear death, but does anything else?

My first thought when I awoke was that I should not sleep with my finger on the trigger. The second was that it was time to begin marking my territory, which I did. I urinated on each post, with a double dose for the steps. From there, each chance I got, I radiated out in ever widening circles until I had a fairly large perimeter claimed. It must have worked. I wasn't eaten.

I was sitting on the steps, enjoying the morning, when my crew arrived. I leaned inside the door, pulled my knife out of the floor, and held the scorpion up, still impaled.

"Tmisri." Eddie said nonchalantly. "Fella hurt."

'Misery', I translated for myself. It was appropriate. "Say that again, Eddie?"

"Tmisri", he repeated. I forget how you call it."

"What does it mean?" I asked.

"Scorpion." Mudi declared.

"Yes, I know that's what it is. What does 'Tmisri' mean?"

"If that fella did strike you," Eddie answered, "you would right now know what it mean." He flipped his wrist and snapped his fingers when he said, 'strike', and everyone laughed. Apparently it wasn't fatal. Just miserable.

We fished again in the morning and in the evening, but not as hard as the day before. I became accustomed to the boat and they to me. We caught more fish in a shorter time and made it look easy. They began to respect me as a fisherman.

Between fishing trips we worked on making my camp more

livable. They set about cleaning the old well beside the house and building a cooking shed and an outhouse.

They did not understand why I didn't want the outhouse near the well and the cooking shed. I suppose they thought it would be more convenient to have it close by, but there is an old axiom everyone should understand: Don't shit where you eat. Apparently they hadn't heard about it.

And apparently they hadn't heard about the germ theory of disease. My explanation of why it had to be away from the house made no sense to them. They humored me by placing it well away from the hut toward the swamp, where I was sure it was on the downstream side of the drainage.

I thought about explaining what bacteria are, but shelved it for another time. How would I convince them that the world is teeming with creatures that can't be seen?

With that thought a little shudder hit me. Am I to something else as they are to me? Is there more here than meets my eye? What if there was something else - some other creature that could reveal another world to me? Would it surrender without attempting?

"Do you ever get sick?" I asked.

"Sure we do," they agreed.

"What kind of sickness?"

"What you mean?" Mudi asked.

"I mean how do you feel? What happens when you are sick?"

They thought for a moment, perhaps wondering more about the questioner than the question.

Eddie spoke first. "Sometimes you get hot-hot and then cold-cold and then hot-hot and on until the bush doctor find the medicine." His face was pained, as if the memory was too fresh.

It sounded like malaria. "Do you know what causes it?" I asked.

They were stumped. A cause hadn't occurred to them. It was just something that happened.

"It is caused," I said, "by an animal so small that there would have to be tens of thousands of them piled up together before you could see them." I don't know whether or not 'tens of thousands' meant anything to them.

"They are carried by mosquitoes. The mosquitoes put them in your blood when they bite you, and those multiply until there are enough to make you very sick."

Mudi cocked his head to one side and said, "Looky dat."

"What else?"

"Lots of people get the diarrhea," Ferlan said, pleased with his offering.

"Know what causes it?"

"No, sar," Mudi answered. "What that thing?"

"Something called bacteria," I explained. "Living things so small you can't see them. Sometimes you get them in the water you drink and sometimes in the food you eat. You can never see them to know if they are there, so the best way to keep from getting sick is to do everything you can to keep them out of your food and water. That's why I want the toilet as far from my food and water as I can get it."

Each explanation led to another question and another explanation. I did my best, but if they understood, I saw no sign of it. It appeared to be contrary to everything they believed, and I was just passing through. There was little chance that I would change their lives in a week or two.

I was there to fish, not to crusade. I wanted to see as much of the water as I could in the time I had. I didn't have a schedule to meet, but I couldn't expect Hendry and Lyman to wait forever.

As my crew turned to leave at sunset the second day, I asked Eddie if we couldn't get an earlier start the next day.

"You want go soon?" He asked.

"I'd like to be on the water when the sun comes up," I said.

"You want go soon-soon," he declared.

I took a chance. "Yes." If my interpretation was wrong, I

41

would have to roll with it.

Like the day before, they were gone before the colors faded. Where there had been people coming and going during the day, there was now not a soul to see.

The aloneness and the weariness were a welcome part of the evening. I sat and looked across the canopy to the west, into the sunset, and thought how easy it would be to do this every day for the rest of my life. What better way could there be to end the day? What better way could there be to spend the day?

I sat and watched and thought until the mosquitoes became a bother. It was almost too dark to see when I got up and went inside. Once inside, there was nothing to do but slide under the bar and relinquish my existence to the sense of sound.

I made an attempt to count the different voices and songs that came across the clearing, but it was too much like counting stars. Soon I was drifting, not hearing. Two days, I thought. I have been here two short days and it seems like a month. What would a month seem like? I have seen fishing found only in dreams, and I have stepped back in time to a simpler world where the corrosion of innocence is not so conspicuous.

I drifted off to sleep thinking about Karawala.

*

It was still pitch black dark when I was awakened by Eddie's voice saying softly, "Mr. Bet?"

I wasn't sure I had really heard it. It could have been a dream. I lay motionless, holding my breath, until it came again. "Mr. Bet?"

Yes, it was Eddie, and he was very close, standing outside no more than two feet from my head. I cursed myself for letting him get that close without waking.

"Yes, Eddie," I answered. "What is it?"

"Is soon-soon, Mr. Bet. You want us to call you soon-soon."

"I want you to call me McBeth, I muttered."

"What that?"

"Nothing. What time is it?"

He paused. There it was again.

"Soon-soon," was all he said, very softly. ˙

I got up and pulled on some clothes. A fire crackled to life outside, claiming a handful of the void. By the time I joined them the smell of coffee was in the air. Eddie, Ferlan and Mudi stood around the fire, but not for warmth.

I wondered why they dared not let the sun set on them here, but would return before it rose. I asked.

"The blood man," Ferlan answered.

"The what?!"

"The blood man," he repeated. A spasm wracked his body.

"Who is the blood man?" I asked.

Eddie answered. "He is a white man gone wild. He come after dark and back you to the bush and drink your blood. He dead you right out, and when he done drinking blood, he done with the body."

I tried to look serious and properly respectful. "What does he look like?"

"Him is a giant," Ferlan said. "Him is a red....," he lost the word and pulled on his hair and face.

"Red hair and beard"? I prompted.

"That the one, but long-long, and long teeth. Him look like de debil."

A vampire! They have vampires in Karawala! And he was very real to these three, if not all. I was amazed.

"Does he ever catch anyone?" I asked.

"All the time he does catch," Eddie said. "Sometimes we does find them and them is white-white. More white than you, Mr. Bet.

"Has anyone seen him?"

"Only those that dead out," he said.

I wanted to ask how they knew what he looked like, but demurred. Too much like asking how anyone knew what Christ

43

or the Buddha looked like.

"But why are you here now? It's still dark."

"Sun soon come. Can't stand the sun. He gone down a hole." They laughed. The thought gave them confidence and relief.

We finished our coffee and walked off toward the village. Lamps were burning in open windows and people were out and about all over town. I saw men and older women as we walked, but no children and no young women. We were greeted by everyone we passed, and even though it was too dark to see faces, everyone knew who they were greeting. It was all "Naksa," him and, "Naksa," them, except for me. For me, it was, "Marning, Mr. Bet. How is it?"

I made a game of it. "How is what?" I would ask, my voice smiling.

"The marning," they would answer, smiling back, some laughing.

As the light began to grow, I saw them carrying tools, long paddles, coils of fishing line and harpoons. How energetic, I thought. How industrious. I heard no grumpy voices; only their sing-song language and laughter.

We also passed houses still boarded up against the night, no light streaming from the cracks in the walls, no voices inside getting a start on the day. We passed Mundo's store, dark and shuttered, the long veranda empty.

"Poop..........poop........poop......poop....poop..poop-poop-poop. The Poop-poop came to life and we set out down the Karawala to the Rio Grande. We were on our way to a new place; one where the snook are big-big. They promised me snook bigger than snook can grow at this place they called Jamaima Key.

The Miskito word for snook is mupi, Eddie told me. There are mupi sirpi and mupi tara. Little snook and big snook. Jamaima Key is the home of pure mupi tara.

I sat on the roof of the "Poop-poop" and watched the river

slip by. It was all I could do to keep from throwing a jig at every rolling tarpon I saw.

The river was like a mirror. Every fish that pierced the surface gave himself away to me. Spanish mackerel slipped out of the water, arced across it, and slipped back in with hardly a ripple. Tarpon exploded into schools of mullet like hand grenades.

Wait a minute. Spanish mackerel in a river? Those are ocean fish. "Eddie," I yelled, leaning down from the roof.

"Yessir, Mr. Bet."

"Are those mackerel I see out there?"

"Yessir, Mr. Bet."

"But those are ocean fish."

"Yessir, Mr. Bet, but everything come in here."

I rolled back up on the roof. The river was wide here, perhaps a quarter of a mile. As far as I could see, the surface rippled from feeding fish. I shook my head slowly. They are not going to believe this back home.

We chugged down river past Pigeon Key and Baboon Key, and as my crew gave me names and pointed out landmarks, I noted the places that should hold fish.

The sun filled the sky with cloud streaks and color as it rose. I could not help but feel euphoric. I began to laugh. I stood on the roof of the old jungle trader and began jumping up and down, laughing gleefully. My senses tingled, stretching out to enter the purity of this world. I was earth, water, wind and fire; no less wild than any creature here.

And if there was any question, it was answered now. My guides leaned out over the gunnels and looked up at me, startled at first, then convinced. I was stark raving mad.

I laughed even harder. The people in our cities can't begin to imagine this world, and the people here can't begin to imagine ours. I cast it from my mind and lay down to catch my breath. I faced forward, on my belly, and watched the river. We rounded a slight bend and straight ahead, two or three miles into the sun, I saw white water crashing over the bar, and beyond that, the Caribbean. I could see forever.

Eddie slowed the engine and Mudi handed me a trolling rod. "We try this side first," he said, "then Jamaima Key."

I let out a large Tony Acetta spoon, far behind the boat, and settled down facing aft with my bare feet dangling off the roof. We trolled along a drop-off, well out from the shore, in fairly open water. Here is where I would be able to land a big snook.

But there were few snook there, and they were not the big ones. Eddie headed for the south side of the river where a line of mangroves separated it from a lagoon beyond. There was another drop-off here, sharper than the other, and there was much more cover. Great tree trunks were lodged in the sand along the drop, offering the snook a perfect lair more than a mile long.

I let the big spoon slip slowly back into the wake. If anything I had was stout enough to hold a big snook, this was it. I had given instructions to Eddie to steer the Poop-poop to the middle of the river the instant I hooked a fish. Even then, it would take lots of luck to keep it out of the logs.

Eddie steered right along the drop, and as the spoon neared the first big tree, everyone tensed with anticipation. We didn't have long to wait. At the center of the tree, my rod bent over with the heavy weight of a hard strike.

"Fish on!" I yelled, and Eddie spun the wheel and pointed the bow out like he did it every day.

The drag was as tight as I dared make it, and still the fish took line. Big fish feel big. The frequency of the movements of head and tail are slower; the power generated much greater. This fish felt huge. Within a few seconds I knew I had a monster on the line. My heartbeat quickened. I became as excited and nervous as a rookie.

She could have gone anywhere she wanted. She could have gone up onto the bar and into the logs and there'd have been nothing I could do about it. She could have cut me off before I'd even felt her great weight.

But she didn't. She moved out away from the drop-off and the logs into the channel of the river and began swimming toward the booming thunder where the river met the sea.

Eddie followed as best he could. Every time the fish turned, Eddie overshot the turn and had to circle back to it. Fifteen minutes into the fight, I still hadn't seen it. Eddie, Mudi and Ferlan were debating the possibilities.

"Mebbe june fish," Eddie said. "Not do like mupi."

He was right, I thought. If it was a snook, it should have jumped. Maybe it was a jewfish.

"Mebbe shark," Mudi offered. "Mebbe big Sandy Bay shark."

"Not likely," I said. "A shark would have cut the leader."

And then the fish put an end to the speculation. She jumped. She came out of the water like a slow motion movie, broadside, gills flared. There was a big, black, unmistakable stripe down her side. Snook. Mupi tara. I almost lost control of myself. This fish was easily twice as big as the all-tackle world record of fifty-two pounds.

There was cheering and jabbering below as if they knew they were watching a long-standing world record fall. I couldn't understand what they were saying, but their excitement needed no interpretation. They knew it was a giant fish.

And I knew there was no way I could land it. There was no place on this boat where I could follow the fish under and around the stem, stern and bottom. It was only a matter of time before she cut me off.

But for now, she was away from the boat and away from the logs. She swam and fought and jumped for thirty minutes or more, demonstrating her power and her speed. I savored every moment of it, thinking not of the impending loss, but of the great opportunity. I might be the only person in the world who has ever hooked such a great snook, and this might be the only snook in the world that has ever attained such great size.

Here we were together, this snook and I. It didn't matter

that she didn't know I couldn't kill her or even that death was a possibility. I wasn't sure I wanted to kill her, even if I could. There would be no point. It could never be weighed or certified; it could only be taken back to the village to be eaten. For me, it would only be another fish story, and they would never believe it back home.

For a short while, I had a love affair with the greatest snook ever. And then she decided it was over. Slowly, deliberately, she began peeling line from the reel, moving straight for the cut that drained the lagoon. There was no way to stop her or slow her down. The line came up. She was swimming near the surface. About two hundred fifty yards from us there was an explosion when she hit the mangrove roots at the shore. The line went slack.

I nodded my head in respect. I had been given a unique and priceless event. "You know I can't tell this story," I said to the snook, the river and the sky.

Below, I think they cursed the fish or the river or the gods, but my ears were not hearing just then. I sat down and began reeling in the line, slowly, watching every last trace of foam and concentric ripples from the last effort of my fish.

She would wear the spoon in her mouth for a week or so, like some tribal ornament, until the hook rusted out and she was free of it. I would wear her memory forever.

"You have a next spoon hook?" Ferlan asked, leaning out to look up at me.

"Yes, I do, Ferlan, but I think I'd just as soon rest on this one for awhile. Let it soak in."

Eddie didn't like that. "Oh, no, Mr. Bet. Plenty big snook here. We catch more."

What I really wanted to do was drift the area, casting into the logs. Trolling wasn't really my style. But controlling a drift in this boat wasn't possible. The tide and wind would have us either aground or out in the channel, neither of which would be a decent vantage point for catching snook.

But they could have it their way and I mine, too. "Ferlan, come up here."

Ferlan climbed up, with a boost from Mudi, and joined me on the roof. "Here, hold this." I handed him the rod and began tying on a new leader and spoon. He sat beside me, legs dangling, looking aft.

Through with the knots, I tossed the spoon into the water and started showing him how to put the reel in and out of gear to let out line. Realizing that I was going to let him fish, his eyes got big, his mouth dropped open and he said, "You want I catch fish?"

I nodded, smiling. He got so excited he could hardly talk. "Eddie! Eddie! He want I catch fish!"

"Hoopah! Looky dat!" Mudi exclaimed. He and Eddie babbled at each other, each claiming the next turn for himself. I laughed with them and caught their excitement. I think I was giving them something bigger than the great snook they gave me. And such a simple thing it was.

Ferlan did as I instructed. No sooner had he set the reel in gear than he had a snook on the line. It was not a giant, but by normal standards, it would have been a trophy. We swung out away from the logs and in a few minutes Ferlan had a twenty pound snook slapping the deck below.

As if he had never seen a fish before, he shoved the rod into my hands and swung out and down to the deck and the fish. Such whooping and hollering would have befit the discovery of gold in one's own back yard.

In Karawala, boys are not allowed to fish for anything but panfish for fear of losing valuable hooks and line. I had promoted Ferlan to manhood. It was a cause for celebration. It would be another year or two before biology promoted him, but this day he would carry his trophy home to his family and be declared a man. No warrior ever claimed a victory with greater exhilaration.

"If you can be one fisher-man, you can be one engineer,"

Mudi declared. And the two traded places.

In turn, I showed Mudi and Eddie how to fish, and each caught fish. We stayed in the area for a couple of hours, catching fish one after another. Each one caused as much excitement as the first.

We would have stayed longer, but they would not hear of releasing fish, and I would not hear of killing more. We stowed the rods and began poop-pooping against the tide toward the mouth of the Karawala.

A light breeze had come up, hiding the evidence of fish eating fish at the surface. Pairs of parrots winged across the river, talking to each other as they flew, coming and going I knew not where. They mate for life, they say, and a long life it is. They've been known to live for eighty years. Would but could I do that, and fly, too!

As we began the turn into the Karawala, I saw the last telltale traces of foam from an outboard motor. I looked up, and far upstream, almost out of sight, I saw it. Eddie and Mudi saw it, too.

"Is that Hendry and Lyman?" I asked, not wanting to hear the truth.

"Haps to be," Eddie answered. "Only motor here."

I didn't have to ask where they were going. I was stranded. I didn't know how bad it was, if bad at all, but surely there was another way out of here.

*

I could hear their excited cheers even before we rounded the last bend. The novelty of having a white man in the village was not so great as the novelty of having someone there who went out to fish every day, caught lots of fish, and then gave them away!

They were cheering now because I was bringing them something to eat. And they needed something to eat. It was gradually dawning on me that these were a very poor people. I saw the distended bellies of malnutrition in the children - the children waiting at the wharf for my fish.

Their parents, some barely beyond childhood, were too proud to come ask for a fish, so they sent the children. I was blind to it at first. I saw smiling faces wherever I looked, but I wasn't looking deep enough. I didn't see the old and worn clothes. I didn't realize that the children were naked because they had no clothes. I thought they preferred to go naked.

What had appeared to be paradise at first impression was beginning to take on a hint of sorrow, even though I had yet to see sorrow on a single face.

As I walked from the landing, I looked more objectively at the life around me. No newspapers. No televisions. No telephones. How fortunate could one get?

But neither did they have electricity or gasoline. Their lighting was by kerosene or candles when they could get them. They chopped wood every day to cook with. They ate only what they caught or grew. There was no running down to the store for a gallon of milk and a loaf of bread.

The nearest medical doctor was far enough away that one would either get well or die before one could get to him. They lived in a world hundreds of years behind ours.

Ferlan steered me to the right, away from the direction of my house. "Mundo say you fix up today."

"Huh?"

"He say to fix up. Come."

I allowed myself to be led to the Chinaman's store, assuming I would have an answer soon enough.

It took my eyes a moment to adjust to the deep shade after the bright sun. I saw an old Chinaman, small and thin, dealing out small parcels of staples to women and children. He sold rice and beans, flour and sugar, salt, rum and hot beer to those who had a Cordoba or two. He sold leaves of tobacco and cigarettes one at a time.

Some paid him with a few coins. Others kept a tab. I watched while waiting my turn. It was a bit like a country store in the variety of merchandise. There were cloth, needles and thread under a glass counter. It was the first glass I had seen here. Hanging on the walls were machetes, axes, a shovel and a straight hoe they called a mackinaw. On shelves were spices and cooking utensils. But there was not much quantity in any of these, and the next store was far away. The entire room measured no more than twenty by twenty feet.

I wondered how difficult it would be to survive if one had no tools; no resources.

"Hello, Missa Bet."

I looked up to see the Chinaman's hand extended in my direction; a broad smile on his face. I took it. Like the others, it was weak. I tried a bow, and scored. He returned the bow, looking into my eyes, the smile momentarily gone. I wanted him to be old and wise, with a long white beard and silk clothing, but he was not.

"My name is McBeth Johnson," I said, hoping at least one person would call me by it.

"Okay, Missa Bet. My name Mundo Chow. How is it?"

I chuckled. "It's just fine, Mr. Chow. How is it with you?"

"Okay. Okay. You need anything?"

"A cold beer would be nice," I answered, knowing there was no such thing in Karawala.

To my surprise, he gave an order to a child at his side. She scampered into a back room and returned with a bottle of Victoria, sweating condensate.

After the first long gulp, it occurred to ask how he managed refrigeration without electricity.

"It lun wit kelosene," he answered, his West Indies English thickly oriental.

I understand the physics of it, but it still amazes me that you can get things cold by burning kerosene. It amazed me even more that there was a kerosene refrigerator this far back in the bush. Whatever, I was grateful, and decided to do all my shopping at the Chinaman's.

"Ferlan tells me I need to fix up," I said, ready to unveil the mystery.

"Okay," he replied. He reached under the counter and brought out an old abacus and a wooden box. "Just take a minute."

The wooden box was filled with scraps of brown paper, each one a chit for something sold. He sorted through them, piling the ones with my name to the side. As he did, I realized that I had been shopping at the Chinaman's store since my arrival, but had been naive enough to think the people of Karawala had brought all the food and things for the house out of the goodness of their hearts.

As Mundo tallied the chits, fingers flying, beads clicking, I tried to anticipate the things to be included. I picked up some of the scraps of paper and saw Sanskrit. I was impressed. I wondered how long and how far he had carried his culture, and what stories he could tell.

He wrote the total on a slip of paper and slid it across the glass top to me. I had no idea I had spent that much money in just three days. The bill was three hundred fifty Cordobas. Fifty dollars.

Without hesitation, I paid him. Then I asked him to explain every item, but not before I had another cold beer in front of me. The beer went onto a chit and into the box.

There was diesel fuel for the Poop-poop and wages for Eddie, Mudi and those who helped straighten up my camp. The tijera and mosquito bar were there, as well as the staples that stocked my kitchen. Ferlan had brought me meals cooked by a Miss Pete, who I had not yet met. They were included. And so was the night at Reverend Hooker's house.

And there were four bottles of rum. "Not my rum," I told him.

"Yes, you lum," he replied. "Fo Endy and Lyman, them."

I couldn't very well challenge the man with the only cold beer in the world, could I? But it did bring up another subject.

"Speaking of Hendry and Lyman, where are they?" I asked.

"They gone, Mr. Bet," Eddie offered. "They say look like you living here now. They not want wait forever."

I sighed and nodded my head. "Got another cold one, Mundo?" Then it occurred to me that I was not being polite. "And get a couple for Eddie and Mudi, please."

"Only one mo cold got. Haps to be hot."

So sometimes you had to drink your beer hot. I could get used to that easier than I could get used to no beer at all. We finished our beer, I got another bottle of rum, and we walked off toward my camp. Now I knew the rules, or a few of them, at least.

Ferlan was at my side as we walked. He was at my side or in my vicinity from dawn to dusk every day. I asked about it.

"Ferlan, tell me why you are not at home or off playing with other kids."

He looked up at me with a proud smile on his face. "I work for you, Mr. Bet."

"This place is full of surprises," I chuckled. "What do you do for me?"

"Anything you want. I back things for you. I get things for you. You want; I get."

So I had a house boy and didn't even know it. "And how much do I pay you?" I asked.

He didn't know the answer to that one. I could tell he hadn't thought about it. Or maybe he didn't expect to be paid. Right now he had something more important to take care of.

Eddie had been carrying his fish. We stopped and Ferlan took it from him and dragged it off toward his house. We waited and watched until he was at the steps, calling all to see what he had caught.

Other children had dragged fish home from the landing, where we had given them away, but Ferlan was the only one who could claim to have caught one. His pride beamed.

I noticed then, almost hidden by brush, a massive old engine and walked over to examine it. Eddie and Mudi followed. It was an old diesel, and it looked as if it could have powered a locomotive. I asked them how it got there.

"That from the old saw mill," Eddie said. "Been here long time."

"What old sawmill?" I asked. I thought I was in a virgin forest. It was a little disappointing to think this had once been a logging town.

"Old 'merican mill. Gone maybe thirty years now."

"Was it a big operation?"

"Hoopa! I tell you. Had ships coming and going every day. And planes pitch here. This was a town then, I tell you. Anything you want, you got. Everybody happy then. Not like now.

Ferlan returned and we walked on. "Is there much of this stuff around here?" I asked.

"Plenty here yet," he answered. "When they left off, they just get up and went. Didn't tell nobody nothing. Left everything here. Everything. Trucks, Jeeps, tools, the whole of it. Some people did come from Bluefields later to haul it off, but plenty here yet."

"Planes pitch here," I repeated. "You mean airplanes landed here?"

"Sure, they did. Right on this field." He held his arms out in both directions.

I looked and saw. If he hadn't smacked me in the face with it, I might never have noticed. I was standing on a runway. And it was a good one; about a hundred feet wide and four thousand or more long, crowned in the center to drain water. Clear the scrub brush, and it would be ready for service.

Whatever it had been, this runway and a few heaps of rusting iron were all that remained. The jungle had reclaimed itself and erased the evidence. If this was all re-growth, it had matured quickly. Long gone, too, were the night clubs, the stores and the houses of the bosses.

Still here, though, were the remnants of the cultural contamination that made them call me Mister and nearly caused dysfunction if I became too familiar.

The realization that being an American is not always a source of pride returned to me. The only thing we left in our wake, some thirty years ago, was a master/slave relationship with the Indians. I was embarrassed that because I was an American, their conditioning, even after so many years, forced that relationship on me. We took far more than lumber.

I walked over to another mound, casually curious about its contents. In it I saw the cast iron housing for a huge electric motor.

"Eddie, if I found something I wanted to use, would it be all right to take it?"

"Sure, Mr. Bet. Them things been here all these years and no one take them yet."

"Good. Let's take that old motor housing to my kitchen." It would make a serviceable oven and stove, much better than cooking on the ground, even if all I did was make coffee now and then.

Eddie shrugged his shoulders and said, "Haps to we going to, but that thing surely heavy."

It turned out to be heavier than we could manage, but Eddie assured me that it would be where I wanted it before the end of the day. We walked on.

At the edge of the village, from the veranda of the last house, a woman called to Eddie.

"Miss Pete say you to come pasear her house," he said.

"Miss Pete? Ferlan brings my food from her, doesn't he?"

"Yes, sar, that the one," Mudi answered. "We taking this mupi to her for you."

I looked at the snook and doubted that I could eat twenty pounds of anything.

"Well, let's go and meet her," I said, and I waved an acknowledgement.

She was a heavy black woman, perhaps in her forties, with a bright, welcome smile. Her hands and forearms were covered with flour, which she was wiping away with her apron.

"Hello, Mack Beth Johnson," she greeted when I was a few paces from her steps. She won me over right then. "Come up here and let me shake your hand."

I did, and it was a real handshake. I couldn't help but like her.

"Make I take this mupi and put those picaninny to work." She clapped her hands and shouted a command. From behind the house ran two children saying, "Yes, auntie, I is right here."

She gave them the snook and a machete and sent them off to clean it. Eddie, Mudi and Ferlan sat on the steps and the veranda. I took a seat in a rocking chair offered by Miss Pete. She took another.

"My name is Petrona Antonia Crisanto Gomez," she said, "But all around here call me Miss Pete, even my poor husband, Valdevio."

I laughed. "What would you have me call you?" I asked.

"Whatever you want. I will know it." Then rising, she said, "You need a fresca, Mack Beth. Sun sharp today."

"Just call me Beth, Miss Pete," I called after her.

I looked through the open door into the house. The walls inside were papered with the pages of magazines. The front room was about ten feet by ten. Beyond it, smoke from a wood fire filtered through the thatch roof. To the side, a doorway was covered by a blanket. I guessed it was a bedroom.

A breeze rustled the dry palm leaves in the roof. She has a fire burning in her stove all day every day. I wondered how she kept from burning the house down. The whole thing was a tinderbox.

Like all the others, the house was made of unpainted, hand sawn lumber, was up on stilts about three feet off the ground and had a veranda running its length. A window on each side of the house remained shuttered most of the time. The breeze passed through the cracks in the walls and floor almost unhindered.

It kept out the rain in all but a driving wind and gave them shade in the heat of the day. It held them above the flood waters in the rainy season. It barred the wild animals and the terrors of the night. And it offered privacy. Water came in by bucket from a surface well. The toilet was an outhouse at the edge of the bush. It was no more than the most basic shelter.

This house also had the infectious cheer of Miss Pete, whose voice was at once laughter and song. She came out with a pitcher of orange juice and glasses, laughing.

"Here is your fresca, boys."

When she had poured the glasses, she sat down and said, "You surely showing these boys about fishinin, Beth. All of Karawala eating mupi now."

"Well, it's certainly a good place for fishing, Miss Pete. The best I've ever seen."

"Oh, yes, this Rio Grande is the home of the fish. More better than Tortuguero."

"You know Tortuguero?" I asked. "In Costa Rica?"

"Yes, Beth, I did work there at the fishinin camp long time. You know it, too?"

"I've heard of it. It's a sport fishing lodge. What did you do there?"

"I did cook for the guesses, them," she answered.

"Why did you leave? Why are you here?"

"My family sent for me in Orinoco. When I reach back, they have a next cook. So I come here, and I am here today."

I had other questions, but the beer and the sun were making me drowsy. Against my will, my eyelids were .drooping. When she got up to check on her cooking, I took the opportunity to excuse myself.

"Miss Pete, it was very nice to meet you. I wondered who was sending those wonderful meals to me. Now I know, and I thank you for them."

"Oh, Beth, is nothing much. Thank you for all the big mupi."

We shook hands again and I resumed my walk. My guides excused themselves and went their separate ways.

It was hot. I was beginning to understand what they meant when they said, "Sun sharp." It actually felt like needles were sticking into my skin. It was so humid the perspiration served only to collect dust. A breeze would have made a big difference.

When I came abreast of my place, I noticed a trail leading off through the bush toward the river. It would be too hot to sleep, I thought, even as drowsy as I was. The promise of a refreshing swim won out over a nap. I took the trail.

My feet and legs were bare. I walked slowly, noisily, hoping to see the snakes or scare them away before I stepped on them. I wondered how foolish it was to walk off by myself like that.

The mosquitoes answered me soon enough. I did not move slowly for long. To do so was to be eaten, ever so imperceptibly, by so many mosquitoes I was turning black by them. My pace quickened. I was not so cautious where I put my feet or what I allowed my legs to brush against, but I did not outright break and run.

With nearly every step I saw things I wished I could stop to inspect, but was forced to leave behind. I walked for what I thought must have been a quarter of a mile without coming to the river. The thought of having to backtrack was not appealing, but neither was the thought of not finding the water. If the trail didn't go to the river, there was no telling where, or to what, it would lead.

I looked down and was forced to stop. In front of me was a wide black river of ants. I was spellbound. They were army ants; some an inch long. They carried their eggs, larvae and pupae with them, on their way to their next bivouac. I looked both ways, hoping to see the queen's entourage, but was forced to move on by the biting hoards. As I rose, wondering which way to go, I heard a splash.

A kingfisher cried. The river, still hidden, was only a few yards ahead. But within a few steps, I encountered another obstacle. Between me and the water was twenty feet of mangroves standing in the mud, their roots covered by the shells of barnacles. I looked at my feet, shook my head and promised them I'd wear shoes next time. Then I took a branch and stepped up on a root.

The tops were dry and smooth. I would be fine unless I slipped or encountered something that required speed and agility to escape. Slowly I stepped, from prop root to prop root, choosing and testing each step carefully, ignoring the mosquitoes as best I could.

I made it to the edge of the river without slipping. It looked enticing. I was looking for submerged logs and other dangers when the water beside me exploded. Tranquility became pandemonium in a split second. In the corner of my eye, I saw an alligator quite large enough to do extreme harm. Water was flying everywhere as he charged across and through the roots toward me. Birds screamed and took flight. I responded with a reflex action that put me in a flat dive into the river.

If I had jumped into the tree, I would have escaped. Now I was right where he wanted me. I told myself I had made my last mistake, and what a beauty it was. I laughed. It wouldn't really be death by alligator; it would be death by stupidity.

I turned and looked back, hoping to make a decent fight of it. There he was, up on all fours where I had just been, mouth open, looking straight at me.

And there he stayed. Maybe he thought stupid people didn't taste good. Maybe all he wanted was to get me out of his territory, but he stayed.

Keeping my eyes on him, I began swimming downstream, careful not to disturb the water or make any sudden moves. He not only stayed; he settled down on his belly and laid his chin on a root. I was going to live.

It was almost a mile to the village landing, but I was not going to try to get out of the water until I found a place clear of swamp and trees. I stayed smack dab in the middle, as far away from the banks as I could. It occurred to me that there was no bottom in this river. I wondered what lived in its depths.

The water had become salty. There would be sharks here. I could be mistaken for dinner. All the way, I never quite got over my nervousness. I watched both sides for signs of alligators and snakes, but saw no more. No sharks showed themselves.

I heard sounds from the village as I swam; a voice or work sounds. But the banks were solid walls of trees and vines, orchids and bromeliads. It was as if it was a scene painted on a vast canvas at the water's edge. I could hear behind it, but not see through it into the shade.

What lay hidden in the darkness? Were there things in there that even these people had never seen? I was sure of it. Most of this world never feels the sun. It lives forever in deep shade and the darkest nights.

By the time the landing came into view, I was settled into a strong side stroke, bulging water in front of me, leaving a wake behind. Even before I climbed out of the water, I drew a crowd. The children saw me first and fled in terror from this river monster. When they saw it was me, they came running back, with parents following. Leopoldo was among them.

"How you come out de riber so?" he asked, eyes wide.

"I've just been for a little swim, Leopoldo," I answered nonchalantly. I started walking, once again, from the landing to my place.

He stayed beside me. "From where you come?" he demanded.

I guessed they did not swim well. A one mile swim might be an impossible feat for them. Playfully, I copied his mannerism; I jutted my chin and puckered my lips in the direction I had been.

"From up the river," I said. I laughed and slapped him on the back. Let him figure it out.

"You swim good," he said, changing the subject. "Like a manantee. We can't swim so good here." We walked a little, then he said, "Must be from far up the river, across from Billy Rose House."

We walked a little farther, past Reverend Hooker's house and the church, before he spoke again. "You fright the children, them, you know."

"I noticed that. Why so, Leopoldo?"

"Must be them think you some kind of wild thing come to eat them," he said. "But you fright me, too. Plenty people die there, you know." He stopped, stepped aside and looked up into my eyes. "Plenty people lost in there."

"You mean drowned, or what?" I hoped not eaten by alligators.

"I mean lost." He was very serious. There was no hint of amusement on his face. I felt like he might be ordering me to stay out of the creeks.

"But people bathe there," I countered.

"Only in the....how you say....not profundo, but...."

"Shallow water? I asked. "You only bathe in the shallow water?"

"That right, Mr. Bet. Only in the shallow."

He turned and took a few steps toward one of the houses, then turned around. "Mr. Bet?"

"Leopoldo."

"How you know to come here?"

"Hendry and Lyman brought me."

"No, how you hear about Karawala?"

"Before my grandfather died, he told me to go to his barn and look for something interesting. There was an old letter and map in a trunk. The letter told about the fishing here."

"The old ones tell about a next Johnson was here long time ago. They say you favor him."

"Do they remember his name?"

"Silas."

"That would be my grandfather."

"You find gold?"

I hadn't told anyone about the gold. The letter wasn't just about fishing. It was also about a shallow sea littered with old sailing ships broken apart on the reefs. Some of them had carried booty, and Silas had buried it under his barn.

"There was gold?"

"The old ones say they help him take out plenty from the keys."

"Well, looky dat," I said.

Leopoldo laughed. "Okay, Mr. Bet."

I said, "Goodbye, Leopoldo," and walked on.

Miss Pete waved as I passed her house. Others waved or said naksa as I passed. I was tired by the time I got home. I walked in, raised the bar, and lay down. I had Silas's gold. I didn't need more. I fell asleep immediately.

TIGER

Chapter Four

Walhwal

There is a story from long ago, at least before the time when I was a boy. They say two men in Karawala had the same dream one night. In the dream, a voice spoke to them and told them to go to an old pine tree out in the savanna. The voice said that when they got to the tree, treasure would rise up out of the ground at the base of the tree. The voice said they must give one half of the treasure to the church.

In the morning, the two men met, each on his way to see the other. They told each other about their dreams, and they were identical in every detail. So off they went to the old pine, and as foretold, gold and jewels rose up from the earth. But the two got greedy. They decided that they would give some to the church, but not half by a long shot. In the moment of that decision, the treasure returned to the earth.

They dug all day, but found nothing. The treasure has never been found.

As told by Abanil Lacayo

"Mr. Bet?" I woke slowly, conscious of the voice, but unable to move or respond until I had pulled my mind and body from the quicksand of deep sleep.

"Mr. Bet?" It was Eddie's voice, again just outside and very near my head, loud enough only for me.

"Hello, Eddie," I said as I sat up. "Oh, boy, was I gone."

I heard Mudi laugh and say, "Mr. Bet sleep like bone."

I heard the crackle of a fire and smelled wood smoke. "What time is it?" I asked. Without waiting for an answer, I asked, "What day is it?"

Laughter came from several places. I wondered who else was there.

"Is Saturday yet, Mr. Bet," Eddie answered.

"We bring you comida," Mudi said, "and some casuuusaaa," he sang, to accompanying laughter.

"Okay," I said as I stepped off the porch, "what's casusa?"

"Is rum! Made right here in Karawala," Mudi boasted.

They had rolled three big logs up to the cooking shed and placed them in a triangle around the old motor housing, which had arrived while I slept. The fire was in it. I nodded my approval and smiled a greeting.

Eddie introduced Bruce and Abanil, who had come with them, he explained, for a pasear.

I sat on the log with them and uncovered a plate of snook, fried in coconut oil, gallo pinto and yucca. I ate hungrily.

From a large glass shrimp boat float, Mudi poured a clear liquid into a coconut shell bowl. He grinned mischievously and set it beside me on the log. He poured for each of the others in turn.

They smoked and sipped as I ate. Mudi and Eddie entertained Bruce and Abanil with our fishing exploits. I could not break my gaze from the western sky, where the sunset was painting the clouds. Parrots and parrotlets flew to their roosts above the coco plums and set up their raucous squawking.

When I had finished eating, I picked up the bowl of casusa and held it to my nose. I couldn't help but smile as they watched intently for my reaction.

"White lightning," I said. "The recipe must be the same everywhere."

"What that?" Eddie asked.

"That's what we call this stuff in Texas," I replied. I took a sip. It was clean tasting; no hint of scorching. It burned all the way down. I held the bowl away from the fire and said, "You guys better get this stuff away from that fire. You'll burn my house down."

They laughed. Mudi splashed a little into the fire and it whooshed into flame.

I looked around, just now noticing Ferlan's absence. "Where's Ferlan?" I asked.

"He can't come here now," Eddie said. "Not permitted. Night catch him."

I remembered the blood man. "What are you guys doing here, then? I thought it was too dangerous here for you at night." It was getting dark. They were usually gone by now.

"We got fire here," Midi grinned. "And you got pistol."

No one knew I had that, or so I thought. "What pistol?"

Mudi laughed. He was always smiling or laughing. "Ferlan see it when he clean the house."

I guess it would be difficult to keep anything secret here. Why should I even bother, I wondered. Even if there was something about me that met with disapproval, why should it matter to me? What would they do?

Even as I posed the question, I wished I hadn't. I would be myself, and if I broke some tabu, I would have to trust myself to smooth off the rough edges.

"Bring it now, Mr. Bet," Eddie directed.

"Oh, Eddie, we don't need a gun here, do we? What do five men with machetes and a fire have to be afraid of here?"

"No, Mr. Bet, you must get the gun." It was Mudi, and he wasn't smiling.

I looked at the others. They were serious. I couldn't tell whether it was fear or something else, but it was enough to make me go strap it on. When I returned, their relief was obvious. It was fear, but why were they afraid?

I stood in front of the fire and asked. "What is out there? Is it tigers or is it the blood man?"

"Hoopah, Mr. Bet, is plenty out there," Eddie started. "The blood man is only one. There is lions and tigers and monkey man and..."

"Whoa, Eddie. Wait a minute. What is the monkey man?"

"He is a man...we don't know where he come from...he come out sometime and change to a monkey and kill people."

"Him is a big monkey," Bruce said, standing up with his arms and legs spread, his eyes big in exaggeration.

This was not a campfire story for the kids. These men believed what they were telling me. Not only did they have their own vampires; they also had their own brand of werewolves.

"He does drag off the children, them, and eat them. Some of the time he will kill a man or woman if he can't get the children. And before the moon set and the sun come, he change back to a man."

"The full moon sets just before the sun rises," I said. "You mean he comes out on a full moon?"

"That right," Eddie said, "and tonight it near to full."

Mudi laughed again. "Maybe the monkey woman come to you tonight, Mr. Bet." The others laughed, too.

"Okay, tell me about the monkey woman." They were having fun, and so was I. The more the casusa took hold, the more animated they became. I guessed the big glass ball held more than a gallon.

"Oh, you going to like it if she come. She is a monkey, but she can change to a beautiful young woman when the moon is full. Like you alone, Mr. Bet, she will come naked to a man living him alone and she will get in his bed and grind him all night."

"She is Indian girl with long black hair and when you touch her, she make you stand up all over. She come to my cousin in Sandy Bay last month. He say he knew it was her, but he couldn't stop. He say she feel different, and he knew it, but no way to stop. She was too much sex."

He had everyone's full attention as he told the story.

"He say it was late and he ready to sleep when he look out and see her standing in the moon, naked, looking right to him. He say she slim, but not meager. Her breasts and legs is strong, them.

"He just look at her long time, afraid she turn and run if he move. So he just look and look and study all of her head to toe.

"And then she walk to him and stop just this close." He held his arms wide. "He say his heart try to jump right out his chest."

Their eyes were wide now; they were excited.

"And then she walk to him and put her hands right down in his pants and turn him and pull him to the bed and grind him all the night.

"And before day, when she leave, he watch her walk in the moonlight. And he see her change. First she start walk funny. Then she start grow hair all over. He knew it so. She never say one word all the night. She only make sex."

"Hoopah," Eddie said. "I hear it so, but I never yet see her."

"I going find her for you, Mr. Bet," Mudi said. "You living here you alone, you need a girl. I going find her for you tonight."

He was feeling the casusa. The others cheered for him. "She going be all used up if you find her, Mudi," Abanil said.

"That my brother, Abanil," Mudi said. "Don't study him."

"Ssso!" Abanil said, joking. "You think I lie? You find that monkey woman, you going grind her to dead, Mudi Lacayo!"

"I do better than Monkey Woman! I going go get my wife for you, Mr. Bet. I going go right now and bring her for you."

He stood up to go, but I caught his arm and stopped him. "Whoa, Mudi. Wait just a minute. I can't let you do that."

He looked at me with surprise. The expression on his face asked what was wrong with me?

"Mudi, I really do appreciate your offer. I am honored by it. I think it is one of the greatest gifts I have ever been offered. But I can't accept it. My people do not permit it."

I had not met Mudi's wife and had no idea what she looked

like. I knew very well, though, how uncomfortable I felt about his offer. It was a great relief when he shrugged his shoulders and said I would just have to wait for the monkey woman.

"Maybe Sebm Debls going come instead, eh, Eddie?" Abanil asked with a grin.

"Stop that." Eddie commanded. "No more about that."

His command was on the strong side, so I did not pursue it. Instead, I asked for more casusa, which was having its intended effect on me. The bowls were refilled and they all lit up a cigarette.

Bruce had been looking at my pistol all night. He finally said something. "You know to shoot that thing, Mr. Bet?"

"Sure, I do, Bruce." I put my hand on the butt. "Want to see?"

"No, no, no, Mr. Bet. Don't waste the bullet, them. You will fright the whole town." He paused, then added, "But that thing would surely good for hunt wari."

"What's a wari?" I asked.

"Is a wild hog."

"You have lots of them around here?" I asked.

"Hoopah, this the home of wari." They all agreed.

"Why do you need a gun to kill them? Why not just take a club and whack them in the head?"

That must have sounded interminably stupid to them, from the looks on their faces. Finally, Mudi laughed and said, "Mr. Bet make joke."

They all broke out laughing, slapping their thighs at my joke. So I laughed, too, trying to cover my blunder.

"That fella kill more than tigers and tommygoff snake," Eddie said, "and you want we hunt them with a stick!"

Mudi held his arm out for me to inspect.

"Looky dat," he said. "That from wari."

There was a long red scar inside his forearm, running from elbow to wrist. It had healed without sutures, but it probably took forever. He was lucky he hadn't bled to death, and surviving that, hadn't lost it to infection.

"And I lucky. Was one tree big enough and I did climb it. Whole pack of them stay two days trying to dig it up. They would eat me if they could."

"You gotta be kidding," I said. These are not like our little collared peccary at home. "How many were there?"

"Small pack," he said, "'bout twenty."

"And they were going to dig up the tree? And eat you when it fell?"

"That how they do, Mr. Bet," Eddie said. "Even tiger give them plenty room. Sometime they come through, maybe fifty or sixty, and dig up everything in the way. Nothing left standing. Nothing, nothing. Like a road through the bush. That fella got tusses, I tell you. And sharp! You go up in a tree, you study find a big one."

I was impressed. "How do you hunt them?

Abanil answered, on his feet, smiling and gesturing. "Sometime you hear the wari, them, in the bush and you go ahead of them and find a big tree. All of you climb up, and when the wari, them come, pop-pop, you shoot. Then you wait for the others, them to leave."

He shrugged his shoulders. Simple.

"And then in a day or so when they leave, you climb down and carry them home?" I asked. "Don't they get a little rank?"

"Not so bad," he said. "Sometime they gone soon."

"Is good, yet, though," Eddie said. "Can eat."

I wasn't sure I would eat a hog that had been laying out in the tropical heat for two days, but I doubted that I knew as much about hunger as they. I had to admire anyone who would go to such lengths to get a meal. How many people did I know who would do that?

Yes, I was impressed. The more I learned about these people, the more I was impressed.

"Tell me about the man who lived here before me." -

Their brows creased and they looked away.

"Come on, now. You told me a little. Now tell me the whole story. Who was he, and how did he get eaten by a tiger?"

Eddie fidgeted a bit, then started the story. "He was called Billy Rose and he come to buy tiger skin and parrot and snake. It was a few years ago the first time, when he make us build the house.

"He buy all kind thing, like tiger tooth and sawfish bill and whatever we had around. He buy out all the parrot, them, and some red monkey.

"And as soon as the house was done, he left off. He say he come back soon, and he did. 'Bout every three months he come stay a week or two, then leave off. He take out plenty tiger skin, I tell you. Sometime we take him out to Sumi Laya to kill them, but most he did stay drunk and send for the girl, them."

"That fella could drink a rum, I tell you," Mudi interjected. They all nodded agreement. "Sometime he drink a six medios, he alone, in one day."

"And he get mannish when he drunk. He come to Mundo's and start fight most every night. And if he can't find a fight, he beat the girl, them."

"Son of a bitch. Why did you put up with him?" I asked. "Nobody needs people like that around."

"Money," Abanil said, rubbing his fingers together. "We is poor people here, Mr. Bet. If you can give us work, you can stay. We got nothing here but what we get with our hand, them. That a hard life. But we don't complain.

"If we can't get a few shilling for cloth, then we got no shirt. If we got no cord for machet, then we can't do nothing, nothing. We just going drop down and dead."

I nodded and sighed.

"So you pretend to like him, and you sell him whatever he wants."

"That is it. He come here for one year and a half," Eddie continued.

"The last time he come, he never leave off. We hear it, but

was nothing to do but listen. First we hear him call for help. Then we hear the tiger. We hear it like it was right close. We hear the bamboo crack, but no gun. He got gun, but he never use it.

"Then we hear the scream and the tiger all the same time. We frighted, I tell you. We know he gone dead and we know what that tiger do. We hear him long time while he eat. Rrrruh...rrrruh...rrrruh, like that, like a drum.

"Next day we all fright to go look, but haps to, we gone. Blood all over, I tell you. Even up in the leaf," he said and waved at the thatched roof of my cabin.

Abanil and Bruce were stoking the fire and watching our backsides nervously. The story was not making them feel good about where they were.

"Right here in this house?" I asked. "Right where I sleep?"

"Maybe you not sleep so good tonight," Mudi replied.

"But there's no sign of it. If there was blood, I would have seen it."

"Blood gone quick time here. We fix up the bamboo and the leaf, them," Eddie said.

"I guess I like my little Browning even more, now."

"That tiger here yet," Eddie said. "We hear him."

"Maybe that tiger works for someone around here," I offered. They chuckled. "If so, I shouldn't have to worry about him. Anyway, I'll be careful. And I'll sleep with one eye open."

They looked puzzled. "How you do that?" Mudi asked.

"I don't," I answered. "It's just a figure of speech."

It was getting late. I thought about a bath, and that reminded me of my swim earlier in the afternoon.

"Are there many alligators in the river?" I asked. The odds of meeting my death in the river seemed greater than the threat of a tiger.

"Not round here," Abanil answered. "Plenty small one, yes, but big one far. All dead out round here. Kill them for the skin."

"There's one big one around here," I said. "I thought I was

going to be eaten today."

"You see alligator?" Mudi asked. "Where you see that?" He was excited by the news.

I motioned across the runway at the path I'd taken. "Right down that path; at the river. He was in the mangroves."

"That where you get in the river?" Eddie asked. "You swim from there to the wharf?" He was incredulous. "Leopoldo tell me you come out the river, but he don't know where you get in. How you swim so?"

Mudi couldn't stand it. "Come, Eddie, we get the alligator, then talk. Come." He picked up a pine root torch and thrust it into the fire. Abanil and Bruce did the same, picking up machetes. "How big that alligator?"

I was feeling the casusa. They had put much more of it into their bodies than I, and they were talking about going alligator hunting. It didn't sound prudent to me.

"About eight feet," I said. "Big enough to kill all four of you. You're not going out tonight, are you?" It was obvious they were.

Eddie shrugged his shoulders, stood up, took the fourth torch and put it into the fire. The four torches crackled and spit as the pine pitch heated up, released its turpentine, and caught fire.

"Haps to we going to. Skin get plenty Cordobas," Mudi said.

"How many?" I asked.

"Maybe two hundred," he answered, making it sound substantial.

They were going to paddle a dugout canoe up the creek, torches held aloft, to harpoon an alligator. For less than thirty dollars. But for them, two hundred Cordobas really is a substantial amount, even split four ways.

I didn't get to ask about what else lay waiting in the river for unwary bathers. I watched them leave, torches bobbing, and wondered which of them I would see in the morning.

I drained my bowl, went inside and fell asleep without trying to focus on the sounds. The last I saw was the flicker of dying flames washing the thatch in yellow light.

*

Neither the monkey woman nor the tiger visited me that night. The parrots woke me with their chatter sooner than I wanted. Between going to sleep and waking up, there was nothing. As Mudi said, I slept hard. Too hard. It must have been the casusa.

I wasn't overly pleased with myself for getting a good night of sound sleep. I wouldn't have wanted to miss the monkey woman if she came by, and I certainly wouldn't have wanted to sleep through dinner for a tiger.

I stepped outside to greet the day. I found a world awash in gold reflected from the clouds and in the first rays of the sun crowning the pines. Across the runway a troupe of white faced monkeys had come down out of the trees to breakfast on the low growing coco plums. A few eyed me with suspicion, but kept eating.

There was no smell of wood smoke and fresh coffee. No sign of Ferlan or my crew. I went around to the cooking shed, started a fire and put on a pot of water to boil. As it heated, I watched and listened.

The sounds of the morning are not the same as the sounds of the night. As I listened, I realized that I had been too wrapped up in fishing in the mornings to hear. These were new sounds. I had neither heard nor seen the daytime creatures that shared this clearing with me.

I dumped some coffee into the boiling water and watched it cook. I thought about going to look for Eddie to see if they were still alive, but decided to let the news come to me. I put on long pants and moccasins, poured a cup of coffee through a rag filter, and stepped out to see what could be seen.

I walked slowly at the edge of the trees, taking only a few

steps each minute, sipping at the steaming coffee, searching each leaf, branch and blade of grass for whatever life it supported. At times I stood stock still, gazing unfocused into the deep shade, waiting for something to move.

I knew I would not see anything unless it moved. Most of the creatures here are camouflaged to perfection. They could not have survived otherwise. Even at my slow pace, there was a sphere of silence and stillness around me. The things in that sphere refused to reveal themselves.

I saw the obvious things like birds in flight and harvester ants with cut leaves held above their heads. I saw the things that depend on escape or sheer numbers for survival.

At the far side of the clearing, there was a path that led into the bush. I followed it. About a hundred feet in, I found an old gnarled star apple tree with sparse, dark leaves, living in deep shade uncontested by the dense undergrowth surrounding it. I slipped into its space and took a seat on a heavy branch dipping close to the ground.

There I sat, watching and listening, trying not to let the mosquitoes bother me, as motionless as they would allow. For the first five minutes I saw nothing and heard little more. Then I began to see movement in the bush around me and to hear the calls of small birds as they returned. The longer I sat, the more the things around me lost their caution and resumed their routines. Within fifteen minutes, the bush was alive with movement and sound.

Butterflies opened their wings to reveal bright, glittering blues. Leaves moved on their own six legs. Twigs got up and walked. Tree frogs appeared from nowhere, revealing reds and yellows I hadn't seen before.

I jumped off my branch and out of my skin when a boa struck out from beside my feet at a small mammal that disappeared instantly into its bone crushing coils.

"Motherfucker!" I yelled. "Don't you ever do that again!"

The pounding of my heart must have scared everything else

away. Suddenly it was all gone again. All but the boa and his meal. It wasn't too big as boas go. About as long as I am tall and about as big around as my leg. But for the size of the scare he threw into me, he was as big as a thirty foot anaconda.

I sat back down and watched him eat. I shook my head slowly as I watched. Being wary here is not enough. Here the dangers are likely to be undetectable until it is too late. One must be wary, lightning fast and lucky.

"Hoo! Mr. Bet!" I heard Ferlan call from my house.

I got up and walked quietly away from the snake. It had swallowed its prey and was laying still, flicking its tongue.

Back on the path, I answered Ferlan. "Over here! In the trees!"

I walked into the clearing and saw him standing by the house, dressed in a clean white shirt, navy blue pants and black lace-up shoes. Their clothes were always clean, but they were also old and worn. I hadn't seen anyone dressed like that since Bluefields.

"Well, if you're not all decked out in fine threads. What's the occasion?"

"I going church," he answered, embarrassed at the attention.

I had forgotten it was Sunday.

"Eddie say you must come look the alligator to the wharf."

"They got it?" I asked. "Anyone hurt?"

"Them is okay. Alligator big. Have almost ten feet."

"Sumbitch! That's a big one. Okay, I'm on my way."

"You need anything from Mundo? I bring it after church."

"Yes. Bring me a big bowl of ice cream with pecans and chocolate syrup."

"What that?"

"Ice cream?"

"Yeh."

"You've never eaten ice cream before?"

"No, sir."

"Well, it's something very cold and sweet and creamy

smooth. I don't think I can do it justice. Just take my word for it. It's very good to eat."

We walked off toward the village. Everywhere I looked, people were dressed in the best clothes they had. They wore things that were put up all week, to be worn only on Sunday. No matter how little they had, they were able to walk with pride one day of the week.

As I walked, I was greeted by many I had not met. They came off their porches and walked out of their way to say hello. They stood taller, smiled brightly and shook hands more firmly.

Ferlan said good-bye as we passed the church. I made my way to the wharf, where a knot of people stood around a very large alligator, listening to Eddie and Mudi entertain them with their adventure.

"This the one, Mr. Bet. Right where you say," Eddie said, bursting with pride.

"Did he give you a good fight?"

"Hoopah, I tell you. Took more than two hours to kill this one. Fella had us all up and down this creek."

It was a magnificent animal. He looked deadly even in death, but not so much as the day before. I wondered how often they lost children to animals like this.

"Well, I guess we can swim in the river again," I said.

"Oh, Mr. Bet," Eddie said, "that very dangerous."

"What else is there? If you just killed the only big alligator here, why not?

"What does get, we never see."

"What does get?" I echoed.

He squatted with his knife and resumed skinning. "Can't say. Maybe june fish; maybe mirro maid."

"What? Mirro maid? What is a mirro maid?" It was beginning to look like this was a veritable haunted house. There was a spook for everything.

"She live in the river," he said, still working, not looking up. "Sometime she come up and take a boy or a man and drag him down. She keep him there 'till he dead, then throw him out."

It sounded reasonable. Sometimes drowning victims will stay submerged until the gasses float the body.

He continued, "One time one man did stay down thirty days with her and escaped. I tell you that man never the same. Make his brain weak. He dead now. Not for him, we never know it she."

I threw my head back and looked up at the sky. A man-o-war wheeled in the currents. The rest of the story was easy to guess. A man was given a few days of bliss with a mermaid before they laid him to rest.

"I think I'll walk around some," I said and turned to go.

"Okay, Mr. Bet. We come pasear when we done."

*

I was sitting on my steps when Ferlan came bouncing into the clearing, still dressed in blue and white. He came straight up to me and held out a small bag.

"Miss Irene send these things for you," he said and sat down at my feet.

I took the bag. In it were bread and a sweet roll. I started with the bread.

"She say you not to get hungry."

I chuckled. "Who is Miss Irene?"

"She lady live by Mundo house. She see you plenty."

"I'll have to stop and thank her."

"She say you can eat there sometime."

I changed the subject. "Did Mundo pay you yesterday?" I was curious as to how much I was paying my house boy and guides.

"Yes, sir," he answered, happy and proud to have a job.

"And how much did you get?"

"Can't say."

It occurred to me that he might not be able to count. "Why

can't you say?"

"Take it to the Reverend."

"No!"

"Sure."

"Not all of it."

"Yes, all. He say it must be so."

"But why, Ferlan? You can't give all your money to the Reverend."

"Haps to I going to. He say it only way to keep the debl gone."

"You mean he told you he would keep the devil away if you gave him your money?"

"That the whole of it."

"What if you only gave him part of it?"

"Not enough. Debl come take me."

"Ferlan," I said gently, "no Reverend in the world has the power to buy off the devil. And no Reverend in the world can sell tickets to heaven. If you want to give to the church, give him a few Cordobas, but do it after your brothers and sisters have something to wear and something to eat."

"I did want do that, but he make me give all."

I could tell it bothered him. He wasn't going to cry, but he was close.

"My mother going get vexed. Going make him cross."

Eddie and Mudi came sauntering up, clothes covered with blood and smelling of the sweet meat of alligator. They were both grinning like a Cheshire cat.

"Where is it?" I asked.

"Where what?" Mudi challenged.

"The rum," I said.

They both laughed. Mudi pulled a medio from his belt at his back. He offered it to me, but I declined.

"Eddie?"

"Mr. Bet."

"How much did Ferlan make this week?"

"Haps to ask Mundo. Maybe three-fifty a day."

I sighed and shook my head. It was unheard of for a boy his age to make that much. Most of the men don't make that much.

I handed Ferlan fifteen cords and told him not to give one real to the Reverend.

Eddie shook his head and tsked. "He make you give it all, Ferlan?"

Ferlan hung his head. "Yes," was all he said.

"And your family hungry so," Mudi said. "How you let him do that?"

"Don't know," he answered.

"To keep the devil away," I interrupted. "Extortion."

"He always say that," Eddie said. "Always the devil going get you."

I put my hand on Ferlan's shoulder. "You can tell him no. The next time he tries to get your money, tell him you are paid up."

No one spoke. A light breeze whispered through the pines. The tops looked soft and fuzzy, swaying gently. Sometimes the feeling came to me that I was going to be here for a long time. It felt very strong just then.

I looked at Eddie and Mudi, at the alligator fused with them, and knew that there was a lifetime of experience here. A week or two would only begin to scratch the surface.

"What if I wanted to buy some land here, Eddie? How would I go about it?"

They looked at me, shook their heads and chuckled. "Sun hot burn you brain," Mudi laughed. "Better you get to the shade."

"No, really, I might like to buy a little property here."

"You mean for you alone to own? Like a hat?" He was laughing, as if I had told a joke. Eddie looked worried.

"Well, yes. That's what I had in mind."

Mudi doubled over, holding his sides, rocking on his heals. He laughed so hard he couldn't catch his breath. Then Eddie started.

Still laughing, Mudi said, "We sure going sell all to you. And you going tell all the ant, them, and all the fly, them, they must leave off from your property."

Eddie roared. "And the tommygoff, too!" The rum was in them well.

Eddie looked at Mudi. "Oh, no, Mudi. We can't do it. What if he leave off for Texas and put it in his grip and take it with him? Where we going sit down? The sea going rush right in to Karawala." They slapped themselves on the back and tried to swallow more rum while they laughed.

"Oh, Eddie, yes! Mr. Bet our friend. We not sell it; we give it him. And for us, he going tell the bush where can grow. We never chop plantation again. Throw out the machet."

I nodded my head. They were right, of course. It was my white man's way that made me want to own it. It made about as much sense as wanting to own a storm.

"Okay, okay. I get the point. No one owns land here. So what if I want to use it?

"Can't say. Leopoldo come pasear later. Ask him."

"Why Leopoldo?"

"He the Cindigo. He know these things."

"What's a cindigo?"

"Like alcalde."

"Like a mayor?" I asked.

"Something like that, I think."

"Or like a chief?"

"Yeah, like a chief," Mudi said. "That the one. We is Indian. He is the chief."

Ferlan had been staring at his feet, mulling things over. It was the first time I had seen him pensive or anything besides ebullient. Suddenly he stood up and said, "All right, I going," and strode off toward the field.

Ferlan had taken but a few steps when Mudi repeated, "All right, Mr. Bet," and was gone.

Eddie took a step and turned to look at me. He had a crooked grin on his face and a twinkle in his eye, perhaps from the rum, and somewhere within, a thought gelled in me. 'No man can claim it for his own. We are like the deer. We can own what we are, but we are not the earth. No man has the power to take from you what you are, even in death. That you own. Nothing else. If you have great heart, the earth will let you live here.'

Then Eddie was gone, and suddenly I was alone, sitting on my steps. To myself, I laughed at the abruptness of things here. The moments have no momentum. People and events can flit into one's sphere of awareness like a little bird, unannounced but for the certainty it is always there, and be gone without parting, with no certainty it came.

I sat and watched and listened and felt a tingling. It looked hard, this place, like reality, but I felt that if I tried to touch it, my hand would lose its place. I had shifted out of it, and for the moment was not a part of anything. I sat in it; in this jungle home of ancient people, but I was no more than a wisp of wind in all the wind. I could neither touch it nor escape its touch.

And if I could not change the wind, I knew its strength and its power to carry me along with it. Reality shifts, and my place in it becomes lost, like the unseen gust. It shifts as if seen through the eye of an insect, and there is a jolt as each tunnel falls into focus. Do I see all things at once, or one thing with all eyes?

My attention snapped. Leopoldo, real flesh and bone, came into view around the pines. With him walked Valdevio and Gonzalo Gomez. They all wore their best.

We exchanged greetings and I asked them what brought them my way.

"Just come pasear," Leopoldo explained. The others smiled and nodded their agreement. I noticed, when they smiled, that they were missing front teeth. It hit me that all the adults were missing front teeth, or nearly all. It caught my curiosity, but I filed it away for future reference. Better not to risk offense.

Predictably enough, the weather was there to talk about. No matter what it's doing, it will always be talked about. I've always wondered about that. I can usually see what the weather is doing, and I assume others are as gifted. So why are we always asking and telling each other about the weather? I knew it was hot. I didn't need to be told.

But I was polite about it. I agreed, looked at the sky and offered my own observations. As soon as that was out of the way, I got down to business.

"Leopoldo, Eddie tells me you are the cindigo here."

"That so, Mr. Bet."

"I asked him about using some land here, and he said I should ask you."

They all smiled heartily and nodded approval to each other.

"We is the one, Mr. Bet. We can fix it for you."

Using is second best to owning. I asked how, revived.

"You say what you want. If no one else use it, then it for you."

Distrust, another of the white man's evils, slipped in. "But what if I use it and make something good on it and someone else says it's his?"

"Same-same. We all know it for you. That thing could never happen."

He said it as matter of fact, as if it was a law of nature. And he should have been correct. But when two men say 'mine', the written word is worth more than many memories. I pressed for more, even though I would feel guilt over it. It was like telling them I didn't trust them, and it showed on their faces.

"Okay, we do this before. We go to Bluefields and make writing. You pay each year to use it. Easy."

So I could lease it, or something like it. They told me there was a lawyer in Bluefields who handled all their affairs. We talked awhile about what I needed to do and what they would do. While we talked, my clearing began to fill up with people from the village. They were all "pasearing", I was told.

Leopoldo, Gonzalo and Valdevio were part of the Committee that decided, like a council, upon the affairs of the village. It would be a simple matter for the Committee to meet and approve my request.

"But what you going do with it?" Leopoldo asked.

With a broad smile, I answered, "I going bring people from Texas for pasear and go fishinin."

They laughed and clapped their hands. "Okay, Mr. Bet, we going." And they turned to mingle with the others, pasearing.

Each time they recounted my words, there was laughing and clapping. But there was nothing but laughter and clapping everywhere I looked. Children were singing and dancing. Women and girls talked their sing-song language and stole glances my way. They sat on the grass or stood in groups, while others strolled through the yard.

Many were dressed in blue and white; men and women, boys and girls. But some were dressed in bright reds and yellows in loose, flowing clothing. I enjoyed the sight and the company. And I felt a little honored that all these people would come for a visit on a Sunday afternoon.

It made me wish I had racks of ribs turning over a slow fire and kegs of beer on ice.

I, too, mingled. Not certain of the customs, I was careful not to approach any women of courtable age, of which there were many, but neither did I avoid being approached. They were very shy and would not shake my hand. They blushed, averted their eyes, introduced themselves after I did, did a sort of curtsey, and left giggling to return to their friends.

Some of the younger girls, in their teens, were quite beautiful, but plumpness seemed to be the popular figure, and most of the older girls had been successful in attaining it.

I did my best to recall the names of everyone I'd met, but I had met so many in such a short time, and was meeting more, that I soon had to give up.

My name, McBeth, has always been an easy one to remember. Being the only white man for hundreds of miles made it even easier. They all knew my name, even before we met, but not once was it used. I was Mr. Bet.

We sat and talked about their way of life and mine. I developed a little more respect for their stoic spirit as they portrayed their way of life. The things they took for granted were things we associate with great courage and great hardship. Three generations often share a one-room house of not more than three hundred square feet. They sleep on the floor, and only the elders have covers. I wondered how far down the family tree would I go to find ancestors with similar lives.

And I laughed with them as they told me about their image of my way of life. The legends of the Old West have traveled far. They knew I had a gun the minute they heard I was from Texas. Their only surprise was that it was not a revolver. They were sure I had killed with it, and nothing I said convinced them otherwise.

According to them, I could hit whatever I shot at, no matter how small or how far away. I could whip any man I fought, no matter how strong, big or fast. I had a ranch with horses, cows and oil wells. I could ride anything with four feet. They were proud to have me there.

"And where a Texas man put down a dollar, he pick up two. He can never spend all." I was, they were sure, one of the wealthiest men in the world.

I laughed and shook my head, but it was no use. They were sure they knew.

About mid-afternoon they began to leave, and in twenty minutes I was alone again, sitting on my steps, looking out over the canopy. I smiled and asked myself what McBeth Johnson was getting himself into. I had no plan and no experience specific to this idea, but I saw in my mind a vision, and I knew if I could hold it there, I could make a copy of it in the world.

I was flooded with emotions. If I did this thing, I would be committing myself to living here most of the year. The safety and comfort of the familiar would no longer be a harbor to run to when things got rough.

I jumped, swatted and cursed all at the same time as a short-jacket fly stabbed my leg. The flies were part of it. Everything here wanted to take a bite out of me.

How would I stand up to that, day after day, month after month? I got up, got a lime and a medio of rum and sat back down on the steps.

But how could I leave this place? The things that bite are part of the beauty, and they are the reason the beauty is undisturbed. If this was not a hostile environment, it would be overrun with farmers or loggers or tourists. There would be a Holiday Inn on this very spot.

An image of nightclubs and beautiful women flashed before me. I shook my head. Music and perfume were not enough. What else could lure me back or change my mind? I would miss it from time to time, but I could live without it. We could all live without it, and like living without disease, be better off.

The rum was making me hungry. I put the bottle in my pocket and walked off to find Miss Pete.

KUKU AWRA
Chapter Five
Matsip

They call it a cotton tree. They are few and far between, but the ones I've seen are huge. The biggest are ten feet or more in diameter and one hundred feet tall. The canopy spreads out in a giant hemisphere above everything else in the bush.

There is one at Wankar Laya, about forty miles up the river, that's a wood stork rookery. I saw more nests and storks there than I wanted to count. The first time I saw a stork, close overhead, I thought it was some sort of dragon. They are that big.

But this is about the cotton trees, which get their name from the kapoc fibers that are released when the seedpods open. Inside the largest of the cotton trees is a city populated by magicians. It is possible for a strong-hearted man to be admitted to one of these cities and to be given treasure to take home.

Four weeks before Good Friday, one must visit the tree at night and clear the brush, vines, grass and debris from around it. One must spend the night under the tree and tell it that he would like to come inside, why he would like to come inside, and what he would want from the magicians. The ritual is repeated each Friday night until Good Friday, when the petitioner is admitted to the city. If greed is the motive, or if the motive is in any way disagreeable to the magicians, they will kill the supplicant right then.

But if the heart is good and the motives altruistic, the request is granted. Upon leaving, there is a warning not to look back, no matter what happens. As one departs with his treasure, the black hoard cries from behind, Kill him! Kill him! If one turns to look, they do just that and return to their city in the tree with their treasure.

It appears that no one has ever resisted the urge to turn and look.

As told by Abanil Lacayo

Ferlan Santiago had never been to Bluefields. He had never in his life ventured beyond the area claimed by the Community of Karawala. I couldn't resist it. I had to take him with us.

It is a rare event to watch as the universe expands before someone's eyes. It had happened to me as I journeyed to Karawala. Then, on the dusty streets of Bluefields, it was happening for Ferlan.

It was all new. Like fairy tales come to life, he knew what they were and what they did, but until then, they were all just parts of stories he had heard. The old rusted carcass of a jeep in Karawala, with vines and trees growing through it, roared to life and came careening around a corner in the reincarnate form of a Toyota taxi, chasing Ferlan up Eddie's back like a lizard up a tree.

He watched it disappear in a cloud of dust, horn honking. His eyes snapped from side to side, looking for more. Finding none, he bounced down and into a store, where he found, in one large room, more dry goods and hardware, tools and utensils, than was owned by the entire village of Karawala.

He jumped from rack to rack, table to table, touching everything he saw, chattering incessantly at Eddie and me about the treasures he was finding. What he saw was so impossible to him that he thought it had to be new to us, too.

Then he stopped. His arms fell limp to his sides and his joy crashed. He had found King Solomon's Mine. He stood amid the answer to every prayer in Karawala and knew with numbing certainty that he would walk out without a single scrap of it.

I saw the realization hit him. I knew in the same instant that I had dealt him a blow he would never forget. I had tarnished his innocence, and I would take him back to hunger. But before I did, I would let him feast on what was there.

Eddie saw it, too. "Ferlan!" he laughed. "Why you look on them things so? And why your face so long? Them things not for we."

Sorrow poured from Ferlan's eyes. It was the sorrow of a prisoner who had done no wrong; a victim of a capricious god. What hunger had meant to him before, I cannot say, but now it was the hunger of a starving servant at a feast with the knowledge that he would not be fed. He must leave the feast to scratch at the earth with his own claws.

I put my arm around his shoulder. "Keep your eyes open, Ferlan. Before we leave, we'll all get something we need."

"Looky dat!" Mudi chimed. "Did I told you? He going care for we. He going be like a father."

Ferlan smiled, and some of the light returned to his face.

We left the store and walked up the street to the Hotel del Queto. Ferlan gawked at everything he saw. Eddie walked with a hand on his shoulder to keep him from bumping into anything.

"Look, now," he would say, "what dat ting?" And he would point out each new thing. I let Eddie and Mudi do the explaining while I walked along as an observer. We passed more shops and market areas, and each one was a new wonder. Sometimes they had to get behind him and push him along the sidewalk.

At the steps of the hotel, we turned to look back down the street. The noon hour had come. Shops were boarding up and the people were deserting the streets. It was another wonder, even to me. For the better part, the business of the day was over. The shops would reopen in the afternoon, but there would be few sales. People would be out and about, but generally not on business.

Once checked in, we stowed our bags in our rooms and reconvened on the porch. Ferlan was the last to return. As we started to leave, he tugged on Eddie's sleeve.

"Can't go yet," Eddie said. "Ferlan haps to go to toilet."

"No problem," I said. I looked at Ferlan and asked, "You know where it is?"

He shook his head, "No," so I took him back inside and showed him to the two communal baths in our hallway. I returned to the porch to wait.

After fifteen minutes of sitting and waiting, I returned to the bath where I'd left him, just to check on him. He could have been sick, I thought.

The door was open. I stepped inside. There was water everywhere. The shower was on, the sink was running over, and Ferlan was standing over the toilet, watching the whirlpool as it flushed. He was absolutely delighted with the discoveries he'd made and proceeded to demonstrate each for me.

I had to step back and laugh. Seeing me laugh just fueled his euphoria. He laughed with me and stamped his feet in the water. He had never seen indoor plumbing before.

"Ferlan," I chuckled, "are you ready yet?"

"No, Mr. Bet," he answered. "Where I to go to toilet here?"

I pointed at the toilet bowl.

He looked at it, then back to me. Incredulous, he asked, "You mean I to shit in that?"

"Yes, Ferlan. That is where you will use the toilet while we are here." We were both still laughing. "When you are done, you flush it, like this." I tossed a bit of toilet paper in and flushed it. I turned off the shower and sink faucets, showed him how to lock the door, and left.

I stood in the hallway and listened. I heard the water come on in the shower and then in the sink. On and off...on and off. The toilet flushed twice, and then all was silent. I guessed he had gotten down to business.

A few minutes later, he came bouncing out onto the veranda,

eyes and smile wide, chattering in Miskito at Eddie and Mudi.

"So!" Eddie said as he picked him up by the scruff of the neck. "You make we wait so while you play!"

"Yeow! Eddie! Put me down!"

He dropped him to the porch and stepped back, looking him over. He couldn't help but chuckle. "Ai, Ferlan."

*

The Restaurante Galaxy isn't much, but it's the best in Bluefields. They can make you a hamburger of sorts, and they have potato chips. But the thing I like best about it is the cold beer. I ordered four of each.

Even Eddie and Mudi were impressed. They had never been in a real restaurant before, where they brought ice water without asking. Turtle eggs, gallo pinto and bread came with the beer. It made them wonder why anyone would order anything but beer.

We hadn't been there long before Ferlan asked if there was a toilet there. I told him there surely must be and suggested he ask the waitress.

I got the impression that if he hadn't been with me, he wouldn't have been allowed to use it. As it was, she admonished him not to make a mess. She didn't want any Indian boys playing with the plumbing. I don't think she wanted any Indian boys in there at all.

Sure enough, he was just curious. He tested the faucets and flushed the toilet and came out with a smile on his face. The waitress scowled at him; I scowled at her.

Having satisfied our hunger with a long and leisurely lunch, we left the restaurant and walked to the lawyer's office. Along the way, we passed in front of the only theater in town, where we stopped to read the posters.

"What this thing?" Ferlan asked, shyly. He was staring at a poster of "Gone With The Wind".

"It's a movie," I answered. "I don't think I'd better try to

91

explain it. We'll come tonight and see it."

We had to pull him away from the theater. He wanted to wait there for us to return. Having moved him, though, it was like trying to restrain a bolting dog on a leash. A few doors up the street, he darted into an open store, where the shopkeeper was watching television. He wore a pair of khaki pants and an undershirt and was sprawled out in an old recliner, almost asleep.

I was surprised to find a television in Bluefields and wondered if the signal came over the mountains from Managua. It was weak. The picture faded in and out, and the snow never quite left. I asked the shopkeeper; he just shrugged his shoulders.

But it was television, and Ferlan was entranced. He'd have tried to climb right in if Eddie hadn't wrapped an arm around his waist and picked him up. He screamed like a monkey and thrashed his arms and legs, but Eddie held on and carried him outside. The shopkeeper got up and locked the door behind us.

The phone company, with the only phones in town, was in the post office building. Eddie and Mudi went inside to see if there was any mail for Karawala. This was the end of the line for the mail. It came from Managua once a week and stopped right here. There was no delivery, so if no one came from Karawala to get it, and no one picked it up before going to Karawala, it could sit there for a long, long time, which it often did. It could also be a long, long time between letters even if there was plenty of traffic.

Eddie and Mudi came out with a handful of letters, all of which had been opened. "Already read 'em, eh?"

"No, sar," Mudi replied. "They come so."

I looked again. They had been sealed and then cut open. "You didn't open them?"

"No, sar." They were more interested in reading the addressees and return addresses. They were unperturbed at the apparent rape of privacy. My stomach muscles tightened involuntarily; my hair bristled.

"Who opened them?"

Without looking up, they answered, "The Guardia, I guess, or maybe the Correo, them."

"Why?"

"They looking money," Eddie answered.

"Not censorship?" I asked.

"What that?" Mudi asked, looking up for the first time.

"That's where the government spies on you to silence troublemakers. It's part of the control they need.

Mudi laughed. "Must be brain weak. More easy go Karawala and look. Learn more."

We all laughed, but it really wasn't funny. Not to me, it wasn't. It was chilling. It bespoke of a terrorist government. Or maybe not. Maybe it was just a petty thief or two who abused their post. I said as much.

"The whole of them like that," Eddie replied.

"What do you mean?"

"I mean if they is government or Guardia, they is going thief you. And if they is Spaniard, is worse. Not just one-one; the whole of them." His voice was matter-of-fact.

I began to sense a blanket of oppression laying over my friends. I didn't want it to be there and hoped it wasn't so. At the same time, I leafed through the things I'd heard so far, and it seemed that they reserved their greatest appreciation for those who left them alone.

We turned the corner, and standing in front of a doorway were Leopoldo, Valdevio and Gonzalo. Beside the door was a large bronze seal that read,

SALVADOR SANTAMARIA
ABOGADO Y NOTARIO PUBLICA
REPUBLICA DE NICARAGUA
AMERICA CENTRAL

So there we were, assembled at the appointed hour. Inside this office, I would do what was necessary to formalize a venture into the unknown. Once done, my life would officially change direction. I was divorcing myself from everything I knew. I took a deep breath and opened the door.

Leopoldo introduced us, referring to the lawyer as, "Dr. Santamaria." The waiting room was the only room large enough to seat us all. Even so, it took all the chairs from all the rooms.

He was a small man, a "Spaniard" who was regarded just slightly higher than all others. His manner was formal; very crisp and efficient. Once seated, he began by explaining to me that he was the only authority for the region of the Kingdom of Mosquitia.

Mudi winced and said, "We not flies. He know dat."

The others shuffled uncomfortably.

He went on, ignoring the comment, to delineate the area of the kingdom. As he spoke, I tried to place the landmarks on the map on the wall. If I was correct, the Community of Karawala held an estate of more than a million acres.

It was given to them, as a kingdom, by the Queen of England, in the treaty by which the crown relinquished its protectorate of that coast and gave it all to Nicaragua. The transfer was made during the last decade of the nineteenth century, on the condition that the Indians maintain the collective title to their lands in perpetuity.

"That right," Leopoldo smiled, swinging his short legs in the air. "Is only for we."

I had not been privy to the results of their deliberations in Karawala, so when it came time to divulge the exact provisions of the agreement, I listened with great interest.

The area of the lease started at the Ibo tree by Thomas Gamboa's house. The southern boundary was an east-west line running through the tree from the edge of the swamp on the east to the Rio Karawala on the west. The northern boundary was similar, with the north end of the runway as the relative benchmark. The eastern boundary was the edge of the swamp; the western was the river. In all, I guessed it to be more than one square mile. It was enough.

And how much would I pay for this? "One thousand Cordoba a year," Leopoldo answered.

For how large an area? "'Bout two hundred seventy-five hectareas."

"Not enough," declared Dr. Santamaria. "Make it five thousand Cordobas per year."

The price had jumped from $142.86 per year, for almost seven hundred acres, to $714.29 per year. Either way, it wasn't enough. I told myself that if this worked, they would get a better deal. What would be fair?

"And how long will this be in effect?"

"For the life, I guess," Leopoldo said.

"Too long," the lawyer said. "Ten years is the longest I can authorize, with another ten at Mr. Johnson's option."

He then turned his attention to me. "What will you call this enterprise?"

I hadn't thought about it. "I don't know. Does it have to have a name?"

"You must register a company name if you are to conduct business in Nicaragua."

"How do I do that?"

"Just give me a name. I'll do the rest."

"Karawala Tarpon Camp," I said. It came out of its own volition. I looked at Eddie and Mudi for approval. They grinned and nodded their heads, as did Leopoldo, Valdevio, Gonzalo and Ferlan.

"Thank you, Mr. McBeth Johnson. If you will return tomorrow at this same time, I will have all the papers ready for your signatures." He extended his hand to each of us as we filed out the door.

Leopoldo and his cohorts could hardly contain themselves. "Five thousand Cordoba! Five thousand Cordoba!" They giggled.

I patted them on the back, smiled with them and asked them

to have dinner with us. But they couldn't. They were on their way to the church, where they would remain, to thank god for five thousand Cordoba.

As they walked off toward the church, Eddie shook his head and said, "You mark this: Karawala never going see even one Cordoba."

"Why not?" I asked.

"The church going take all."

"Sure is so," Mudi agreed. "Peter going back it right to god, what them don't keep."

"Who's Peter?"

"That Leopoldo church name," Eddie offered.

"You gotta be kidding. Leopoldo plays the Apostle Peter."

"No, sar, is truth," Mudi protested. "Plenty them do so."

"They is the boss of it," Eddie said.

"The boss of what?" I asked.

"The church and Karawala," he sighed.

"What about the Reverend Hooker?"

"Is he going get," they agreed.

So the Reverend Hooker would get whatever the committeemen didn't put in their pockets. Religion is a good business no matter where one stands. I didn't want to say anything I didn't want repeated, and I didn't want to make any promises I might not keep. I shook my head and started down the hill to Avenida Comercial.

At the corner, we were stopped by a man who greeted Eddie and Mudi with the familiarity of old friends. I stood by while they talked, not understanding anything but an occasional word in English.

After awhile, Eddie turned to me and said, "Mr. Bet, he say he have a dori for sell."

"Have motor, too. Good motor," the man said, smiling.

I thought about telling him I wasn't interested. It couldn't possibly be what I wanted, but any boat is better than no boat at all.

"Let's go have a look," I said.

"Not here," he answered. "Is to El Bluff. I bring it this side tomorrow soonsoon."

"Okay," I agreed. "Soonsoon. At the wharf?"

"To the market better."

"At the market, then."

"Okay, Mr. Bet; okay, Eddie; okay, Mudi; okay, Ferlan," he said with a wave as he turned and walked away.

"Who was that?" I asked.

"That Bofu," he answered, offering no more.

*

We had spent the night before bobbing around in the Caribbean on an old coastal trader. She was identical to Mundo's Poop-Poop except for her slightly larger size. It had taken about sixteen hours to jump the Rio Grande bar, run eighty miles south, pass through the channel at El Bluff, and cross Bluefields Bay. I was tired enough to need a nap before dinner. We went back to the hotel.

That night, we let our hair down. We had a big Chinese dinner, took in the movie and probably had a drink in every bar in town.

It rained twice while we were in the movie. The only roof over the theater was tin. Even a light rain drummed out the soundtrack. Heavy rains were thunderous. They said some nights in the rainy season it rained all the way through the movie, but people still came.

There was no concession stand. Instead, there were people walking the isles, like in a ballpark, selling fresh squeezed fruit juices, fermented fruit juices and frozen fermented fruit juices. They advertised their wares at the top of their lungs, making it difficult to follow the movie.

But if the vendors and the drumming of the rain were too loud, one could still read the subtitles. And if the movie was boring, one could sit and wonder why they call them subtitles.

*

I awoke to hear Eddie's voice just outside my door. It was still early. Too Early. I mumbled something in response and looked up at the ceiling, first remembering where I was, then trying to piece together the night before. Mostly failing that, I searched for some reason that would cause Eddie to call so early.

"What is it, Eddie?"

"Go look Kuku Awra."

It didn't register. "What?"

"Look dori. Bofu bring dori."

I swung my feet to the floor and stood up. "Oh, shit. I don't feel too good," I said to myself.

I heard Mudi laugh quietly from the hallway. "Mr. Bet got goma?" He asked Eddie.

"If 'goma' means hangover, then I have one," I answered. "I'll be out in a minute."

The intoxication of the night before wasn't all rum, or so I believed. I couldn't verify it, but I strongly suspected an additive of some sort that made the seduction of the night seem dreamlike. And the hangover was gone almost as quickly as I had noticed it, as if it was a wave just passing through.

And like a dream, some of the night was gone, with only wisps of almost remembered scenes. I knew I hadn't gotten drunk. Or had I? Was I real, or was I a dream?

We found Bofu sitting in a rocking chair on the veranda, drinking a cup of coffee. He wore a blue and red leather cap, with the visor pulled down over his eyes. With his feet on the rail, he affected a comic pose of an affluent hotel guest, prompting hoots from Mudi.

The boat was tied alongside the market wharf amid a flotilla of dugout canoes. Even if she hadn't had a motor on her transom, I'd have known immediately which one she was. All the other dories were almost identical in size; none of them were painted. Then there was this one. She was a full twenty-five feet long and four in the beam, painted blue, easily dwarfing the others.

She'd been hewn from a single enormous mahogany log, by hand, where the log had been felled. From the felling to the launching had taken six months. It was obvious that whoever had done the work had made many more before. She looked like she'd been pulled from a mould, but an axe, a machete, an adze and a draw-knife were all the tools the shipwright owned.

She was nothing more than a giant canoe, but she possessed a beauty beyond that of the most expensive production boats. Her beauty was the love of her creator and of the great tree she was. It was in the hundreds of generations of refining the perfect hull shape for mahogany logs in jungle rivers. It was in the sacrifice for a coat of paint.

"What's her name?"

From behind me a voice answered, "Kuku Awra."

I turned, and there stood an American couple. "It's Miskito for drifting coconut he said. "I'm Brian, and this is Carol." We shook hands. "You going to buy my dori?"

"I'm McBeth Johnson. Where did you come from? Why are you here? Why do you want to sell her? And I might." I was surprised at seeing another American.

"I'm afraid that will have to wait. We're on our way to Managua for a little R&R. Two hundred dollars and she's yours. You can give her a test cruise to Karawala, if you wish. I'll be back in Sandy Bay in two weeks. If you want her, you can send me the money. If not, send the boat."

"Sounds fair enough," I said.

"Good. I'm off. See you in two weeks." They turned and walked away.

Like in a dream, characters came from nowhere and vanished, and it was as if nothing out of the ordinary had happened. Bofu started the motor and said, "Let's go."

She ran well, and she was dry in the choppy bay waters. I was told that almost every outboard on the coast was a twenty horse Johnson and that several stores stocked parts for them. This one was a year old, had been used lightly by its original owner, and was in good condition. It was an easy sale.

When we returned to the market wharf, I told Bofu I would take her to Karawala, but I wouldn't take possession of her until we were ready to leave.

"And who is this Brian?" I asked.

"He live in Sandy Bay," Bofu answered.

"Where Is Sandy Bay?"

"Near to Karawala," Eddie said. "Not far."

"What do they do there?"

"Can't say. No one know."

"How long have they been there?"

"Near to one years," Bofu answered. "I do work for them. They leaving off soon, though. Going back to Michigan. Where that, Mr. Bet? Is in Texas?"

"No, Bofu, Michigan is far to the north of Texas, almost to Canada. How could someone live here for a year and no one know what they do?"

"Can't say," he said, unperturbed. "Is important?"

I thought about it for a moment. Here was a man who had worked for another for almost a year and had watched his comings and goings. Not only had he not figured out what this other man was doing; it was not important to him. Nor was it important to anyone else. No one knew.

"No," I said. "It doesn't matter what one does." I shook my head. "Not only does it not matter; it doesn't even matter that no one knows what one does."

How alone we can be in this world. We can float around in a bubble so nearly unseen and so completely unimportant that we can drop into the lives of an alien culture and not make a ripple in their curiosities. Our vanities are sheer frivolity. I would have to find out, somehow, what they think is important.

In the meantime, there I stood, so insignificant that if I were to vanish into thin air, right before their eyes, they would do no more than shrug their shoulders and go on about their business. They would forget me like I forgot last night's dream.

I wondered if I was remembered. Was there anyone down the winding tunnel of my past who thought about me? I remember people and things well enough, and the memory for some is strong. But is any of it important? Would it matter if none of it had ever existed? What if this universe popped into existence just this morning, complete with all our memories?

I looked down at the Kuku Awra. If there was no past, perhaps there was a future. Floating there at my feet, in Bluefields Bay, was the conduit to my future. I could see into it, but not much farther than I could see into the jungle. It was all blue and green.

"Eddie!" I barked. "You know the way to Karawala on the inside?"

"Sure, Mr. Bet."

"Good. Let's go shopping."

We bought five drums of gasoline, five cases of outboard motor oil, a spare prop, shear pins, plugs and points and a few basic tools. All but what we needed for the return trip went on the trading boat, to be accompanied by Mudi and Ferlan.

I made good on my promise to Ferlan. I gave them a shopping spree of their own, with fifty dollars each to spend. It was more money than any of them had ever seen. It took them awhile to grasp how much it would buy.

My only instruction to Ferlan was that if any of it went anywhere but to his family, he would have to pay me back. I've never seen anyone so happy.

That afternoon, we met Leopoldo and the others at the lawyer's office to sign the papers. They were all in Spanish legalese, which made it slow going for me. But after many questions and many explanations, it was done. We shook hands all around.

On the way out, Dr. Santamaria asked to see me privately for a moment.

"Please sit down, Mr. Johnson. I feel that I must tell you a little about these people before you begin this venture."

I sat. I was eager to learn and hoped this man, with his experience with them, would have some insight to share.

"You must treat these people like children," he began. "They have not learned moral values, and they are completely ignorant of how adults should behave. They know nothing at all about responsibility."

His expression was severe and serious. He believed he was sharing wisdom.

"They will lie to you and steal from you and cheat you any way they can. Especially the pious ones. When you catch them, you must punish them severely. If it is a serious crime, you must send me a message. I will have them brought here to Bluefields where we can jail them and beat them properly."

I was flabbergasted. "I had no idea..."

"No, I'm sure you didn't. But I do, and thanks to me, now you do, too."

I couldn't get out fast enough. I thanked him and left. With the door closed behind me, I stamped off down the street in a huff, my contingent following. Halfway down the block, I turned and said, "Now I know why you hate the Spaniards."

They laughed. Leopoldo smiled, and shaking his head, said, "Him give you 'stupid Indian' speak."

"That doesn't make you angry?"

They feigned surprise and turned, clowning, to inspect one another.

"Got dirt on you?...No...Snake bit you up?...No...Got cut?...No...Make you belly hurt?...No...Broke bone?...No...Give you fever?...No."

"Okay, Mr. Bet," Leopoldo said, slapping his hands. "Look like we is no damage. Only you. We don't study him."

If they could laugh about it, I could, too. But if this doesn't rile their anger, what does? What makes them hate the Spaniards?

Leopoldo took his friends back to the mission; Eddie took me to meet Sunshine Down. Sunny had a little shop on Avenida Comercial, but his main business was outfitter for whoever happened to be going into the bush, for whatever reason, to stay.

I could not tell what nationality he was. Everyone else was immediately recognizable as black, Indian, Spaniard or Chinese. He was a very strongly stocky man of average height. His hair and beard were black; his eyes were sharp and clear and smiling. Everything about him seemed to speak of efficiency. There was nothing about Sunny's voice or appearance that gave him away, but there was a certainty that he had been there for a long time.

And there was a certainty that he was no ordinary shopkeeper. Without asking; without being told, I could tell he was a trader of the more exotic wares of the coast. Everything that couldn't be bought over the counter could be found in his back room. If it wasn't there already, he could get it for you. There was a bit of the scorpion in him, but no sleaze.

After an introduction and small talk, he set up an account for me. "Whatever you need, just send a list with one of the captains. I'll gather it up and send it, along with the count. You can send the money with the next boat."

It sounded like a service I would need. There was a sense of honor in his voice and a warning to trust only what he said. Make no assumptions. He has a knife.

"And I might add," he said with pride, "that I am most famous for my entertainment. My clients often return somewhat the worse for wear. I wine and dine them and offer them a few pleasures they can't find elsewhere. Why don't you drop by this evening for dinner?"

There might have been more there than I wanted to bargain for. It was easy to imagine dark rooms full of thieves, cutthroats and smugglers. This man was on the shady side, if not altogether the dark side. But I wanted to know more.

"It would be an honor and a pleasure," I answered.

"Good. Come by at about eight."

It was the first reference I'd heard to the hour of the day in weeks.

We left Sunshine's shop and returned to the hotel, where we sat on the veranda sipping a beer and watching Bluefields complete the day. I made a list of building materials I thought I might need in Karawala and gave it to Mudi. There were tools and raw materials enough, but no hardware. We would need nails, screen, wiring and plumbing.

That done, I showered and laid down to rest. I closed my eyes, but there was too much to think about. I couldn't sleep. My mind jumped from short term to long term and back. The more I thought about it, the greater my logistics problem became.

I couldn't expect to build a few huts and a few boats and have people flocking down for great fishing. I would have to offer a safe and comfortable, if rustic, hotel, along with the boats, motors, tackle and guides that world class sport fishermen were accustomed to.

And I would have to offer dining and drinking that was worth the trip even if the fishing was off. The more I thought, the bigger it got. How would I get restaurant equipment and supplies to Karawala? From where? I needed outboard motors and generators and a reliable supply of fuel.

I needed to plan this thing from the ground up, until I was sure I had every detail covered. I had taken a little fantasy and leapt into it. Now that it was hardening into reality, it was becoming extremely complicated. I still couldn't see the whole thing, but I could see bits and pieces popping out of thin air and dropping into place. I could see that the numbers of bits and pieces were like the numbers of ants in the bush.

I got up, dressed and walked to Sunny's. It was eight o'clock and dark. Sunny's door was open, but the lights were off and no one stood behind the counter. Behind the counter were racks of cloth and clothing, and behind that, I couldn't guess.

I knocked on the open door and called. From the back room I heard Sunny's voice boom, "Ho! That must be McBeth! Coming, Beth." And in a lower voice, he paused and said, "That's odd. Why did I call him Beth?"

The door opened and he walked through a part in the clothing racks, extending his hand and smiling.

"Good evening," I said, accepting. "I'm called Beth everywhere except here on the coast, where everyone insists on calling me Mr. Bet."

He laughed and led me through the door to the back room and up the stairs to a large dimly lit room above the store. It was like stepping out of Bluefields and into a place and time far more affluent and sophisticated.

"Have you listened to them speak? That's the Spanish influence in the language. No th sounds. Dat for that and so on. You are Mister because the familiar is impossible for them, and you are Bet because that's their equivalent of Beth.

There were two small windows on the street side through which nothing could be seen from outside. The walls were rich, deep mahogany wood panels hung with art, artifacts and tapestries; the ceiling and floor were of a light colored wood. In the center of the room was a massive, square wooden table, perhaps twelve feet on a side, with four equally massive chairs around it. Both table and chairs were ornately carved.

Against the walls stood eight other chairs equal to those at the table. With all twelve at the table, there would have been more than enough elbow room. I was very much impressed. The room said a great deal about the wealth, the power and the taste of my host.

"This was done during the early days of this century, when Bluefields was a thriving, prosperous port. It was mostly an American town then - a lumber town. All the old colonial houses you see on the hill were American houses, and very fine houses they were.

"This," he said, motioning around the room with

outstretched arms, "was built by the British Consul. The only consular offices in the country now are in Managua, but there was a time when there were as many here as there."

He motioned to one of the chairs and said, "Please, sit down."

There were two places set on opposite sides of the table. On the other sides were baskets of fruit and orchids. As soon as we were seated, he clapped his hands twice, loudly. From a room I guessed was the kitchen, opposite the stairwell, came two young women, each with a bottle of wine; one for each of us.

"Ladies, this is our guest for the evening, Mr. McBeth Johnson. McBeth, this is Trina to my left and Angelina to your left."

I was impressed with their beauty. They were innocently sensuous, without the raw eroticism of the girls on the streets. Their clothes were soft and flowing and almost revealing; not an open invitation to sex. "My pleasure," I said.

Angelina stepped close to pour. She put a hand lightly on my shoulder. Her hair brushed my cheek, and a breast pressed my arm. Her perfume came to me as a faintly scented flower.

And then she was gone. Sunny's eyes twinkled. "Intoxicating, aren't they?" Then, lifting his glass, "to your health and prosperity."

"And to yours," I replied, "both of which seem to be considerable." We drank. The wine was excellent.

"Ah, McBeth, merely appearances. Take no stock in it."

"As you say."

"Now where was I before we were so wonderfully interrupted? Ah, yes. The old days. When the last log was shipped to New Orleans, your imperialistic, plundering ancestors packed up and went with it. They left this coast to rot and be consumed by re-growth."

He wasn't scolding. He was telling a story; setting the stage.

"But they left enough for those of us who stayed and those who followed. Being lumbermen, they saw only trees, and when the trees were gone, they thought there was nothing left."

He turned his glass and brought his gaze directly to my eyes. "Which brings us to you, Mr. Johnson. What brings you to our coast? What riches do you expect to find to reward you for the hardships of the bush?"

So. What he really wanted was information about the competition. Or perhaps he wanted to make sure he was in on the take. I could only hope my little endeavor would be insignificant to him. I redoubled my caution and began to examine the room for things other than local interest.

"Is important?" I asked, smiling, remembering the morning.

"Yes. You will find there are many here who will take a great interest in your activities." He paused, letting me think about it. "And they will take more than interest if they can."

"I've already found my riches," I answered, "in the little village of Karawala. They are the riches of the soul; things one can see and hear and breathe and eat. I've come for something no one else seems to care about."

"Come, now, McBeth."

"Really. I came as a tourist to go fishing. I like what I found, and I'm going to stay awhile. And I'm going to bring others like me when I get my camp built. Nothing more."

The door opened. Trina and Angelina came out with more wine, moving slowly to our sides, leaning closer. Their clothes were a little looser; a bit more revealing of cleavage and thigh, but still concealing. Angelina's cheek touched mine as she poured.

As she stood, her blouse brushed my face and she pressed a leg to my side. No accident; she was deliberately arousing me. She smiled and nodded as she left.

"She's a little flirt, that one." Sunny said, smiling. "I think she likes you."

Whether she did or not, I thought I liked her. I thought about drinking faster so she'd come out more often, then thought better of it for several reasons.

"Now, McBeth, no one comes out here for the fun of it. You are obviously not one of those peace corps beggars. And you are not one of those university students like Brian or Barney. You have strong hands and money in your pockets. You are not here for your health. Give me a hint. Maybe I can help."

My attention was diverted to our waitresses bringing bowls of steaming soup. I'm afraid I may have given all my attention to her, to the neglect of my host. But it must have been his intention.

With the bowls before us, they moved to the sides of the table and began peeling and slicing fruit for us. Angelina allotted half her attention to me, and I most of mine to her. Her blouse was now loose enough that her breasts were revealed when she bent. She watched me until she was sure I had noticed. Her nipples hardened.

The wrap of her skirt was now more open, and the slit moved from the side toward the center, revealing flesh all the way up the thigh. If it were moved a little more to the center, there would be nothing concealed. My heavy breathing was not lost by any of the three. Trina smiled and winked as they left.

Sunny laughed heartily. "At this rate she'll be naked before we finish dinner."

I could only laugh nervously and shake my head. He was maneuvering me. When he sensed my guard was up, he brought it down with his girls. He was not doing all this, as he said, for his health. I had the feeling he knew everything I had said or done since I got there. It was not a bad practice. I would follow his example.

I was savoring every bite of the soup without having any idea what was in it.

"The Indians call it run-down," he said. "They take the head and feet of a green turtle and the head of a barracuda and cook it in coconut milk for a day or two until it reaches the right consistency. I've taken their recipe and refined it a bit. Do you like it?"

Kuku Awra

"It is wonderful. I'll have to serve it to my guests."

"There you go again. Whatever you are up to, you'll find it impossible to conceal. In a land considered unexplored, you'll think you are the focus of network TV."

"So I've seen. And so by the next time you see me, you'll be convinced."

"If you are still claiming to be setting up a fishing lodge in the middle of nowhere, I'll be convinced that you have succeeded in slipping one by a people who never miss a thing. And I'll know you are a very dangerous man."

I didn't want him to think I was dangerous, but there was nothing else I could tell him. I needed a moment by myself.

"Excuse me, but is there a restroom nearby?"

"At the bottom of the stairs, to your right."

I thanked him and stood up. When I started down the stairs, I heard him clap once. I hoped I wasn't going to miss anything.

As I stepped from the bottom tread, a figure stepped from the shadows to face me, poised for attack. I saw the glint of steel in his hand. Reflexively, I jumped, faked with my left foot, turned my hips in mid air, and caught him in the jaw with a spin kick-heel kick combination that snapped his head from side to side and dropped him to the floor like a sack of rice.

I turned and looked back up the stairs. Sunny stood at the top. He applauded me and said, "Well done. Much more than I suspected."

I picked up the knife, stepped over the man, and went into the restroom. I had been tested. My reaction would surely make my intentions more suspect now than before, and there was nothing I could say or do to change it. How quickly and how far would this news travel?

I returned to his side and tossed the knife on the table in front of him.

He looked up at me and said, "He would not have used it. It was, as you probably have guessed, an experiment. I'll have to pay poor Bofu very well for your punishment."

"Bofu!? The same Bofu who brought me the boat?"

"One and the same."

"I thought he worked for this Brian guy from Michigan."

"He does, or did, but he has always worked for me. Working for Brian was part of his employment with me. You really reacted much more violently than I expected. You'll be safer than most out there."

I returned to my seat, and as I sat, our main course arrived. "Please relax, Mr. Johnson. You are an honored guest in my home. And you are perfectly safe."

I believed him. If there was a threat in him, it would come from what he didn't say, and I would never see it coming.

I turned to look at Angelina. She stood at my side with her back to my host, leaning against the table. There was nothing left to the imagination. She smiled, stepped aside and disappeared into the kitchen.

My mouth was open. I could have been slobbering for all I know.

"Let's eat. She'll be yours soon enough. We still have some talking to do."

"You don't believe me, do you?"

"Of course not. But I believe you are an honorable man, and that carries considerable weight here. That's turtle, and that's red deer," he said, pointing with his fork at the trays of food. "You'll find the venison here to be infinitely better than that bitter meat you have in Texas. And the turtle is better than any meat you may have eaten anywhere in the world."

We ate, and what he said about the food was true. Angelina left my mind as I let the scents and flavors of the food claim me. Sunny, too, fell silent for awhile. I was hardly aware of my glass being filled when empty, or hot food replacing warm. She was there, but unobtrusive.

Finally, Sunny spoke again. "Stay away from drugs. If you are suspected of drug trafficking, you will die a horrible death. That is all controlled by Somoza's lieutenants. Your CIA lets them get rich and keeps them under control by giving them the drug trade. Don't fuck around with them. They enjoy killing."

"I'm not interested in drugs."

He went on as if he hadn't heard me. "If you want to take out a little gold, keep a low profile, stay away from the mining concessions, and don't get greedy. There's enough there that they don't mind us taking out a pound or so now and then as long as we uncover a new deposit for them while we're at it."

He thought for a minute while having some more turtle. I, too, thought. Why was he telling me this? Was he accepting me? It seemed so. But how? Into what?

Our empty plates were cleared and coffee appeared in their places. I looked up at Angelina, but she was all business now.

"As for the fish, you can have them. If your tourists are rich or influential, you'll please Somoza, which never hurts. But be careful not to please him too much. A volcano is going to erupt here some day. Don't take sides.

"As for the rest of it, most of this country is here for the taking for those who are strong enough. Just be very careful that what you are taking does not already belong to someone else. Our jails are reserved for political prisoners. Criminals are dealt with by those who catch them."

He took the last sip of coffee, pushed his chair back, and said, "Now, I think you have something much more important than conversation to attend to. You are a guest in my house until you decide to leave. You will be a guest when you return. Please don't stay at that thing they call a hotel. This is really a very large house.

He disappeared through a door with Trina. I followed Angelina through another, to a room with a large four-poster bed. The door clicked shut. She turned to face me; her clothes fell to the floor.

DAVIS MORALES
Chapter Six
Matlalkanbi

Look, now. You put it to sleep if you touch it. (He bent down and touched it, and the leaves folded up.) We call it the sleeper.

The day of the full moon, a suitor will go to the bush to find a handsome specimen. He will go alone, and he will not tell anyone. Once the plant is found, he will return to the village unseen. Secrecy is of utmost importance. He is going to ask the sleeper to help him win his girl.

He will spend the rest of the day alone in his house. Near evening, he will dress in his best clothes and leave the village. He must leave before the sun sets, but he must not approach the sleeper until the full moon rises. Then he approaches it from the west and sits by it. He will have a calabash bowl, which he places to his right, and a shilling, held between his thumb and index finger. Once he sits, he cannot move for the rest of the night.

After he is seated comfortably, he introduces himself to the sleeper and begins to make casual conversation with it. The topic is not important. His goal is to please and become friends with it. When he thinks he has won the sleeper's confidence, he tells it about his girl. While he is doing this, he slowly works the shilling into the soil below the stalk. This could take quite awhile, because he must do it so gently that the plant will not go to sleep.

Once this is done, he will promise to keep other plants from growing around it and to bring it food if it will help him win his girl. He will assure the sleeper that he loves the girl and has good intentions. If he is clumsy with the shilling, it will go to sleep and will not hear him.

At dawn, he will excuse himself and go to another area to look for another sleeper. He will take some leaves from that plant and mash them up in the calabash bowl along with the leaves of sweet smelling plants. The juice from this mixture is rubbed on his face, arms, chest and legs.

He then goes to visit his girl. If he has done everything well, she will not be able to resist him.

As told by Ferlan Santiago

It is not comfortable to lean back against the end of a fifty-five gallon drum for long periods of time, but it's better than nothing. The alternative was no backrest at all, so we rolled our drum of gasoline into the Kuku Awra amidships, right behind a thwart, and I sat down.

Mudi and Ferlan got up to see us off. They helped us load and then stood on the wharf and watched us disappear into the blackness of the bay. "Safe pass," they said, and we the same.

Even before Eddie settled into our heading, I found the little light across the bay that marks the only real channel into the Escondido. There are other places deep enough to cross that would cut several miles off the trip, but they silt up and shift with the storms. The light marks the only sure channel. Even small children know it.

There was a cool northeast breeze blowing into our faces as we crossed. It kicked up a chop on the water and wetted us with a salty mist from each wave. By the time we turned into the Escondido, I was cold and wet and wishing I was upstairs at Sunny's in a warm bed.

But I wasn't. I was miserable. How could it be so cold in the tropics? I dipped my hand into the water. It was warm. I put my hand against my chest. My shirt was wet and cold. I looked up at the sky. No stars. We'd get no help from the sun.

The corridor of the river was sheltered. We motored along the north side, upriver, as close to the bank as we could get. When the light began to grow, I watched for familiar landmarks, hoping to find the little tributary to Pearl Lagoon before Eddie turned into it.

I felt it before I saw it. We hit a wall of colder air as we crossed the line from warm salt water to cool fresh water. The tide was ebbing, sucking the water out of the creeks. We would not feel the warmth of the sea again until we hit the Rio Grande.

The sudden change seemed to have chilled the animals, too. There were no birds in the air or in the trees by the river. Nothing moved but the leaves in the canopy. I kept my legs together and my arms crossed close to my chest to hold my heat. My muscles soon began to ache from being tensed against the cold.

About halfway between the river and the lagoon, we were waved down by soldiers standing on a dock in front of a station of some sort. I was surprised to see them there, and more surprised that I hadn't seen the station on the first trip. I must have been watching the opposite bank.

We came to a stop. The warmth of calmness felt good enough that I welcomed the intrusion. They directed their questions first at Eddie. Where were we coming from and where were we going? Eddie answered stiffly, his resentment barely hidden. When they asked for the boat's papers, he told them exactly how obvious it should be to them that it was not a commercial boat.

They let it pass and turned their attention to me. I answered their questions politely enough until they asked for my mother's maiden name. I laughed. I couldn't help myself. The threat of execution couldn't have kept me from laughing.

I stifled it as quickly as I could and apologized for my impudence. One of them spat and hitched up his pants. I was sure they took their assignments very seriously, to the point of being deadly serious. In a land of resentment, without witnesses, these shake down stops could backfire violently.

After being instructed in the extent of their willingness to abuse the power they had, and just how serious my predicament could be, I gave them each a ten dollar bill and they waved us on, smiling and wishing us well. I smiled as we left. It was exactly like getting a traffic ticket.

I was soon chilled again and paying attention only to our progress as we wound along the creek. An occasional insect smacked into my face and left me stinging for a moment, but aside from that, there was very little stimulus. The monotonous drone of the outboard drowned all other sound.

When we finally broke out into Pearl Lagoon, it was as bad as I had feared. We had forty miles of open water to cross, quartering into the wind. The waves were building and almost capping. We had no choice, unless it was to turn around and go back to Bluefields.

Eddie slowed to idle speed, perhaps hoping I would tell him to return to the protection of the creek. I shook my head and pointed to the north.

Half speed was all we could manage, and at that, the waves began breaking over the bow. Eddie tossed me a calabash bowl, and I started bailing.

We motored into the wind and waves long enough that I began telling myself that I had never been warm and dry, and this was the way I would spend the rest of my life - out of sight of land on a steel gray bay under a steel gray sky, sopping wet, cold and hungry.

Mechanically, I bailed. Eddie bailed and held the tiller, changing hands to ward off numbness. I had always thought hypothermia was only possible in freezing conditions, but this was proving me wrong. I was chilled to the bone, even though it couldn't have been below seventy degrees. Every muscle in my body was tensed against the cold, and shivering was becoming more frequent.

I looked up. There was a thin dark line that separated the

bay from the sky. We were off course. I cursed the loss of time and turned.

"Eddie! Where are you going?"

"Orinoco. Can't let night catch us in the canal."

The village must have been in the middle of the line, but I couldn't see it. I watched it, trying to pick it out, wishing it would hurry.

For a long time it didn't grow. I had the sensation it was moving away from us as fast as we moved toward it. I wanted to tell Eddie to speed up, but I knew it was impossible. And I knew he had to be as cold as I. If he could push her any harder, he would.

Things finally began jumping out of the horizon into view. First the trees stood up, as if they had been crouching down all that time. Then there were houses under the trees. But we saw no people until we were almost on the beach. They were all inside where it was warm. The wind had blown away the sound of our motor.

When we were finally heard, there were shouts all through the village, and people poured out of the houses. There was great excitement at the coming of a boat. The children ran up and down the shore waving and laughing and calling back to those in the village.

In short order Eddie and I were in a crowded kitchen with a hot fire blazing, a blanket around us and a cup of coffee in our hands. Women chattered and children squealed. Men asked about the boat, the pass, things in Bluefields and Karawala. They crowded into the little house and spilled out on the ground around. They came to give us their greetings, stayed briefly and scurried home to their own fires and blankets and coffee.

I was beginning to feel almost comfortable when a woman came to fetch me. I heard her voice before I saw her. She came giving orders to children, who laughed and ran off to do her bidding. I heard the floor boards creak under her weight, and there she was.

"Your house ready, Mr. Bet. Come now."

"Aren't you going to say hello?"

"Hello. Come now." Her smile so big it almost forced her eyes shut. Everyone laughed.

"Hello," I said. I got up, thanked my host and handed him his blanket, shrugged my shoulders and followed the big, black woman who had come for me.

As we walked, I said, "Excuse me, but I don't know your name."

"My name Miss Erma," she said very politely.

"Miss Erma?"

"Mr. Bet."

"What about the house? You said my house was ready."

"Is so."

"I don't have a house here."

"Look, now!" She pointed ahead. "Is your house."

"But how did I come by a house here?"

"I make it for you."

"What? It was built before I got here."

"Is so."

"Then how could you have built it for me?"

"I know you coming."

"Oh, Miss Erma, how could you know that?"

"Not said you, understand, but I have a wish, and I know that wish to come truth. And now you are here. The house for you."

I started to protest, but she stopped me. "No more from me. You want more, you ask the girls, them."

All the while, she had the same placid look of contentment on her face. Now she smiled and bid me pass through the hedge to my grounds. I did so and heard her chuckle as she walked away.

I was still a bit chilled or I would have taken some time to look around. Perhaps this was mine. If so, I didn't think it would get much use. I was there by serendipity; not by choice. As soon as the wind laid, I would be gone again.

Someone had brought my saddlebags. They were on the porch. And someone had lit a fire inside. Smoke fled the house through the eaves. The bougainvilleas would have to wait until I was warm and dry. I pushed the door open and walked in.

There was a large bed made of rough sawn mahogany under a mosquito bar tall enough to stand in. There was a table for eating and rocking chairs for resting. In one corner there was a large earthen hearth with a warm fire, and next to it was a washtub full of steaming water.

I saw no more. I dropped my saddlebags, pulled off my clothes and stepped into the tub. It took some doing to get my stiff legs crossed just right and my butt settled in, but I made it. And heaven it was. I sat and soaked and wished it was long enough to stretch out in.

The chill went away, but the water was still warm, so I stayed where I was. I pulled my saddlebags to my side and retrieved a puro and a medio of Flor. I had a smile of contentment on my face when the door opened two delightful young women walked in. My skin tightened.

*

The girls talked with their eyes and with a tease. The way of a laugh and the set of a hip bespoke volumes that words would have failed. Rarely did a moment go by that I could not feel one or both of them holding close and watching me. Never did I want for food or clean dry clothes, and at night they shared my bed.

I could not have talked to them. They did not speak my language. But I gazed at their nakedness and their innocence and wondered what purpose I could have in their lives. I asked why they had come to me, but for that, they did not answer.

I was so comfortable in Orinoco I soon forgot why I was there. Every time the thought of Karawala popped into my mind, I thanked fate for nasty weather and begged for more. I got my wish. For four days the clouds shut out the warmth of the sun and the wind churned the lagoon.

I was drunk - drunk with sex and the purity of my lovers and with the perfection of having nothing and everything all at once.

I woke up one morning to a warm, calm day. The norther had passed. The sun was shining and the humidity was like being inside a cloud. It was time for me to go.

They would not go to Karawala. I coaxed and pleaded, but they would not budge. Nor would they see me off. They wouldn't even say good-bye.

And I was as loath to leave. Twice I fell back into bed with them and lingered. I studied their bodies and their eyes and told them how I would long for them while I was gone.

And it was true. I knew I would. I wanted to feel their flesh against mine. I wanted to bathe with them in the river and to see their eyes sparkle when they smiled. I wanted to hear them whisper my name while they went about the business of the day.

*

The door shut behind me as I stepped off the porch. Reluctantly, I set off on the path that would take me to the landing. The next thing I knew, there were three young men standing in front of me, blocking my way. Their belligerence shook me to my senses. The machetes they carried were not tools; they were weapons.

I looked around quickly. I was out of sight of every house. There was no one in view.

One spoke: "Orinoco not your town, mon. This my town. I don't want see you here again, hear?"

I didn't have to weigh my odds against these guys. A challenge cannot be justified unless talk has failed and flight is impossible. Both were still options.

"Now what have I done to provoke your anger?" I asked. "I

can't recall seeing you before."

He tensed, ready to pounce. There was hatred in his eyes. I wanted to know why it was there.

"You come like the world for you and you grind de girl, them."

"I what?" I asked, incredulous.

"Fuck!...Fuck!...You fucking our girls!"

"I didn't come here for your girls," I protested. "I came to get out of the cold." I started to tell them the girls had come to me, but I thought better of it.

"I going cut you now," he growled.

Just as he raised his machete, I heard Eddie's voice behind them. "Mr. Bet?"

He let the machete down easy and changed his expression.

"Let's go, now, Mr. Bet. I waiting long time for you."

As if nothing was happening, he walked up, took my saddlebags and led me away. It could be said that I felt great relief.

We walked quickly, saying nothing. I had a great sense of unfinished business. One thing was certain: I would be back. I would have to face them again.

There is no fear, I told myself. The thing I feel is excitement. Get him out in the open and let me have him.

Miss Erma was at the landing, along with half of Orinoco, to see us off. As happy as the mood was, they could not have known about my confrontation. Perhaps they never would. Perhaps I would not dream that dream again.

Miles from Orinoco, close to Top Lock, Eddie stopped the boat, turned off the motor and let her drift. Kuku Awra. Drifting Coconut.

"What that fella say?"

"What fella?" I asked.

"Davis Morales, with the machete. He was to cut you?"

"Davis Morales," I repeated. "Yes, I think he was going to try to cut me. I might not have been able to get away from all three of them."

"So! That fella cross, Mr. Bet. He get vexed and kill a gal one time. And some claim he kill his brother."

"I don't think he wants me to go back there. I think he might get violent if I did. What did they do to him for killing the girl?"

"Nuttin, nuttin. They all fright of him. Never even report it to Bluefields. They too fright he find it out."

"What do you think he'll do?"

"I don't study that, Mr. Bet. Only he is Davis. Better you not go back there."

He cranked up the outboard and we were off. Discussion ended. He looked none too happy - preoccupied; detached. I thought he might be rolling scenarios over in his mind, trying to guess what Davis might do. We hardly spoke again that day.

I rolled the scenarios over in my mind all the way home. For every action he might take, I planned a reaction. For everything he might say, I planned a retort. The only thing I accomplished was blinding myself to the beauty around me. I kept myself wound tight and bent out of shape all day.

I was angry that I had been challenged. I was angry that he was ruining my day in absentia. I was angry about the cowardice of his ambush, out of sight of witnesses and with odds that precluded a fair fight.

Under the sound of the outboard I muttered, "I will be back, Davis Morales. I will be back." It was not a threat. It was a statement of fact, with a question at the end, "What will you do?"

*

The thought and feeling of anger was lifted when we rounded the bend and saw a crowd of cheering children on the Karawala wharf. I smiled and then laughed, with them and for them, for the very simple things that made them so happy.

My heart softened. I felt joy and sorrow. I felt surprise in knowing there were loves growing in me and perhaps in them for me. It would have been easy to cry just then.

They all wanted to touch me and hold my hand and ask, "How the pass, Mr. Bet?" All with smiles and sparkling black eyes that made me think there was light shining through. They could have lit my way in the dark.

I stopped at Mundo's for a beer and listened to the talk about the coming rains. It was time, they said. The clouds were building in the west. Flood soon come.

I stopped at Miss Pete's to see what she had cooking. I was just in time for a fresh batch of hot bread right out of her earthen oven. To go with it, she gave me a bowl of run-down and a plate of gallo pinto. More glamorous meals there are, but none much better.

After I finished, I walked into her kitchen to thank her. The rains were on her mind, too. As we talked, I happened to look into the pot of run-down, and a smile spread across my face. Resting in the middle of the pot, half submerged, was the skull of a green sea turtle.

Miss Pete laughed and asked, "You don't know you eating that turtle head?

"No, I didn't. But it was good. What else is in there?"

"Oh, just some of what we got. The foot is there, too, the head of a barra and some platano, some coco root, some casssava root, dasheen, coconut oil.....I forget all is in there. If it fall in there, it get cook and eat. Tomorrow I put in something new."

I thanked her again and walked home. Parrots, parrotlets and parakeets by the thousands were in the coco plums, eating, squawking and screeching. I supposed the din was a protest against the darkening sky.

As soon as it was dark, I pulled off my clothes and went to the well for a bath. I drew a bucket of water, took a deep breath, and poured it over my head. My warm, sweaty skin drew up tight against the cold. I lathered soap from head to toe, scrubbed it in, and washed it off with buckets of water. As I bathed, I looked up at the stars.

No moon, no clouds and no haze meant the sky was a crisp black, with sharp stars stabbing through. The Milky Way was a bright wash all the way across. It looked like it was almost close enough to touch.

After being hot and wet and salty all day, I felt clean and crisp. I toweled off inside and slipped into bed under the bar, naked and uncovered. It felt good to give my skin some air. The sheets were clean; someone had done my laundry and cleaned my house while I was gone.

I listened, and I began to hear. I focused on sounds and amazed myself again at how selective our senses can be. I could pick out one frog and listen just to it, while thousands of others like it trilled at the same time.

As I listened around my sphere, I began to drift, and almost asleep, I saw their eyes, like stars piercing the sky, and heard their voices, softly singing. I could not make out what they said, but I could feel their breasts and their thighs and their hair.

LI AOLA

Chapter Seven

Matlalkanbi Pura Kum

One morning Eddie brought me a small, smooth stone. He was beaming with pride as he put it in my hand, as if he was giving me something precious. It was a lightning ball, he said. It had split a tree the night before.

The next day he showed me a puddle of water full of tadpoles and said the savanna had lots of puddles with little fish in them. He said those were strange little fish that came from the sky, and he asked me if there were rivers up there.

One night I asked him how far the stars were, and he said he had never climbed high enough to touch one.

From the Journals of McBeth Johnson

The rains begin in the west, in the mountains of Matagalpa, and move east down the river. First there are heavy black clouds on the horizon and lightning in the night, but no thunder.

For a week or so we watched it brew. There was a charge in the air. Every living thing waited eagerly for the end of the dry season. One could feel electricity and smell the moisture. Each day the darkness grew nearer.

It was the time to fish. Everything that had followed the salt and tides up the river was now returning to the sea ahead of the flood. They had to pass by us on their way out.

As the clouds grew near, the river began to rise and the current quickened. The flood was on its way. At first I was truly amazed at the quantity of life flowing by me. The fish were in tremendous, hungry schools and were stacking up near the river mouth, waiting for the cold, brown fresh water that would force them out to sea. Above them were gulls, man-o-war and pelicans filling the sky like swarming insects.

My amazement gave way to anxiety as the voracity increased. At times we were showered, as we sat in the boat, by big fish thrashing at the surface in chase of prey. All over the river we could see them exploding: big after small; giant after big; a few after the many. And at times the river roared like thunder with the sound of thousands upon thousands of mullet taking flight and falling back into the water.

More than once we covered our heads with our arms as fish and water showered down on us. Birds wheeled and screamed, beating our backs with their wings; predators jarred the boat. We sat defenseless in the midst of pandemonium and often stopped fishing and just sat and watched, enthralled and nervous and excited. The Indians kept their little dories out of the water and neither bathed nor swam in the river.

We fought fish until our arms ached. While we rested, the fury continued, oblivious of our presence. We were no more than a log drifting along the current. Here before us, nature was having an orgy. I laughed aloud, unheard; I stood and screamed and waved my arms, unseen and unheard. I sat, exhausted, and shook my head. I am nothing, I thought. I am not even as much as a bird. The birds eat, and they are eaten. They are players. I am only something floating down the river.

We caught few fish. Most of those we hooked were eaten by something else before we could get it to the boat. Our lines were broken, cut and stripped from the reels as fast as we could get them rigged and in the water. We soon gave up.

But we couldn't go home until darkness made it foolish to stay any longer. We watched, entranced, never dulled by the scenes before us. I was struck again by the violence and the beauty of nature. I compared it to the acts of man and decided we are too slow and weak to be violent. Inhumane and cruel, yes,

125

but only in our most arrogant moment could we claim to be fit
for violence. And if that is so, we could only have survived by
avoiding it.

*

The rains came. Black clouds settled over Karawala and
opened up. The rain and lightning and thunder were continuous.
I made myself a rain gauge and measured thirty-six inches of rain
in three days, and each time I went to look, it had overflowed. I
lay awake at night listening to the thunder, which was literally
ceaseless for hours at a time.

Sometimes the wind drove the rain straight through my
house, soaking me and everything in it, and I understood why all
the other houses were made to be boarded up and shuttered
against the storms. Other times the air was dead calm and the
only sound was that of the rain falling steadily on the leaves of
my roof and the trees of the jungle. Everything else held its
breath - everything but the tree frogs and the toads, and if the
rain slackened for a moment, they could drown it out. All night
they sang, and only the boom and crack of nearby lightning was
louder.

For three days, the only person I saw was Miss Pete, when I
slogged through the rain to her house for meals. No one was
about. They were all shut up inside where it was warm. Miss
Pete said they would be out in the wind and rain soon enough.

"We all must eat," she said. "The only way to do that is to go
out and get it."

And sure enough, they did. I saw them walking by on the
runway on their way to their plantations, and I saw them when
they came back carrying heavy sacks of roots and nuts. Their
backs were bowed under the weight. They were sopping wet and
splashing water with every step, but they always waved and
smiled when they saw me, and I waved and smiled back.

I tried for awhile to stay dry, but soon surrendered to

overwhelming forces. The best I could do was stay clean. Every night I stood out in the rain and took a long shower, scrubbing with the strong soap that Mundo sold. After toweling off as best I could, I sat in my chair, naked, and had a shot of rum and a cigar. Then, air-dried, I slipped under the bar and into the sheets, which I took great pains to keep clean and dry.

On the fourth day, I awoke to a world of water. I stood on my porch and laughed aloud and waved at the people passing by in their dories. The rainfall was steady, as if it was now settled in for the duration.

Eddie and Mudi paddled up and stopped about twenty feet from the house. I smiled and said, "Good morning."

But they didn't return the smile. Eddie said, "Walk here to we, Mr. Bet."

I wondered what was up. Was there something in the dory they wanted me to see? "Okay, Eddie," I replied, and waded out. The water was knee deep and cold.

When I got there, they bade me turn around and look. A chill shook me, and then I laughed in surprise. Snakes were everywhere. They were literally dripping from the eaves. Everywhere there was a purchase, I saw a snake. First I saw only a few, but the closer I looked, the more I saw. They were all over the house, and I had been sleeping with them and standing with them on the porch.

They had come in the night to escape the rising water. These, I thought, must be the ones living close by and on the ground. Surely there were many more in the trees. These were the ones I lived with on a daily basis, but never saw. What else lived here unseen, so close that I could touch? What else had touched my skin that might find a bite a treat?

I waded closer, against the advice of my guides; it made them fidget. Around the house I went, keeping them at a safe distance. They were in the kitchen, too, but nowhere did I see yellow beard, bushmaster or coral snakes. There were brightly colored snakes like false corals, and there were snakes that could hardly be seen, even though they were exposed. There were big, fat boas and long, pencil-thin vine snakes.

"How am I going to get rid of these?" I turned and asked them. But I knew the answer. I'd just have to room with them until they left.

"Can't say," Mudi replied. He was smiling now, amused at my predicament.

"Is the water going to stay like this all through the rainy season?"

"Nah," Eddie answered. "This just top gallon. Soon gone. Always like this. First flood top gallon, then just flood."

Very carefully, I inspected every square inch of house around the front door. Satisfied that none of them were poisonous, I climbed the steps, lifted one from the door pull, and went inside.

Eddie and Mudi had a conniption fit. "You crazy, Mr. Bet. Get down out that house." They paddled another twenty feet away, too frightened to stay and too loyal to leave. "Please come from out that house."

"Oh, Eddie," Mudi quavered, "he gone dead out in there. He gone dead."

I opened the door and tossed a fairly large snake into the water. "If I die, Mudi, it ain't gonna be a snake that does it. These are my friends. Treat them with proper respect and they'll share the world with you."

"Well, better you treat them with respect from out here. Not safe in there. You going get bit up, you hear?"

At that, I let out a yell. Sure enough, I got too close to one and got a few dozen tiny, recurved teeth snagged on my cheek. I hadn't seen him. I grabbed him by the neck, jerked him off my skin, and threw him out the door.

If they were afraid before, they were panicked then. Blood streamed down my face. The cuts were tiny, but facial cuts bleed profusely. I left the house and waded toward them, blood dripping into the muddy water. I watched the snake that had bitten me swim off slowly toward the bush. I dipped water and washed the blood away.

Eddie and Mudi were nearly panicked, and I couldn't understand why. I tried to tell them it wasn't a poisonous snake, but that didn't calm them. For a moment, a chill ran through me. What if I was wrong? What if it was a poisonous snake? Was I going to die?

But the thought passed as quickly as it came. Not a chance. Why were they so afraid? It took awhile, but I finally came to understand that to them, there is no such thing as a non-venomous snake.

Mudi kept trying to get me into the dori, but Eddie kept saying, "Haps to wait for dark." I just stood there shaking my head.

They argued about what to do with me, and they fretted about my health, and when they did, they threw their heads back and wailed.

I tapped Eddie on the shoulder. He jumped. "Why do you have to wait for dark?" I asked. "If I really needed help, I'd likely die waiting for dark."

"That what I telling him," Mudi said, "But he not listen."

"If a woman look on you, and she in her time," Eddie said, bewildered, "she going dead. Haps to wait for dark. Can't see then."

Mudi disagreed. "Haps to go now. Tell the woman, them, hide."

I was intrigued. How could snakebite have become so firmly associated with menstruation that the very sight of a snakebit person would cause a woman to die? This was their knowledge, and I could not make light of it. They must have seen some terrible deaths by snakes.

Ask questions later, I thought, after the fear has passed. "Where would you take me?" I asked.

"To the bush doctor."

"I'd like to visit him, but today is not the day. The worst that can happen to me is infection."

"It hort bad?" Mudi asked.

"It doesn't hurt at all."

"Must be it hurt," Eddie said. "Is snake, ain't?"

"Is snake," I nodded. "But fear is the greatest part of pain, and I am not afraid."

*

The top gallon flood turned out to be a good opportunity to bring in the building materials. About mid morning people began arriving in dories towing logs to be sawn and poles to erect for framing. I sat on my porch and watched them bring it and tie it off so it wouldn't drift away.

The water began to recede as suddenly as it had risen. I tried to imagine the fury of the bar as all this water met the tide. It must have been vicious.

All day I sat there, with nowhere to go and nothing to do but watch. Now and then someone paddled up to talk, but when they saw the snakes, they left. Miss Pete sent Eddie down with food, and he made me wade out to get it. As I ate, we talked.

"No fishinin now," he said.

"Why not?" I asked.

"All out to sea."

"Surely there are fish here. Maybe not snook and tarpon, but if there is water, there are fish."

"In the lagoon, them, have tapom and mupi yet. They stay all time. Water not get salt there and no flood. Always clear. But no fish here. Only pis-pis. Karawala get fish when the flood low, but not Rio Grande."

"What do you eat when the fish are gone?"

"Same-same. Rice and beans."

"No meat?"

"Sure, we got give-nut and deer and wari."

"What's a give-nut?"

"A little animal in the swamp by the river. Is good."

"Are there lots of them?"

"Hoopah, this the home of them. I going bring you one tomorrow."

I ate slowly, standing in the water, enjoying talking as much as eating. I always enjoyed talking with Eddie. He was a quiet, self-conscious person, and didn't say a lot, but what he said was often animated, and his gestures and expressions said more than words. I was learning to watch him closely for the little nuances that revealed what he was thinking.

There was one thing I saw in him I really liked. I don't think he could lie. If I got too personal, he blushed and fidgeted and laughed nervously, but gave no answer. If I pried where I shouldn't, his expression would harden just for the instant it took to notice, and he would wash it away like a wave on the beach.

"You are not like the people I know," I told him.

He looked at me out of the corner of his eye. "Sure is so," he replied.

I looked at the trees, listened to the silence, and sighed heavily. I could read nothing in his expression. He looked at me as if what I'd said was unimportant. Whatever my people were, they were not here. They did not matter.

"That's why I like you, Eddie. The only thing that matters is what's right here right now, and it's all laid out where we both can see it."

*

I love the way snakes move. Without a sound, they can disappear even as you watch them. The night of the top gallon was not my best. I lay in my tijera, with the bar pulled tight under the mattress, and strained my every sense for the intrusion of snakes.

I knew they were there, and I hoped they were harmless, but in the blackness, they were hidden. I could not detect their presence by any sense, but in the absence of anything real, I felt them turn toward me. Their eyes pierced the darkness and found me in my bed, helpless but for my faith in nature.

In my aloneness, I allowed them to conquer my imagination. That which I could not sense became visions that fed my mind in great magnification. I could as well have been turning in the fires of hell, with all its serpents wrapped around me: cold scales and flickering tongues against my naked skin; fangs and venom tearing deep into my flesh.

At times my heart raced with fear; at times I floated in it, wondering at it, savoring this glimpse of myself. I turned inward and confronted things that could not exist elsewhere, created by me from nothing. It was like being awake in a dream.

I was wide awake, but there was nothing real to grasp. Reality had vaporized and drifted off, leaving me in the void with nothing but a mind full of snakes. Even the shelter of the house had proven to be an illusion. It kept nothing out and nothing in. As sanctum and territory, I had only my ego.

Bits and pieces of me were peeled away and fed, like the house, to the snakes. I realized there was no one to cry out to for help; I was as much alone as the only human on a faraway planet, without a ship to carry me home. I would come through the night or perish by my own wits, and there was no refuge. I could neither move nor utter a sound, lest I alert something in the night to my presence. I could not ignore it, and I could not escape it.

I don't know how long it lasted; I suppose it doesn't matter. I exhausted my fear and myself and lay in bed thinking about the cool of the night air and the sounds of the bush. The snakes lost their importance. I decided they'd have to share this with me until the water receded. I would not leave.

I went to sleep, and if I dreamed, it was not about snakes. It was a deep, comfortable sleep, and when I woke, there were two worlds to greet me. One was all that was familiar. The other was the illusion of the first. I knew they were both the same, and I knew how fear was playing its part.

I awoke to the sound of sloshing feet in wet rubber boots. The water was gone, the snakes were gone, and everything was coated in a layer of mud.

Half of Karawala was standing outside. When I stepped through the door, a cheer went up. Children ran off to tell the others. I was alive! I had spent the night in a house full of snakes, and I was still alive!

They had come to see my corpse and count the bites. Finding me alive elevated my status. The day before, they had thought me stupid to walk into a house full of snakes and lay down to sleep with them. I had frightened them. Now I was a wonder.

"How you live yet?" They all wanted to know. "How is the snake not make you dead?"

Some went about their business, some stayed to stare in wonder, and some set about the preparations for building my camp. Miss Pete's husband, Valdevio, and his brother Gonzalo brought their carpenter's tools. While others brought poles and leaf and bamboo, they started laying out the first new cabin.

I was excited. The place was bustling with activity, and everyone seemed as happy and excited as I. The reason was simple. No one here had worked for pay for many years before I came. Now they were going to be able to buy things. The uncertainty of gathering food in the jungle was being replaced, at least in part, by the confidence of currency.

In spite of the rain, it seemed that most of the village was there. The men did all the heavy work, while the women and children ran errands and brought food. I counted at least thirty people coming with materials and working during the day. Eddie told me there were more in the bush cutting stick.

It was still raining too much to get much done. Wet machetes, axes and hammers are hard to hold. When the rain broke, they worked. When it poured, they stayed home. I sat on the steps and watched things happen.

I learned to hear the rain when it was still far away, and to tell whether it was coming to us. "Li aola," they would shout, when the sound was just right, "rain coming." And they would put away their tools and seek shelter.

I watched the sawyers struggle with poles and ropes to erect their tapesco. It took them all day, between the rains, to get it done. It was a scaffold, built to hold a heavy weight. It was wide at the base and narrow at the top, with legs splayed out to buttress it. I had no idea what it was for.

The next day, I found out. They came early, boots sloshing, with ten men to help. They brought a big log alongside it, and by pushing, pulling and much grunting and groaning, hoisted it to the top, where it lay cradled.

I was impressed with their strength. They must be like ants, I thought, with the power to lift ten times their weight. They were short and slight, but things moved when they pushed.

With the log hoisted, the helpers left. The sawyers began marking the log with chunks of lead salvaged from old batteries. As I watched, it dawned on me what they were doing, and soon it was confirmed.

One man stood atop the log; the other on the ground below. Their saw measured eight feet in length. With a slow, measured cadence, they began the first cut. The man on the ground pulled; the man on top pulled. The blade moved imperceptibly through the log.

I shook my head in disbelief. It would take forever to saw the log into lumber, but they were going to do it. They were going to saw lumber for all the floors in all the houses I was going to build. This little project was going to take some time, but we had time on our hands. I had nowhere to go: no appointments; no time clock; no calendar. If you had asked, I would not have been able to tell you the date.

They made good time that day. They squared the log and sawed the first plank. It took them from first light to last to do it. When it rained, they stopped to sharpen the saw. They told me they would be lucky to saw a log a week.

I told them about the sawmills I'd seen that could cut a log like that in just a few minutes. They nodded their heads. They had worked at the old sawmill here in Karawala. They had seen the work of machines. There was a hint of sadness in their eyes.

"Your way is best," I said. "It is back-breaking work, but you will never clear the jungle at this rate."

"You take de saw. I think you soon change de mind."

"No, thanks," I said, smiling. "I'll take your word for it."

*

I did take the saw. Over the weeks I tried my hand at everything they did. I sat with the women and tied the palmetto leaves, preparing them for the roofers. Cross-legged on the grass, we pulled a strand of leaf from the fan and tied a pair together where stalk met leaf, then set it out to dry. The same strand would be used to tie the leaf to the lattice-work roof.

Throughout the day they sat, working ceaselessly, fingers and hands flowing, sing-song voices never stopping. Even though the sun and humidity neared the unbearable, I was softly comfortable with them. They taught me Miskito words and phrases and opened the door, just a little, into their world.

With a family, I walked out into the savannah to gather the leaves, and I backed the bundles to the camp. We walked a mile or more north, just outside the winding corridor of the Karawala, into the grasses, popta and pines.

Winston Davies, the husband and father of this Miskito family, showed me which leaves to cut, and how. The leaves, he said, must not show signs of insects or insect eggs, lest the roof be eaten quickly. He worried some about the moon, but I assured him that it was more important to me to get started than to wait until he liked the moon.

As we cut, the children gathered them up and took them to their mother, who bundled them for the walk back. I assumed that Winston and I would carry the bundles, making trip after trip until they were all there, but when it was time to go, everyone in the family picked one up.

When it came time to clear the road to the river, I took a machete and wore blisters in my hands. We felled trees and cleared brush from the runway to the river, widening the path to twenty feet. It took a month to complete, but when it was done, the walk was safe.

I was both student and teacher. I learned not only what materials they used, but where to find them and how to gather them. Each time I went out, I came back with more knowledge than baggage.

I soon learned that telling them how I wanted things done didn't work, and for the most part, drawings were useless. I had to show them. They could follow an example or a model, but they had no mind for abstractions. No matter how well I thought I had described something, or how good I thought my instructions were, nothing worked out right until I gave them a tangible example.

And so I worked. I worked at first to break the boredom, and then I worked because there was so much I could learn about them and from them that could only be had by sweating and bleeding with them.

When work started on the first boat, I spent a great deal of time at the village wharf, where the shipwright Poi had set up shop. Poi was a black man from Tasbapauni, a village about thirty miles down the coast. His given name was Roderick Christian, and when I asked why everyone knew him as Poi, he just shrugged his shoulders and grinned. Like Eddie, he had come to Nicaragua with his father, when he was a boy.

I made drawings of what I wanted, but Poi couldn't visualize it, so we made models until he understood. These were not to be dugout canoes. They were planked boats, made from mahogany sawn in Karawala.

Poi had made the Poop-Poop and other trading boats, so I knew he could make the boats I wanted. Mundo had arranged to bring him to Karawala.

The first time I saw Poi, I liked him. He had a huge smile on his face, sawdust and shavings in his hair, and a medio of Flor de Caña in his hip pocket. He wore an old blue cap and had a carpenter's pencil stuck behind his ear. I'm not sure I ever saw him without the cap and the pencil, except the time he had the fever.

Poi went to the savanna himself to choose the tree for the keel. I tagged along, and when we stopped in front of a stand of pines, I admitted to surprise.

"Wait a minute," I said, "these are pine trees. You're not going to use pine in my boats, are you?"

"Sure I is," he answered. "These Karawala pines the best. Come from all over looking Karawala keel. They say it never rot."

It was a dense stand of pines; so dense the trees had little girth compared to their height.

"These trees old, old," he explained as he walked through the stand, examining each tree. "They hard like stone and heavy. Cut with axe and it spark." He looked at me and laughed. "You think it not so, haint?"

He took up an axe and waved us back. With his strength and bulk, I expected the axe to sink in deep, but the first swing took only a chip of bark with a metallic ring. And sure enough, after he got through the bark, I actually saw sparks fly.

After felling, the log was trimmed to thirty feet, stripped of bark and hoisted onto the shoulders of a dozen men to be backed to Karawala. They were almost staggering under the load, but off they went.

With an adze and a draw knife, it took Poi three days to square it off into a four by six to his approval. In four days, all we had was one piece of lumber.

He was not so choosy about the mahogany. He selected the planks carefully, but he didn't go into the bush to select the trees.

First there was a keel and stem. Then came the ribs, and it

looked like the skeleton of a whale. Each piece was tried and trimmed again and again before he allowed it to take its place. Day by day I came to see, but sometimes the progress was imperceptible.

Every cry of, "li aola," sent him to Mundo's store to wait out the rain, and while he was there, he laughed at the rain and drank some rum. If the rain lasted long enough, his day was over. Even if it had just started, it was over. His eyes would brighten, his smile would spread across his face, and he would sway away to find a bed.

Casual was the best way to describe it. He, and everyone else, was glad to have an income of more than what one could grow, pick or catch. But work was something one did in proportion to need. Unnecessary work was not a consideration.

It was the process, not the product, that floated them. If work did not get done one day, it would another. So why worry? The current will go where it will, and they knew no person could raise a hand to stop it, or even divert it. The notion of schedules and deadlines struck them as humorous.

Thinking I could change that, and trying, could only have been frustrating and stressful. If a day dawned without a single person coming to work, I thought nothing of it. Now is all the time there is. We had plenty of time.

I was not surprised to look for Poi one day, only to find him gone to Tasbapauni. I stood with my bare feet in the mud, looking at a boat with shavings piled around her like shorn locks. I was disappointed, but there was nothing to do but walk back home and wait for word.

And so it went. Some days the stillness was broken by the ring of blades and the pounding of hammers, others by rain, and some by nothing but the songs of birds.

I cannot imagine anything closer to living in a dream. I pictured myself unheard and unseen for all the effect I had, while I was at once the focus of attention. My turns and twists at times seemed unrelated and random. I learned not to expect.

*

Late one afternoon, after everyone had gone home, but before the parrots began their chatter, I looked up to see a man and woman walking in from the savannah, and to my amazement, they were white. I sat on my porch, agog, and watched them approach. And then I remembered.

I had met them in Bluefields. The Kuku Awra was theirs, and I had come to Karawala in it. I was going to buy it from them. I had forgotten them entirely and had come to think of the boat as mine. They came now, I assumed, either to collect or to repossess.

"Naksa," I greeted when they were appropriately close.

"Naksa," they answered. We were all smiles and handshakes.

All of a sudden, I was a host, with nowhere to put my guests. We walked around to the kitchen shed and sat on the logs.

"You must be here about the boat," I offered. "Yes, I want to buy her. Sorry I didn't get back to you earlier."

"We just got back from Managua," he said. "Carol had a little medical problem that held us up."

As we talked, I rummaged around in the dishes for three clean cups and some rum.

"Nothing serious, I hope."

"I almost lost my leg," she said.

That caught my attention. I turned to look. She was wearing shorts, and on her shin, I saw an open chancre, about the size of a quarter, that looked bone deep.

"How on earth did you get that?" I asked, pouring rum and handing her the first cup.

"It's a fungus, and it was necrotic," she answered. "The Indians get them now and then. It's the damned humidity. You can't get dry in this place. I hate it."

I believed her. There was disgust and hatred in her voice. I wanted to ask her why it wasn't bandaged, but wanted to change the subject more.

"I asked around about you, but no one seems to know why you are here or what you are doing. So now that you're here, I get to ask you."

"I'm an anthropologist," he laughed. "And no matter how many times I try to explain it, they never understand. I'm here to work on my thesis. Carol came with me because we thought it would be a grand adventure. You know. Coconut palms and deserted beaches, like a post card."

He paused to suck on a lime and swallow some rum.

"It's been an adventure, all right. Two more weeks and we will have been here thirteen months, and that's the end of it. We'll go back, I'll write my thesis, and we'll never see this place again."

He was calm, not bitter, but I could tell that neither of them saw what I did. I was glad I wasn't here to study and analyze. The adventure had run its course a month or so after their arrival, and the rest of it was boredom and biting insects.

With deep fatigue in his voice, Brian looked into his glass and said, "It isn't sudden death you have to worry about here, although the tigers and snakes are real enough. It's the slow debilitation of the heat, the humidity and the parasites. It's the steady onslaught of the struggle for survival. These people...." He looked into my eyes, pleading. "There are no survivors."

We talked into the night about what they had seen and done and learned, and what I was going to do here. Time and again I asked myself if Karawala would lose its luster for me, too, and if I would die here of some dread disease.

They were excited about going home to the university and about snow and Christmas and the comfort of civilization. Talk about leaving was the only thing that animated them.

They went off to the village to sleep, and long after they left, I was still awake, staring up at the bar, trying to see through now and into the future. I fell asleep with the conclusion that there is no past or future; time does not move. There is nothing but now, and it is infinite.

If I am alive now, I am a survivor.

I awoke the next morning to the steady drumming of rain on the thatch. Without looking, I knew what surrounded me. Everything had a green cast to it, the sky was on the ground, and the grass grew up through little pools of water. No one came to work.

Brian and Carol slipped out of Karawala, and I never saw them again. Two weeks later, Bofu brought me a trunk filled with the things they wouldn't need at home. Some of it were things I would never need, and some were things I could have done without, but there was real treasure in it, too. There were books. If it was worth writing, it is worth reading. I had not realized, until I opened that trunk, how hungry for reading I had become.

On the top of the heap was an old copy of a news magazine. On the cover stood Brian, dressed in cap and gown, wearing a giant peace medal and grinning through his beard. The caption was, "The Graduate, 1968."

A note was clipped to it. "The story was about Berkeley. In my whole life, I've only spent one day in California, and it got me on the cover of TIME. Good luck, Brian."

I read the magazine first.

I never threw any of it away, and even though there was only that one evening, I have never forgotten them.

*

I had another hunger that was growing. I wanted to go to Orinoco to see those girls. Not a day passed that I did not think about them. When the rain fell steadily all day and all of Karawala stayed inside, I ached for them. "Woman Rain," they called it. Nothing to do but get a woman and spend the day in love. But I was trapped In Karawala, a day away, and all I could do was nap, read and sit and watch.

Eddie said we were cut off from Orinoco as long as the water was up. The tunnel through the swamp was gone. Impassable. I wondered whether it was true, or if he just wanted to keep me away from Davis Morales.

If my hunger had been only for sex, I could have satisfied it easily in Karawala. The young women made no secret of their willingness. But it was more than that. I wanted to be with the Orinoco girls. I wanted to hear their laughter and to feel their touch. I wanted to look deep into their eyes and find their spirits and then to flow inside and look outward from their minds.

What does the world look like without knowledge of the unseen? How does one cope in a world where cause and effect are disconnected? What populates a thought? I could only guess that they are to me as I am to something else, and that intelligence is both relative and relatively meaningless.

What celestial music did they hear that was only a ringing in my ear? What string, unknown to me, tied this earth to the moon? Are there as many worlds as perceptions? Is there more than one perception? If this cannot be known, can it matter?

I wanted them to look out through my eyes. It is that hunger that made me feel lonely. The hunger for sex can set one on fire and send you out in bold pursuit, but it does not cause loneliness. The hunger for sharing does that.

I asked myself why I had this longing for two girls in Orinoco, so very far apart, but got only a shrug for an answer. Having no answer, I let the question sink, not to rise again. The feeling was enough. It was good. It was the answer.

But if I could not satisfy that hunger, I could at least quench the other. With a gleam in my eye, I began to smile back.

On the river, when I took the Kuku Awra out by myself, I sometimes passed by young women bathing in the river. I motored on, without slowing or acknowledging them. Never were there men with them; they were hidden from sight as best they could. They covered their breasts when they saw me coming and stood still, half out of the water, until I passed.

And then one day I waved, and their hands left their breasts to wave back, and they smiled cheerfully. I slowed and passed nearer. One said, "Okay, Mr. Bet, let's go." She slithered into the boat, naked, and I motored up the river until we were secluded.

CHIGGERS
Chapter Eight
Matlalkambi Pura Wal

There are horses here, but no one rides them. They don't even use them as beasts of burden. These people are incredibly strong. If you sit here on these steps and watch the things they carry into town on their backs, it will amaze you. One man will carry a log that weighs several hundred pounds. They stagger under the weight, and they stop to rest every hundred feet or so, but they will not harness that log to a horse and let him pull it. They would rather walk to Sandy Bay than bridle a horse and ride it.

From the Journals of McBeth Johnson

I sat in Miss Pete's house, eating fried snook and chatting about impersonal things, when she noticed me rubbing my toe against the chair.

"You got itch?" she asked.

I showed her my toe. It was red and a bit swollen. I figured it was an insect bite of some sort: nothing to worry about.

"Oh," she said, brow furrowed, "Must be you got chigger."

"Maybe so," I answered. It seemed reasonable, although it must have been a very serious chigger.

"Make I send for Jane. She got good eye for that thing."

"Now, Miss Pete, no need to go to any trouble. I'll be okay. A chigger is nothing to worry about."

"Haps to you going take it out. That bad thing."

I was in no hurry to go anywhere, so I decided to find out who Jane was and what she was going to do with my toe. Miss

Pete barked orders at one of the children and off he went.

Within a few minutes, I heard bare feet on the wooden steps and a shy knock on the open door.

"Miss Pete, is I, Jane." Her voice was little more than a whisper.

"Come here, girl, and look at this man's toe. I think he got chigger."

I turned and saw a young woman shuffle through the door, her long tattered dress brushing the floor. Her head was bowed; her eyes averted. She was blushing. Miss Pete took her by the hand and led her to me. She knelt at my feet and held the inflamed foot with both hands cupped around the toes. "This Jane, Beth."

"Hello, Jane. It's a pleasure to meet you." She was quite beautiful, and very shy.

"Tanki payn," she answered, blushing through her dark skin. "Is chigger," she announced. "Need a razor."

"A razor?" I asked, surprised. "What are you going to do with a razor?"

"I going take out the chigger, them."

"Them? You think I have more than one chigger?"

"Only one, but got plenty egg. Soon have plenty chigger." She took the rusty razor blade from Miss Pete and wiped it on her dress.

"One moment," I said. "If you are going to cut into my toe with that, I'm going to sterilize it first." I got a match and heated the edge.

With a quizzical look and a shrug of the shoulders, she took the blade from me. I watched as she studied my toe, looking for the best place to cut. She chose the edge, next to the nail, and made an incision about a half inch long. A mass of tiny eggs flowed out with a trickle of blood.

"I'll be damned," I said. "Looky dat."

She smiled. She squeezed gently, pushing more eggs out, and wiped the eggs and blood away. She began pushing the skin back and trimming it off with the razor, and soon I saw the chigger. It was deep under my skin, growing fat and bloated on my blood. My amazement kept me from being disgusted.

Very gently, Jane lifted it out of my toe. It was about the size of a pea and was nothing but a red, swollen egg factory. There was a gaping hole where she had digested the tissue of my toe to give her the stuff for making eggs. I examined both with great curiosity.

"Have creoline?" Jane asked Miss Pete.

"Right here." She handed her a bottle with a dark liquid that looked like tobacco juice. There was an old cork in the bottle.

"Haps to kill the balance", she said. "Going hurt."

I had been around enough to know that these people are very stoic about pain. If she said it was going to hurt, she meant it. It was going to hurt.

"The balance of what?" I asked. "My foot?"

They laughed. "The egg, them."

She poured creoline into the wound. It hurt. I could not believe how a few drops of liquid could make me feel like my entire foot had been shoved into the glowing coals of a fire. I let out a yell more in surprise than anguish. Miss Pete and Jane thought it was funny.

"Haps to wear shoes if no want chigger."

"The chigger wasn't all that bad. What I no want is more creoline."

The fire subsided quickly. I wrapped a rag around my toe, thanked Miss Pete for lunch and Jane for the surgery, and left. I walked home on the heel of my foot, holding the toes as high as I could to keep the wound clean. There was no pain.

I sat on my steps, unwrapped the toe and examined it in the sunlight. If there were any eggs there, I couldn't see them, and surely the creoline killed them.

Didn't it? What if it didn't? What if they hatched in my toe? What if I awoke some morning to find hundreds of chiggers, bloated on my blood, eating the flesh of my feet and laying more eggs by the millions?

The thought was not pleasant. I got out a medio of rum and lit a cigar. Arms on my knees, I sat hunched on the porch, giving equal attention to the medio and the puro, surveying my domain.

I had no idea what kind of animal this chigger was. Arachnid? Probably. No way to tell. The head and legs were almost microscopic. I examined my other toes for signs of chiggers, but found none. I squeezed a drop of lime into the hole and poured some rum over it, just in case the creoline didn't work.

Miss Pete and Jane had been unimpressed. The little parasites must be common; I had more of these to look forward to. And what else, I wondered. What other tiny little creatures lay waiting for my blood? Should I be more wary of creatures akin to chiggers than tigers and snakes?

The sky began to darken with heavy clouds. Thunder rumbled. The percussions sometimes felt like soft mallets against my skin. There was excitement in it, and power. It is easy to see how our distant ancestors perceived the universe as having but four elements. Those four seem to possess all the power there is. All else fails to compare.

There are the quakes and volcanoes of the earth; the great waves of the sea; fires that consume entire forests; and the thunder, lightning, wind and rain born of thin air. Any one of them can snuff out the existence of any living thing - and do so with absolute indifference. The power of the elements is to this day all but incomprehensible.

Sitting on my steps in the jungle, exposed to it and completely vulnerable, I caught a glimpse of what the eyes of the first man might have seen. I nodded my head in acknowledgement.

The rumble grew to booms and then sharp explosions. When the rain was so heavy I could hardly see through it, I got a bar of soap, stripped and stepped out for a shower. The wind drove each drop into my skin. It stung at first, and I had to turn my back to it, but it was also primal and sensual, and I lingered.

Even without the thunder, the rain roared as it beat against the leaves. The sound was loud enough that I could hardly hear my own laughter. I held my arms out to it and turned full circle, catching frozen images of the storm and the jungle with each flash of lightning.

As I turned, soap in my hair, I imagined the response I would get if I tried this at home. The neighbors would call the police. I would be arrested for indecent exposure. I could go to jail for this! With that image and the storm and the rum, I laughed at our illusions of freedom.

I stood in the rain until it began to slacken. Inside, I dried with a towel as best I could. Still naked, I sat with a lime, a glass of rum and my puro and looked out through the open door at the remnant of the storm. As the air dried my skin, I thought of Orinoco.

In bed that night, I lay in the cocoon of the bar and listened to the night celebrate the water. They are especially loud, these myriad unseen voices, after a good storm. With my eyes closed, the illusion of being inside evaporated, and I floated like a wisp of fog. The tendrils of life reached into me and curled about my being.

WHAT'S FOR DINNER?

Chapter Nine

Matlalkanbi Pura Yumhpa

*Oh, Mack Beth, the bush doctor have his way and I
have my own. Take this bottle of rum and this bowl of lime
and go to bed. Drink the rum and eat the lime, and
tomorrow the fresh cold will be gone.*

Instructions from Miss Pete

I heard their feet sloshing in their rubber boots before they
rounded the trees. Their voices were low, almost inaudible, but I
knew them. Eddie and Mudi and Ferlan never failed to appear at
first light to start my fire and put on a pot of coffee. If there was
no coffee, they made a brew from parched corn. It wasn't much
good, but it was hot, and with a little sugar, it passed.

We were alternating between coffee and corn to conserve the
coffee. During the rainy season, the boats couldn't get to
Bluefields very often, and supplies became scarce between trips. I
had the last medio of rum in town, and the butt of the last puro
lay soaked in the grass by my house. No one had seen a cigarette
in weeks.

Those things we can live without, albeit grudgingly, but
Mundo's stocks of rice and beans were running low. Flour and
sugar and salt all came on the boats, but the boats were not
coming. The choices became fewer and fewer.

Eddie was pouring parched corn into a pot when I walked
out.

"Things not look good today, Mr. Bet. Look like parch corn
and fry bread is all we got to eat."

Unleavened dough fried in coconut oil, washed down with parched corn, was our breakfast.

"Why so, Eddie? It looks to me like this place always has food."

"Not in this time," Mudi said. "The bar is too cross to get out. We got no gun for shoot deer and wari. The flood have all the fish, them out to sea. Umpira yang nani."

"What's that, Mudi?"

"Umpira yang nani. Poor we. Going get meager before the dry. You, too, Mr. Bet." The thought was comical to them; they laughed. "We is all right here together. And no boat up the river. You going be meager just like we. No dollars gold can buy what not here."

We shared the hot brew and what little sugar I had left. I was finding it hard to believe that this place that had seemed so bountiful was now slamming the doors shut. And they were unconcerned about it. Stoic.

"Is this a bad year, Eddie?"

"A little worse, maybe, but no big storm for long time, so not bad."

"This happens every rainy season?"

"What that?"

"Running out of food."

"Oh, we not out. Just down to bread-kind."

"What's bread-kind?"

"Have plantation yet, with yucca and dasheen and coco root. Plenty kuku all time. Sometime we get lucky and catch a deer or something. Is hard, though."

Mudi and Ferlan nodded their agreement. Until the rains let up and the river returned to normal, we were isolated. We would eat nothing but what we caught or gathered. If infection or injury brought us down, we would get well or die without the help of medicine or doctor.

It was a sobering realization. The world did not exist outside the accessible realm of this community. It was no more than the memory of a dream. Upon waking, we know they are not real. This isolation was hard enough to touch.

"Gentlemen, there is plenty here to eat," I declared. "We will find it together."

During the next few weeks we found all sorts of things to eat, not one of which would they touch. We tore open a big rotting log and found it full of grubs. They thought I was out of my mind for suggesting we eat them. I caught a three-toed sloth and told them it was a delicacy. They looked at me and shook their heads in sympathy.

I caught a big boa and they screamed and ran as if I had pulled a demon straight out of hell. Even after I had killed it, cleaned it and steaked it, they kept their distance. I put it in a pot and walked off toward Miss Pete's house to ask her to cook it for me. They ran ahead to warn her, and before I got there I saw her run from the house, screaming, her children right behind her, escaping this crazy fool with a snake.

I stopped, mouth agape, and watched the hysteria in amazement. They disappeared into a house and slammed the doors and windows shut. I shrugged my shoulders, turned around and carried my snake back to my kitchen.

I could not let it go to waste. I killed it; I would eat it, even if it was a bit much for one person. I would have preferred it battered and fried, but salted and grilled was all I was supplied for. I cooked it all, ate my fill, and covered the rest for later.

My friends did not return that day, but they were back the next morning. I met them with a mischievous smile and offered them a bite of breakfast. Eddie and Mudi declined and backed away from the kitchen, but Ferlan was hungry and did not quite understand their fear. He accepted.

Fire ants had discovered the pot. They added a peppery taste to the heated boa. Ferlan was very tentative, watching Eddie and Mudi for their reaction as he first smelled it, then took a small bite and chewed. They, in turn, were intensely curious, but kept their distance.

A smile spread across Ferlan's face, and he lost all fear. "This uaola good, Eddie. Come and try it." He reached into the pot and held a piece out to them. They shrank back. Ferlan and I laughed and ate some more.

"You going dead out, Ferlan Santiago," Mudi warned. "That thing not for eat."

"Mudi," I lectured, "This snake is as good as a chicken. You eat chicken, don't you?"

"So snake does, too," he replied, "Serpent is evil thing, Mr. Bet," he warned, but I could tell he wasn't convinced.

"There is one and only one creature in this universe with the aptitude for evil," I growled. "This animal is not it."

"What that creature?" Eddie asked.

"Mankind," I answered.

Ferlan stopped eating. Eddie and Mudi stared at the ground and thought.

"Beyond the mind of man, there is no evil. There are no demons or devils or hells to house them. No burning fires beyond our guilt. We are it."

"I don't want study that," Mudi whispered.

I spoke gently: "A snake is no more evil than a butterfly or a flower. It is impossible for any of those things to be evil."

"Is I, the evil?" Ferlan asked, shaken.

"No, Ferlan. Only those who choose evil are evil. No one is born with a black heart; it is something one creates.

There was a clumsy silence while we finished the snake. It is too easy, I thought, to accept authority without question. Blind acceptance is drummed into us from birth, and so seems like the only way to think. If there is any greater barrier to enlightenment, I cannot imagine what it is.

"You must learn to think things through for yourself, Ferlan. Question everything you hear. Ask yourself if it makes sense; if it fits the world you live in."

"The Bible is wrong?" He asked, piercing. Eddie and Mudi looked up.

"Where it teaches the right way to live, it is mostly right," I answered, and paused. "But the rest of it can be very misleading. About the snake, the Bible is wrong. But mostly people are wrong about the Bible. They make the meaning of it fit their own behavior to make them feel right about themselves. They corrupt it."

I wondered where this might lead. The church had a strong hold on him. Many times I had watched him in spontaneous play, curious and animated, only to be jerked tight by some reminder of the way someone else thought he was supposed to behave. I wished I could free him of that.

"You see?" Mudi exclaimed. "Mr. Bet got strong brains. Did I told you?"

"Yes, I hear it," Eddie answered. "You listen good, Ferlan. He tell you right, like we. You too much in the church. You gone from sense."

"Want some snake, Eddie?" I asked, smiling.

"Maybe next time, Mr. Bet. I eat already." Eddie had a way of showing self-consciousness when he was embarrassed. He averted his eyes to the ground, held his arms close to his sides and shuffled his feet.

"Come, Eddie, make we eat some," Mudi challenged.

They agreed with what I'd said, I could tell, but their conditioning was strong. Rational thought was finding emotional bondage difficult to deal with.

Eddie hesitated. Mudi grinned and stepped forward, reaching for one of the two remaining pieces. "Okay, then. Make I try it."

Not to be outdone, Eddie stepped up. Both were soon chewing hungrily and remarking about the taste.

"Mr. Bet?"

"Yes, Eddie."

"Animal don't come in the night to get your food?"

I hadn't thought about it, but he was right. One shouldn't present too much temptation to the beasts of the night. In bear country I would have gone to great lengths to secure my food away from my bed.

"Only fire ants," I answered.

"We eating them now," Mudi laughed.

"I guess I feel secure here."

"Some night they going wake you."

"Maybe soon-soon the monkey going carry all," Ferlan said.

"Okay," I said, "We'll build a locker for it."

"Better," they all agreed.

SANI TINGNI
Chapter Ten
Matawalsip

The monetary system on this coast is Spanish, British and Nicaraguan. Their nickel, or five-cent piece, is called a Real, from their Spanish heritage. Cincos Reales, or five nickels, equals a Shilling, their quarter. They are all Cordobas, of course, and everything else is counted in Cordobas.

As told by Sunshine Down

"They say tapom to Sani Tingni," Eddie said. "Can catch today."

That was all I needed. "Where's Sani Tingni?"

"Up the river some. Little creek at Sani Warban."

Sani Warban. Where the river narrowed and flowed deep. The water was more than a hundred feet deep there, straight down on the north bank. Within a few minutes we were loading our gear into the Kuku Awra.

The Rio Karawala was clear, but the Rio Grande was still swollen and muddy, like chocolate milk flowing to the sea. Entire trees, uprooted from the banks by the current, floated down the river. Some measured more than two hundred feet in height. Debris of all natural sorts littered the water. Conspicuously absent was the trash of human origin.

From the mouth of the Karawala to the mouth of Sani Tingni is only a couple of miles, but being in a straight stretch, the distance was deceptive; it looked much less. Against the current, dodging flotsam, it took forever to close it.

This creek, too, was clear. The floodwater was coming from the mountains in the west, a place unknown by me. These waters were from the sky above our heads. Sani Tingni was narrower than the Karawala. The canopy closed over us, sealing us in a long, winding green tunnel. The air was still. The water was a deep green mirror, broken only by our intrusion.

I let a red and white Super Bingo slip into the wake and dropped it back as far as I dared.

"Yes, yes, yes. Look, now." Eddie pointed ahead. "They here."

He spoke quietly, but if excitement can be transmitted, the fish knew we were there. I turned to look and saw the dark back and silver sides of a tarpon as he rolled. Big bubbles rose from the tarpon below; there was a school. More rolled at our sides as we passed, gulping air to fill their bladders. I felt adrenaline pump into my blood.

I felt a tap and quickly flipped the reel into gear. As if the hook was snagged, the line became taut and the rod bent. My hands tightened around the fore grip and I heaved back on the rod to set the hook. As if my arms had launched a rocket, a Silver King shot up out of the creek, shattering the stillness, and crashed into the foliage above. In a tiny instant of time, he was back in the water, his explosion dripping down behind him. I held a rod attached by a long thin line to a tree.

Limp, I sat and watched the concentric circles be swallowed by the mangroves, until there was no evidence that anything had happened. What a rush! There was now a place in time and space where that animal and I were tied together. I would keep that picture forever, and I would remember how weak I felt after the charge of excitement, with adrenaline pumping in my blood and nothing to do with it. How could so much emotion be packed into such a small frame of time?

But it was not the sort of connection I sought. The creek was too confining; it was unfair to the fish to have his flight cut short by branches. I reeled the line in and laid the rod across the thwarts. A hooked tarpon was more likely to kill himself in the branches than to be caught fairly by me.

Mudi understood, and without hesitation, unwrapped his harpoon.

"Better I strike one tapom, Mr. Bet." He said excitedly, working quickly to lay out the line and tie it off.

I nodded my assent. In this place, at this time, with these people, notions of sportsmanship were a bit absurd. If we managed to get one stuck, he'd probably turn the dori over on the first run. Failing that, he'd most likely land in the boat after a jump and break every bone in our bodies. Either way, the odds were stacked heavily against us. There is great eagerness and excitement in hunger.

Standing on the bow, Mudi readied himself. He stood poised, with the harpoon raised, aiming at a window of water in front of us. The fish would have to roll where he aimed.

Eddie killed the motor, and he and Ferlan picked up the paddles and dipped them quietly into the water, keeping us in the school. Mudi was transformed. Now he was a hunter, strong and intense. His entire being was focused on the water where the fish would roll. As if aiming him, Eddie and Ferlan moved the dori to the fish, in concentration as deep as his.

The scene was ancient and primitive. I had managed to travel in time far enough that the time could not be identified. I was part of a prehistoric hunting party.

A tarpon rolled, and Mudi's body snapped so suddenly and so violently I was startled even before the harpoon struck home. There was a swoosh and a thud and then water filled our sphere of existence. The soft green tunnel was suddenly sharp and piercing. The violent thrashing of the tarpon rocked the dori even before the line snapped tight.

"That's it, boy!" Eddie shouted as he grabbed the gunnels. "Now hold him!"

The jolt knocked Mudi off balance. He fell to his knees, and without flinching or taking his eyes off the fish, took hold of the line and braced himself. The Kuku Awra lurched sideways, very nearly tipping, before straightening out behind the fish.

One wild, gill-rattling jump brought him falling back toward us. No reflexes were quick enough; we could not have dodged him. Mudi had struck well. He landed alongside and lay still in the water, dead.

We pulled it in over the gunnel as quickly as we could and set out to find another, but the school was gone. After paddling around for a few minutes, Eddie started the motor and headed out of the creek.

"Plenty fish there, boy." Eddie smiled, proud of the catch. "Karawala going eat good tonight."

I guessed the fish would dress out at about one hundred twenty-five pounds. It was enough to feed every person in the village, just once.

"What you going do with your half, Mr. Bet?" Ferlan asked.

"My half?" I asked, surprised.

"Is the law. The owner get half, if is dori or rifle."

I looked at Eddie for an explanation.

"We here in your dori," he said. "Not for you, we be in Karawala. If you have gun and we use to kill wari or sula, haps to we going carry you half."

"So half of this is mine."

"Is so."

Then I will give it to Karawala.

No hay ron. No hay puro. No hay nada. But the tarpon was good. Miss Pete cooked a big chunk of it over an open fire for about an hour. Then she brought it inside, where she "take the bone out, them". She chopped it up, added whatever spices and herbs she had or could find, flattened it out into patties, and fried it in coconut oil.

It could not be served in a seafood restaurant, but we were happy to have it. All over Karawala, women and girls were frying patties of roasted, chopped, spiced tarpon, and everyone was celebrating.

My mouth watered as I waited. There was an emptiness in my stomach that had been growing harder with the weeks. At times it burned, not like indigestion, but like a sense of sorrow I could not explain. I had to cinch my belt tight to keep my pants from falling to the ground. I was getting meager. I had never known hunger before.

It did not take much to fill us up. In better times I could have eaten twice as much. Miss Pete was very careful to put away the leftovers so that the scavengers could not get to them. Rats and roaches came and went as they pleased while people slept.

Jane came by after dinner to thank me for the fish and to bring me a small pouch of coffee beans.

"Where you get them coffee, Jane?" Miss Pete asked.

"My brother come from up the river," she answered. "He not bring much, but he say Miguel Vidori coming soon."

"Aiee! He bring rice and bean?"

"Haps to, he going to. My brother say El Milagro going leave off for Bluefields before the Krismis."

Miss Pete looked at me with a troubled face. "I guess you going, too, Beth?"

"Does he go to Orinoco?" I asked.

They all but gasped at that. "Davis say he going kill you if you go back there," Miss Pete warned. "Better you not go."

"Worse yet," Jane said. "Davis to La Cruz now. Say he going come here to kill you."

I sighed deeply. "Looks like trouble either way."

Running away did not even occur to me. I had a problem, but the only possible solution lay in stopping Davis Morales, not in letting him chase me away. Could I turn him into a friend? Buy him off? Fight him? Have him jailed?

"What does Davis do?" I asked.

Miss Pete harrumphed. "That fella no good, Beth. He thief and drink and beat the girl, them. Some one of these boys going kill him some day, I tell you."

"How does he get away with it? Why doesn't someone stop

him?"

"He too mannish. He got them all fright right up." She paused. "And these boys not like that. They not so mannish."

"What about the police? Why not go to Bluefields?"

"That Guardia too cruel. They only want kill we. Guardia is for the Spaniards, not we. We don't study them."

So they didn't have a solution, either. I walked home wondering how far crime had evolved here. In a place where there are no locks, no jails and no means of dealing with threats of violence, one would think the people would live without the fears we have. I wished it was so, but I am enough the skeptic that I could not believe it.

KILL A TIGER

Chapter Eleven

Matawalsip Pura Kum

There is an animal we see in the bush at night. It flies slow through the bush, and it sounds like airplane, but can't be airplane. Airplane can't fly through trees. It is about the size of a child foot. It has a green light on the front, yellow lights on the sides, and a red light on the tail. I don't know what kind of animal that is, but we fright of it.

As told by Abanil Lacayo

As often as not, I did little after the sun went down. Sometimes I never even lit a lamp, choosing to sit or walk in the darkness. In all but the darkest nights, there was enough light for anything but reading.

And so I sat, many a night, and thought about the things I was experiencing, trying to see into the people far enough to understand them. That night I thought about all the hungers that were growing within me. A yearning for my native soil began to percolate among the fleshes of that stew. A boat was going to Bluefields. I was already on it.

I listened to the night sounds, but not for long. I fell off early, but not for long. At about midnight, I woke up with fear charging through me like pulses of electricity. I wanted to jump and run, but I forced the impulse down and remained frozen, listening for a hint of what danger had come to me.

I heard nothing. Nothing. Never had there been a moment of complete silence in the night. Far away, I could hear the chorus, but here there were no sounds nearby. Nothing but cold dread.

I knew there was something there, beneath audible sound, and when it moved, it tore at my nerves. But I could not hear it and dared not move.

And then it coughed. It was hardly a sound, so quiet, but it froze me with fear. Although I had never heard it before, I knew there was a jaguar stalking my house. The tiger was here.

Surely it knew I was here. There was nothing to keep my scent from wafting to it on the breeze. By now, he could hear my heartbeat and my breathing. He might even have been able to smell my fear.

Where had the fear come from, and why couldn't I calm it? What sense had wakened me?

If I lay there, hoping it would go away, I would be eaten. I had to get up and get my gun. Slowly and carefully, I began moving to the edge of the cot, trying desperately not to make a sound. Every move I made was amplified a thousand times. I felt like a worm on a hook.

It sounds so simple, but swinging your feet to the floor and standing up is a long way when skin moving against cotton sounds like thunder. I picked up the pistol and stood, searching for the tiger.

It coughed again, close and loud. I looked and saw him step out of the bush at the edge of the swamp. My skin tightened, my nipples hurt and every hair on my body stood up. No one to call to; nowhere to run. One of us was soon to die.

He stood there for a moment before walking slowly and deliberately toward me. I cupped the butt of the Browning and aimed, cocked and ready to fire. About twenty-five feet away, he stopped and sat on his haunches and stared right into my eyes, as if I stood in plain sight. I dared not lower the pistol. If it was down when he charged, he would get his meal.

Knowing that even a thought could slow my response, I kept my mind clear and breathed deep to calm myself. There was no twitch or warning when he charged. I have never seen anything move that fast. His leap stretched him out to full length, and I realized he would not run up to the house and claw his way through the wall; the one leap would take him from sitting on my lawn to crashing through the thin, flimsy bamboo.

I started firing just as his feet left the ground. My fourth shot met him as his front feet hit the floor beside me, bamboo and popta flying. His charge carried him past me, and before he could turn, I hit him four more times, once in the heart, once in the head, and twice in between. He dropped. I hesitated an instant before pumping the rest of the clip into his heart.

I dropped the spent clip and shoved in a loaded one. I didn't know how many times I'd hit him, but I was taking no chances. If he so much as batted an eyelash, he was going to get another clip. Not for an instant did I take my eyes off him.

Blood spread out from his chest and head and ran through the cracks in the floor. I smiled. There was no movement. Neither breathing nor twitching of muscles could I see, but it was too dark to trust my life to what I thought I didn't see. I held the pistol aimed at his heart while I looked him over.

Here in my thin little house was a jaguar, the largest spotted cat in the world. I couldn't suppress a chuckle. Twenty-five feet was a short leap for an animal that measured more than half that when he was fully stretched out in a flying leap. What a magnificent animal, I thought, and how close I stood to my own death.

"I won, motherfucker," I said softly, and tensed at the possibility that my voice might have stirred him to life. When he remained dead, I continued, "Tomorrow morning, I'll cut your balls off and hang them on a string around my neck."

My mouth was so dry I could barely talk. I tried to swallow, but my tongue got in the way. If there had been a bottle of rum in the house, I'd have chugged the whole thing. I didn't even have a cigar.

After five minutes of focused concentration, I relaxed, but I didn't put the gun down. Nor did I poke the cat in the ribs. I sat down and waited for the day. When the adrenaline began to wear off, fatigue replaced the excitement. I sat and stared into his open eyes.

It is a wonder how little difference there often is between fear and excitement. Perhaps it is no more than one's interpretation, but I know what it means to taste fear. It is a literal taste, not figurative, and I will never forget it. Pain and great sorrow are forgotten, but the fear I felt upon waking that night will never leave me.

I may never understand how the fear came to me before I knew the tiger was there. How did he do that to me? Was it a sense I have that warned me? Did I, in peaceful sleep, feel his presence enter my sphere? If so, why did it almost freeze me?

I became connected to that tiger, like a thin filament of mono connects me to a tarpon, when he began stalking me. Along that connection, he transmitted the fear intended to freeze his prey. It is the fear that makes him so successful. The predator is not the enemy. It is fear. If you can overcome fear, you will not be eaten. When you overcome fear, you cease to be prey.

"Why," I asked the tiger, "couldn't you have gone after Davis Morales? You could have solved a great problem for me and fed yourself at the same time. We both would have been happy."

I fell asleep in the chair with the Browning in my hand, wondering about what was within me.

When I woke, there was a low murmur of voices outside. I woke with a start. It was daylight. The tiger lay in front of me in his own clotted blood, looking very dead. I stood up and pushed the door open, the gun still in my hand.

A cheer went up when they saw me. "He live!" They yelled. "He live!" A crowd had come to see what had passed in the night. They stood away, ready to run at any sign of the tiger. When they saw me, they rushed in.

Eddie shook his head and smiled. "We thought you dead," he said. "We thought you like Billy Rose, gone to feed tiger."

Miss Pete and Jane bawled into their aprons. Mudi called from inside, "Come look, now, Eddie, this fella big tiger, I tell you."

"Yeeow!" I heard Ferlan yelling and bouncing around inside. "Yeeow!"

They called for more men to help them drag it outside, and they called for the women to come clean up the blood.

"Aiee, looky dat thing," Miss Pete cried when they dragged it down the steps. "Big fella, I tell you."

Ferlan walked around me, looking for damage. "You not hurted?" He asked.

"Not like him," I answered, pointing at the tiger. Several men were standing over it, examining. "How many times did I hit him?"

"Plenty," they said. "Sound like war last night," Eddie said. "We know is big trouble."

It would have been pointless to ask why no one had come to see what happened. They hadn't even called out. Perhaps if I had only frightened it away, they would have called attention to themselves.

All of a sudden I was very, very tired and very, very hungry. I looked at Miss Pete and asked, "What you got for eat?"

She laughed a hearty, deep laugh and said, "Oh, Beth, you not going ask me to cook no tiger?"

I laughed, too. "No, Miss Pete. I don't think I'm ready to try tiger."

"Come, then. We go."

She fed me well, with things she'd been saving. She gathered eggs and killed a chicken, and handed me a bottle of casusa to sip while she cooked. "To kill the fright," she said.

While I sat and waited, Ferlan came to tell me the bush doctor was there, "for the seed and the tusk, them." He said he was going to make something for me.

The casusa warmed and relaxed me. I sat with my eyes closed and listened to the soft, sing-song voices around me. The voices of women came from the kitchen. I understood none of the words, but the tone was one of contentment. It seemed they were always happy when they were cooking, as if the fire and the food were all the security they needed. Sometimes they would all talk and laugh at once, and I imagined that they understood it all.

I heard birds singing in the coco plums, and I heard the voices of children playing. Even those in the distance were clear, and listening to sounds in the silence was like looking through a telescope at the edge of the universe. The hearing gave me knowledge.

I ate, and when I had eaten, I laid my head back and nodded. There was nowhere to go and nothing to do. I couldn't get back into my house until it was scrubbed and cleaned and repaired. There were people working on those things, and there were people skinning the big cat.

Ferlan sat patiently beside me on the porch. Now and then I opened my eyes and caught him watching me. I had done something to make him proud.

A little later Eddie and Mudi came sauntering up and took their places on the porch. Their pride, too, was obvious.

"Tomás Gamboa say you must go with him to the bush tomorrow," Eddie said.

"He say you take the tiger spirit," Mudi added. "You not only man, now."

"Okay," I said. "What will we do in the bush?"

"Not we," Eddie answered, "You alone."

"You alone going see," Mudi said.

That was all they would say. I could get no more out of them.

Eddie broke the silence. "Make a good skin, I tell you."

Mudi broke out laughing. "The girl going come to you now, Mr. Bet. They going come and grind the tiger man and you going have tukta all about Karawala."

The floor was still wet when I got home, and it was as light in color as fresh sawn maple. The tiger's blood was gone. The bamboo and thatch were repaired. There was a green patch where the cat had come through.

I stood in the door and inspected it. The physical evidence was gone, but I could feel a ghost in my mind. I accepted him as a permanent guest.

It was hardly dark when I lay down, hoping to sleep. My eyes burned, and my brain felt swollen. I did not care what sounds came from where and what. I knew there would not be another tiger for a long time, if ever, but I could not stop listening for that cough that would pull my skin tight and stand my hair on end.

I would have greeted the sound with pleasant excitement. Images swirled through the darkness. There was a connection between me and the cat and the earth beneath the cat's big paws, and there was no real difference in any of them. I flowed through them all, and they through me.

HILL PAUNI

Chapter Twelve

Matawalsip Pura Wal

*All this world and the sky are here if you are looking or
if you are not. No matter. You paint the color from all you
ever saw: not from what you see. Is nothing more. Is what
you think. You see it, sure, but you can't be sure what it is.*

As told by Tomás Gamboa

Tomás Gamboa is not big; none of the Miskitu are big. He
came into sight from around the pines and stood at the edge of
the runway, looking at me, waiting for me. I picked up a knife
and a bag of carefully dried matches and walked out to greet
him.

His expression did not change as I approached. He was
examining me from head to toe, weighing my strengths and
weaknesses. I did the same. I could not be sure how old he was,
but his face had weathered many years. It was like old leather.
His eyes were black and as bright as those of a boy. I wondered
how such young eyes could be surrounded by such an old face.
They were not hard, piercing eyes, but they were looking into me
and through me, as if he could see inside. It was not an
uncomfortable feeling. I felt relieved by it.

He didn't say a word. Before I extended my hand, he turned
and walked toward the path to the river. I fell in behind him,
content with the silence. There were things I wanted to ask him
about the bush medicine, but I followed his lead and felt assured
that he would offer more if I was patient.

We crossed the Karawala in a canoe so small I was sure it

would sink beneath our weight. Tomás poled us well into the bush on the other side and hid the dori under roots and bushes that hung over an unseen inlet. It could not have been for theft; perhaps his motive was privacy.

He set out toward the west, along a well worn path, but after a mile or so, he left it for a lesser trail. His pace was steady; neither fast nor slow. Not once did he look back at me or say a single word.

So be it, I thought. If this is nothing more than a walk in the park, I have the time and interest. If it is more, it will come to me soon enough. Neither lagging nor gaining, I kept a constant distance between us. I looked into the bush as we passed.

To my surprise, the land began rising. I had thought it was flat along the coast. As the land rose, the trees became taller and greater in girth, and the light at the forest floor dimmed. The undergrowth thinned; for the first time I could see more than a few yards through the leaves. Looking up, the canopy was unbroken.

Tomás Gamboa came to a stop in the middle of a large clearing. He turned and smiled. "This it," he said, "We here." He held out his arms and turned, inviting me to look.

It looked planned, as if this was no accident of nature. In a circle around the clearing were five of the greatest mahoganies I have ever seen. Their buttresses and trunks were huge; their highest branches somewhere beyond my sight. Within the circle, the ground was clear of twigs, branches and leaves. I nodded.

Beyond the circle, there was a mound. Undappled sunlight fell on tall, soft grasses that covered it like thick hair. I guessed it to be about fifty feet high.

"Where are we?" I asked. I was not sure I could hold my curiosity in check any longer.

He smiled and said, "Hill Pauni."

"Tell me about it," I pleaded. "What sort of place is it?"

"You soon tell me. Get stick for fire." He waved me off, out of the circumference of the circle.

I obeyed. I was excited. I had no idea what to anticipate, but I had a feeling I was about to experience something unusual. As quickly as I could, I picked up all the firewood I could carry and took it to Tomás.

"Make you get more." He smiled and winked. "Going be long night."

He told me where to stack the wood, and off I went for more. It took more than an hour of gathering to make him happy. When it was done, I had a respectable pile of wood stacked just outside the gamba of the tree opposite the mound.

The tree made a perfect camp. Its trunk and gamba protected us on three sides; the fire on the fourth. I sat, hoping to relax and talk a bit, but as my butt hit the dirt, he got to his feet. "Come." He returned to the center of the circle. From a small leather pouch, he took a necklace of tiger teeth and put it around my neck. He stood back and looked at me and the teeth, and he grinned. "Good works. Now you safe from bad spirit."

I, too, smiled. In a world dominated by bad spirits, I would take all the help I could get. "Are these from my tiger?"

"Sure. Only you alone can wear. When bad spirit molest you, tusks explode." He held out the big canines, and with hands and eyes, feigned an explosion.

"What bad spirit?"

"Can't say. Could be anything."

He picked up a calabash bowl and said, "Come."

We walked beyond the circle into the bush, where he slowed and began searching the ground for something. When he found it, he smiled and sighed deeply. "Look, now," he said softly, reverently. "You lucky fella."

We bent over a small herb. He showed me, without speaking, the difference between it and the other similar plants around it. Satisfied that I saw, he motioned me closer, pulled it from the ground, held it to my nose, and said, "Smell."

I did. For one brief instant, the essence of all that is sweet and pure rushed in, filled me entirely, and vanished. For one brief instant a door had opened, and I had seen through it into paradise. It had to be magic. Nothing else could explain it. Nothing had ever made me feel that good before. I looked for more, but Tomás caught my arm and pulled me up.

"Only one. Only get one. But now you know. Can give to next one."

"What next one?"

"You will know."

"You mean I could bring someone up here?"

"I could stop you?"

"Would you want me to?"

"Not for me to want."

I looked around me, and then at him. "Thank you."

"Is good," he said. He began searching the ground again, parting the foliage and plucking leaves and berries, making sure I saw which plants. With the bowl about half full, we returned to the center of the circle. It was darker, but the sun still had a long way to go before night.

From another leather pouch, he poured a powder, and from a small gourd in his pocket, he poured a clear liquid. We sat cross-legged; I watched while he ground and stirred the mixture with a pestle of wood. When he was done, he handed me the bowl.

I looked into it, then into his eyes, searching for a hint. "What is it?" I asked.

"Drink," he commanded, with a devilish grin.

First I sniffed. There was a faint hint of the little root in it. I needed no more enticement. Down it went.

"Good...good...good," he smiled and nodded as I drank.

When I had finished, he stood. "I going now. Until tomorrow."

I had just quaffed I knew not what, and my guide was abandoning me for the night. A twinge of fear knotted into a ball in my stomach, but I pushed it away. Sitting where I was, I watched him until he reached the edge of the circle, where he turned and faced me.

"Two things we are: spirit and animal. If you want see the spirit, you must let die the animal."

I don't know how long I sat there watching the trail. I thought briefly about following, but there was a reason he brought me here, and perhaps there would be something worthwhile in it for me. What did I drink? What was going to happen? There was nothing I could do but wait and see.

I relaxed. Tomás had not given me any reason to think there was danger here. To the contrary, I felt a sense of confidence that belied my situation. I was about to spend the night alone in the jungle with no more protection than a knife, a few matches and the gamba of the mahogany, and I felt good about it.

I began to feel very good, as a matter of fact. There seemed to be a faint hint of the sweetness of that little root rising from my skin. I became more relaxed; there was a sensation of great strength coming over me.

From a cross-legged position, I stood without effort, as if I had levitated. All was well within me and around me; I could feel it as an absolute. The sense of well-being increased, and I seemed to grow, as if I was expanding to fill more space.

I took a step and felt the incredible machinery of my body in fluid motion. Millions of muscle fibers pulled in perfect coordination to move, with perfect balance, this mountainous hulk of flesh and bones. That one step was a celebration of the evolution of life. Every fiber cried out in joy.

The things around me began to change. Each hot breath roared through my nostrils with scents I had never smelled. I looked at old familiar things with new wonderment. I looked at my hands and saw complexity unequalled anywhere else in nature. Looking inward, I saw a mind cognizant of its own complexity and knew it had no boundaries. I was waking up.

Without volition, I took the red bandana from my head, and it was as if I had uncaged myself. I unbuttoned my shirt and laughed gleefully as it fell to the ground.

'Why am I doing this?' I wondered. 'Why does it feel so good?'

I stood naked in the clearing. To the birds and the trees, I said, "You don't care. I look no different to you dressed or not. My clothes do not define me."

I did not wonder at my immodest behavior; it was insignificant. I stood for a moment, looking down at my clothes, and wondered what they were. I held the jeans and felt the texture; I looked and saw the miracle of tightly woven fibers. The invention of cloth is one of the wonders of the world. It plays to our vanity so well that we see the swagger, but astonishment is lost. Our machines have made it ordinary. Art by machinery has made us ordinary.

But there is nothing ordinary about us. Like our inability to see the depth of fabric, we fail to see the depth of our beauty. We are far, far beyond what we see in the mirror. Could we but release it from prison.

I left my clothes where they were and walked toward the mound. Backlit by the setting sun, it had a golden halo. It was the only place where sunlight came to earth. I was drawn to it like a moth to flame.

I stood at the base and looked straight ahead at the grass. I was mesmerized by the way it undulated. As I watched, it began to weave patterns, and the earth beneath it began to rise and fall as if it was breathing. Everything I saw or felt or heard was sensuous, and this moving, living mound heightened the feeling. My entire being glowed with primal sensuality that was at once carnal and metaphysical.

I climbed to the top to lie in the grass. I was in a pristine world with the bluest sky ever seen. The trees danced with pliant limbs to the music of the wind, and every cloud took living shape. Things that were once one thing became another until it became pointless to think of recognition. Nothing was what I thought it was. The veneers of the world I knew had fallen away, like my clothes.

My world was carefully ordered; this world had neither arrangement nor permanence. I closed my eyes for a moment, thinking that when I opened them, I would see reality. I saw nothing, heard nothing, felt nothing and thought nothing. Time stopped. If it lasted an instant, it lasted an eternity.

There was a terrific explosion somewhere within. From above the mound, I looked down at my body. It was beautiful, but it was not me. Was I dead? No. The animal was dead, and that lump of clay was not what I am. I am spirit. I can fly.

I was startled to see that the mound had suddenly become populated, as if by picnickers in a park. A little girl stood by my body with her mother and asked, "What is it?"

"That is where we live," she answered.

I was incredulous. "What?"

All of them looked up at the source of my voice. "Who are you?" I asked. "How did you get here?"

"We're the voices inside," she answered. "You brought us here. You went out, so we came out. Isn't it nice to be out?"

I nodded my assent.

When I opened my eyes, I looked out upon myself. Not one thing but many, I was at once everything and nothing, existing beyond myself in space and time. Whatever existed within me also existed beyond me. I was everything there ever was.

The earth still rose and fell like a sleeping giant; I knew it was aware. The grasses weaved their patterns with a wink and a come-on smile. The branches did their best to seduce me.

There was an overwhelming sense of love coming from everything. It was not directed at anything, like a mother's love for a child, but it bathed everything in its light. This is what we had to suppress to get where we are. This is the meaning and the purpose we lost. For what?

The sun began to set, and there was a sudden urgency brought on by darkness. This was not the darkness of sleep; this was the darkness of hunters and their prey. I was naked and felt like prey. I needed shelter.

I went quickly to the center of the clearing and retrieved my clothes. Clutching them, I went to the giant mahogany, where I had piled the firewood, and settled down between the gamba. Watching the open side, I pulled on my clothes. It was not enough. I needed to be hidden, and the flimsy clothes did nothing to make me less visible or less vulnerable. They were a false promise.

The last light was sucked away. It was a pitch black night; my sense of sight was gone. I pushed myself into a ball, deep between the gamba, and listened. The silence roared.

There was then no separation in time between me and my primitive ancestors, who spent their nights in fear of being eaten, curled up in some hollow that offered a sense of protection. Every leaf that rustled, every twig that snapped, every sound, real or imagined, was magnified a thousand times, and was each and every one a savage beast come to drink my blood and gnaw my bones.

There was an image of lightning striking an old dry tree. It burst into flames and fell to earth. I remembered why there was a pile of wood in front of me. My hand went into my pocket and pulled out the package of matches. I discovered fire. The beast of night was slain.

The kindling caught and grew. I fed it well, and when it was blazing, I pulled out a torch and held it aloft. With a roar, I proclaimed my territory and dared the world to cross the line. With unbound ecstasy, I danced around the flames with the firebrand in my hand, taunting the darkness I had escaped.

Somewhere beyond the light, where darkness hid all, I heard a sound. Not from within; this one was hard reality. I retreated to the safety of my gamba, behind the fire. I had no voice to call, "Who's there?" I tossed more wood on the fire.

A branch cracked. A foot stepped lightly on leaves. Was it human? Would it charge through the flames in one great leap, like the tiger, to disembowel me and tear the skin from my face?

From deep within me came an inhuman growl. Like a low

bass chord, it reverberated its warning, dripping death into the ears of whatever stood beyond the light. Reaching into the fire, I pulled out a perfect club, ablaze on the end, and charged out into the blackness, roaring, where the terror stood.

I heard it bolt and run, but I never saw it. My club thudded into the soft earth where it had stood, and a shower of sparks traced the arc. The feel of the club, the sound of the thud, and the crackling sparks gave me an exhilarating sense of power. Again I roared and brought the club smashing to earth, and again I felt my strength increase.

Over and over it fell. I watched the sparks shower down, and with my breath aflame, I dared the world to challenge me.

These things I did without thought. The drink had rid the world of McBeth Johnson and had loosed the contents my mind and spirit on the night. I was like a wild animal gone berserk over the discovery of the weapon. The things I felt were the same things my ancestors felt aeons ago when they discovered fire and weapon. Had anyone told me these things were within me, I would have thought them mad.

I grunted my assent. I am my ancestors. I carry them within me. I can share their experiences. I am a million years old; I am a newborn infant. I am all male, and I am woman. I am pure and innocent, and I am rotten with corruption. There is nothing I am not.

The moon began to rise and wash the night in its pale light. No longer were the beasts concealed from me. The sensuality grew stronger; a steady yearning. Seeing the mound bathed in moonlight, I walked to it and to its top.

Walking and climbing, I moved without effort, as if I was the driver of a wonderfully fluid and powerful machine. I was detached from it, but it followed my every direction as if we were one. It was my body, just as anything else I own is mine. I possess it, and it is my set of senses and my means of transportation, but I am not it, and it is not me.

Being disassociated from it, I lost my fear of damage to it.

Being removed from pain, I lost my fear of everything. And having lost it, I came to understand that most of life is governed by the fear of pain.

A wave of sadness swept over me. What a waste, I thought, to become so closely associated with a body that one is consumed with the protection of it. From this springs the ego and our vanity. What a waste that this is the preoccupation of humanity.

I laughed. What does it matter what I look like?

I trotted off the mound, opposite the clearing, and found a path leading away. Without breaking stride, I took it. There was just enough light on the path to see by, but only with peripheral vision. The shadows were without light.

Without seeing, I knew where things were. I could sense the animals and the trees, and I knew that I was seen as if in broad daylight. I was bathed in a barely visible blue fire that swirled outward from within. I was invisible, hidden by the darkness, but my ghost was out for all to see.

Life was so heavily concentrated that I could feel it like wind against my skin. It moved through me as I passed; not I through it, and as it did, it caressed me and sent me on my way.

I walked long into the night, never caring where or how far. At times I stopped and stood still to watch and listen. Sometimes the familiar melted and flowed and the irrational danced before me. At times it was a dream, but still I was awake. I was more awake than ever before. I came to understand. I saw each living thing connected to all living things, and all of them to the earth.

I came to a pond and saw my reflection beside the moon. I was surprised at what I saw. It was me, but it was not what I thought of myself. I saw a different person there: perhaps the me that someone else knows.

Could there be more than one me? Could there be a different me for everyone I know? What do they know that I don't? Why can't I know all of them? And if there are more than one, which is the real me? Is it my me, or is it my brother's me?

There before me, staring back from bottomless blackness, was I without my self. On all fours, I stared into my eyes. I came closer, and we kissed. Who knows me best? I am only water.

*

With the milky light of the moon giving way to the faint glow that promises morning, I found myself standing on the mound again. The things around me were becoming firm. The trees ceased their undulating dance, the grasses their weaving. The earth was still, but I knew it was alive. The show was over; it was time to get back to normal. I was exhausted. I lay down to sleep.

The animal was dead.

LONG WALK
Chapter Thirteen
Matawalsip Pura Yumhpa

Those boys are going to get up tomorrow morning, walk the beach to Tasbapauni, spend the night, get up the next morning and play a double header. Then they are going to spend the night and walk back. That tells you how much they love to play ball. And some of those girls are going to walk, too. They're going to be in a hurt when they get back.

As told by Miss Pete

I knew he was coming before I heard or saw him. My senses were sharp, and there were more of them. Not everything had worn off.

"I was beginning to wonder if you were coming back."

He smiled. "But I know sure."

He had known exactly where to find me, and he seemed to have known what I saw and what I did during the night. When I tried to talk about it, he shushed me and said, "See better in the darkness."

"Has anyone died doing this?" I was thinking about the folly of roaming the bush alone at night.

"Aiee! So much question," he laughed and walked on. "Can't die."

I wasn't satisfied. I wanted to hear his explanation for everything I did and saw, as if it was his invention. I wanted him to tell me it was a mystical experience that only a select few had ever known.

Just as we reached the creek, he lost his patience with me. He spun around to face me and said, "This thing got no words."

"Can I do it again?"

"Do what?"

"Go to Hill Pauni and take the drug."

"Is no place to go. You there now," he said. "Is no drug. Is no Hill Pauni." He touched his fingertips to his temples. "Is only whole world right here. Everything fit right in here."

He wasn't going to talk. If there was no drug, then what was the drink? I had just had a mystical experience, or at least I thought I had, and I didn't want to do anything but talk about it. Impasse. He probably couldn't answer my questions. Reality is independent of the observer. What his senses told him of this world might not be related to what I thought of it. I had to concede that there is more here than meets the eye, but I was more determined than ever that there is nothing here that can't be seen. One must learn to look.

In the middle of the river, he stopped and said, "Think too much. Not to think. Only do. Only be."

"Okay, Tomás," I smiled. "No more think."

*

I lay on my back and listened, but the night was unfamiliar. I heard the same sounds in the same places and connected them to the same animals, but there was something fundamentally different about the night. If everything around me was the same, then I must have changed.

I could feel a difference in myself. Without having grown, I was larger. My clothes still fit, and I lay in bed the same, but part of me spilled out beyond my clothes and my bed and reached into space around me. Had it always been there? Was my awareness of it the only thing that was new?

A new realm of mystery had opened to me - a realm extending as far within as the universe did without. I was delighted and squirmed a bit in anticipation of the wonders I might discover - and let loose. I promised myself never again to become imprisoned.

Was it a hallucination? Was I now insane? No to both, I decided. I had not imagined it. Of that, I was sure. And if it was not imagined, then at the least, it was an opening, and if it was too small for me to pass through at the moment, I would pry at it until I could.

I fell asleep with resentment that there could be more to me than I had ever imagined, and I was being denied access to it. Who else knew, and why hadn't they told me?

I went about my business the next few days reexamining all I thought familiar to see if it had changed. And I looked into the eyes of those I knew to see if there was a hint of a secret kept from me.

I found that I could change the world simply by looking in a different way. It is what I choose it to be. Nothing more and nothing less. As for the secrets within, I found no knowing eyes. We are all secrets, and being so, cannot know ourselves. How presumptuous I was to think that the world looks the same to others as it does to me. And what of the image in the mirror? Only I can see.

My mind adds all my life to the world as it flows about me. No other could see it as I. And if that is true, then reality is independent of perception. There is only interpretation.

Who dares to conceal me from myself? If I am bound to this planet, I can explore it, but only dream about the stars. This inner world is here, within my reach. Can I uncover it? It is me, and I am mine.

*

"Mr. Bet?"

That was Eddie, who stood just inches from my ear. It was little more than a whisper, which was all it took to wake me. He whispered my name just once through the bamboo slats and stepped away. Ferlan started a fire and put water on to boil. Mudi sat down and stared at the outline of the trees against the sky.

"Day soon come."

I stepped out and greeted them.

"Miguel Vidori soon leave off." Eddie said. "Maybe reach Kara tonight."

The El Milagro was on its way. It would be full of people, cargo and livestock from La Cruz and all points between. Since the first flood, no one had tried to jump the bar for the passage outside, but stocks of staples were running low, and it was time for someone to go to Bluefields, rough though it may be.

They knew I was ready. They knew that if there was a way, I would leave. Nothing I said could convince them that it was only for a month or so. The news that the El Milagro was sailing had turned their mood somber. They feared that if I left, I would never return.

"I'm just going out in one big circle that leads right back to Karawala," I explained. "From here to Bluefields to Managua to Texas and back again."

Texas. It's the place where everyone rides horses and carries guns and never runs out of money. When they heard that Miguel was leaving off, everyone in Karawala brought their shopping list to me. If they were sorry to see me go, one couldn't tell it by the lists. Watches and radios were the favorites, but shoes and clothes and baubles and beads were high on the lists, too.

All day they came. They came in groups, pairs and singles. Some dressed in their best, for a special occasion, and some just dropped by on their way to or from wherever their day took them. Ostensibly, they came to wish me a safe pass, but each had his little list. The girls blushed and averted their eyes; the men apologized and offered to return the favor or to work it off.

None of them had the money to pay for anything, but it may never have occurred to them that they should. I was a man of immeasurable wealth, was I not? Wouldn't I be pleased to come back bearing gifts for all?

I could not disappoint them, so I took each request and promised to do my best. To please them all, I would have to drag a department store behind me, sneak it past customs and load it all on a jungle trader. I promised myself that I would do something for them, if not exactly what they wanted.

Two days later, Eddie, Mudi, Ferlan and I were in the Kuku Awra, sitting at The Bar, waiting for El Milagro. But the miracle never came. Miguel Vidori sent word that he was having mechanical problems. He wouldn't be going to Bluefields.

"He like the girl and the rum too much," Mudi said. "That man no good."

"Sure is so," Eddie replied. "Look like you is right here, boss."

"Do we have enough gasoline to get to Bluefields?"

Eddie raised an eyebrow at me. "Water too high. Can't pass the canal."

"I wasn't thinking about the canal," I said. I jutted my chin toward the bar. "Outside."

On the bar, the surf built into sudden ground swells and crashed down in white water. Where the current met the swells, there were deep troughs filled suddenly by waves crashing in from all sides. The sound was of continuous thunder. To most eyes, it was pure chaos, but I could see a narrow ribbon of current in the deepest part of the channel that was less furious. And outside, beyond the bar, the sea looked manageable.

Without waiting for a verdict, Ferlan got out of the boat and waded ashore. I saw fear in his eyes.

"Got enough, I guess," Eddie answered. "You want we jump the bar?" He was tense. I could tell he didn't want to do it.

"Do you think Miguel will go to Bluefields before Christmas?"

"Don't look so now."

"That's what I thought." January would be too late. If I was going to find fishermen for the spring season and get all my equipment bought and shipped, I had to go now.

"What if I say we go?"

They shrugged their shoulders. "Haps to, we going to."

We eased out into the middle of the river and watched the bar, looking for the best way through. There wasn't an easy way, but Eddie finally chose the place to hit it and started out. I looked back at La Barra, the little village near the mouth. A crowd had gathered to watch our attempt.

The current swept us out quickly. As I had promised, we were in a calmer corridor, with mountains of white water building and crashing in on both sides of us. One moment we were falling toward the bottom, as the water was sucked from under us; the next we were rising or spinning or trying to dodge tons of water as the waves dragged and the tops came crashing down. Always we looked up to the tops of the waves around us. Even the tallest of the trees were lost to sight.

The water was churned to foam. It was in the air, in our eyes and in our noses. The sting and burn and smell of salt was strong in us, but raw excitement kept our eyes wide open and our nostrils flared. Our chests heaved and we held fast as we slammed against the waves and walls of water. We could see neither the open ocean beyond nor the river behind. Our only reference for direction was the rising sun.

And then, without warning, a wave built up directly under us and catapulted us into the air. Looking down, I saw patches of bottom exposed where the swells swept over the bar. Like they were frozen, I saw plumes of waves reaching skyward. Waves crashed into waves and into the river's current, sending them vertically as much as twenty feet. I had not guessed even a fraction of this bar's fury.

Hanging in mid-air, frozen in time, I had two thoughts. The first was for the beauty of all that raw power. The second was that I had killed us. Why hadn't Eddie refused? Why hadn't he and Mudi jumped out with Ferlan?

In the air, we turned. I expected the fall to break the boat apart, even if we didn't hit bottom. And if the fall didn't kill us, we would surely be pounded to death almost instantly. We hit hard, and nearly swamped, but the boat held together, and the motor stayed alive. We had turned around completely and were headed back into the river. My decision was overturned; we were not going outside.

"That bar kill plenty people," Mudi said when we were safe inside. "We got good luck."

"She cross today," Eddie added. "Maybe big boat not get out."

We had just offered ourselves up to death and lived through it, and Eddie and Mudi talked about it like it had happened to someone else. How could they be so nonchalant? I was excited. My pulse was racing.

Eddie turned broadside to the bar and looked out to sea. "One time a boat go out loaded with people. They saw her go up, like we, and they saw her go down, and they lost sight of her." He paused. "Never did see a stick of her again. All of them gone."

"Must be sharks eat good," Mudi said.

"Peter say some Karawala boy going walk Tassapauni," Eddie offered. "You want walk the beach?"

I had heard of Tasbapauni, but knew nothing about it. It was south, on the beach.

"How far is it?"

"'Bout twelve leagues."

"How many miles?"

"'Bout twenty-five, I guess."

Twelve leagues is about thirty-six miles. It was possible that he didn't know how far it was.

"How long does it take to walk it?"

"Eight, maybe ten hours. Got boat there every day. Can go inside from there."

I was sopping wet, and my saddlebags were soaked, but I was determined to go. "Okay. Let me out."

"I see them pass to the bight not long. Can catch," Eddie said as he started south.

We left the river at Jamaima Key and headed into the lagoon. Far ahead, near the south end, I saw two dories. Eddie went directly to them.

Leopoldo and Abanil were in a dori together. I had to laugh when I saw them. I turned to Mudi and asked, "How did your brother get paired up with Saint Peter?"

Mudi laughed, too. "Can't say."

Abanil had a liking for young girls and rum, but not for the church. Peter did his best to keep the young girls in church and chaste and as far away from the likes of Abanil Lacayo as possible. There couldn't have been a more incompatible pair to share a dori.

When he heard I was joining their party, Abanil said, "I is glad for having you, Mr. Bet. I surely is." He smiled broadly and shook my hand. Reaching for my bags, he said, "Make I back this for you."

"Thank you, Abanil, but I'll carry it. You've got plenty of your own."

Leopoldo was happy to see me, too. I said good-bye to Eddie and Mudi and five of us set out through the swamp toward the beach, with Leopoldo and Abanil both chattering away at me.

"Yessir, Mr. Bet, not for you, Peter would surely make me a Christian today," he said with a big smile.

"So! You think you could be a Christian!" Peter scowled. "Even God can't make you a Christian."

We walked slowly through the swamp. The path was clear, but still I heard the clanging of machetes up ahead. It was noise for the sake of noise, to let whatever lay ahead know we were coming. The saddlebags were comfortable, if a little warm against my back and chest. The weight was evenly distributed. It made me wonder why anyone would wear a pack.

There was no undergrowth in this swamp. A tangle of prop roots spread out from the tall, shining trunks of the red mangroves. There was no walking over those roots. We waded around them, picking our way carefully lest we step on something or into something that might prove to be uncomfortable or inconvenient. It looked to be the perfect setting for a prehistoric beast to rise up out of the water.

It was dark in the swamp. Red mangroves are not tall trees. They stand in water that is sometimes fresh and sometimes salty, but usually brackish. And usually no other plant grows with them, other than epiphytes high in the branches. The tangle of prop roots keep the trees from falling over in the soft mud. Aerial roots dangle from the branches. The boles of the trees are straight and round and shining with wetness all the way to the canopy, which spreads out to form a thick green blanket over the swamp. The water is always in shadow.

Soon I saw coconut palms ahead and heard the surf. The land rose and firmed. We left the dark and humid swamp and stepped out into the bright sun. A line of coconuts stretched away as far as I could see in both directions, and in front of them a uniform fifty feet of sand and driftwood separated them from the sea. The line of the surf curved gently seaward north and south, and as far as one could see, there was not another human being.

Taking his shoes off, Peter said, "Is easy going now."

"Better take the shoe off, them," Abanil said.

I looked down. My moccasins were light and very comfortable. I thought I'd leave them on, and said so.

Abanil and Peter shook their heads. "Sand soon grind off the skin. We not want back you."

I took them off.

"Tide low. Good for walk," Peter offered.

I could see the high tide line. Before the day was out, we would be climbing over driftwood and walking in soft sand. We set a fast pace to minimize the rough going at the end.

It felt good to walk. The sand was firm, but not hard, and it was cool. The breeze was refreshing. I was carrying more than sixty pounds, but its heft was even. It didn't feel that heavy. I knew I couldn't have carried that much weight any other way. None of my companions carried more than ten.

Sand crabs scurried out of the way with every step we took. About every kilometer, a big black crab hawk with a white tail guarded his stretch of the beach. We saw no other animals, but tracks were plentiful, if indistinguishable in the sand. I asked my friends what kind of animals might be found here at night.

"Hoopah! Plenty animal here," Peter said. "Raccoon all along here at night. All come eat crab."

"And the tiger come eat raccoon," Abanil said. "They say is white tiger here. Can be white tiger, Mr. Bet?"

"That would be an albino. If the sunlight catches it right, you can see the spots, and the eyes are pink."

"That the one. That just like they say it. Must be so."

"There is also a black phase," I offered. "A melanistic jaguar. You can see the spots on that one, too, and the eyes are black as coal."

"I hear about him, too," Abanil said. They were both pleased to have the stories verified by me. If I said it, it must be true.

"Never can let night catch we here," Peter said seriously. "Tiger eat we sure."

"Not now, Peter," Abanil corrected. "We with Mr. Bet now. He tiger and snake. Got tiger spirit. No tiger going molest we now."

"Stop that talk, Abanil," Peter admonished. "We not study that now. Not part of the church. Must be Christian."

"You be Christian. Old way better. What you think, Mr. Bet? You study that Bible story, them?"

Uh-oh. Trapped. I really wanted to hear more from Abanil and less from Peter, but what I wanted most was to keep from offending anyone.

"Sure, I know the Bible stories, but I know nothing about your way. Tell me more about your way."

"Can't say just what, but we got no church in it."

Peter was scowling at Abanil, but Abanil ignored him and refused to meet his eyes.

"No dieties?"

"What that?"

"Gods. Powerful spirits. Did you have them in the past?"

"We never hear about that."

"Why do you say I am tiger and snake?"

Abanil slowed his pace and then stopped. He shrugged his shoulders, then cocked his head to the side and answered, "If is said so, must be you. Is said so."

"Said so by who?"

"All of we. Must be so." And with that, he strode off.

We walked, and I wondered. "...nothing to ask...know." There was a point beyond which no one was willing to talk. The way they greeted the world, they seemed to be possessed of a knowledge that our more educated society lacked, but it was one that was neither taught nor discussed. I could feel something of it in myself. It had been growing in me for months and had taken a quantum leap at Hill Pauni. I knew without basis for knowledge. I understood just by looking.

What else comes of sitting in the dark and staring into a fire? What unseen threads connect us?

The sun climbed into the sky, and it began to get hot. My companions kept a steady, forced pace. Conversation ceased as the sweat began to drip. The march became serious.

We began to stagger out. I walked at a fast pace, I thought, but I could tell that Peter and Abanil were holding back to stay with me. The two younger men gradually widened the gap between us. I stopped watching the crab hawks. I stopped looking out to sea. I fell to watching the sand before me, and my footsteps began to pound into me the realization that I had underestimated the magnitude of this walk.

Perhaps I should have waited for Miguel. What first seemed attractive was now beginning to look like something to be undertaken only with reluctance.

The straps of the saddlebags began to weigh heavily on my shoulders. The muscles in my neck tightened against the strain, and I could feel it all the way to my temples. It was not pain, but it was fatigue that would become pain before we were there. I guessed that we were half way there, and said so.

"Peter smiled. "Not even to Karas Laya. Got 'bout two times more to reach."

The news was demoralizing. I thought about lightening my load, but could not decide what was least valuable to me. Already my legs were beginning to hurt, and the sun had become sharp against my skin, like the shards of broken glass.

I had no thoughts of turning back. My pride would not allow it. Nor would I allow my expression to communicate my discomfort. I bent to the load and trudged on, determined to complete the ordeal without complaint.

We passed a lone house, set back in a clearing in the coconuts. "Ralph place," Peter offered. "He got plantation here."

It was a small thatched-roof house set up on stilts, like all those in the area. The ground around it was clean and bare, with the exception of a mound of coconut husks to one side.

"He live alone?"

"Got girl, them."

No more was said. Ralph apparently was not at home.

We stopped at Karas Laya to rest a moment and to drink a coconut. Peter scampered up a palm like a monkey and loosed a cluster of young coconuts with his machete. Back on the beach, he and Abanil cut away the green husks with quick strokes and whacked off the end of the shell.

The young coconut drink was not yet full enough to be called milk. It was surprisingly cool and refreshing and almost effervescent. It was always the young ones, full in size, but not yet ripe, that they chose to drink. The meat was thin and soft, and after they drank the liquid, they would break one open and have a bite of it.

I drank my fill and leaned back on my saddlebags for a rest, but they would have none of it.

"Can't rest," Peter said, "haps to walk. Never reach if stop to rest."

It wasn't the first time they would have to get me up, but it was the easiest.

Karas Laya was closed. Alongshore currents and wave action had moved the beach right across its mouth. The nearest part of the creek was some twenty feet from the sea, its water a good two feet higher. It was as if the creek had flowed this far and stopped, so close to the sea. A long pool lay alongside the beach, half in shade and half in sunlight. Winding away into the swamp was a narrow ribbon of creek cloaked in darkness, its path a tunnel into the unknown.

Storms and heavy rains open it up periodically, and it trades its waters and its creatures with those of the sea. In the calm months and in the dry season, the sands seal it off again, and it incubates its soup of tiny shrimp, larval tarpon and the trillions of eggs that went in with the tide.

Abanil picked up the branch of a tree that had a stub on one end, like a hoe. "Going open her up," he said.

Peter was flustered. If I could have read his mind, it would have said, "Abanil, you put that stupid stick down and get on down the beach."

But he didn't say it. He dropped his bag and picked up a stick. I dropped my saddlebags in the shade and flopped down to watch.

Fifteen minutes later, they had a trickle of water flowing to the sea. As it flowed, it picked up sand and widened and deepened the cut. When the flow was heavy enough that they were sure it wouldn't close off again, we left.

"Soon be plenty fish going out there," Abanil said, smiling at the thought and shaking his head.

"What kind?"

"Hoopah, this the home of mupi and tapom!" Peter exclaimed. "Inside the lagoon, can catch all ever want."

"And big, I tell you!" Abanil added. "Got mupi tara here big as a dori.

I took that one with a grain of salt. A monster snook might be three or four feet long, but hardly as big as a boat. Nonetheless, I knew I would be fishing this lagoon as soon as I got back.

"People don't molest much here. Hardly come."

"Why is that?"

"Too much trouble, suppose to be."

"Are there any more places like this?"

"Only snook creek," Abanil answered. "Is north."

"And got more mupi than here," Peter added.

Funny. I felt less tired with the talk of fish. But when the talk stopped, the sun resumed its relentless burning, my joints began to ache, and my neck reminded me of the strain. Salt was crusting on my skin and mixing with the sand. Every little nick and cut stung. Sweat, fortified with sea salt, dripped into my eyes.

There were no landmarks or milestones along the beach. It all looked exactly alike to me. Try as I did, I found nothing that might serve to mark our progress. The coconuts were all the same height and set back the same distance from the beach. The curve of the shoreline never changed, and nothing lay seaward. We might as well have been marching in place for all the change I saw in our progress. There was no way to tell how far we had gone.

The only certainty that we were moving at all was the trail of footsteps in the sand, and now and then I turned to look at them to verify their existence. They stretched back only as far as the last wave to wash the beach, and beyond that, there was no proof that we had passed.

I wanted to ask how much farther we had to go, but I was always too afraid of the answer. The fatigue and the pain continued to grow, until I was reduced to marking each step as an accomplishment. I experimented with walking, comparing the pain of short steps to long steps. The skin on the insides of my thighs began to chafe, burning at first, and then becoming raw. I was forced to walk with my feet apart to keep from rubbing the skin.

At some point, I think my companions became tired and uncomfortable, too. All talk ceased. No one paid any attention to the others. For each of us, there was but one awareness; one objective - the next step. Even so, they could have walked away from me at any time. I wondered whether it was out of loyalty to me or some other motive less complimentary. I appreciated it, and I resented the necessity as much, I think, as they.

Into the afternoon we walked. The shadows swung out from the coconuts, and the tide forced us up the beach into the loose sand and over the driftwood. I began to stumble. My legs were so weak I could hardly lift my feet over the logs. My vision began to blur. The straps of my saddlebags finally wore through the skin on my shoulders, and I began to bleed. My lips cracked, and when we stopped to drink coconuts, I tasted blood.

"I don't think I can make it," I finally admitted. My voice cracked; they couldn't hear me over the roar of the surf. I stopped.

I heard shouting and looked up to see Winston, one of the two ahead, running back, obviously alarmed. He spoke in Miskito, and his alarm spread.

"Bruce cut up." Abanil told me. He and Peter ran ahead with Winston. I hurried along as best I could.

When I got to Bruce, I found him laying in the sand in a pile of driftwood. His heel was laid open: sliced by a broken shell.

"Help me with these bags", I ordered.

Each took a strap and lifted, but the bags were much heavier than they thought. They lifted again, harder, and eased them off my shoulders and over my head.

"These heavy", Peter said with surprise. "Why you walk the beach with such heavy grip?"

"No one never walk with heavy grip," Abanil said, a little angry that I had tried it. "Most don't back nothing, nothing."

Suddenly sixty pounds lighter, I felt like I was going to float away. It made me feel giddy, and I laughed. But with the next step, I was reminded of the sunburn and the pain and the blood.

"Let's get that wound cleaned," I instructed. We picked Bruce up and carried him into the surf. He howled when the salt hit raw flesh. The heel was wide open to the bone. He had taken his last step for the day. I made a bandage with a clean shirt and pulled the wound closed.

I stood up and sighed. "We'd better get moving," I said. "We need to get him to a doctor."

"Too late," Peter said. "Night catch we. Haps to we going sleep here."

Tasbapauni was only a few more miles. As tired as I was, the prospect of a night on the beach was less appealing to me than carrying Bruce to town. But their minds were set. They told me to stretch out on the sand and wait. I obeyed, and my fatigue overcame all else.

Like a dream, the world slowed and flowed and I imagined that little snakes came out and slid into my clothing, next to my skin, and covered me with their coolness. Mudi and Abanil were the shadows of wraiths carrying big snakes out from the coconuts and piling them in front of me. I watched as the pile grew high; I watched as they dug five holes in the sand, never wondering what they were doing.

I watched the waves reach shallow water, climb up, loose their power in an unending roar of white, and wash hissing up the beach. They had come to me to die. My pain became a separate thing; as enormous as the sea. It was as intense and as crippling as ever, but I no longer cared that it was there. I observed it as I observed the surf and the preparations of my guides. I was impartial, indifferent to any outcome, waiting patiently for the womb of sleep.

As the sky darkened, they came to me, pulled me to my feet, and led me to one of five trenches: five shallow graves that radiated out from a fire pit. "Mahong soon come," Abanil warned.

I lay down, and they buried me. Only my face protruded. They stuck four sticks into the sand around my head and made a tent of my shirt. The sand flies could kill as surely as a tiger. "Not to move," Peter said. "Not for nothing."

To keep the fire alive without exposing themselves to hoards of biting flies, between the trenches they had laid long poles that they could push into the fire during the night. Abanil helped Peter bury Bruce and Winston, then he buried Peter, lit the fire, and slid into his own grave. I heard him pushing sand and grunting at it, and I wondered if he might have had to sacrifice a few square inches of exposed skin.

The fire crackled and hissed, and firelight danced on the shirt over my face. The surf lessened and withdrew, and a new sound came to my ears. It was the cumulative sound of sand flies and mosquitoes that outnumbered the stars. Even through the sand, I could hear their tiny wings above my face, threatening to devour me the way piranhas devour a cow.

"Mr. Bet?"

The voices again, I thought.

"Mr. Bet?"

A little louder this time, it was Abanil's voice.

"Yes?"

"If tiger come, get burning stick."

"You are a comfort."

He was quiet for awhile, til again he spoke, "Mr. Bet?"

"Abanil?"

"Is a hebm and hell?"

I chuckled. "My body feels like I'm in hell, but everything around me is heaven."

"Not answer."

"It doesn't matter if there is or isn't. I have no way of knowing, short of dying."

"Read Bible," Peter interrupted. "Is word of God."

"It's someone's word, for sure," I answered. "But I'm not convinced it came from god."

"Who, then?"

"People, same as us, but without much understanding of nature." My guard was down. I wasn't thinking about who I was talking with.

"How that?"

"Two thousand years ago we didn't know much."

"Had God."

Then Abanil again. "Mr. Bet? Is a God?"

"If there is, I must have pissed him off."

"Is a God." Peter retorted.

"No matter. Find the right way to live."

"Why not matter?"

"Because the way you live is all that matters. What's in your heart? Maybe heaven and hell are nothing more than a carrot and a whip. Maybe religion is nothing more than mysticism gone awry."

If they said anything else, I didn't hear it. The last thing I remember was becoming aware that the creatures in the sand were moving. I wondered how much of me they would eat. It seemed that everything had an interest in my blood.

*

My eyes opened, and I saw my shirt above my eyes. I was still buried. I smelled wood smoke and heard the surf moaning softly. Abanil and Peter were up. I pulled my arms out of the sand and moved the shirt. The sun was not yet up, but already there were bananas and coconuts ready for breakfast. Abanil dumped an armload of mussels into the fire.

"Naksa, Mr. Bet."

"Naksa, Abanil."

"Got hunger?"

"Yep."

The mussels began to open; they were ready to eat. When I moved to rise, I was reminded of the pain. My hips screamed in pain. My crotch and the insides of my thighs reminded me that there was no skin there. I sighed deeply, shook my head, and looked down the beach toward Tasbapauni.

The air was calm. The sea breeze met the land breeze at the beach and both stopped. Less than a mile away, I saw plumes of smoke rising from the breakfast fires of the village. We were almost there. We could have made it. I could have been well fed and well bed. I could have had a bath. Instead, I was caked with sand, salt and blood. Not one square inch of me was clean. I tried to mutter an epithet, but only croaked.

I could neither walk nor eat like this. I waded into the surf to bathe. Abanil watched, perhaps too tired of caring for me to try to stop me.

Nothing had ever felt better. Belly down, I floated like a dead man, and the waves washed away the grit. Weightless, I rose and fell with each wave, dangling my arms and legs below like tentacles. I closed my eyes and could have slept again if I'd had a snorkel. Gravity was defeated; the pain was gone.

Looking up, I burst out laughing. An alongshore current was sweeping me south at a pace faster than walking. I could have floated there. I could stay in the water and float to Tasbapauni faster than Abanil and Peter could walk.

But I couldn't. I had those saddlebags to carry. If not for them, we would have waltzed into Tasbapauni long before dark. Instead, I would hobble in twenty-four hours after the start. How humiliating. They would make good sport of that. Never again would I carry more than survival tools: a blade and a flame.

DAVIS, AGAIN
Chapter Fourteen
Matawalsip Pura Walhwal

I told Beth I wanted to catch a big shark. He took me out to Man-O-War Key, where the Jamaican fishing boat was anchored. They were cleaning fish and throwing guts and heads overboard. I've never seen so many sharks. We caught a ten pound jack, McBeth rigged it up and went to the foredeck to throw it to the next big shark. He saw one and heaved. I saw it, too. It must have been twenty feet long. I got that bait away from that shark as fast as I could and told him we needed a bigger boat.

As told by Carlos "Charlie" Aguas

It is spelled Tasbapauni, but everyone calls it Tassapauni. It is a thin strip of a village, bounded on the east by the Caribbean, on the west by Pearl Lagoon and on the north and south by swamps and the endless swath of coconuts along the beach. You can almost throw a rock from the sea to the lagoon. Maybe a mile long, the houses face the sea on one side and the lagoon on the other. They all have a view; they all have waterfront lots. The architecture, the people and the livestock are much like Karawala.

But unlike Karawala, they have commerce. The trading boats find easy passage from Bluefields to the towns on the lagoon. The people of the lagoon frequent the shops and bars of Bluefields whenever they please.

The economy is not that much better. The people are poor and dependent on the land for what they eat. But any excess finds a ready market. There is cash. They can buy things. Those who have never known a life without money cannot grasp the significance of never having any. I had not grasped it until this day, when I was struck by the difference it made in this village.

It is freedom. Even if one possesses very little of it, it is freedom. It gives one options and opportunities that cannot be had without it. And then a little farther down the road, it steals that freedom with dependence. Having money, one cannot live without it.

"I understand you had a rough journey."

I turned toward the voice. It was that of an Englishwoman, and the surprise made me laugh.

Holding out her hand, she said, "I am Sarah Becket, and you are McBeth Johnson. They call me Miss Bucket."

"They call me Mr. Bet." I shook her hand, not sure this was real.

"No need to be so talkative. I know you are tired. As soon as I take care of your friend's foot, we'll have some tea."

She turned and walked away, long thin skirt swishing just above the sand. I followed. I suppose she thought it was inconceivable that I would not. So did I.

Her hair was short, with a hint of gray. Her face was thin and strong, and middle age was beginning to line it. She wore no makeup. And she was small, without being the least bit frail. She put a smile on my face. I was drawn to her, and walked more easily behind her.

Two boys of about ten years shared the weight of my saddlebags. I was not allowed to carry them.

A bath and clean clothes were of the highest priority. I accepted all the hospitality Sarah offered without reserve or modesty, but with gratitude. I soaped and rinsed until the boys bringing water asked if I was going to drain the well. Sarah gave me a salve to put on the raw places.

Dried and dressed, I hobbled to the veranda, where Sarah waited with tea and soda cakes. I smiled with all the warmth I had in me. Here was Florence Nightingale, in the middle of nowhere. I sat, and she handed me two pills.

"Take these. They'll make you feel better."

I did as ordered. Before I could ask, she answered, "Muscle relaxants. I'm a nurse. I came over here with a church group last year, decided they needed me here, and stayed."

She wasn't abrupt, but she was to the point. She had heard a great deal about me, but I had never heard a word about her. I wondered why.

She told me I had ended the walk in pretty good shape compared to some. It was common for feet to swell so much that walking is impossible for as long as a week. Most, she said, require some bed rest.

It made me feel a little better to know the walk stressed even the hardy folk who live here, but I was not in the mood for conversation, even though I was indebted to my hostess. She understood, and after Abanil came by with the news that a boat would leave the next morning, she sent me to bed, where I stayed until I heard the stirrings of early morning.

Before daylight, I thanked Sarah again and boarded a trading boat. I took my place among the cattle, hogs and chickens and awaited our departure. Leopoldo and Abanil greeted me as I boarded.

"Mr. Bet supposed to be happy man, now," Abanil said with a sly grin.

"And why is that?"

"Going see the Orinoco girl, them." His teeth flashed in the dark.

"Are we going to Orinoco?" I asked, surprised.

"Haps to."

I hadn't asked where the boat was stopping. At that point, it was enough that I was under way again. A stop in Orinoco had been a certainty when I left Karawala, but by the time I got to Tasbapauni, I was not thinking about much more than the next step. If the boat had gone directly to Bluefields, I would not have objected.

A smile came across my face, and that made Abanil laugh. "First time I see you smile long time," he said.

"Mr. Bet smiling and all Karawala got cabanga negra," Leopoldo said.

"What's that?"

"Cabanga negra. The black blues."

"That right," Abanil agreed. "Karawala got cabanga negra now you gone. All crying."

"But, why?"

"They not think you coming back."

"Of course I am. I told them so."

"Too much time it happen. Man leave off for go far and never reach back. Poor Ferlan crying hard. He love you like a father. Eddie, too."

"When you reach back, you tell everyone that I will return, in one month, just as I said. Have the field ready. Plane going pitch."

"See that?" Abanil asked Leopoldo. "Like I tell you?"

They seemed reassured. "And tell them that if I can carry all of Karawala to Texas, then Karawala can carry me around for awhile. Karawala can never leave me, and I can never leave Karawala. There is no reason for cabanga negra."

"Is truth," they nodded.

The sky began to lighten and stayed that way for awhile before it burst into flame. Daylight come on Pearl Lagoon. Seagulls wheeled in the air, screaming over schools of feeding fish, calling every bird in the world to come to the table. Bottlenose dolphin charged through the schools of fish, sending them flying, bulging water and leaving a wake.

I could not hear the sounds over the engine, and I could smell nothing but diesel fumes. I had to imagine the things my sight told me were there.

Right in the middle of the lagoon, chugging along like we knew what we were doing, the trader slid to a sudden stop, sending cows, pigs, chickens and people flying forward into the first immovable obstacle. We were aground on a sandbar. It was an occurrence repeated on nearly every passage through the lagoon. After the multilingual swearing died down and the cargo was moved back in place, the men jumped out and rocked and shoved while the captain ran the engine full speed in reverse. After half an hour of grunting and sweating, she slowly inched off the bar, and a cheer went up.

We had a determined captain. He backed her up a few hundred yards, glared at the roiled water where we'd been, and told the engineer to give her all she had. He was either going to slide her over the bar or get us so grounded we'd never get off. There was no going around for this man.

I was bewildered, but everyone else flowed with it. They moved to the best bracing position they could find, where the danger of being gored by a flying cow was minimized, and waited for the impact. Who was in a hurry, anyway? Let the captain have his sport.

'All she had' was just about all she could take. The pounding of the wheel in shallow water shook the boat from stern to stem each time a blade turned through the bottom of its arc. The vibration of the runaway diesel was sure to shake the caulking from the planks. She was sure to fall apart when we hit the bar.

There must be a rational reason for this, I thought. Somewhere along the way, these people had determined that this was the best solution to the problem. Else, why so nonchalant? Why else would the captain endanger the integrity of his ship, humble though it was, and the safety of his passengers?

We hit, and we did slide. Pigs squealed, cattle bawled, chickens squawked and babies cried. Everything that was loose crashed into something. I think we almost made it across. It felt like the bow had nosed down after riding high up on the bar.

But we were stuck, and I figured our center of gravity had to be at the high point of the bar.

No one moved. The engineer killed the diesel, which was turning nothing but mud. No one said anything. The livestock settled down, and still everyone just sat there. I couldn't help myself. I started laughing. It was a chuckle at first, but it grew. I looked around at our situation, and the worse it looked, the harder I laughed.

And then Abanil started, and he made me laugh even harder. My gut muscles hurt and I cried with laughter. I looked up and everyone on the boat was laughing. They were holding their sides and slapping their thighs and laughing their hearts out. What else could we have done?

It died down, and still no one did anything to get us off the bar.

"Are we going to stay here forever?" I asked.

"Waiting high tide," Abanil answered, still smiling and wiping tears. "Mr. Bet surely make we laugh."

"High tide? High tide must be six hours away."

"Not going get her off more soon," Abanil answered, unperturbed. "Make I take a little rest."

At about ten in the morning, the land breeze gave way to the sea breeze, and we were saved from the heat that was building in the calm. Waves began slapping at the stern, and people began moving about again. In another hour, I could feel the trader trying to float. No one got out to push or rock. We just waited until the tide lifted us up and the wind pushed us toward Orinoco.

As we neared the village, Abanil and Leopoldo called me to the bow, where we could watch our landing.

"What's up?"

"Soon see. Mr. Bet going get big surprise."

I saw someone point at me and run off toward Miss Erma's. A dozen dories set out to meet us as we set the anchor. Some brought things to sell. Some brought passengers and cargo, and some came to get whoever might be going ashore. My saddlebags were dropped into one of the dories, and I lowered myself down gently. Standing in the canoe, holding the boat, I saw Miss Erma start toward the shore with two lovely Orinoco girls close behind. It brought a smile to my face.

When we beached, each girl took an arm and led me away to the house and the bed and the feeling of complete contentment. Every step of the way they held me close and chattered about how long it had been and how happy they were to see me. A crowd of laughing children followed with my bags.

The door had hardly shut behind us when their hands began exploring me. Laughing and cooing, clothes began falling to the floor.

I stayed for three days. Again, I asked them to come to Karawala with me, but they were adamant. I told them they needed someone to take care of them.   They threw back their heads and laughed. "You think we need husband?   Husband nothing but someone else to feed and care for. Orinoco woman keep man for work and grind, but not for husband."

"Husband going leave. He going leave off and drink rum and get behind next woman. And when he stinking drunk, he going come home to sleep. And if the woman put up a fuss, he going beat her. Husband nothing but trouble, and make the woman do the work, too."

I guess that put me in my place. "But what about me?"

"You live Karawala. Come pasear Orinoco. We going be here for you any time you come."

"All Miskito Kingdom going know we your family. We going tell them so. No next man going come this house."

And that is the way we left it. Having gotten the family arrangement straightened out and understood, we settled into a very leisurely relationship. I left them in the house and started toward the landing. Around the bend in the path, there stood Davis Morales, alone, a machete hanging loosely from his hand. He put me in a bad mood.

"Davis, I'm getting tired of fucking around with you."

He took a few steps forward, closing the gap almost within striking range. "I told you stay away."

"Did you think I would?"

"I told you I going kill you."

I suppose he thought he could scare me away. "Do you think you can?"

His eyes flashed. Lips pulled back, he took one step forward and swung the machete back for a slash.

It was a stupid mistake. Before he could start forward with it, I stepped, folded and kicked. I watched his face change, first to surprise, and then anguish, as I drove my heel into his rib cage. I felt them break. I heard them pop. The machete flew out of his hand, and he went down.

As I stepped around him, I warned, "Don't fuck with me again."

EARTHQUAKE
Chapter Fifteen
Matawalsip Pura Matsip

If you know how to look, you can see the beauty in everything, and you can hear the music everywhere. And it will make you so happy you will cry.

Tomás Gamboa

It was hot, and Lanica was late. The airport at Bluefields isn't much. There is one dirt runway just barely long enough for a DC3. The take-off is uphill half way and downhill the other. The crown is pronounced. Lift-off is just before the trees and houses at the end of the runway. There is no room for error or mechanical failure.

Passengers wait outside for their flight. Tickets are bought and bags are checked at the LaNica office in town. The one small concrete building at the airport houses the radio operator and a guardsman or two. The boarding agent appears in his car after the airplane buzzes the town.

"You must be Johnson."

The voice was American. I turned and looked, first for weapons, then at his face. It was only a split-second glance.

He laughed and extended his hand. "I'm Halley. Sunny told me to keep an eye out for you."

I had looked for Sunny in town, but was told he was at the mines. We shook hands. Halley wasn't much bigger than I, but his grip was strong: much stronger than a handshake needed to be.

He was dressed in khakis, darkened by sweat. On his feet were army issue jungle boots. Everything about him was well worn, but recently cleaned. He stood militarily erect, and I couldn't tell whether he was sneering or grinning or just smiling. His expression seemed to say we had something in common.

A guardsman stepped out and said something to the crowd that I didn't catch. People started moving down the road to town.

"Flight's cancelled," he said, squinting at the old DC3 at the end of the runway. "Looks like we'll have to hitch a ride."

He walked over to the guardsman, and after a brief conversation, motioned to me to join them.

"Hope you don't mind the smell of shrimp," he said as we walked toward the plane.

As we climbed the metal stairs to the belly of the plane, I understood what he meant. It was a freighter. The entire fuselage was stuffed with boxes of frozen shrimp and fish from the Boothe Fisheries plant at El Bluff. And it stank.

"She had to make an emergency landing a few months ago. Whole fucking cargo thawed out and spoiled before they could get to her." He laughed. "Froze it again and shipped it off to the states anyway."

There were no seats. She'd been stripped down to a bare fuselage. Even the insulation was gone. We sat down between the forward bulkhead and the crates. The guardsman and the pilot shut the door and banged on it. A moment later we heard the starter groan.

The engine coughed and sputtered, but did not start. He tried again. And again. On the fourth try, there was a loud boom, a moment of sputtering, and it started. The starboard engine was the same.

"I'm glad we can't see out of this fucker."

"Why's that?" I asked.

"If we go down, we'll never know it. We'll be crushed into a glob of protoplasm before we know what's happening."

"You're a big comfort, Halley."

"This sumbitch flew over a million hours in Southeast Asia. Before that, she flew a million in the states. She's gonna die here."

"You're a big comfort, Halley."

He lit a cigarette. I looked at him like he was crazy.

"What the fuck, man? You're gonna die down here, too. We all are. Don't you know? You've been sent on your last mission. You're in the asshole of the world, and it's fixin to shit you out."

The pilot started his run-up and ended our conversation. The roar was deafening. He didn't go through a normal preflight. He just ran 'em up and nodded to the guardsman to pull the chocks.

As we gained speed, the tail lifted. I felt us rise to the hump, and then I felt the attitude change as we started downhill for the takeoff. It was all wrong. An airplane is not supposed to take off downhill into a town. My gut rolled.

The end of the runway was rough. We began to bounce. I had no way of knowing even if we were still on the runway. I would know nothing until I felt us lift off and begin to climb. It was not a comfortable feeling. I suppose that was as close to Russian roulette as I'll ever get. One doesn't know unless one hears the hammer fall on an empty chamber. I kept myself clenched against the impact until we left the ground.

We did not climb fast. I pulled myself up against the increased gravity to look out a window. Stone did the same, still smoking. With conversation made impossible by the roar, we stayed that way, one on each side of the plane, all the way to Managua. Occasionally, I glanced his way.

It was a low level flight. He seemed to examine everything we passed. And he seemed to be perfectly relaxed and at home on this rather unconventional flight. I wondered what he was looking for, and I wondered who he was working for. I hoped it was us, and not them, and I hoped I hadn't stepped into something I couldn't clean up.

There were roads and trails leading out of Bluefields, but they didn't go far. Like the tentacles of a coelenterate, they radiated out and stopped. Beyond them, the cover of the trees was unbroken. It looked like one giant, flat broccoli. Only the major rivers could be seen, without shores, meandering like an endless snake through the green. There were no houses or clearings or any signs of humanity. Lush and crisp and clean, it was a place that did not belong to man. Perhaps there were places there where no man had ever walked.

This was the majority of the territory of Nicaragua - uninhabited tropical rain forest. Human habitation was the strip of land along the west coast partitioned from the wilds of the jungle by the Serranitas Darien. Nature placed a barrier there, and on the one side we ignored the delicate balance by which she had nurtured abundance. On the other she enforced her laws, and her laws assured perpetuity.

As the land began to rise to the eastern slopes, I saw signs of man. First there were small clearings with a house and perhaps a trail or two. Then there were large tracts of land that were cleared and burned, and on the eastern slopes, the browns and blacks and reds of earth began to dominate the greens of life.

Across the divide, there was a haze of smoke in the air, not from the machines of man, but from his burning of the forest. It lay as a blanket over the valley and gave it a look of desolation. This land belonged to man. It was dirty and burned and denuded of everything that once gave it beauty. The only green was in the neat rows and perfect squares of agribusiness. I saw a wasteland and felt relief that the mountains had it contained on the Pacific coast.

I felt a much greater relief when I stepped onto the tarmac. We had only walked a few yards when a black '57 Ford pulled away from the terminal area and headed toward us. Halley stopped and waited.

"It's Emilio," he said. "My driver."

We left the Aero Club and pulled onto the north highway just as it was getting dark. I was tired. "Can you drop me off at the Gran Hotel?" I asked. "I want to get the first flight out in the morning."

"Oh, horse shit, Johnson. We just got out of the bush. What we need is wine, women and song. You're coming with me. You hungry?"

"Yes, I am. And thirsty. And if we're going to spend any more time together, we've got to get a few things straight."

"Like what?"

"Like names, to start. Mine's McBeth, but I go by Beth."

"McBeth? McBeth Johnson? I like that. I really do. That's the best damn name I ever heard. How in hell did you come up with that?"

"It's on my birth certificate. Now, what's yours?"

"Hanover Stone. Call me Halley."

"Good, Hanover Stone. That one rolls well, too. So, Halley, what makes you think I'm on a mission?"

"Huh?"

"A mission. You said I'd been sent on my last mission. What did you mean?"

"Come on, Johnson, don't give me that shit. You're a spook, just like me."

"What makes you think so?" I didn't know what I should think about this man, so I kept my guard up.

"Because it's obvious. You're trained in martial arts, and you strip-searched me with the blink of an eye in Bluefields. We're trained to spot each other."

Sunny must have told him I laid his bodyguard out. "Would it do any good to tell you I am nothing more than a fisherman?"

He huffed. "I'm supposed to think you've been living alone in that jungle all this time, and you come out without a scratch, and all you did there was go fishing?"

"You've got it."

"No, I don't have it. I think you've been through every survival school we've got. I think a man who works alone like you probably knows how to kill better than anyone I've ever known. And I think you must outrank me by a long shot, so I'm not going to ask any questions."

I shook my head. "You've been in intelligence too long."

He shot back, "How do you know I'm in intelligence?"

"I'm not stupid. You said so. But you made some assumptions about me that were wrong."

"Have it your way, Johnson. I'll find out who you are at the embassy."

"Who's embassy?"

"Ours! Who else?"

"Not answer."

Trust was out of the question for men like Stone. It could be a deadly mistake. Suspicion was the order of the day for every relationship. Survival depended on it. There were too many thieves, cutthroats and smugglers who looked friendly and dependable. When I walked out of the bush, I walked out of an elysian field of sorts where trust was not only possible but necessary. Even though I couldn't trust him, I felt a kinship.

We pulled up at Restaurante El Retiro, an open-air place on the south highway. Emilio stayed with the car. Halley chose a table where our backs were protected and there was an easy escape over a wall. I smiled and shook my head.

"What got you into this business?"

He looked into my eyes, perhaps remembering and perhaps deciding whether or not to tell.

Finally, he said, "I got trapped."

The statement conveyed dismay and betrayal. I waited.

"When we came back from 'Nam, we landed in San Diego. The first thing we did was go across the border to Tijuana. On the way back, I got busted. I had some grass in my pocket, and the bastards busted me for it. I had just spent a tour of duty fighting for my country in a dirty war and on my first day back in America The Beautiful, they put me in jail."

The waitress put two cold cervezas Victoria on the table. We poured and drank until they were gone.

"They gave me a choice of five years in prison or five years doing our embassy's dirty work down here. I took the least confining prison." He paused for a moment, looking away. "Criminal justice is either a double entendre or an oxymoron. I haven't figured out which."

"The difference between government and organized crime is pretty tenuous, isn't it?"

"I get raped every day. I get robbed and beaten every day, and it's always by smiling men backed by the full trust and faith of the United States government. It sucks."

"I'm sorry." I didn't know what else to say.

"I'm just one of thousands."

We looked up when a big, black, chauffeur driven Mercedes pulled up and two young, beautiful, well dressed blondes got out and took a table near us. I smiled at them as they sat, and they smiled back. I started to get up and introduce myself, but Halley grabbed my arm.

"Don't even look." His voice was urgent. "Don't look, don't smile, don't even think about it."

"Con calma, Halley. You don't like girls?"

"Somebody skipped something in your briefing, Johnson. Those are Pepe Amorette's pretties." He was speaking in a low voice, and he was serious.

"Okay, who's Pepe?"

His mouth fell open. "You are good, Johnson. No one on earth could possibly be that stupid. You are in deep, aren't you?"

"Who's Pepe?"

"Okay, I'll play. He's one of Somoza's lieutenants: Coronel Pepe Amorette. He's in charge of all the cocaine traffic through here. And he'd just as soon kill you as look at you. If he thought you'd even winked at one of his women, you would be dead. Talk about something else."

We did. Over hamburgers, fried potatoes and beer, I told him about Karawala, some of which he believed. The hamburgers were almost good and reminded me of home.

As we were finishing, there was a low rumble, and our beer bottles, of which there were many by now, began to walk across the table.

"Terremoto," he said casually. "Earthquake. Happens all the time."

A few minutes later there was another, a little stronger. "I guess that cuts it short. We don't want to be around here when a big one hits."

I paid our bill, and we left.

In the car, I asked, "So when does Amorette get busted?"

It was an innocent question. I assumed that if our intelligence knew about it, they must be planning a bust.

"You know something I don't?"

"No, no, I' don't." He still wasn't sure who I was.

"Nobody's going to bust Amorette. Not unless he fucks up big time. We're here to make sure he doesn't run into trouble. Hell, man, we're here to help him."

"You mean we want this stuff to get to the U.S.? We're not trying to stop it?"

He shook his head. It seemed that everyone I met thought I was naive. "How do you think we control these countries?"

"You've got to be kidding. You mean the U.S. government is trafficking drugs?"

"Where have you been, Johnson? This isn't even classified. There's a Pepe Amorette in every country down here, and we're making every one of them rich. They love us for it. Democracy? Fuck, man, these people could care less about democracy, and so could we. This is all about money and power. We make them rich, and they keep things safe for our businesses. And look at all those armies we get to sell guns to."

I wasn't very happy about what he was telling me, but I thought better about voicing my displeasure. It wasn't direct, but I could sense his disillusionment. He didn't like it either.

"And we keep throwing our children into jail," I said, looking out the window.

"Huh?"

"Oh, I was just wondering how it's all kept so quiet back home. You'd think there would be an uproar."

"Are you kidding? Who would ever believe 'liberty and justice for all' could be mixed up in something like this? Nobody." There was bile in his voice.

He's probably right. And if anyone ever said so, he'd either be discredited or he'd disappear. We control Latin America through the drug trade. I don't suppose anything could be more corrupt or hypocritical. We keep drugs flowing onto our streets while we mount a war on drugs. We give our children cocaine and then throw them in jail for taking it. For power and money, we do all this.

In Latin America, we keep the corrupt in power so that we can pillage their natural resources and their people. I began to feel dirty, as if I was an unwitting party to the ignorance and poverty and decay I saw along the streets. For the first time, I saw the huge difference between the people of Karawala and the cosmopolitan, and it was ugly.

These people between the Pacific and the mountains were enslaved as much by the United States as by Somoza and his lieutenants. They were a nation of slaves owned by the military and the wealthy, which were one and the same.

I was too tired to feel anger; an overwhelming sense of sadness surfaced, and as we pulled into Stone's quinta, I had to choke it away. I had seen the desolation spilling over the mountains. It was only a matter of time before it followed the rivers to Karawala.

We sat in the garden, overlooking Managua, and Emlio's wife brought us a bottle of Flor de Caña, a basket of limes and two Hoya de Nicaragua, cigars of unsurpassed excellence.

"I think you are what you say you are," Halley said after we had poured and lit.

"But I do not know what you are," I replied.

"You know enough. I work for the C.I.A. I've already told you too much. Sunny told me you were one of us. I believed him. But your innocence is real. Either that, or you have me in your sights. Are you going to kill me, Johnson?"

"No. Am I safe with you?"

"In my business, I would say yes and mean no. Nothing I say or do can be trusted."

"You're a big comfort, Stone."

"I wish I was a fisherman. I wish I could go where you go without having to sneak around like some fucking peeping tom looking for someone else's secrets. I get tired of picking up dirty underwear and smelling it."

He had been looking at the ground, talking to footprints and gun oil. He turned to me. "Is the fishing all that good?"

I nodded.

"I've been down here for two years, and all I've done is run dirty errands for the embassy. I think I'd like to go fishing."

"I think I'd like a shower. When I get back from Texas, we'll go fishing."

I didn't feel threatened any more. He was tired of what he was doing. Maybe he was looking for a way out. I fell asleep thinking about Texas.

And then I woke up. The rumbling sound was back, as loud as thunder, and my bed was heaving and rocking. I didn't have to think or guess; it was an earthquake. The first wave was under us and the second was roaring up the mountain. It hit just as I was trying to get out of bed.

I was thrown into the air with the bed and everything else in the room. I landed on my feet and the floor heaved me into the air again. The lights were out; it was pitch black dark, and I could not find the floor. Every time I came down, it rose up to hit me. I tried to crawl on my hands and knees, but all I felt was the earth slamming into me.

I knew where the door was, and I tried to make for it, but all I got was a kick in the face from the floor. Things I couldn't see were falling on me, thudding into my back, hitting my legs like baseball bats. And all the time there was the terrible thundering roar of the earth moving its mountains against one another, splitting my ears with its anger.

I stopped trying to move. It was pointless. I listened, and I heard, and I felt the unimaginable power of the earth kicking down its mountains and all the things man had put on its back. It was on a rampage, and I was a witness.

I smiled. "So this is what it's like," I said to the earth. "I am going to die tonight, and you will not even know you killed me. But first, you will flex your muscles for me."

I was amazed that the house had not collapsed and buried me. I was battered and bruised, but I felt neither pain nor fear. I felt extreme excitement, and I felt grateful for having been introduced, in the darkness, to a strong and vigorous earth.

The wave passed, and in the relative calm, I made for the doorway.

"McBeth! Get the fuck out of here."

Stone was nearing the door, his voice just ahead of me. I was still on my hands and knees, moving as fast as I could. I could hear another wave starting up the mountain. Before it hit, we were behind the house, in the orchard, looking toward Managua.

There is no experience that can prepare one for the pain and suffering of a natural disaster. It is mind-numbing. I do not remember having any concrete thoughts. What had been excitement - almost amusement - was shifted at a glance to a sense of absolute loss. It was as if I could feel the pain of thousands of people dying together and the anguish of those still living. I cannot imagine anyone so hardened by life that he could not have been affected by what was happening.

The sight down the mountain was nothing less than horror. The lights were out everywhere, but we could see the extents of the city by the fires that were burning and the explosions that rocked Managua even as the earth shook it down. Without seeing anything else, we knew the city was destroyed. All at once, as if it was soaked in gasoline, it was on fire. All the thatched roofs and dry wood were ignited by gasoline stations and LPG tanks and kerosene lamps.

Standing up was too risky. We stayed there on our hands and knees and watched it burn. There was nothing to say. There were three hundred fifty thousand people down there, and in the past ten minutes, most of them had become homeless. Many of them had died or were dying. I could think of nothing but the horror they must be feeling as they left their homes to flee the fires.

Where could they run? What could they do but cower in the streets and call out to their families? There could be no protection from the heat. How much like hell it must have seemed, with pandemonium loosed upon them. What did their strong catholic beliefs tell them was happening?

"You okay?" I asked.

"I guess. You?"

"Alive."

"This is bad," he said, and his voice echoed my emotions. "It's all gone." He snapped his fingers. "Like that, it's all gone."

The earth settled into gentle rolling motions, and we were able to get to our feet. At times it was stable, but now and then the rumbling started again, and we got back down on the ground. The fires burned all night, and for most of it, we sat and watched.

We were joined by Emilio and his family. None of us were willing to go back inside, even though both houses were still standing. And so we sat or tried to sleep, curled into a ball on the ground.

It got worse as the light grew. We looked for landmark buildings we should have been able to see from there, but saw only rubble. I felt hot on the inside; my mind was hot, like an ember. And I felt hollow. The earthquake had emptied out all the old familiar things that one likes to hold to and find comfort in. They were all shaken out onto the ground, and in their place was the void of an unknown future.

"We've got to go down there," Stone announced. "We've got to find out who's still alive."

He didn't say it, but I knew he meant our people. And I knew we couldn't just sit around at the quinta. If I had been on my own, and had a car, I might have taken the south highway to Costa Rica. But I wasn't, and I didn't, and it wouldn't have been right to let Stone go down there alone, imprudent as it was to go at all. No doubt people were still dying down there, and no doubt they were desperate.

Cautiously, we entered the house. "You got a camera?"

"Yes."

"Thirty-five millimeter?"

"S L R."

"Get it. Got a gun?"

"Left them in Karawala. Didn't think I'd need one."

He gave me an old Colt 1911 forty-five and a handful of loaded clips. I dropped the clip, cleared it and reloaded. I got a raised eyebrow from Stone.

"Keep it out of sight unless you need it."

The cistern was full. We filled everything that could carry water. For the next thirty minutes we scoured the quinta for anything that might be useful. We took first aid supplies, shovels, a few changes of clothes, flashlights, rope, blankets, machetes, cigarettes, rum and food.

Not a mile from the quinta, we ran into the first obstacle. The road had buckled to a peak, and the side of a mountain had moved itself into our path. Big slabs of roadway poked up through the red volcanic earth.

We climbed to the top to assess the damage on the other side. It appeared clear enough to pass if one was very careful. We backtracked and tried another route via a dirt road that led to the Masaya highway. By picking our way carefully, driving across things that rational men would avoid, we drove into town about midday.

The U.S. Consulate was Halley's objective. We stopped in front of the embassy just long enough to see that it was relatively undamaged. Other than that, he seemed to concentrate on getting through the rubble to the exclusion of witnessing the destruction.

I was focused on everything but our path. I saw people walking the streets in a daze. I saw people standing in front of homes, naked, in shock, not seeing or hearing anything. I saw bodies piled on the sidewalks, their arms and legs twisted and frozen in rigor mortis, their mouths and eyes still open in the scream of death. I smelled burning human flesh in the smoke that covered us like a fog. Infants and young children sat on the sidewalks, their little bodies burned and broken, crying through oblivion to a world that could not hear them.

I could take no interest in Halley's mission. When he got out to clear debris, I got out to offer comfort as best I could. I tried taking pictures, but soon put my camera down. It seemed an obscene thing to behave as a tourist in the midst of devastation.

The consulate was a pile of rubble. "Wait here," Halley said as he got out.

We were on the top of a hill, where I could see everything in a wide radius. There were no people in this area. I assumed that everyone in a business district would have been home for the holidays. I got out, with my camera, and took some pictures. It seemed acceptable without people around.

I noticed an old woman in rags walking slowly up the hill toward me. Through a telephoto lens, I watched her. The clothes she wore were made from brightly colored scraps of cloth, perhaps saved from other garments long worn out. I took her picture. On she came.

Now and then she stopped, I suppose to rest. When she drew closer, I saw that she was crying, but she had long run out of tears. Her eyes were dry, and her face was twisted with pain. Her gaze was fixed in front of her. She neither blinked nor moved her eyes. I took pictures until she was at the car.

"Señora?" I asked. "Necessita ayuda, señora?"

She didn't respond.

"Tengo agua, señora. Tiene sed?"

No response. She kept walking, eyes ahead. Nothing I said or did drew a response. I don't think she knew I was there.

Halley came out of the consulate sobbing and slumped against the building. I hurried to him.

"She's dead," he said through the pain.

"Who's dead? Who's in there?"

"You've got to help me get her out of there," he said, and he turned and went back into the building.

In the back, behind the offices, there were living quarters for staff members. In one of the bedrooms there was a pile of adobe rubble with a pair of women's legs protruding stiffly. Someone very dear to him had lost her life here. I asked no questions. I moved rock until I had her uncovered enough to pull her out. She was cold to the touch.

I told Halley to go to the car. If she was disfigured, I didn't want him to see it. When he was gone, I pulled her out. She was young, blonde, shapely and undressed. Apparently she had been buried in mid-scream. Her mouth and eyes were full of debris. I think she died quickly. She was gashed deeply in a few places, but hadn't bled. I wrapped her in sheets and went outside without checking for more bodies.

Halley had his head buried in the steering wheel. He didn't look up when I got in.

"She never knew what hit her," I said.

He didn't respond. "Who was she?" I asked.

He didn't answer. He started the car, put it in gear, and moved off slowly down the hill.

We continued our tour of the town, stopping here and there to inquire about someone he knew. Most were dead or missing. We stopped at the Gran Hotel, where I had stayed and drank with others like me and Halley before I went to Bluefields. The shell was still intact, but inside, the lobby was filled with the floors above.

"This was a landmark." It was the first thing he'd said since the consulate. "This was the Rumor Room Bar, where we came to get drunk and get laid and find out who was still alive and who had found out what. Crop dusters and thieves and smugglers and stringers all working for Uncle Sam.

"This is where Pepe Amorette put down the last attempt at revolution. They called themselves Sandinistas, and they had some politicians and businessmen held hostage in there. He had 'em surrounded. No way out. Someone asked him to negotiate, and he said, 'Go ahead and talk. I'm going to kill them all anyway.'

"They did talk, and the hostages were released. Amorette killed all the rebels."

He pointed at the walls and balconies around the second floor. "They never patched the bullet holes. The guardia wanted them to stay as reminders. Bummer. It was a great place."

He started to drive away, then hit the brakes. "Consuela! We've got to get Consuela's things."

I knew Conseuela. She had a shop in the lobby.

"What are we going to do with her things?" I asked. "Where are we going to put them?"

He thought about it and started off again. Halfway down the block, he said, "We gotta go see Willy."

"Who's Willy?"

"My boss."

He wasn't very talkative. We wound our way through downtown and started out the south highway. Just past the Masaya cutoff, he turned off on a dirt road to the left that led to Willy's house.

We found him in his radio shack. He was a ham operator, among other things. The first thing I heard him say was, "Yankee November One Papa Kilo, clear and standing by."

He turned and faced us. He looked like old leather. I was a passenger, and I felt like it. He stared at me too long. I suppose he wanted to ask who I was, but conditions precluded that. He turned to Stone and said, "Go to the Intercontinental. The Hermit needs a ride to the airport."

"Lisa's dead," Stone said.

Willy looked saddened, but replied, "I'm sorry, but she's not the only one. We don't have time for grief now."

Someone called for "Papa Kilo", and he turned to answer. We left.

It wasn't a long drive. The Intercontinental was surrounded by Guardia. Somoza's bunker was nearby, and this was a well protected area. We parked, and Halley ordered, "Take the gun."

There was an old man sitting on the curb, next to the main entry. He was dressed in a blue jump suit. He looked like a derelict.

As we approached the entry, Halley ordered, "Go sit by him and don't let anyone get near him. If he dies, you die."

"If you slip, you slide," I answered. It was the Miskito equivalent.

"Huh?"

"Go do what you gotta do, Halley." He was disappointing. I wanted to tell him that making threats was tantamount to failure, but that would have given my hand away. I saved the lesson for later.

I sat down on the curb, next to the old man, pistol in my hand. "Bad day, huh?"

"Bad day," he agreed. "You my savior?"

"More like watch dog." I noticed his fingernails. They hadn't been trimmed in awhile. They were long and curled, like what you might expect from a witch. "What's your name?"

"Howard."

"You're shittin' me. Hughes?"

"I'm caught."

"And I'm sitting here guarding you." I laughed. "I heard rumors you were here, but I didn't believe them. And here I am with a gun in my hand pretending I'm a secret agent. Bad day. Hope it doesn't get worse."

"What do you mean, pretending?"

"Hell, I'm just a tourist, Howard. A fisherman. I ran into this C.I.A. guy in Bluefields yesterday and he thought I was a spook, too. One thing led to another, and here I am."

"I guess a lot of things are turned upside down today."

I stood up and took my post a bit more seriously. I didn't like the fact that I had been thrown into a situation that could lead to bullets and blood. Where was Halley? Why had I been left holding the bag?

When I saw him strolling out of the hotel, I wanted to shoot him. Just let him get within ten feet of Howard Hughes, and I would execute my orders.

He raised his hands. "Don't shoot," he pleaded.

"You sorry motherfucker," I accused. "From now on, you tell me where we're going before we get there."

"Your car will be here in a minute, Mr. Hughes." And then to me, "We're going to the airport."

We were assigned to follow the Hughes Mercedes to the airport, protect him along the way, and get him on board the Lear Jet that was coming to pick him up.

"Tell me, please, just one time, how we came to be assigned to Howard Hughes. Why am I not having a beer at the bar while you follow Hughes to the airport?"

"I told them you are deep undercover. 'Need to know' basis, and all that. Congratulations. Like it or not, you are now one of us."

"Not for long, I'm not."

He answered seriously, with a twinge of sadness, "No one quits."

We cleared Howard Hughes through security and took him onto the tarmac at Las Mercedes. Halley had me get out of the car, to be visible.

"For what?" I asked.

"People are watching. Who you are doesn't matter as much as who you are with. I want them to get a good look at you. If you become familiar, your credentials will not be challenged. Trust me."

"You are not trustworthy."

"No matter what you do down here, this will be valuable. Look at it as a gift. It gives you power."

The Lear came in, landed, pulled up next to us, picked up Howard Hughes and left. I was relieved.

Driving back to the quinta, it became obvious that the shock had worn off for some. The looting had begun. Everywhere I looked, people were coming out of stores with all they could carry. My guess was that some of them had family buried in the rubble but couldn't pass up the opportunity.

Those who were not looting were leaving. Both sides of every highway were lined with people on their way out with whatever they could carry. The looters were laughing; those leaving were still in shock; muted. In never ending lines, like ants, they followed the person in front of them.

I was totally exhausted when we got back to the quinta. We showered under the cistern, using the water sparingly. Olivia fed us, and we went to sleep under the coconuts, where Emilio had moved our beds.

The next day was more of the same. Stone went to the embassy to report on what he'd seen and to find out what others had seen. Among other things, we learned that the airport was closed to commercial traffic until they could assess the damage. The only thing coming in or going out was a C-141 Starlifter from McDill Air Force Base in Florida. They were bringing emergency medical supplies and reinforcements for the embassy.

When we left, I said, "Looks like we're going to spend Christmas in the rubble."

"Cheer up, Johnson. The U.S. Air Force is flying you out of here this afternoon. "You're going to spend Christmas Eve at the B.O.Q. at McDill. They'll put you on a plane for Texas tomorrow morning.

That afternoon we drove out onto the tarmac, right up to the belly of the plane. As I started to board, a young first lieutenant asked for my credentials.

"His credentials are buried in the rubble, asshole," Stone scolded. "He carries a red passport, and that's all you need to know. Don't talk to him. Don't ask him any questions. When you get to McDill, you take care of him, and you get him to Texas first thing tomorrow morning. Understood?"

"Yes, sir," and he saluted. To me, he said, "We're not ready to leave yet, sir. You'll be more comfortable waiting out here."

"Thank you. I will."

When he was gone, I said, "You're going to get me into trouble, Stone."

"Probably, but this ain't it."

Someone Halley knew drove up in a jeep, grinning. "You're not going to believe this," he said. "Someone stole Tachito's Corvette. He's called off the relief effort, and he's got the entire Guardia Nacional out looking for it."

"No shit? Must be nice to be the president's son."

"No shit. Gotta go. Lot to do. You going back?"

"Nope. Johnson is."

"New guy, eh? See you when you get back, Johnson." He drove off toward the military end of the airport.

I was asked to board. Halley handed me a slip of paper. "Mail the film to this address. Might as well make a few bucks out of this."

I walked up into the cavern that was the belly of the ship. At the top of the ramp, I turned. "Had a great time, Stone."

HUEHUETE

Chapter Sixteen

Matawalsip Pura Matlalkanbi

If you put a few drops of trunk turtle oil in the palm of your hand, within a few minutes it will penetrate the skin, pass through your hand and fall to the ground. If you eat the meat of this turtle, within a few minutes you will begin to sweat the oil. Everything you wear or touch will become oily.

Eating this turtle is good for cleansing the body. It is also a good liniment for rheumatism and arthritis.

As told by Bugs Sinclair

"Yo, Beth!"

It was Halley. He couldn't have known I was coming. Coincidence.

"How were things in the Untied Snakes?"

"Well, it didn't take long to be reminded why I left. The apple pie has been trampled."

"Oh! Merry Christmas and a Happy New Year."

"That part was okay, but don't look past the surface. What brings you to the airport?"

"Just shopping," he answered, smiling.

I laughed. "You're standing here watching people come out of aduana. Are you expecting someone?"

"Always, and here you are."

"But you weren't expecting me."

"Correct. Let's go." He picked up one of my bags and headed for the door.

I had primed myself for caution and suspicion around Halley, but finding him here lifted my spirits. He was someone who had not asked for trust, had made no promises and had no expectations. In those qualities, he was unique. There was something reassuring about hearing a man say, "I cannot be trusted; do not believe me."

Honesty so revealing might be disarming to some, but it carried strength and confidence to me . It also meant, "I will never depend on you for anything; I will never expect anything of you." It meant self-reliance. It was a reminder that we are all alone. Utterly alone. It meant that every alliance is temporary. Because he couldn't be trusted, he was the most trustworthy person I had ever met.

Emilio was waiting with the car. He was all smiles and eager to try out some new English he had learned from Halley.

The smiles disappeared with the first whiff of rotten human flesh. A month after the earthquake, they were still digging out bodies.

"There is a common grave not far from the quinta," Halley explained, "where bulldozers bury corpses brought out from town. They bring them in dump trucks, dump them into the ravine, douse them with gasoline, burn them and cover them up. All day every day. I think it will go over twenty thousand before they're all buried."

"The papers in the states say it's no more than five thousand," I offered.

"The same assholes who write the stories have seen the same things I've seen," he sighed. "They know better."

"You see our pictures?"

"Yep. And I know the slob who stole them."

One of my photos was on the cover of a major weekly news magazine. It is impossible that anyone else could have taken it. No one else was there at that moment. Not even Halley. They scooped everything else in print, and they used our photos to do it. We got neither credit nor pay.

"I called him and told him I was sending it. I called him again, and he told me he never got it. And there they were. Anything we can do about it?"

"Nothing legal," he answered, smiling devilishly. "But we'll find a way to let him know we are displeased."

"I'm a little more than displeased," I said angrily, "I'm royally pissed. The son of a bitch took credit for my work. He stole it and put his name on it. He deserves a red hot poker up his ass."

"A red hot poker it is, then, but man, you are vindictive." After a moment, he changed his mind. "That's a little much, don't you think? That's damage that can't be corrected. Broken bones heal. How about a couple of broken bones and a retraction and credit and money?"

"It's up to you. I'm not in this picture." I would never meet the man, and I had already forgotten his name. My anger was that of a sucker. Whether Halley did anything or not, I would hold on to the anger to remind me of the way the world works.

The city was dark; the electricity was still not on. We drove around rubble still in the streets, and for long stretches saw no habitable buildings.

"I've been driving around in it so long it looks normal. The people here still live like animals or cave men. They have no more than what they've pulled from the ruins. They burn furniture for cooking fuel. They eat dogs and rats and lizards. They sleep curled up on a floor wherever they can find cover."

He spoke softly, without looking out. There was sadness in his voice, and there were human beings in the desolation who would never again know the slightest comfort. Those who had not died of injury were dying of disease and hunger. They were forsaken.

It reminded me of the old woman I had seen at the consulate. I wondered if she had ever recovered from her shock.

He rapped my rod tube with his knuckles. "Fishing rods?"

"It ain't a bazooka."

"Tomorrow we go fishing."

"I'd like nothing better," I said, "but I've got to get to El Bluff to get my cargo off the *Red Dawn* and through aduana."

"The Red Dawn, eh? Don't worry about your cargo. It will be in Karawala when we get there."

"And how are you going to do that?" I asked. Getting my cargo through customs meant days of negotiating in a sweltering dockside office with some Colonel who was an expert at extracting the largest bribe possible. It meant forcing myself to be pleasant when what I really want to do is drown a rat.

He smiled and said, "Sometimes my line of work has advantages. Tomorrow I take you to Huehuete, and in a few days you can take me to Karawala."

I had been in Nicaragua long enough to know that almost nothing was done legally. Those who worked through the system were those without the right friends, and they were generally skinned alive. I decided to let Halley take care of it rather than risk making a mess of it myself.

"Where is Huehuete?"

"On the Pacific side, a couple of hours south of here, about halfway to Rivas. Emilio told me about it. Said they catch some big robalo there."

"Snook?"

"Same fish."

That made a difference. I am always ready to catch a snook.

"Johnson."

"That's me."

"You'll need to send the Colonel a little present. It will make him feel better the next time you see him."

"Understood."

*

Huehuete was down twenty miles of dirt road after we left the South Highway. When we forded a river near the beach, I knew we were going to catch fish. The river forms a small lagoon where it empties into the ocean, and that is where we stopped.

As we rigged our rods, we saw requiem sharks finning in the shallow water near the beach. A line of black rocks jutted out of the sand farther out and stood as a barrier to the waves. An old man and a boy fished with hand lines in the lagoon, throwing spoons on heavy mono and winding it in on coke bottles. When we walked up with our fishing rods, they stopped to watch.

We asked, and they told us where we could find fish. We showed them the lures we brought, and they told us which they thought would catch fish. But our line, they said, was too small. They shook their heads and told us we'd never catch these snook on that line.

I gave Halley a spinning rod rigged for the surf and put a big Rapala on both rods. We fished along the beach for awhile without success. I waded out to the rocks, and just as I found a place to fish, I turned and saw Halley standing on the beach with his rod bent to a heavy fish, the old man and the boy cheering him on. By the time I got back to him, they were dragging a thirty pound snook onto the beach and howling at the clouds.

"Damn!" was all he could say. "Damn, Beth! Damn, that's fun. Would you look at that sumbitch! Damn, I can't believe I caught him."

It was a beautiful, heavy-bodied fish, not at all like the scrawny little snook you find in the Florida mangroves. This one had shoulders and a belly. It was the kind of snook dedicated fishermen dream of. It was one hell of a fish for a first snook. He gave it to the old man.

The fish turned on. We stood there side by side and caught snook after snook. At times we had on doubles, with drags screaming and fish crisscrossing in front of us. Before long the entire village of Huehuete was behind us, cheering every fish, unhooking them for us and dragging them off. We were tired when they quit.

We hooked a few that took off for the opening in the rocks and never slowed down. All we could do was watch the line disappear from the spool. Others got into the rocks and broke us off, and some ended up in a boiling patch of red water where a shark made a meal. By the end of the day, Halley was a snook fisherman, and even Emilio had caught a few.

Along about sundown, we built a fire and sat down with a bottle of rum to watch the sun slide sizzling into the sea where the big snook had swum away with our line and our lures. There was nothing to say and nothing to do but sit and watch and savor the day and its movement into night.

There was salt and sand caked on our skin, and the hot rum stung the little cracks in our lips, but even those things were part of a perfect day. The dryness of the Pacific side allowed us to stay on the beach after dark without being eaten by insects. I did not want human sound to intrude on the crackling of the fire and the pounding of the surf against the rocks.

"They are going to recruit you."

"Who?"

"I don't have to tell you who."

"I am not going to be recruited," I said, and I meant it as a matter of fact rather than a protest or denial.

He stared into the fire and poked at it with a stick.

"They will win. You can fight it if you want, but they will win. They can make it very easy for you, or they can make your life miserable. How much is it worth to you to have your cargo arrive in Karawala ahead of you? How much was it worth to be able to ship it on the *Red Dawn*?"

"So they sent you here to sign me up. They are you, and you are they, and all of you want to drag me down with you."

He looked at me then. "I knew you'd see it that way. But for all it's worth, I'm just telling you what lies ahead."

"It doesn't matter," I said. "I expected it. I knew it would be you, and I knew there would never be any way of knowing whether you brought me a warning or a proposal."

"All you have to do is tell me what you see and hear in Karawala. Say yes, and you will never have to talk to anyone but me."

"If I say no?"

"Why?"

"Because it won't end there. It will start with a little control, but it won't end until they have complete control."

"If you say no, they will send someone else, and if he fails, the Guardia will show up at your door. Sooner or later, you'll say yes."

"I know."

"So what's the problem?"

"The problem is that there is no escape. No matter how deep you go, you find Uncle Sam sitting there on a log, with a shit-eating grin on his face, waiting for you. *You* thought *you* were through with them when you got back from 'Nam, but you stepped off their ship right into their pocket. They want control, and they won't rest until they own every breath of air and every heartbeat. I left to get away from that, and now they are stepping into my life bigger than ever. If I'd stayed at home, all they would have done was tax me to death."

"Yeh," he sighed. "I know."

"But why?" I asked. "Why me? What possible interest is there for the C.I.A. in Karawala?"

"There is going to be a revolution. The Sandinistas are gaining strength. They are communists, and we think they are getting help from Castro. If the Cubans come, they'll walk right through your kitchen."

He turned to meet my eyes. The moment remains frozen in my memory. The firelight made his face dance; the wind moved a lock of hair. His look was apologetic: almost embarrassed, as if he were somehow at fault.

I felt vulnerable and angry and confused. The truth was out. Help had been offered and an alarm sounded. Unless I broke and ran, I was a piece of the puzzle.

"When?"

"Not for a few years, we think, but this earthquake thing has gotten everyone pretty well pissed off."

I laughed. "Somoza caused the earthquake?"

"If they thought they could hang it on him, they'd try. It's the way all the relief supplies wound up in the hands of the Guardia. Read *La Prensa*. Chamorro is holding their feet to the fire. They'll probably have to kill him."

"Who's Chamorro?"

"Pedro Joaquin. Owns *La Prensa*, the opposition newspaper. He's a real thorn in Somoza's side."

"Wait a minute," I said. "I didn't come down here to get involved in a revolution. I came to go fishing. And the people of Karawala want no part in a revolution." Anger boiled up. I pointed at him and said, "Keep your people out of Karawala."

He nodded. "Enough for now. Tomorrow I'll introduce you to a few people in Managua who can make things easier for you, and then we'll fly over to Karawala." After a pause, he added, "You might make it without us, but it won't be easy."

I never said yes, but I didn't say no, either. We finished the rum, doused the fire and left.

FLOGGING

Chapter Seventeen

Matawalsip Pura Matlalkanbi Pura Kum

The CIA was going to use this runway for air support for the Bay of Pigs invasion. There would have been fighter jets and bombers right here in Karawala.

They sent Cuban expats here to improve and extend the runway. They only worked at night. During the day, they hid the equipment and stayed out of sight.

The commander of the Cubans was one of Castro's boys. After awhile, the people in Karawala were picking up news reports on Radio Havana about a secret Cuban training base here. Obviously our boys heard the news, too.

"Aha," they said. "There must be a spy." So they sent someone down here to find him.

It must be that the commander heard the news and figured his time was running out. He fled. They caught him at Monkey Point, where he was hanged.

The project was abandoned. It was one more failure in a long list of failures that came to be known as a fiasco. They managed to keep this one a secret.

As told by Hanover Stone

Willy Walker was a retired USAF colonel who owned a ranch, a crop dusting service and an air taxi service in Nicaragua. I never asked, but I always wondered how his retirement pay had enabled him to put all that together. Whenever I was around him, I listened and watched for anything that might betray a connection to the intelligence community, but there was never a hint. I didn't pry; he remained an enigma. He was Halley's "boss", but he did not know I knew that, and I never said so.

He became my pilot. Halley said he was the best there was.

Halley was setting me up, but I couldn't decide whether it was positive or negative. Was Papa Kilo a way to keep tabs on me, or was it a truly helpful gesture? Was Tom Richardson part of the web, or was he, as the owner of Ferreteria Richardson, nothing more than the best source in the country for building materials and hardware?

There were more, and they were all Americans. Every time I needed something, Halley knew an American supplier, and he was always the best in his field. Coincidence? Maybe. I never knew. They were all like Papa Kilo. There was never the slightest hint, from them or me, that anyone was even aware that there was an intelligence community in Nicaragua. I always wondered if they had the same suspicions about me as I had about them.

Where did it start, and where did it stop? And if all they wanted was information, they could have gotten it without "recruiting" me. The right question, at the right time, would have gotten them all the information they wanted.

I needed all of those contacts. Most of all, I needed a good English speaking pilot whose presence would summon the confidence of his passengers. Willy made you feel like he extended into every nut, bolt and rivet of the aircraft and that flying was as natural to him as dreaming is to the sleeper.

Two days after Huehuete, we left Aeropuerto Los Brasiles in his Aztec. On the other side of the mountains, we flew into the clouds and did not emerge until well into our descent to Karawala.

With nothing but dead reckoning for navigation, he was right on the money. If he hadn't flown over it, we might never have found it. The ceiling was little more than a hundred feet above the treetops. Visibility was limited to a small cone below the plane. We went around once, to give them time to clear the livestock off the runway, and started our approach.

"Looks wet," he said, just before we touched down. "Might be a little sloppy."

The moment the wheels touched the ground, a sheet of muddy water covered the windshield. We could not see. I cinched my seatbelt tighter and looked at Papa Kilo, expecting intense concentration and concern. He appeared relaxed.

"Oh, shit!" Halley swore from behind me as we drifted broadside to starboard. I braced, waiting for the landing gear to collapse and send us cartwheeling down the runway.

But he corrected, and he overcorrected, sending us into a drift broadside to port. And still we were blind. If we drifted off the runway, we would go into a drainage ditch and tear the gear off before we slammed into a tree. Our odds were not good.

Papa Kilo said, calmly, "We don't have any brakes." I thought he might be too busy to listen to my reply.

It was not fun, and it was not exciting. We only had about twenty-eight hundred feet of runway to use up before we were in the brush at the north end. It wasn't the appropriate time for it, but I wished I had taken the time to clear it out a bit farther. It seemed a certainty that we were not going to get out unscathed.

Our imperturbable pilot got things under control after most of the energy of the aircraft had been damped by mud, water and soggy turf. When we came to a stop, we let out a unanimous sigh of relief. But for liberal amounts of skill and luck, that could have been the last landing any of us would ever make. It was this thought that kept any of us from speaking. I imagined an Aztec careening end over end until it hit the trees and burst into flame.

Rain began to wash the mud and grass away. There was a cow standing in front of us, not a foot from the nose, peacefully chewing her cud. I looked at Halley, and he at me, in disbelief.

"Runway's in pretty good shape, McBeth." Papa Kilo said. "If I remember right, it has a good bed that runs another quarter of a mile into the savanna. You might want to give us a little longer roll."

We were cheered when we got out. A crowd from the village surrounded the plane, and all of them were delighted with the show we put on. The plane was a comic mess. Her red and white paint was obscured by mud and grass from nose to tail. She would need a good cleaning before she was airworthy again.

"We thought you dead," Eddie said as he shook my hand. Ferlan was bouncing and jabbering so fast I couldn't understand him.

"Why?" I asked.

"The terremoto. They say you buried in Managua Centro."

"Well, here I am. Still alive."

I started toward the camp. Not much had been done since I left.

"Mr. Bet?" Eddie's voice carried worry. He stopped, as did everyone. I looked around. Everyone looked worried.

"What gives?"

"We thought you dead, Mr. Bet."

"So? What is it, Eddie?"

"When we think you dead, we think you don't need your things, them."

So my things, them, were scattered about the village.

"But no worry. We going fetch them back."

Mudi was grinning. "I tell them, Mr. Bet, but they don't listen. I tell you going reach back."

I laughed. "Okay, okay. No harm done, but I want it back." The word was given, and they scattered.

The cargo from the Red Dawn was all there, stored in the big house, except for the generator, which was on skids in the boat shed, which housed a freshly varnished fishing boat. Poi waved and grinned.

"Look like three fingers time," he laughed.

"Look so, Poi," I answered. "Come on in."

The grin spread, revealing the gaps where his front teeth had been. "Haps to I going to."

We sat in the big house amid the tools, lumber and equipment and poured a round of rum. We told the Karawalans about the earthquake and they told us about things on the coast. The rain washed the Aztec. It was such a steady, gently drumming rain that it gave the impression of having no beginning and no end. It could not have occurred that there was something else to do. We sipped our rum, sucked on limes and looked out at the plane and the trees and a peace as gentle as the rain.

Papa Kilo wasn't going anywhere until the rain stopped and the water drained off the runway. Halley wasn't going anywhere until Papa Kilo did. I had nowhere to go. When we got hungry, we sent for food. When it got dark, we lit lamps. When we got tired, we strung hammocks and went to sleep. No problem.

The next morning dawned clear and calm. It wouldn't have been proper to let them go back to Managua without going fishing. Anchored at Sani Warban, we watched the sun emerge from the river, dripping gold. One could not but be at peace in that setting.

Looking into the mirror of the river and listening to the chords of green, Halley said, "Man, you have got it made."

Silently, I agreed. "It feels good to be in balance."

He sighed and shook his head. "I had forgotten what it's like."

"Most never know."

"This would be a good place to write."

"What would you write about?"

"The shit I saw in Nam was a horror story. It made our government look as bad as the Nazis, but it got covered up. Government is nothing but one big conspiracy against the people. They say they are against organized crime, but they *are* organized crime. Either no one notices or no one cares.

240

"Do you think anyone would listen? Faith in government is as strong as faith in God. It's unquestioned. You'll be labeled a heretic. Maybe worse; maybe the Big Boys will think you need to be silenced."

"I don't know. Maybe. Maybe not, but I've got to try."

"Isn't this a bit of a contradiction? To sit amid the best of the world and talk about the worst?"

He didn't get a chance to answer. A tarpon took his bait and launched itself like a missile into the air. Serenity was transformed in an instant into bedlam. Papa Kilo began reeling in his line to clear it and a tarpon took his, too. Ferlan bounded to the bow and heaved on the anchor rode. Eddie started the motor, but with tarpon in two directions, there was nowhere to follow.

With every jump, we heard gills rattle and bodies slap heavily on the water. Papa Kilo was a fisherman and smiled pleasantly as he leaned back against the rod. Halley had never caught a big fish and cranked furiously as it peeled line off the reel.

Neither fish was much over one hundred pounds, and after we got Halley calmed down, the Penn Thirties wore them out. Lines crisscrossed, and we uncrossed them. They sounded and were worked back to the surface. Papa Kilo and Halley popped a bead of sweat and complained about the rod butt in their gut. I waited patiently for one or both of them to throw the hook or break the line.

But they didn't. In a half-hour we had two beautiful tarpon at the side of the boat, cobalt blue and silver, exhausted. Quickly, without asking or waiting for instructions, Eddie and Ferlan gaffed them both and slipped them over the gunnels.

"All Karawala going eat tapom this night," Ferlan said with a proud smile.

We whooped and hollered and celebrated, and our boisterous noise echoed off the walls of the jungle at the edges of the river. Everyone on the east coast knew we had caught a fish.

"Okay, Willy, time for a picture," Halley said.

Rods in hand, they sat on the foredeck, feet dangling just above the heads of their tarpon laid side by side in the bottom of the boat, and I took pictures. Eddie and Ferlan stood behind them, and I took pictures. Halley got down in the bottom of the boat with them, and I took pictures. From somewhere, a medio of rum appeared, and I took pictures.

"Are they good to eat?" Halley asked.

"Not very," Willy answered.

"Not so bad the way they fix them here. We'll have some for lunch."

Eddie dropped us off at the village wharf. I took them to Mundo's for a cold beer, and from there, we walked through the village, past Miss Pete's, and down the runway to the camp. I named the trees and the birds and told them what I knew about the village.

By the time we got back to the camp, the tarpon had been dressed and distributed, and there was a big chunk of it roasting in my fireplace. After an hour of roasting, Miss Pete removed the bones, chopped it up, mixed in spices, patted it into patties, coated them with flour and fried them in coconut oil.

It made it edible, but there is nothing you can do to tarpon to make it taste good. For Karawala, it was a much needed source of protein, and they were always happy to get it. With such an abundance of tarpon in the river, I was always happy to give it to them.

"I guess if this is all you've got, it isn't too bad," Halley said after his first bite, "but let's catch something else to eat next time."

Our morning on the river had given the Indians a chance to bring back the things they had taken, believing I was dead, without being seen by me. Things were stacked on all the porches, and Jane was sorting through them and putting them away. Most of it, if not quite everything, was brought back in good condition. The things that were lost or damaged might as well have been written off as depreciation.

Neither Halley nor Willy could find an excuse to stay, although Halley's expression suggested a reluctance to leave. He had been quiet and pensive all morning. With a foot on the wing, he turned and said, "In all my time in Viet Nam, I never saw the jungle as a place of beauty and solitude. It was always a place of fear. In twenty-four hours, I've seen the jungle, and I've peeked through a window into myself. And now I've got to go back to the ass-hole of Central America and eat shit."

He shook his head slowly, got in and shut the door. He didn't say goodbye or shake hands. He just got in and left.

I stood at the edge of the field and watched them take off. The Aztec had plenty of room, but I saw plenty of room for improvement. There were things at both ends of the runway, and at the sides, that could cause trouble. Before Willy brought the first customer, I would make it safer. I did not ever want a customer to have a landing like the one we had.

I asked the girls if they could sew. Of course they could. Most of the time, the only thing they had to wear was what they had made themselves. Understanding the concept of a wind sock was another matter, but it finally got through.

I approached the Cindigo, Leopoldo, about the idea of a fence around the field, but he wagged a negative finger at the notion.

"How we going play baseball?"

That was another thing. The pitcher's mound had to go. It was right in the middle of the runway.

"Sho! You think them boys going stop play baseball?" His expression made it quite clear that we could land nose first for all he cared. The mound was there long before I came, and it would be there long after I left.

"Maybe we could compromise."

"No. What that thing is, no."

"Okay. Okay. How about if the baseball players help work on the field and I bring some baseball equipment?" The equipment was already there. It came on the Red Dawn.

That got him. "What kind of equipment?"

"Like balls and bats and gloves and things."

"Is truth?"

"It could be."

"If you do that, them boys and we going make this campo the best in all of Nicaragua."

He had a grin on his face and a sparkle in his eyes. If I couldn't get rid of the pitcher's mound, I could have a long runway with clear approaches. So I lost a hundred feet or so on one end. I had a long way to go on the other.

I went to Mundo's that night for a beer and a game of casino, and every ball player in Karawala crowded in after me.

"Is truth?" They all wanted to know.

"It's up to you," I answered. Come to the big house before the game tomorrow. I'll let you try it out."

That got me all the beer I could drink, but with hungry families at home, I couldn't let them buy. A cold beer was worth fifty cents gold, and fifty cents gold was a half a day of work. A good buzz could cost two day's pay. I bought.

They offered to let me play casino, but it was just a polite gesture. The first time I played with them, I cleaned out the house. If I sat down at their game, they would quickly find a reason to leave. I thanked them and said I'd just come to watch. It was always that way.

They played sitting on old oil drums, and others watched from oil drums, and the table was a piece of plywood on an oil drum. Kerosene lamps were placed around the room to illuminate the hands and the table.

It was hot. No wind stirred the air. Sweat ran down the faces of the players; the cold bottles were held to cheeks and brows. But there was laughter and banter that filled the air and overcame the heat. The sweat was worn like another article of clothing, and the night had a special excitement for the anticipated Sunday game.

I went home with a swagger, feeling like a hero. I had never been thanked so much for so little in all my life. Baseball was a very big deal in Karawala.

The feeling came again. I felt bigger than I was, and if the moon cast a shadow, I couldn't find it. I went inside, got undressed, lay back and closed my eyes. My dreams were clear, if meaningless to me. I saw powerfully muscled feminine bodies and gentle, aqualine faces from other rooms. None spoke or noticed me. There was no turmoil; my house was in order.

They came early. Not long after the sun cleared the pines, ball players began walking up, hands in hip pockets, smiling missing-tooth smiles. They came to see the baseball stuff. They came to stake a claim.

Before I opened the first box, I explained that it was all team equipment. No private ownership.

"Yessar," they agreed.

I cut the tape on one of the boxes and opened it. There was silence, as if the sound of a breath would awaken them from a dream. "Who plays first base?" I asked.

"Is I," answered Dexter Levy, cautiously.

I tossed him a new first baseman's mit, still wrapped in tissue paper. He held it, examined it, smelled it, and finally slid his right hand into it. The silence was broken by every voice in the room jabbering at the same time.

Balls, gloves and bats swept through the room and out the door as fast as I could open boxes.

"Aie, we going play ball now, papa."

There was a game already going when I got to the field, and every man, woman and child in Karawala was there, if not to play, to watch the game. I sat in the shade of Tomás Gamboa's ibo tree, in deep left field, and became part of the audience, which cheered, heckled and razzed as well as our best.

Their skill was surprising. Without coaching, they had picked up the mechanics of pitching, fielding, throwing and batting, and they had strategies for everything. I asked Tomás where they had learned to play.

"From the 'mericans," he answered. "From the sawmill."

"But that was thirty years ago."

"Not good now?"

"Yes, it is. I'm just surprised to see it. I'm surprised they know the game so well after all that time."

"Them boys play ball every Sunday. Sometime they got to play with a wood ball and no glove, but haps to they going play ball, and haps to we going watch."

And so I, too, watched. They asked me to play, and I wanted to, but decided against it. Failing that, they asked me to be the umpire, but that was a position I really didn't want. I told them I was best suited for drinking beer and razzing the batter, which I did with relish. El juez, I offered, should be the umpire, and I would be the commissioner of baseball, which meant that all I would do was drink beer and razz the batter. I explained that mine was really a participatory position and was essential to the game.

Playing for an audience is at least half the fun of baseball, and it can be argued that the players have a secondary role to the fans. At least eighteen people have to get out of the shade to entertain the picnickers and beer drinkers and young lovers, and in so doing they miss out on all the fun. They stand out there in the sun to be the butt of the heckling and jeers and throw-the-bum-out for the off-chance of the occasional cheer and rare heroic play.

If the salaries remained the same, how many of our major league hot-shots would play without an audience? They play for money, but without adulation, they would be like carpenters or shoe clerks. In Karawala, the enthusiasm of the spectators was the only reward. The game was still a game played for the joy of being part of something bigger and greater than one person trying to make a life.

Sundays were heady days. I was a child again playing sandlot baseball. I sat in the shade and let myself become absorbed by the event. It was the closest tie I had with the people of Karawala. It was a language and a culture that we could share without misunderstanding or misinterpretation. We all knew the game. They had no idea what Yankee Stadium looked like, but there was no difference in the game played there and the game played here.

On this day, they played for Roberto Clemente, who had gone from a setting like Karawala in Puerto Rico to major league baseball. The news had just come in that he had died in a plane crash on a relief mission for the earthquake victims. It was no less festive an occasion for his death, but every pitch was in his honor. Aie, Roberto!

I walked home with a satisfied glow. For the first time, we were all the same. The chasm of disparate cultures and experiences had been closed for the duration of a baseball game, and when it opened again, it would not be so wide.

I had not been home long before the Sunday visitors began to arrive. They were effusive in their thanks for the baseball equipment, and they were awed by the tons of machinery I had brought, now uncrated and laid out for inspection. It amounted to wealth beyond imagination.

After an hour or so, most of my visitors walked off to pasear somewhere else. Eddie and Ferlan remained in the big house sorting and storing fishing tackle and kitchen equipment. Jane and Teresa sat on the porch steps with me, making small talk and watching the shadows grow.

Teresa saw something that made her gasp, and before I could ask what it was, she and Jane ran off toward the village. I shrugged my shoulders and went in to help Eddie. A few minutes later, a crowd began to gather across the runway. I didn't pay it much attention until I heard someone yelling in an angry voice. I looked up.

The crowd had become a circle, with Teresa and a man in the center. He was chastising Teresa in the harshest of ways.

"What's happening?" I asked.

"Look like Teresa going get beating."

"No." I replied, as if I could stop it.

"Look, now."

The man reached out with both hands and ripped her blouse off. She tried to run, but he caught her by her hair and jerked her violently back to the center of the circle. Next he tore her skirt from her, and her underwear, until she stood naked and humiliated. I could not believe what I was seeing.

"Why doesn't someone stop him?" I asked, incredulous.

When he whipped off his belt, I started looking for a gun. I heard the first lash slap her body and heard her scream in pain. Finding a shotgun, I started toward the door. "I'll stop him," I said, blood red with rage. He held her by a hand to keep her from escaping while he struck savagely with the belt, striking her breasts, her belly and her pubic area again and again while she screamed in fear and pain and struggled desperately to escape his grasp. The crowd watched, but did nothing to help.

Eddie caught me before I got to the door. "Not for you to stop," he said, and his look conveyed a warning. I stopped.

She was on her knees, still screaming, and the belt fell on her neck and back. Blood ran down her skin from open wounds.

"Why? Are you all going to stand here and watch him kill her?"

"He not going kill her," he said confidently. "He see her pasear here to you. He think she want grind with you."

"He's beating her because she came here?"

"Must be."

The beating stopped. Teresa's husband pushed her over onto her back. Satisfied with his brutality, he turned and looked defiantly at me, with the belt hanging from his hand, threatening or daring, I know not which. He left, and the crowd dispersed, leaving Teresa lying on the ground, naked and bloody and weeping. Miss Pete came and wrapped her in clean sheets and took her home.

It was the most barbaric thing I had ever seen, and it almost made me abandon Karawala. Eddie told me a man has a right to beat his wife, and even if he kills her, no one can interfere.

To this day, I become enraged when I think about it, and I suffer guilt for letting Eddie stop me. That night I lay in bed and replayed it again and again. Never before or since have I wanted so much to kill another human being. But he was not human. He was a jealous and cruel monster that deserved the same fate as a rabid dog.

Had an animal attacked her so savagely, no time would have been wasted in hunting it down and killing it. Not only would he go unpunished, but she would go back to him and lay with him in his bed. She would allow him to fuck her, and she would bear a child a year by him until she could no longer bear children.

And if she was a perfect wife, still his suspicion and jealousy would call up his rage, and he would beat her. She could not escape it. No matter if she was a saint or slut, she would be beaten, and she would accept it. Perhaps she would even believe it was part of his love for her. It was their culture, and I hated it.

ANTS

Chapter Eighteen

Matawalsip Pura Matlalkanbi Pura Wal

A fish washed ashore at El Bluff some time ago. It measured thirty-seven feet in length and was eighteen feet from belly to back. They say it was a blackfish. It was the second one of that size to wash up there.

As told by Rudy Sinclair

"Miss Pete?"

"Yes, Beth." She was in the camp kitchen, happily surrounded by refrigerators, freezers, a commercial gas stove, and a big double bowl stainless steel sink. She was making my lunch; I was sharpening hooks and cleaning reels in preparation for our first guest.

"How important is a job here?" I knew the answer, but I wanted her to know my intent.

"Oh, Beth, that is the most important thing."

"And people who have jobs have more status than those who don't?"

"What 'status'?"

"Importance; power."

"Is certain."

"Even more than farmers or hunters or fishermen?"

"Oh, yes."

"And in the family: the most important person is the one with the job?"

"In the family, too." She had stopped what she was doing and was looking askance at me.

"What if I gave Teresa a job? How would that effect her relationship with her husband?"

She began to grin, and the grin widened to laughter. "Aye, Beth. I see it. I see it. Can try it if you want."

I smiled, too. "Ask her if she wants to work here. If she does, she can start tomorrow."

"No need to ask. She will be here."

I helped Teresa avenge the beating and humiliation at her husband's hands. He was forever subordinated to her and dependent on her. I let it be known that he was not welcome on my property, and that he would never have a job with me. I also let it be known that if any man in Karawala was stupid enough to beat his wife in my presence, I would put a bullet through his head.

It was a bluff, but they believed it. The mystique of Texas preceded me. They believed that if a Texan pulled the trigger, the bullet would find its mark. Whenever the subject of shooting came up, Ferlan was always proud to announce, "Mr. Bet never miss". I knew that I was more likely to break his bones with fists and feet, but they had more respect for bullets.

Teresa's husband let it be known that I had made an enemy. He also ran off at the mouth about what he was going to do to me, but as far as I know, he never beat Teresa again. He put up with her being the head of the household for the better part of that dry season, and then he left. They say he went to Tasbapauni, where he got caught stealing an outboard motor from one of the Jamaican fishermen. His death was not announced, but it was generally acknowledged that he did not survive the incident.

Teresa let it be known that she had had her last husband.

*

The camp took shape, and about mid-March I got word that the first customer was on his way. I hadn't expected a flood of fishermen, but I had hoped for more than one single guest at the grand opening. So be it. We set about making ready.

Along about ten in the morning the day before his arrival, I noticed the ground turning black around my house. Walking over to investigate, it seemed to be moving. As I got close, I saw why.

Army ants were encircling the house. They came in solid black streams a yard wide from three directions, and they were piling up so thick around the house that no ground or grass could be seen. They were several inches thick and still coming.

As if a command was given or a bugle blown, they moved en masse to the posts supporting the house and began their invasion. I was awestruck. Scenes from *The Naked Jungle* flashed through my mind. Surely there were as many ants here, with millions more coming, as in the movie. But their interest was in the house – not in me.

Within a few minutes, one could see nothing of the house, either inside or out. It still had the same shape and outline, but nothing could be seen but ants several inches thick. I called to Eddie.

He thought it was funny. "You got the marching army now."

"Great! How do I get rid of them?"

"Too late now. Only for wait. Soon leave."

"What is 'soon'?"

"Sometime today. Maybe tomorrow. When they get done eat."

"Eat what?" I pictured a house eaten to the bone.

"What in the leaf."

I knew there were all sorts of things in the thatch of the roof. There were insect eggs, insect larvae, insect pupae and adult insects. There were also occasional mice, lizards, frogs and snakes.

With a bundle of popta leaves, I swept the ants off the steps and porch and took a look inside. Solid ants. I opened the door, swept a path, and went inside.

Eddie laughed again and warned, "You going get bit up."

By sweeping continuously, I was able to keep them from climbing up my legs. They fell on me from the roof, but not in great numbers, and only the big ones with the giant mandibles were painful. The things they were taking out of the roof were amazing in their variety and their quantity. No wonder there was so much noise up there at night.

On the center post, at about eye level, there was a green and red tree frog. There were no ants on it and none around it in a four-inch radius. Either they thought it was divine or it was poisonous. Not one ant crossed that invisible barrier.

I went outside. Eddie was still there.

"What if these things come while we have guests? What if they come at night and get into a guest's house?"

"Haps to he going get out," he said with a shrug.

He was right, of course. This is their jungle, not ours, and they had us outnumbered by a few billion to one.

The invasion was well organized. They had come from the east, through the swamp, in a river of uncountable ants. They were ants without a home, carrying their queen, her eggs, larvae and pupae with them wherever they went.

Near the house, they had split into three columns that approached the house from three directions. They left as they had come; at a signal unseen and unheard by me, they began to leave. Even as the main column continued to arrive, they began their retreat from my house, carrying their booty away.

Throughout the day, I came and went, observing. As the sun began to set, the house was mostly clear of them, but still the black river flowed as if it had no end. I slept in a hammock in the big house that night. The next morning, all I found were stragglers, or perhaps it was a rear guard.

The thought of being in the house asleep, perhaps soundly by the grace of rum, when army ants came was unpleasant, but it wasn't something I could afford to dwell upon. The jungle presented a long list of potentially unpleasant things, but only the hard reality of the now deserved my attention. I could erect defenses for the rest as best I could, but one cannot deal with something that is not present, so why worry? The task at hand is to make the now a good adventure.

*

The minute Tom stepped out of Papa Kilo's Aztec, it became my job to create an adventure for him. Most of it was already done. The setting was adventure enough. To him, and to everyone who followed, Karawala Tarpon Camp was more remote and more primitive than they had imagined.

Tom stuck a puro in his mouth, walked a respectable distance from the plane, lit it, and turned to watch the village children unload his gear and carry it to the big house. I walked over to him and introduced myself. He was already sweating, but he was at ease, as if this was something he did often.

Having verified that everything was unloaded, he said, "Let's go fishing." Willy waved goodbye, cranked her up and took off.

It was midday. We never fished during the middle of the day for two reasons. The heat was one; the absence of feeding fish was the other. Tom had come to fish. The sweat was pouring off him as he rigged his tackle, but he had no interest in anything but getting out on the river. As he rigged, he asked questions.

"How are we going to fish?"

"Probably just troll until this evening."

"The river looks big. How deep is the water?"

"A hundred feet in places."

"What's your best trolling bait?"

"A jointed red and white Creek Chub Pikie."

"How about the big Rapala Magnums?"

"They get strikes, but they get torn up. You can't land anything with them except snook."

"Got any Russellures?"

He knew what he was talking about. He was a tarpon fisherman, and he had fished for them everywhere they were found. He had broken two IGFA line class records and was looking for the place that had the all-tackle fish. I told him Karawala was the place, but I suppose every camp owner he had ever met had said the same. He just kept rigging.

Sundays were supposed to be preparation days. I had it all planned. My guests and I would get acquainted, they would get settled and get their tackle ready, and maybe we would fish a little before dark.

But Tom wasn't listening, and neither did anyone else. The guides were off from noon Saturday to noon Sunday, because that's when the camp was empty. Fishermen go to fish, not to sit around talking and making camp.

I hitched up my enthusiasm and said, "Let's go catch some fish."

Tom nodded and winked. He approved.

I knew that tarpon were out of the question in the middle of the day. Our only chance was snook, and that wasn't much better. There were two places we could go: the deep water at Sani Warban and the drop-off at Jamaima Key. Neither place was likely to yield many, but they were sure to be big. All I wanted was one big snook right off the bat. Without that, I was in for an unbearably long afternoon.

Albeit one man, this was what I had been working for, and this had been my only worry: that some who came would not catch fish. My own slow days on the river had tortured me with the prospect that there would be disappointment for some. I had not come to terms with it and never did.

Tom wasn't worried about it. He watched the water and puffed on his cigar and asked about the things that were unfamiliar to him. Trolling away the afternoon was just fine with him. He was rigged for big fish, which meant either bait or trolling, both of which lend themselves to a more laid back style of fishing and enjoyment of the day.

On our third pass along the steep north bank at Sani Warban, Tom's rod bent. He shook his head and pulled back. "Snagged."

He was snagged, all right. He was snagged into the biggest snook he had ever seen. A twenty-eight pound snook wasn't a great fight on thirty pound class tackle, but because it was a personal best for Tom, it thrilled me. We were off to a good start.

Eddie sat in the stern, motor off, guiding the boat with a paddle. He wasn't impressed. "Not so big. Can catch plenty more bigger."

That evening when we returned to camp, we were met by a troupe of musicians and dancers, all dressed in costumes and masks. They followed us up the trail, dancing around us and taunting us, and when we reached the big house, they blocked our way. We stood and watched.

Masqueraded as they were, without a square inch of skin revealed, they could dance and act without inhibition. For a people who spoke of sex only in the third person, they became very suggestive. There were six dancers; three each of male and female, and there were three musicians. The drummer had a drum that could only have been his own creation. There was a guitarist, and there was a bassist who played on a jaguar call made from a calabash with a hide stretched across it and with one rawhide cord in the center.

Miss Pete brought glasses of rum for everyone, and she and Jane and Teresa joined us on the steps.

"This the Masagaret, Beth."

One by one, they danced by Miss Pete, swallowed their rum, and continued their dancing, becoming even more suggestive as the rum soaked in.

"Damn, Beth, what are they going to do if we get them drunk?"

"Can't hurt to see," I answered. "Jane, toss 'em a medio."

The medio was tossed and quickly quaffed. The tempo increased.

"They dancing for the fiesta, Beth. Tomorrow is the planting moon. You are to give them something for the fiesta."

I had never seen anyone in Karawala act with such abandon. And they were good. As primitive as the music and the dance were, they were arousing. I looked at Tom and saw that he, too was enthralled.

"What? What do they want for the fiesta?

"Any little thing you have. Maybe some Cordobas to buy bread kind."

If this was a fund raising dance, I wondered what the fiesta would be like. "How much do they need?"

"Oh, whatever you can spare. We are a poor people. You want we have a good fiesta?"

"Yes." Both of us answered.

I reached into my pocket. Two hundred cords. River money, but not enough.

I rose to go to my cabin, but Tom said, "Wait."

He pulled out his wallet and handed me a hundred dollar bill. Seven hundred cords. "Will this do?"

The dancers stopped and looked at me. I could feel them thinking, 'Take it!'

I did, and I put my two hundred with it. One of the dancers leaped at me and snatched the money from my hand.

It was over. They bowed, leaped into the air, turned and were gone.

I wanted to go to the fiesta, but Tom was there to fish, and so we fished. The next day, we heard music and voices in the village long into the night, but could only guess at what was happening. If it was a ritual of a more pagan origin, I wanted to be there; I wanted to be part of it. Planting is fertility. What more could I say? Next year, I would be alone in the camp when the dancers came for the Masagaret.

*

Tom caught fish while he was there, but they were not what he was looking for. The tarpon he caught were not much over one hundred pounds, although he watched the big ones roll at Sani Warban. He knew they were there.

We fished for snook some, too, and he caught many that bettered his previous personal best. But the fishing didn't excite him, and the camp was a little too rustic for his liking. When he left, he said he'd be back, but we both knew it was just a courtesy in parting.

The Grand Opening wasn't that grand. It came and went without recognition.

POLITICIANS & STRINGERS

Chapter Nineteen

Matawalsip Pura Matlalkanbi Pura Yumhpa

We were in that little lagoon just inside the Karas Laya creek mouth, and tarpon were rolling all around us. Mr. Bet cast out that fly he made from chicken feathers and one took it right when it hit the water. That fish jumped right into the boat and POW! landed right on that open tackle box, and then he had hooks stuck all over him, and he flopped and landed on my foot and stuck a hook in it and flopped again and jerked the hook out and landed on Mr. Bet and stuck a hook in his leg and flopped again and jerked the hook out and landed back in the water with the hook still in his mouth. We had fish blood, my blood and Mr. Bet's blood all over the boat. Mr. Bet caught that fish and said because he gave us so much trouble, he deserved to be eaten. That was one mannish fish, I tell you.

As told by Eddie Wilson

"Somoza is as corrupt as they come."

There was often an after-dinner discussion of Nicaraguan politics and politicians. It usually came as a question directed at me, but there were a few experts who offered an opinion without being prompted. Considering the source, I had to listen. The reporter leaned back in his chair, puffed on the Joya de Nicaragua I had given him, and watched the smoke rise up toward the thatch of the big house.

"I thought they all came corrupt. What's different about Somoza?" I asked.

"When it comes to corruption, these Latinos have a lock on it."

He was there to interview me for a story he was doing on the Nicaraguan elections. The longer he stayed, the more it looked like he was there to tell me about Nicaraguan elections and to avail himself of my hospitality and fishing.

"I haven't noticed any more corruption here than I have in Washington," I offered.

"Then you haven't had your eyes open."

"So tell me about it."

"How do you think he got to be one of the wealthiest men in the world? Right up there with the Shah of Iran and Ferdinand Marcos? Corruption."

"Simple. He got it from Washington, just like all the rest. All he did was play their game."

"But that money was supposed to be for aid to the people here. He stole it." It appeared as if he was letting me in on some privileged information. And he looked a bit smug about it.

"If it was supposed to be for the people, it would have gone to the people." I wasn't very patient with his kind of argument. Like all good patriotic Americans, he was conditioned to believe that the bad guys were all beyond our borders. "If Washington wanted the people to get our aid, they would have pounded Somoza to a pulp the first time he tried to steal it. Huh-uh. The wrinkles around their eyes are from winking at each other."

He looked offended. "Now why in hell do you think we would let him get away with stealing foreign aid?"

"Because foreign aid makes Americans feel good about themselves and putting it into the pockets of foreign leaders gives us complete control of their governments and the drug trade."

That set him off. "God damn it!" he yelled. "You mother fucking expatriated sons of bitches all think you're smarter and better than we are, and we're all so fucking stupid."

"Where did that come from?" I asked honestly, if not a bit amused. That stick must have been sharp. "Calm down. You said you wanted to know what I had seen. What I think comes with it."

I knew without doubt that he couldn't print what I said, but I honestly thought it was worth discussion. We sat under the glow of kerosene lamps with our voices the only evidence of humanity. I could not imagine a more peaceful setting anywhere on earth.

"I'm not sure I give a damn what you think," he said, and poured himself another shot of Flor. "You're full of shit if you think we use our foreign aid to buy off governments. Sometimes it gets stolen by corrupt leaders."

"Come on, Tom. Pull your head out. When did you ever see our foreign aid make a difference in the standard of living anywhere? We give them arms and armies. Name one head of state who receives our aid without getting filthy rich."

I wasn't being all that aggressive. My voice was low and calm, but I must have pushed him into a corner. His reaction was entirely unexpected.

"Fuck this shit. I'm going to bed."

The next morning, I took them into the village, where the voting booths were still set up. It was no coincidence that the booths looked like outhouses. "If you are red, you go to that booth and vote for Somoza. When you come out, your hand gets stamped with red ink. If you are blue, you go to the other booth and vote for the blue candidate."

"Doesn't sound like a very secret ballot," Tom said. Everyone knows who voted for who."

"For whom. Yes, it's an interesting phenomenon. They go out of their way to make sure everyone votes, but the entire election is reduced to voting for a color. No one has any idea what the color means. One of them is Somoza and the other is the one they are not supposed to vote for. They are entirely ignorant of every aspect of government, but we're proud to say it's a democracy."

"Who did they vote for?"

"Everyone voted for Somoza."

"Everyone?"

"Everyone."

"Why?"

"He leaves them alone. He doesn't tax them, he doesn't make any rules for them to follow, and he doesn't police them. They like that. They don't even know the name of the opposition candidate, but they suspect that he might be a Sandinista, and the Sandinistas have told them that they will take this coast away from them when they gain power." I looked Tom in the eye. "And the Sandinistas are rabid communists."

"How do you know?"

"Because they say so. They don't even try to hide it. They say they are going to kill Somoza, and they say they are going to take this coast."

"That's not what I heard," Tom said.

"And what did you hear?"

"I heard they are nationalists, and all they want to do is rid the country of a dictator."

I laughed. "And Castro is their patron saint. Why do you suppose they spend so much time in Havana? Why do you suppose there are so many Cuban patrols along this coast?"

He ignored me. "What about the other candidates? Other offices?

"Oh, they don't have the foggiest idea what any of those people do or why they might be qualified to do it. Red means red, and blue means blue all the way down the ballot, and there's probably not more than a handful of people in the country who know more than that."

"How do they get the election results back to Managua?"

"Well, I'm not sure that matters too much. Right now the Guardia has the boxes."

"What Guardia? Is there a garrison here?"

"Not unless one man makes a garrison." I pointed at the house where the Guardia lived. "One man without a uniform. He has a rifle and a CW radio."

He looked at me with a curious expression. "Country western radio? Out here?"

I laughed. "Dadidadit didada. CW. Continuous wave. Morse code." I wanted to add, "You stupid shit," but I held my tongue. It all happened in front of Mundo's, and the Guardia lived across and up from Mundo's.

"I'll be damned. He has electricity?"

"He has a little gasoline plant that he runs once a day at four P.M."

"So what will he do with the boxes?"

"I guess he'll either keep them until someone comes to get them or another election comes up. Last week two boats came in here. One was Somoza's and one was the opposition party's. Each one was loaded with fifty-five gallon drums of rum and cases of cigarettes. Each one unloaded a drum of rum and a few cartons of cigarettes and went on up the river. They had enough rum to pickle every liver on the Rio Grande. Everyone here was drunk for a week. They timed it so that the rum ran out the day after the election. Then everyone here got goma."

"Goma?"

"Hangover. Big time. They don't get enough to eat as it is. They eat even less when they drink. I'm surprised it didn't kill some of them."

He had what he wanted from me, and beyond that, all he wanted was air conditioning. A week later Willy brought me a copy of *The Miami Herald* and a story by our reporter, in which I was quoted, as a seasoned observer, as saying Somoza was a strong-arm dictator and should be defeated.

Had he stayed one day longer, he would have had a much better story. The next day there was a solar eclipse, and the memory of that day makes all others like it a non-event.

There must have been some announcement of the event either on the radio or by word of mouth from Bluefields. In the morning, they began gathering all the dogs in the village and tying them to trees near their houses. The moment the moon began to obscure the sun, an insane fear struck every man, woman and child.

Women and children ran screaming from their homes and crawled under them to be shielded from the evil thing that was swallowing the sun. Old men began beating the dogs with sticks to drive away the evil spirits. At the height of it, when everything looked for all the world like a cloudy day, the dogs were howling in real pain, the women were wailing, and the children were screaming in mortal terror. I cannot imagine a more cacophonous orchestration generated by living beings. If Hell has a sound, that was it.

As proof that the dog beating and the wailing were successful in driving evil from the village, the moon began to yield up the sun to the sky. As the light grew, the wailing and the beating diminished, and when it was clear that the sun was no longer in danger, those under the houses came out, and the dogs were released. Every face wore the trauma of a fear I could not understand. It was as if they had each come face to face with the demons of Hell - as if they had felt the icy breath of death.

I tried to explain what had happened, but no one could hear my words. After sunset, kerosene lamps glowed through the night in every house, and throughout Karawala there were seizures brought on by the fear.

MEASLES

Chapter Twenty

Yawanaiska

Before we had that fence, the baseball team would clear the livestock off the runway before we landed. Then one day a colt broke loose and ran out in front of us. I got us slowed down to about twenty knots before we hit it. I thought for a minute we were going to push it along in front of us until we stopped, but the nose gear collapsed and both props hit the dirt.

It took two months to get all the parts. Beth and I rebuilt it in two days, and when we flew it back to Managua, it was as smooth as a brand new plane.

Everybody in Karawala threw a fit when Beth told them he was going to build a fence, but there wasn't any choice.

As told by Col. Willy Walker

It was an easy landing. We circled while they chased the stock through the gates and off the runway, and then we landed. It was almost too easy. No calves or ponies darted out in front of us. It was dry; no skidding, no sliding and no mud on the windshield.

There was a crowd gathered at the big house before we taxied up, but they were not smiling. Instead of children looking for candy, there were women wearing worried faces. I got out and looked at Eddie. "What gives?" The bell at the church was tolling. It rang clear in the morning stillness.

"Is a terrible sickness here. The children, them is all dying."

"Umpira yang nani," said a young woman near me. She held a child wrapped in an old cotton blanket. I could not see the child, but the hopelessness and despair on its mother's face was heartbreaking. "Help. Please help."

I looked from face to face and saw the same thing in the eyes of everyone. Their cheeks were streaked with tears; grief and exhaustion lay on them as if at any moment their strength would end, and they would be crushed.

"Tomás trying his best, but steady we bury the children." Jane's choking voice came to me through the sobs.

What could I do? I was suddenly completely and totally inadequate. I could not pretend to be a doctor for them, but they knew, and I knew, that I was their only hope. I turned to Willy. "Go to Bluefields, Willy, and get a doctor and medicine and bring them back here."

"Is no good, Beth," Miss Pete said. "The sickness is all about. We try already. No doctor going come. Is all too busy."

"I'll see what I can do in Managua," Willy said. "But you already know what I'll find."

"I know," I answered, "but thanks for trying."

The Nicaraguan government, indeed most of the Spaniards [spit] on the west coast, saw the Miskito Indians in the same light that our own compassionate government and people saw our native Americans. They wouldn't piss on one if he was on fire. Asking for their help only gave them the pleasure of turning them down.

I had no idea what I was going to do, but I asked a few of them to bring their children inside. They were all wrapped in blankets and burning with fever. "Miss Pete, the first thing we've got to do is get these children unwrapped. The blankets make the fever worse. Tell them to take the blankets and clothes off."

I looked at each child and saw the same thing. Their bellies were distended from malnutrition, they were dehydrated, they had a rash on their bodies, white spots on their tongues, and their chests were congested. I had walked into a measles epidemic, and it looked like they had pneumonia, too.

My choices were limited, but there were things I could do. We brought the mattresses from the cabins and spread them on the floor of the big house. I sent word to the village that I would try to help anyone who wanted to bring their children. I sent Mudi to Mundo's to bring all the condensed milk he had, and I told the mothers to make soup. I couldn't cure the virus, but maybe I could keep them alive long enough for their immune system to take over.

Into the night, they brought their children. We lay them on the mattresses, unwrapped them and washed them with cool, wet towels. We spoon fed them broth and condensed milk, sometimes a drop at a time. Some of them were so weak they could hardly swallow, and all of them labored to breathe. I had antibiotics, but I was afraid to use them on children so young. They were all between eighteen months and four years old, and I did not know if the drug might contribute to death.

But when I was asked, I admitted that I had a supply of tetracycline, and I gave in to their pleading. That I might withhold it was incomprehensible to them, and none of us would ever know whether it helped or hurt, even though they swear I saved every child that lived.

I had never noticed before, but there were disproportionate numbers of children in the age classes, as if there were cycles in the birth rate. I had wondered why there seemed to be so many young children and so few older, and now it was obvious. Every few years an epidemic sweeps the coast and wipes out most of the children. Only the survivors are left. The time between epidemics determines the population of an age class.

I asked Miss Irene, and she confirmed it. All of her children had died in epidemics. All nine of them. When her husband died, she thanked God that she would never have to bear children again. She loved her husband, and she misses him, but she is glad he is gone.

I fed and washed and watched. In my arms, I held an infant who could not swallow. There was almost nothing left of him. He had not been in good health before the epidemic, and he had been ill for five days. The measles had almost run its course, but pneumonia had him now, and every breath was a struggle. He was little more than skin draped over a skeleton, and every bone threatened to poke through.

With a whittled stick, I placed one drop of broth at a time on his swollen tongue. As the sky began to lighten with the coming dawn, I heard his last breath escape his lips and felt him go limp.

Others had died, and more would lose their struggle, but this one died in my arms, and I didn't know his name or who his mother was. The world slipped away, and I felt as if this was happening somewhere beyond me or within me, but not to me. It was a scene without reason. It was Hell, inflicted in the real world on living people. Why is there life, if this is the only outcome? What became of the Promise?

My trance was broken by the heart-rending wail of the child's mother as she took him from my arms. I was crying, but I knew not for how long. I stood and watched, helpless, as she fell to the floor with him.

Beyond the glow of the kerosene lamps, the world went about its business, oblivious of the pain and bewilderment of disease and death in Karawala. I could not be indifferent. I watched the radiance of life ebb and become so dim as to be almost undetectable, and in some, I saw it flee entirely, escaping the terror of life. If life is sometimes difficult to detect, death is not. It pierces everything around it with its presence.

By the third day, I was numb. I had seen too many children carried into the big house to die. I had seen too many families carry a lifeless bundle down the runway to the village. The bell in the Moravian church had not stopped.

An unfinished house near Mundo's had become a wailing room. The mourners went to it to pour out their grief. They took with them sheets to cover themselves so that they could mourn their loss and express their pain uninhibited by the fear of revealing weakness. With their faces and bodies covered completely, they were both anonymous and in the company of others. They had both comfort and privacy.

They screamed out their anger, and they cursed the devil that took their babies. They writhed on the floor; they stomped through the room; they lay on the floor and banged their fists. They were more than a mile away, but we could hear their wailing and moaning throughout the night.

We do not cleanse ourselves of pain and grief the way they do. We hide it; we do not give it recognition; we pretend to be strong. Perhaps our pain is not as deep. They who have so little throughout life seem to lose so much more in death. Their pain is unfathomable. Latwan. Love and pain are all the same.

I went out and sat on the steps, facing the dawn. Some of them were recovering. With them, we were winning, but those little victories would never outweigh the devastation. Inside I heard soft voices of comfort for the grieving and the ill. I heard boards creak under the weight of the women, and I could tell who was walking where by the sounds. I tried to tell myself that if I didn't go back in, I could withdraw from the misery and give it back to the people of Karawala. But that would be desertion, and only cowards desert.

I could not help but compare this scene to the security of the American child. The average newborn infant outweighs the three year old child who had died in my arms. Ours is a sterile, well-fed life even for the least fortunate among us. No community need fear the loss of an entire age class in a delirium of fever, debilitation and death. No mother need go through childbirth knowing that another epidemic would come to wreak its havoc.

Ferlan brought me a medio and a puro and sat down on the steps with me. My eyes burned, and my head felt like a bowling ball. I accepted his offer gratefully. The rum burned and the smoke was harsh, but they were welcome.

"Mr. Bet, how you know these things?" Ferlan asked. I think he was assuming far more than I knew.

"A very dear friend of mine teaches me a little and gives me medicine."

"We going thank God for him and you," he said.

"Thank you, Ferlan. Yes, thank God for him."

"Look like plenty going live, now. Not like last time."

"You remember the last time?"

"Sure. Same like now, only you not here. Plenty children dead out."

We sat for several minutes without talking, and he said, "Better you take a rest now."

I was brain-dead tired, and the rum was beginning to make my lips numb. "Yes, better I take a rest."

Latwan, I thought as I walked to my house. Perhaps they know something we have forgotten. Love and pain are the same.

*

The plane came on Saturday mornings to take the fishermen back to Managua and on to the Untied Snakes. It came back Sunday afternoon with another load. For about a day, I could relax. It was a time to sit on the steps and visit with those who pasear. It was a time for a medio and a puro when the sun grows shadows as it slips away to the other side of the world. It was a quiet, peaceful time, even when the parrots drowned out the silence with their squawking. Two by two and in flocks, they flapped and babbled their way to their roosts. There were ibises calling come-come-bucket from the bush. There were chachalacas and a cacophony of others. The noise was part of the peace.

As I sat so one fine evening, I looked up to see a young white couple approaching. Being whites not brought by me was surprise enough, but these were a sparkling clean, brightly smiling gangly young man and woman. They walked and talked and I watched them approach. It was inconceivable that they had a destination other than my camp.

German? Too young and too clean. The Germans I had seen were parrot hunters. They wore a perpetual snarl. Brit? Not here. Not comfortable. Yanquis? Most likely. But these were not hippies, and they had not been on the road.

"Hello, I'll bet you're Mr. Bet," the pup said as he extended his hand. His grin said he was proud of his little quip. "My name is Don, and this is Freida."

I stood and shook hands. "I am the one they call Mr. Bet," I acknowledged. "And if that is the only way I am known, then I must be a Bet. Please come in and tell me what brought you here." I had long since grown weary of offering a correction, and I was accustomed enough to the name that I had become comfortable with it. I was, in fact, Mr. Bet. My customers had even taken to the name, always with a smile.

I offered drinks, which were accepted, and as I poured, I asked, "What brings you to Karawala?"

"We're here to build a clinic."

I raised an eyebrow and asked, "You're in construction?" I had been around people who build things, and these two did not fit the mould. The answer to the question was too obvious.

"Oh, no. We're in the Peace Corps. We're not actually going to *build* the clinic, but it's our job to get one built."

"This is certainly a place that needs a clinic." I set glasses on the table and poured rum over the ice. "You're going to be heroes here."

We sipped and I puffed, and they told me about their plans. They were nurses, and they had joined the Peace Corps with a noble sense of altruism and the mission of changing the world. Why else would anyone join the Peace Corps? They had it all figured out. All but one small element.

"When do you start?"

Freida didn't talk much, didn't drink much and didn't like the smell of my cigar, but she responded like she'd been waiting for the question. "That's up to people like you, Mr. Bet. Before we can start, we need materials, and we've got to have money to get materials. We're depending on American businessmen to give us the money."

When she talked, she didn't waste words. It was getting dark. I struck a match and lit a lamp. The light plant had been off all day, and I didn't plan to listen to it until I had to. "Well, if it's up to people like me, you've got a long wait coming. People like me have just enough to get by on, and if there are times when there's a little surplus, we stash it for meager times. What you've got in that glass is about all you'll get from me."

She was much more taken aback than I expected. Did she really think that they would arrive on the spot and have everything fall into their laps? They couldn't be that naïve. "Who sent you here?"

"The Peace Corps."

"From where? Where were you when you were told to go to Karawala and build a clinic?"

"Well, it started in Washington, and then we went to Managua."

"Who told you there would be money here when you got here?"

And then it came out. They said they had been told that American businessmen would take care of everything they needed, including food and lodging. Wherever they went, there would be an American, and he would take care of them. And they believed it.

"Do you mind if we stay here tonight?" Don asked.

"I'm sorry, but I have a full camp tomorrow. The girls won't be coming back until after the plane lands." I had turned down the same request often enough that it no longer made me uneasy.

"They said you have a restaurant here. Do you mind if we eat here?"

As politely as I could, I said, "I'm sorry. I have a kitchen here for my guests, and my guests have exclusive use of all my facilities."

It was obvious, of course, that I would have to put them up for the night. Sending them out on a pitch-black night would have been traumatic for them. Freida was already distressed. She looked outside and saw nothing but blackness. Her glance went first to Don, who would not be of much help, and then to me, pleading. They hadn't brought a flashlight. Even if they had, they wouldn't be able to find anything. The uneasiness was becoming visible in both of them. And if the thought hadn't gelled, the knot was the knowledge that this was not a campout. They brought the heart of darkness with them, and it was coming out.

I picked up a flashlight and put the beam on the cabin closest to the field. "You can stay there tonight. There is a lamp on the table, and the beds are clean. Get up when you hear the piam-piam cry. The birds will wake you. There will be light in the east. Go to the village and ask for Eddie Wilson. Tell him to send Teresa."

Part of me was a little contemptuous of them and of a society that raises its children to be afraid of the dark. The other part was sympathetic to two young people on a mission to save the earth. I knew how easy it was to slip from nervousness to fear and into madness, and once there, to stay until the sun comes up. It's the darkness and all the things it conceals. When the lights go out, there are the sounds outside – new and unknown sounds that may or may not carry threat, and the tenderfoot doesn't know what to listen for. It is that first shriek of fear or mayhem that silences every voice in the bush and freezes the heart. That's when the voices from the inside begin to haunt.

The first tentative peep of a tree frog brings reassurance that the horrors may not be so close at hand, but it doesn't last long. The door is ajar, and the ones inside are awake. I have been there, but I have long since made friends with the voices. Some, once out, were not allowed back in, but for each one I threw out, I created another. My guests did not suspect that this was where they would meet themselves. But not tonight. I poured more rum.

The Nicaraguan jay insists that nothing sleep past first light. They begin their cries at the first hint of light, and once they wake the world, they cease their ruckus and go about their business. When they woke me, I dressed and went to the porch. From their cabin, I saw a match flare, a wick light, and the yellow light of a lantern fill the cabin. Satisfied that they were up, I went to the big house for a cup of coffee. The next time I looked, I saw them walking toward the village.

I didn't see them again for a few weeks, but everyone was talking about what they were doing. It was as if everyone was part of my own private intelligence network. I hadn't thought about it like that before, but they were, in fact. I had so many eyes and ears that not much happened on the coast that I didn't know about. Karawala was so excited about a clinic that Don and Freida couldn't sneeze without making news. It made me wonder if they talked about me as much.

I looked up one Saturday evening, startled by the sound of a woman choking on a scream. It was Freida. She was running and stumbling toward the camp, retching sounds coming from her throat. Don was behind her, helpless to do anything but follow. As she neared, I saw that she was splattered with blood. It wasn't hers, but she had been very close to something that had horrified her. I knew what it was. They had been asked to assist at a birth. I had been asked to help once, and even though I protested that I wasn't a doctor, they insisted. They thought I had magic. I had left immediately after the birth. Don and Freida must have stayed.

I took a deep breath. This was not going to be easy. As if in a nightmare, she tried to run and couldn't. Deep sobs racked her chest. She advanced as if she moved in slow motion. I stood up and walked to meet her. I reached her just as she collapsed. I caught her and picked her up in my arms. I thought she was amazingly light, and then I reminded myself that I hadn't carried a girl in awhile.

From behind me, Don said, "Oh, God, Beth, you wouldn't believe what we just saw."

"I'm afraid I would, Don. There are things about this place that are not very pretty."

"You know? You know what they do?"

"I've heard. I've made sure I never had to watch."

As we neared the cabin they had used before, Freida came to. When she saw my face and realized I was carrying her, her fury woke, and she nearly shook herself out of my arms. I put her down as gently as I could. Once on her feet, she turned on me, slapping and scratching at my face. At that moment, she didn't know who I was. She saw only a man, and it was a man who had sickened her. I let her flail away until she tired, and then I pulled her gently to my chest.

"He killed her." She sobbed. "She's dead. He cut her clitoris, and she bled to death. She was only an hour old."

"I know. I know." There was a scent that I had not known in a long while. "Are you all right? Are you steady on your feet now?"

She took a step back and said, "Yes." And then she looked from side to side, stamped a foot, and said, "They're so fucking barbaric! I hate them! I want to get out of here!"

"Come," I said, and motioned both of them to the big house. "Rum has many uses, and some of them are medicinal."

"No. You have a gun. I know you have a gun. They said so. Give it to me. I'm going to kill that bastard."

"That's not what guns are for," I said. She was pissed, and rightfully so. I thought it best that they stay at the camp that night.

"You need a shower. Let me get you some clothes."

She looked at me and down at herself and said with indignation, "I can't wear your clothes."

"Something wrong with my clothes?"

"They'll fall off."

"Cinch 'em up with a belt. Come on. I'll get you a towel and something to wear." I turned and walked to the big house. I didn't look back. They could follow, or they could walk back to the village. Once inside, I went to the bar, got glasses and a medio and started for a table. Don and Freida were at the door.

"Really, Freida, the blood," I said.

She looked again, and for a moment, the horror returned. She looked up. "Okay, but I can't go over there alone. You'll have to come sit on the steps."

Those were the ones outside. They were the real ones, even though they might not have been present. The ones inside would make themselves known later, when she closed her eyes. It was dark when we walked her to the shower. I could see well enough, but they wanted a flashlight. It would not have helped to tell them that they could see better without it. I would have to prove it some other night.

We heard her gasp when she stepped under the shower. The water in the pipes underground is cold, and it takes awhile for the warm water, heated by the sun, to reach the shower head. It is always a surprise. One is not supposed to be cold in the tropics. But the warm water arrived, and she lingered. She lingered a long time. The only limit to her cleansing was the water left in the tank. The pump would not come on to keep it full. The night was clear; the stars were bright. Don and I sat on the steps of the bath house and listened to the night.

Don heard the ones inside. His breathing betrayed the turmoil, and his flinches were those of one fending off the shades of wraiths. I could not tell him why he felt the way he did, and I could not calm the fury. They were coming for him, and if he didn't discover that they were his creation, they would get him. As if I, too, was his creation, my voice could do nothing but add to the thunder. He was on his own, on the outside, without the soothing fall of water.

She drained it. All five hundred gallons of it. Two times I walked back to the big house for ice and rum. We knew she was alive. We could hear the changes in the water as she moved under it. We heard the soap hit the floor when she dropped it. But throughout the five hundred gallons, not one sound came from her throat. She was in the moment of the water. The ones inside could not reach her, and the ones outside were barred from the door. As the last drops fell, I smiled. It was good. She was winning.

The first thing she said was, "Jesus! I need suspenders." The door opened, and she stepped out on the porch. We couldn't help it. We had to laugh. She was the girl in the too big clothes. She had the belt cinched as tight as she could get it, and still the jeans hung low, just catching her pubic bones. The pockets of the shirt were below her breasts. If she wasn't careful about the way she walked, the jeans might well slip off. Had I been in the bush too long, or did she look sexy?

It didn't matter. I wasn't going to get close to either of them. I would help them in little ways with the clinic, and I had contacts in Managua that might give them what they needed. It's not that I didn't welcome company, but that my customers would not.

There would be a clinic, and the health of Karawala would improve, but the mutilations would not be stopped.

MUPI TARA

Chapter Twenty-One

Yawanaiska Pura Kum

One night a tiger chased a hog under that cabin. Two fishermen were asleep in there. That tiger and hog sure made a racket until the hog was dead. We could hear the tiger roaring and the hog squealing and the two of them banging against the floor of the cabin. It stayed right there and ate the hog, and the fishermen couldn't make a sound.

Mr. Bet got his rifle, but he couldn't shoot. The bullet might bounce up and hit someone. He waited all the rest of the night, but the tiger never came out. Just when the piam-piam cried, it ran into the bush, but a shot might have gone into the village.

That tiger sure gave those boys a fright, I tell you.

As told by Eddie Wilson

Ariel came over and sat beside me at the rigging table. His friends were opening rod tubes and fitting reels to rods.

"I'm not here to catch tarpon or little snook. I'm here to catch one monster snook, and that's it. I don't care if I only catch one fish the entire week, as long as it's a huge snook." He was matter-of-fact about it, not asking if it was practical or possible.

"How huge is a monster snook?" I asked. "Most people turn cartwheels over a twenty-five or thirty pound snook."

"I caught a thirty pounder the last time I was here. That was huge then, and I was thrilled by it. But there are bigger snook here. I want one over forty pounds."

The way he said it, I could tell he had set a goal for himself -

not for me or for the guides. Most people want action, and if a big fish comes along, more the better. Most are rigged for action, not for one big fish.

"I'll take you myself," I said, "but let's go for fifty. You'll still have to reel in some smaller fish, and you will probably hook a tarpon or two, but if you're up to casting all day without much to show for it, I've got the place for you."

"Now for the big question."

"Oh, what's that?" I couldn't imagine a bigger request. A forty pound snook was enough for one sitting.

"What's it going to cost me for a boat to myself? I suppose we pay for double occupancy."

I got a big smile on my face. "The boat is a pittance compared to the cost of a forty pound snook. I'll let you know at the end of the week."

His response was a laugh and a shrug.

What I had in mind wasn't going to use much more fuel, and even though the camp was full, I had enough boats. If he was successful, and that was a huge *if*, a snook over forty pounds would be a good promotional fish. There were lots of huge snook in the river, but hooking and landing one was a whole 'nother story. I'd lost count of the ones that got away.

"Eddie?"

"Right here, boss." He had been helping the others rig their rods.

"We're going to take Ariel out to catch a mupi tara tomorrow."

He looked at Ariel. "Plenty big snook here. You know that."

"I mean really big. Forty pounds or more. Maybe fifty."

"Got plenty, but can't catch."

"Yes, I know," I said. "We'll start at Sani Warban."

"Sani Warban?" Ariel questioned. "That's the tarpon hole. I don't want to waste even one minute fighting a tarpon."

"That the home of big fish," Eddie replied. "Plenty tapom there, but that place got big snook, I tell you."

*

Up at four. Start the light plant. Ring the bell. Eat a little fruit and drink some coffee. Out the door. Go fishing.

We eased into Sani Warban as it was getting light. Success depended on many things, but the perfect positioning of the boat was primary. The outside bend of Sani Warban went straight down more than one hundred feet. The snook would be snugged up right against the bank; the tarpon were out in the current. If Ariel's plug was out too far, a tarpon would take it. We tied the bow off on a branch and let the stern swing out.

Tarpon were rolling not thirty feet from us. Big tarpon. "Dammit, Beth, I told you I want nothing to do with tarpon."

I held out a one-ounce Boone Tout with a six-inch shrimp tail. "So don't throw it at a tarpon. Drop it as close as you can to the bank and let it sink. Six inches out will do. That's where the snook are, and that's where the tarpon are not. Work it just enough to keep the line tight."

Eddie tied a Bimini twist in the line, tied it to a leader and tied the leader to the jig, both with a perfection loop knot. I leaned back and got comfortable. From then on, it was up to him. We were in it for the long haul.

"You can work it downstream, but the current will keep it fairly shallow. Your best bet is to cast upstream, let it sink, work it past the boat, and when the current brings it up, start over."

He did as I said, and cast after cast, nothing happened. Tarpon continued to roll, and when they found something to eat, there was an explosion in the river, sometimes close to the boat. An exceptionally big tarpon rolled right in front of us.

"Holy shit! Did you see that?"

"Yes, I did, but you have no interest in tarpon."

"How much did he weigh?"

"Maybe two twenty-five."

"My god, that was a big fish!"

I shrugged. "We see those every day. You'll see some bigger, and probably today."

The sun climbed into the sky. Ariel was tireless. He was on a mission. If I said there was a monster snook at Sani Warban, he was going to catch it, even if it meant ten thousand casts to do it. Along about nine o'clock in the morning, he snagged something. He was three hours into his week without a nibble, and all of a sudden his rod was bent double.

"Shit! I've snagged a log."

"No stick here," Eddie said. "Haps to be a fish."

It did look like he had snagged something. His rod was bent, but nothing else was happening. It was like he had hooked the bottom, but there wasn't anything down there to hook.

"Snook!" Eddie yelled. "Big snook!" The giveaway was a few slow tugs seen through the rod. He had a fish. Eddie bounded to the bow to untie us so we could move out into the river to fight it.

Line began to peel slowly from the reel. Then it quickened. And then the run began, and water flew from the reel as line was stripped away in a blistering dash for freedom. For the fish, it worked. The line went slack, and Ariel reeled in an empty feeling. Gone. Whatever it was, it was gone, and no one would ever know if it was a snook. For less than a minute, he had known a big fish.

Eddie tied us off again. There hadn't even been time to start the motor.

"What happened?" he asked.

"Who knows? Maybe a nick in the line. Maybe a toothy critter after a knot. Doesn't matter. Big fish do that."

Ariel's hands were unsteady. He had felt it. He had known, just for a moment, what it was like to be connected to his quarry, and it had sent him home with his tail between his legs. He lost. He did nothing wrong, but he lost all the same.

"The odds are against you," I said. "The little ones are easy; the big ones are hard. The monsters are almost impossible.

Check your line, tie on another tout and start over."

And that he did, when his nerves calmed. He stood in the stern and began casting upstream. I wasn't going to say it, but that might have been the fish of a lifetime. He might have been thinking it, but neither of us would talk about it.

When the line went slack, Eddie had but one thing to say. "Mupi tara. That fella big, I tell you." He said nothing else, but began tying on a new plug, as if nothing unusual had happened.

At about 10:00 A.M., the land breeze gave way to the sea breeze, and the wind came up. It was no more than ten to fifteen knots, but it put the tarpon down. From then on, we saw no fish. At 11:00, the heat began to become oppressive. Ariel was soaked in sweat, but still casting. It had become mechanical, with brief rests for water.

I felt the heat. Eddie felt the heat. Every living creature felt the heat. It was only ninety degrees, but with the humidity and the tropical sun, it felt like being inside a pressure cooker.

"Ready for lunch?" I asked, hoping he was.

"You brought lunch?" he asked, surprised.

"No, but the camp is close. We can go have lunch, rest a little, and come back out this afternoon. There won't be much happening until then."

"Let's go," he replied, with relief in his voice.

"I don't have to twist your arm?"

"Not even a little," he said as he stepped into the cockpit, stowed his rod and sat down, blowing air through puckered lips. "I couldn't have done that until dark. I need a cold beer."

The water in the Karawala was frothy from the props of six boats racing back to camp for cold beer and lunch. At the dock, there were nine fishermen showing off the morning's catch. Everyone had brought something back for the table, and some were impressive. Ariel was the only one with nothing to show.

Barry patted him on the back. Chiding, he asked, "Where's your fish, Ariel?"

"I had him on," he answered, shaking his head.

Barry looked at me. I nodded assent.

"Big?"

Eddie answered. "That fella one big snook."

"How big?"

"Can't say. We never see."

"Then how do you know it was a snook?"

"Was snook." He was certain.

Barry looked at me again. "Only really big snook do that wallowing thing with their heads before they take off," I explained. "It was a snook."

We had a cold Victoria, ate a lunch of fried snook and took a nap. A little after three, we were back at Sani Warban and Ariel was back on the stern.

"Am I going to throw this tout all week?"

"That's the best we've got for what you want."

"Am I going to throw it at this same water all week?"

"No to that," I answered, getting up. "As a matter of fact, let's move."

We motored to the next warban, just below Kara, and tied off in the deepest water along a bank sheltered from the wind. The tide had just begun to ebb.

Within five minutes, he was hooked up, and again it looked at first like he had snagged a log. I started the motor just as Eddie released us, and we moved out, in reverse, into the river, where we hoped to pull the fish away from the bank. The fish sounded. There was no stopping her; she was going to the bottom, and I worried that it might not be a snook. In shallow water, snook are acrobats, but in deep water, they often do not jump until the end of the fight. They keep you guessing.

After five minutes of a bulldog tug-of-war, Ariel started gaining line. It was still strong, but tiring. I watched for the telltale bouncing and circling of a big jack, but when I saw neither, I knew.

"You've got yourself a good sized snook," I announced.

Eddie concurred. "Is sure." He picked up the gaff. The fish

and the boat were being carried downstream by the current.

"It wouldn't do for you to catch your fish on the first day," I offered. "You should have to work much harder for a monster snook."

"I'll take it when I can get it," he answered. He had moved to the bow, where it was easier to fight and land a big fish.

The line began to rise.

"Going jump!" Eddie said, a little charged up. I picked up my camera.

The fish's ascent quickened, and then there it was at the surface, head shaking and tail thrashing. It was a fine snook, but it was shy of forty pounds. Down again it went, and there was nothing he could do but watch the line peel away.

"Son of a bitch!" Ariel shouted. "That's it! That's the one!"

"Careful, now. She's not in the boat yet."

Ariel worked it back up, and within a few minutes, it was at the side of the boat. Eddie slipped the gaff in its mouth and heaved it in. Ariel was lit up with excitement.

"Tell me it's over forty. Tell me."

"We'll have to hang it on the scales, but I think it's closer to thirty-five."

Eddie nodded. "About that."

"You're not there yet, but you're in a very select club. Not many people have caught a snook like that on a rod and reel, and fewer still with a casting rod. Congratulations." We all shook hands.

"Do you want to take her to the scales now?" I asked. "She's already losing weight."

"You're sure it won't go forty." It was a statement and a question.

After a pause, I answered, "Not absolutely positively. I can usually get within a pound for snook up to thirty, but for one this big, only the scales can tell for sure."

"Then let's go weigh it."

Eddie and Ariel sat, and I pushed the throttle all the way

down.

"Thirty-six and one half pounds," Eddie announced from the scales. "Mupi tara."

"That surely a big snook, Beth," Miss Pete said from the big house. "Can feed plenty."

I looked at Ariel. "You want to have it mounted?"

He was puzzled. "How am I going to have it mounted?"

"We'll freeze it and build a balsa coffin for it. When you open it at home, it will still be frozen."

"Balsa?"

"Yep. Four inches thick."

"Damn right. Freeze it. But I'm still after a forty pounder."

"As is everyone else who fishes for snook. But why not go for the all-tackle world record? Why forty?"

"I guess it sounds more attainable. I don't like to fail."

I had to laugh. His was a monster snook even if it didn't weigh forty pounds. He had bragging rights for the rest of his life. "I hate to tell you, but you've probably come as close as you're going to get. We hook lots of huge snook, but very few are landed. You probably caught the season record today."

Miss Pete had it laid out and ready to wrap when the rest of the fishermen returned. They all wore big smiles and came to tell about all the fish they caught. Ariel sat at the table with a beer in his hand and a sly grin on his face, waiting for the inevitable question, which would come with a little razzing.

Danny asked it. "Where's your monster snook, Ariel? What did you catch today?"

"Just one," he answered. The grin was growing.

"Is right here, boys," Miss Pete said. "Come look before I lock it up."

Danny and Barry walked around the counter and looked. "Holy shit!" They said in unison. That started a stampede, and each one said pretty much the same thing when they saw it.

"And on the first day," I said.

*

It was getting light when we tied off at the same spot at Sani Warban the next morning. Ariel stepped up on the stern and started casting. Cast after cast, like a robot, he covered the bank from his farthest cast to a lob near the boat. The sun climbed the sky, and the heat climbed with it.

"Sun prickly," Eddie said. "Sharp like knife." Trickles of sweat ran down his face. I was sweating, but Ariel looked like he had just pulled himself out of the river. I gave him some water and asked him to rest.

"Are these the only places where there are big snook? These warbans?"

"Oh, no. There are lots of places with big snook."

"Then why aren't we fishing them?"

"Because all the best snook holes are full of logs. The big fish are there, but no one is going to catch them. They go straight for the logs, and there's no stopping them. That's why the season record is never much over thirty pounds. We catch some bigger fish in the fall at Snook Creek, Karas Laya and on the bar, but we can't get into Snook Creek and Karas Laya right now, and the bar isn't fishable."

"Why so?" he asked as he stepped back onto the stern.

"The bar is too rough to wade, and Snook Creek and Karas Laya are closed. Their mouths are behind the beach."

He started casting again. "So every morning we will be right here, and every afternoon we'll be up the river a bit."

"Maybe not. We might run up to Tulu Warban."

"Where's that?"

"About thirty minutes up river from here. It's a pretty place. I like it, but it has a problem."

"I'll bite. What kind of problem?"

The *bite* was appropriate. "A resident croc about twenty feet long. He could be a problem if he took a fancy to us while we're tied off at the bank."

Ariel looked at Eddie. "That true, Eddie?"

Eddie smiled. "Maybe more than twenty feet. We never measure."

"I'd love to see a twenty foot croc in the wild, but I wouldn't want that to be the last thing I ever saw. You actually fish that place?"

"We don't tie off, and we don't anchor. We stay ready to move. You'd have to cast to the bank from a drifting boat."

"I'll have to think about that. Do you think it's dangerous?"

"Not as dangerous as a freeway. The river is the freeway for the people who live here. They paddle by all day and all night in their dories, and if he's eaten any of them, there were no witnesses." I thought for a moment about saying more. What the hell? "Fishing isn't so much about catching fish as it is about being there. That means being here with everything that lives here. It means butterflies, orchids and crocodiles big enough to eat a man. I would rather be eaten by a croc than to die in a burning, mangled ton of metal. The odds are better here and a damn sight better to look at."

It took him a minute to answer. "I'm accustomed to mangled tons of metal. I see it every night on the news. I'm so accustomed that I have no fear of it. Someone else always dies. If we go up there, it might be me. Three men, one croc. The odds have changed."

I shook my head. "I can only tell you that those who live here rarely ever die a violent death, and they are surrounded in every moment by the things we fear most. They are surrounded by things that can eat them."

He was casting as we spoke. Again, he looked at Edie. "Does that croc bother you?"

"I don't study that," he answered. "He there, we there. He fish, we fish. Same thing." He was characteristically brief, with little facial expression or body language. One could not tell from looking what his true emotions were. The croc was somewhere else. It was not a consideration until its teeth could be seen. It had no substance until it was a threat, and it couldn't be a threat until it burst out of the water and attacked. No problem. Not to worry.

"I never ceases to amaze me," I said, "that we have become so inured to the everyday murder and mayhem of the industrial world that we no longer think about it, let alone fear it, yet we step into a place like this, and we fear it. We fear nature. We are so out of place that we fear the most beautiful things on earth."

He fell silent for several casts, and when he spoke again, he changed the subject.

"What's the biggest fish you ever caught here?"

"It was too big to weigh."

"Too big to weigh? Those scales must be twelve feet off the ground."

"I put them there to weigh big tarpon. This fish was eighteen feet long."

He turned and looked at me, his expression incredulous. "Get out."

Eddie laughed. "That was one mannish fish."

"I guess you've got a story to tell."

"I guess you asked for it. It was a sawfish. One of my guests saw a sawfish bill at the camp and wanted to catch one. We went out after dinner one night to Jamaima Key with a bucket of mullet, a thirty pound class rod and two medios of Flor. I took a pistol along for just in case. We anchored and set out a mullet on the bottom. The hook was attached to thirty feet of five hundred pound cable with a thirty foot double line above it. There was nothing to do but sit and wait.

"Out came the Flor, and the weight of the day's fishing, a big dinner with wine and lots of Flor finally got to him. He fell asleep. I decided to keep fishing and wake him if we got a take.

"We sat, and we waited. Just as I was about to give up, something picked up the mullet and started moving off with it. I picked up the rod and put the reel in freespool. The lips of a sawfish are two thick bony plates used to crush oysters and other shellfish. The only way to hook one is to wait until he swallows the bait. I let him swim away with it for thirty seconds before I put the reel in gear. I let him pull the line tight before I set the hook."

"Wake him up, Eddie"

"He woke up, and I tried to give him the rod, but he just mumbled something, waved me off and closed his eyes again. I didn't want it, but the fish was mine.

"So off it went, toward the bar and the open sea. The run was almost casual, but the power was undeniable, and as the line disappeared, I wondered if I was going to be able to stop it. I had no intention of following it out to sea. We left the anchor on the bottom. If it wouldn't turn, I was willing to give it a spool of line.

"It took about three hundred yards of line before it turned, and when it did, it swam slowly back to the boat. Maybe twenty yards away from us, it turned again, but it only took a few yards of line, and I thought, 'this is too easy.'

"That's when he charged the boat. The first time, he just smashed into the bottom, nearly throwing me overboard. The second time, he came up out of the water and brought his bill down hard on the starboard gunnel, thrashing his tail and throwing water all over us. That's when I pulled my pistol. I yelled to Eddie to get our sleeping guest down on the deck.

"The third time he came up, I started shooting. He started near the stern and chopped his way up to the bow, wood and water flying everywhere. Leaning against the port gunnel, I emptied the pistol in him. Fourteen shots, and that's all I had. I hadn't brought another clip.

"When the water settled, I looked at Eddie. 'You okay?' He nodded. 'And him?'"

"Asleep yet. Man sleep like bone." Looking at the water around the boat, he asked, "Fish gone?"

"I don't know. The line is slack. Let's have a look."

"I picked up the rod and slowly began to take up the slack. I reeled until the swivel on the cable touched the rod tip, and then

I put the rod down and took the cable in hand. I pulled it in until I felt the weight of something very heavy. If it had any fight left in it, I didn't want to piss it off again."

"Looks like we still have a fish."

"Better we cut the line?" Eddie asked.

"Nope. I want to see this thing. Give me a hand."

"It was not easy to lift, even with two men and neutral buoyancy, but we managed to pull it up enough to get a rope around the bill. The bullets had done their work; there was little life left in the fish.

"Eddie looked at the bill and the rope protruding from the water. He looked at me and asked, 'Now what you going do?' The question implied very clearly that we had done little more that subdue the fish and substitute a rope for fishing line. We still did not have the fish. It was still in the water, and no two men on earth were going to pull it over the gunnel.

"It would be easier if we swamp the boat," I said.

"He looked at me like I was crazy. 'What?' was all he could say. He was afraid I was serious." I looked at Eddie. His expression said he still thought I was crazy.

"I might have been crazy. You have to be crazy to go out at night on a jungle river in search of prehistoric monsters, but I was not about to swamp the boat. Sooner or later, the sharks would come, and some of them would be bigger than our fish. If we didn't do something soon, we would have no choice but to cut and run. The glow of kerosene lamps came from windows across the river at The Bar."

"Wait a minute," Ariel interrupted. "You keep talking about the bar, and all this time I've thought you were talking about the river bar at the mouth, but now you're talking about houses. Just what are you talking about?"

"Both. The Bar is the village at the bar. La Barra del Rio Grande. Obviously, it's inside the bar on dry land. Sort of dry land. It's just a little higher than the swamp behind it."

"Okay. Continue." He was still casting. Maybe the story

drew his attention from the monotony and the heat.

"There was shallow water at The Bar with a hard sand bottom. We hauled the anchor and towed the fish across the river, where we drew a crowd. With help, we pulled it out enough that its back was out of the water. It was quite a show. They kept going from the fish to the boat, and, 'go fetch so and so' was heard enough that I think everyone in the village was there before we left. I heard, 'hoopah, looky dat' so many times I dreamt about it that night.

"We untied the fish, stretched the rope from tip to tail and tied a knot in it. Someone showed up with a saw, and we cut the bill off. It was almost five feet long and a foot wide, tooth to tooth. When we measured the rope, it was eighteen feet to the knot."

"What did you do with it?"

"It's at the camp. I'll show it to you tomorrow."

"The fish?"

"No, the bill. We gave the fish to The Bar."

"What did they do with it?"

"They ate it."

"They ate an eighteen foot sawfish?"

I never answered the question. His tout was deep and almost directly under the boat when something took it. The fish was big enough to put a good bow in the rod, but it was almost immediately obvious that it wasn't the fish he was looking for. He started hoisting it toward the surface with all the pressure he could muster.

"'Bout ten pounds," Eddie guessed.

And then it stopped, as if the fish had thrown a clove hitch around a log. Ariel wedged his thumbs against the spool and heaved, but gained no ground.

"Shit. I'm snagged," he swore, and he reached for the line as if to break it, but as he did, something heavy pulled down and moved toward the bottom. He took the rod again with both hands.

"What have I got?"

"Can't say," Eddie said, perplexed.

"Let's see what it does," I offered.

Whatever it was, it was taking a leisurely swim to the bottom, if swimming it was. It was taking line more like an anchor that couldn't quite be stopped. Just as we were beginning to think it might not be a fish, it made two powerful pulls against the rod, and having made its descent, it moved out across the bottom toward the other side of the river.

"Must be June fish," Eddie declared.

"June fish? Ariel asked. "You mean jewfish?

I concurred. "One and the same, but not a big one. It ate your snook."

"Not big? He's big enough to eat a ten pound snook, and he's swimming around like he doesn't have a hook in his mouth, and you say he's not big?"

"Okay, maybe he's big, and maybe the hook is in the snook's mouth. Maybe I just hope he's not big."

"Why?"

"Because if he's not big, we might be able to get him in the boat," I paused. "In an hour or two."

"And if he's big?"

Eddie chuckled.

"We'll never see it. He can live, eat, spawn, go wherever he wants and die of old age, and there's absolutely nothing we can do about it."

He thought about that before continuing.

"How big would that be?"

"About the size of a Volkswagon. We had one come up and eat a sixty pound tarpon once. We saw a big, dark shadow rising up out of the depths, and just as it got to the tarpon, we recognized it. One gulp and it was gone, sinking slowly back to its hole."

Again, he paused to think, perhaps deciding what to do.

"What did you do?"

"There wasn't much we could do. Twenty pound test line is not going to lift a thousand pound fish. I cut the line."

"Did you see it, Eddie?"

"No, sir. But plenty like that here."

"How big is this one?"

"Two, maybe three hundred pounds."

"Can we land it?"

"Haps to, we going to."

Ariel was putting all the pressure he could on the fish. For whatever reason, he had decided to try to land it, even though he had said he would break off everything but big snook. The sun was high. It was hot, and it was time for lunch and a nap. Off in the distance, at the creek mouth, I saw one boat, then two, turn into the Karawala and head for camp. They would have their lunch, a nap and return to the river before we boated the fish.

Not much happens in the mid-day heat of a tropical rain forest. Birds, frogs and insects are quiet, and the chop on the river conceals the movements of fish, if indeed they are active. An occasional wading bird is the only sign of life, even though the bush seethes with it. But we humans will suffer heat, cold and brutal exertion in pursuit of entertainment. I watched Ariel strain against his fish and knew that his misery was also his achievement. Even if the line parted or the hook pulled out, there was something going on inside him that made the fish his forever. Catching the fish had less importance than the struggle. He might lose the fish without a single glimpse, but the memory was caught and would never fade.

It took more than two hours. Three times the fish swam into shallow water on the other side of the river, turned and went deep again as if it was patrolling its territory. Each time it went back down, Ariel cursed it and ordered it to the surface. The tide turned, the wind laid, and we steamed in the heat. Then from the deepest water, it relented, and Ariel began pumping it slowly to the surface, arms and legs trembling as the last of his energy drained away down a silver thread of monofilament.

My fear that he had snagged a huge sting ray was allayed when I saw a fin. A minute later, the fish was at the side of the boat. It was truly huge, but it was not the monster he was looking for. This one fish, if we kept it, would feed the entire village.

"How are we going to get that thing into the boat?" Ariel asked as he sat. "I don't think I'm going to be much help."

That was all it took for Eddie to slip the gaff into the fish's mouth and stick it. Hungry people do not release fish. He had shown great restraint in waiting for someone to say something about keeping it, and having heard, he quickly went to work securing it. I helped him lift the head out of the water enough to slip a mooring line through the gills and out the mouth. The fish was ours, even if we couldn't lift it over the gunnel. All Ariel could manage was a weak grin.

I didn't have to ask. His expression told me he was through for the day. He took a seat next to his fish, rested a forearm on the gunnel and reached down to touch it. Just under the surface, it rested, fanning its fins and gills. It was a very quiet moment of wonder. When Ariel looked up, I nodded at Eddie, and he started the motor.

It took the rest of the afternoon to motor slowly back to the wharf and get the fish carried to the scales. By the time the other fishermen returned to camp, Ariel was showered, rested and perched atop a ladder next to his fish. He had a glass of Flor in one hand and a puro in the other. From the place where the path to the river emerges from the bush, it is another hundred yards to the big house. Each of the returning fishermen stopped there, slack-jawed, when they saw the fish. After a moment of amazement, they hurried to the scales, where a crowd from the village had gathered.

As they walked up, Ariel took a pull on the rum, a puff on the puro and said, nonchalantly, "Three fifty-two." His grin and the cheers from the crowd said everything else.

A jewfish is a giant grouper. Its flesh is light and flaky and absolutely delectable when sautéed in butter. We ate until we hurt, and no doubt everyone in Karawala did the same. That one fish was enough to feed three hundred people.

Days three and four of Ariel's quest were nonproductive if the catch was the only consideration. The fishing was mechanical. Cast, sink, retrieve...cast, sink, retrieve, ad infinitum. Tarpon rolled and fed in the mornings, and twice he hooked one only to break it off after one jump. Whenever I thought he was losing confidence, we moved, if only for a rest and a change of scenery, but always we started at Sani Warban. When the others asked, all he could do was shake his head and listen as they told of their many snook and some twenty and thirty pounders.

On the fifth and last day, I suggested we just go out and catch some snook without the focus on a monster, but he was resolute. It was the big one or nothing, so the first rays of the sun struck us at Sani Warban, tied off at the same spot. If anyone was going to pull a really big snook out of the river, it was going to be at Sani Warban, and it could just as well be eighty pounds as forty. Big fish were everywhere, but only at Sani Warban and maybe two other places were conditions favorable for landing one.

At about nine o'clock in the morning Ariel's rod bent double. Eddie and I jumped to our feet to watch the rod and line for anything that might betray what was down there.

"Another fucking tarpon," Ariel grumbled.

"Wait on it," I cautioned.

The rod moved as the fish wallowed and charged away.

"Snook!" Eddie exclaimed.

"Snook!" I echoed. "Big snook."

"Nah." Ariel said. "I don't need any guide talk. It's a tarpon, and I'm going to break it off."

"No!" I yelled. "Don't do it."

The fish ran out a bit and started coming up.

"See? Tarpon," he said, and he stuck his thumbs between

the spool and the bar to break the line. The line rose as the fish came up from the deep. It was going to jump. Up it came. If it had run out, the line would have parted, and we would never have seen it.

Ariel kept his thumbs down and the spool stopped. I wanted to snatch the rod from his hands and play the fish myself, but all I could do was stand down and watch it happen.

Out of the water it came, all five feet of it, heavy-bodied and with a big black stripe down its side. How big was it? No one will ever know. The line broke in midair, and the splash as it returned to the river was the last anyone will ever see of it. Snook. Big snook. Bigger by far than the all-tackle world record. Seventy, maybe eighty pounds. I sighed and shook my head.

"I've hooked a few like that, but never where I had a chance of landing one. I fought one for over an hour before it got into the roots."

There were other things I could have said, but it wouldn't have made things any better. After a long silence, I started the motor and headed for camp.

There is an immense peace in the places of the wild. Even in the teeth of the fiercest storm, even in the uneasy presence of the unseen viper, there is an immense peace. The fish are part of it, but catching them is not.

TOP GALLON
Chapter Twenty-Two
Yawanaiska Pura Wal

He said we are empowered to lie, cheat and steal with the full faith and backing of the laws of the United States of America. It's the way business works, and it's the way justice works. It's the way the politicians have set things up. That's why he quit. He couldn't live like that.

He wasn't going to stay down here. He was going to go back and find a way of life that would keep him away from corruption as much as possible. I guess that's what he found here.

Halley Stone

Top gallon. The river reaches its crest. It rises up out of its banks and spreads out across the low ground, hiding the lakes and rivers and lagoons under a blanket of water. No matter how hard it rains, it just can't get any higher. High ground becomes an island, and the islands become refuge for all that walk on land.

I stayed for it. Since my first season, they had told me about hunting the top gallon flood, but I had always been gone when it came. This season, when the flood came down the river, I was there for the hunt.

"Mr. Bet?"

It was Eddie. It was still dark, and it was still raining. There was no urgency in his voice.

"What in the world are you doing up at this hour?"

"Is top gallon. Must be we going hunt."

We had been getting ten to fifteen inches of rain per day for several days. The river was already swollen, and if it could have been seen from the air, it would have looked like a huge ribbon of chocolate milk topped with cinnamon sticks.

Great trees loosened by the rain from their hold on the banks floated with the current to the sea, accompanied by rafts of hyacinths and flotsam flushed from the jungle. Waterlogged passengers perched or coiled and waited to be swept near enough to shore to swim for it.

It was the time of cleansing and redistribution. The river stuck her muddy tongue far out to sea. Those that still clung to their rafts at the bar were carried out, there to perish or to be blown ashore in some distant land. Seeds and plants from the headwaters and tributaries got planted along the way, and representatives from every green thing in Nicaragua set sail for wherever the winds and currents would take them.

It was the time of mud and wading and of drying the laundry over a fire one piece at a time. One could almost drown just by breathing the air. Entire weeks went by without sunlight or blue sky. The rain drummed incessantly, and the thunder rolled as if at war. It was cold.

Hunt? Who in his right mind would get out of a warm, dry bed and go hunting in a cold, pouring rain?

"Go back to bed, Eddie."

"No, Mr. Bet. Haps to we going."

I got out of bed and lit a lamp. "Come in out of the rain."

Lightning illuminated the outside. Eddie had one of my boats tied to the porch. I imagined snakes hanging from the roof and wondered why Eddie wasn't afraid. The rest of the hunting party sat hunched over in the boat, baling water with calabash bowls. They wore capes and coats and ponchos fashioned from sheets of plastic salvaged from the beach.

"This the time. The flood got all the animals, them, run up to high ground. Easy for catch."

"Where?"

"Mairin Laya."

"Mairin Laya? That's twenty miles up the river."

"Supposed to be."

They would not have asked if it wasn't important. They needed my boat, and they needed my guns. They didn't need me, but this was what I stayed for.

"Okay. Get the guns and an ammo box. I'll be ready in a few minutes."

We motored slowly along the path to the river. The water was up over the wharf some six feet above high tide. When the bow hit the current, it spun us downstream, and we were off.

It was an eerie darkness. I sat not five feet from the outboard, but the rain and thunder reduced it to a quiet purr. The rain beat down our wake as we passed and made the surface jump with millions of dancing drops. We could not have been seen or heard. Our passing could only have been betrayed by flashes of lightning.

We slipped silently into the big river and turned into the current. The night gave way to gray. We hung close to the shore to avoid the full force of the river. If there was an opposite shore, it could not be seen.

"Next side gone," Ferlan observed. I nodded my head.

We watched carefully for sticks, some of which were fifty feet long and ten feet in diameter. Some of the trees, such as mangrove and ironwood, are too dense to float. They just bump along the bottom. Others, like balsa, float high out of the water and are easy to see. And there are those that hardly float and hang unseen just below the surface. Those are the ones that knock holes in boats and shear the lower units off the outboards.

We watched carefully, but still we hit logs. There would be a jarring crunch at the bow, and Eddie would move desperately to pull the prop out of the water before the log traveled the length of the boat. Sometimes the impact knocked the log down into the water. Sometimes not. We carried spare props and a spare outboard.

There would be silence, a collision and excited chatter, an inspection, and then silence. Mudi, Abanil and Narcisso sharpened machetes to a razor edge, but mostly we hunkered down against the rain and watched for obstructions in the river.

And so it went. We passed Kara without seeing a soul. There were no birds at Tulu Warban. Hours passed, and all we knew was wet and cold. Eddie stopped once to try to light a cigarette, but managed only to get his matches and his cigarettes wet.

"Match sure caught cold, now," he joked.

We pulled ashore at the mouth of Mairin Laya. There is high ground there, and a family had made their home at the top of the bank. It is nothing more than a thatched palm roof, where they can cook, eat and sleep without getting soaked. Barnyard animals share the dirt and the roof with little more notice than that of the smoke from a fire that never goes out.

We climbed stiffly up the bank and were greeted by two bashful bare-breasted women, one the other's daughter. They told me the young one had never been more than a few minutes away from their shelter. There were no matches there. It was her duty to keep the fire burning, and so she went only far enough to gather wood.

We stopped to pay our respects to the man of the house and to offer him a few gifts in exchange for information about the movements of game in the area. But he was out on a hunt of his own. We gave matches, cigarettes, rum, salt and flour to the ladies of the house and warmed ourselves over their fire.

I smiled at how appropriate it was that we had met two half-naked women at the mouth of Mairin Laya - *Woman Creek*. They wore short skirts made from flour sacks, and I doubted that they owned anything else. I guessed that the mother was nearing thirty; her daughter was about sixteen. It would not be long before she, too, became a mother. The flour sack skirts were never taken off. They bathed in them, slept in them, and raised them over their hips for a man.

The daughter's eyes were bright and her body lithe, but not meager from hunger. I thought, with some amusement, that she was probably stronger than many of the men I knew. She was a very pretty girl, and I was saddened by the thought that she would never know the slightest luxury. Her world consisted of a straw mat, a thatched palm roof and a fire that must never go out.

As we left, she warned us to watch for snakes. "Real snakes, mind you," she said. She meant poisonous snakes. A few weeks later, I heard that she had been killed by the bite of a fer-de-lance.

A few miles up Mairin Laya, we were stopped by the bush. Driftwood had caught in the overhanging branches and barricaded our way. It was so thick there was no thought of trying to clear it. We left the channel of the creek and anchored the boat. We saw signs of animals where they had browsed submerged grass at the edge of the creek. The tracks were under water; we couldn't tell what they were, but we hoped to follow them to high ground.

We waded in, and as we walked, we began to fan out to cover more ground. With the clanging of machetes and the watery sounds of wading, we hardly went unannounced. Parrots and monkeys squawked and screamed and the bush ahead rustled with things unseen as they moved out of our path.

The going was slow, and the mosquitoes found us to be sitting ducks. We all carried something in our hands that had to be held above the water. We couldn't slap at them. All we could do was rub our arms against our faces and curse the little bloodsuckers as they whined in our ears.

We waded waist deep, but felt our way carefully lest one of us take a step off the edge of something unseen. Low bush concealed by the opaqueness of the water reached out to prick and jab. What else, I wondered, was hidden? It didn't matter that there was nothing there. Being unable to see was disquieting.

It was not a walk in the park. The mosquitoes, and no doubt leaches, were draining our blood and leaving unknown parasites in its place. We were soaked and in danger of hypothermia. And whatever befell us, we were on our own. We had waded away from our only transportation in faith that it would be there when we returned. The rain drummed on. What was it like without guns and an outboard? They knew. I was not of a mind to find out.

We waded and chopped for more than an hour, and I had begun to think that we would never find what we were looking for when the bush opened to a flooded plain that formed a large temporary lake, and in its center the earth rose up in a wooded island a few acres large. We were there, and it had not taken a monumental effort. There, perhaps a half mile away, were deer, tapir, wari and give-nut. I could see deer on the near shore.

I soon became the apex of a vee formation as those on either side of me quickened their pace and moved so as to surround the island. I was motioned to stop. Nothing was spoken; it seemed they knew what to do. It was no longer a hunt. We had found our game. Serious and intent, now, they began the harvest. I waited in the water for them to flush game to me. I watched the mogote, and I watched the water for alligators and snakes.

From the other side, there were shots, and following the shots, a small herd of red deer came into view and stopped. I aimed and fired and dropped a buck. I smiled. I know of no finer venison than that of the little red deer of Central America. Sula, they call them, and venison is sula wina.

More shots rang, followed by whoops and shouts from victorious hunters. I heard the Enfield and knew that Eddie had shot: then the Helice, and knew where Abanil was. They called to each other to announce their kills. From all sides I heard happy voices. I, too, voiced my joy. Many hungry people were going to get some much-needed protein.

When the shooting and shouting started, most of the animals broke through our thin perimeter and bounded into the water. Like radiating waves, they swam out to find other high ground. I watched them go. I thought we had enough.

After the shooting came the counting and the dressing. We soon had our game laid out in one place. We had eight deer, two large turkey-like birds, called guan, two wari and one giant anteater.

Ferlan had killed the anteater, not with a gun, but with a machete, and he was proud of it. He strutted around our deer with his nose in the air.

"So! You got carbina, and all you got is small little deer. Look my antspear. Look, now. Look how big."

I laughed. It had never occurred to me that one might eat an anteater. "Is it good to eat?"

"Is the best." They agreed.

We built a fire, and as we dressed our game, Narcisso roasted livers and hearts on a spit. It was well past noon, and we had only eaten a few pieces of fruit all day. My hunger hastened my work.

Without watching the others, I field dressed my deer the way I would have in Texas. When they saw what I had done, they shook their heads at my waste and salvaged the entrails and head for themselves. Nothing is wasted. In this land where hunger is at best a recent memory, there is precious little of any animal that is not eaten.

The roasted livers and hearts, without spices or gravies, were as good as any meat I had ever eaten. It was fresh, it was pure, and I had a ravenous appetite. We ate with our hands, and as I ate, two things occurred to me. The first was that the boat and its new cargo were separated by a few miles. The second was that we could bring the boat to the cargo much easier than we could back the cargo to the boat. I said as much.

"Sure is so," Mudi answered. "Eddie and I going fetch it for we."

We watched them wade away and disappear into the bush. About an hour later, we saw the boat emerge from the same place. The water was deep enough that we didn't need to stay in the river channels. We loaded up and moved on. I thought we would be going back, but they were just getting started.

Farther in we went, toward a camp built by those who went there to hunt alligators. On the river, I was in the familiar, but now I felt the same things as on the first trip from Bluefields. This was all the world there was, and now was all the time there was. Past and future did not exist, and the universe existed not as what I knew of it, but as what I could see and hear and feel. It had never known the artificial.

I was wet, cold and tired. I had been bitten by everything that could fly through the rain, swim through the water or drop from a tree to draw my blood. I was in awe of all that thrived in this lush and hostile land. The interminable rain was not even an inconvenience to anything but us, the feeble two-legged visitors. To all else, it was nourishment and comfort. None of this could exist without it.

Darkness closed in on us before we found the camp, and with the water up, there was a possibility that we would not be able to find it. I had been thinking about the luxury of a fire for quite some time. I did not like the prospect of spending the night huddled in a boat, in the rain, without the warmth and protection of fire.

In near total darkness, we inched our way through the trees. Eddie steered by flashes of lightning, from one flash to the next, and it seemed that we remained stationary while the trees and the creek rearranged themselves in the darkness, like dancers under strobes.

And then it was there - a landing of mud worn smooth by bare feet and dories hauled out of the water. If a small, worn-out dory hadn't been tied up there, it would have taken the broad light of day to see that it was not an alligator slide. We pulled up, stepped out and hurried up the path.

It wasn't much of a camp. Several lean-tos covered with palm leaves sheltered raised cane platforms used as beds. In the center, there was an ingenious earth-filled campfire at waist height, contained by an inverted pyramid of interwoven bamboo. Three hunters stood at the fire. A fourth was busily skinning an enormous alligator.

We went barging into the camp almost at a run, with no interest other than warmth, but to our hosts to be, it must have seemed like an attack. They were visibly startled and reached for machetes and knives for defense. We laughed as we entered, as much from relief as at our effect, and with much greeting and explaining, began heaping wood on the fire.

Our hosts stood with eyes agape in astonishment. They were all known to one another. If your world has but a few hundred inhabitants, you are likely to know them all. But in an area of thousands of uninhabited square miles, the odds of a meeting like this are infinitesimal. We were as surprised as they to find the place occupied.

And once again, even though I had never laid eyes on any of them, they knew exactly who I was, and again, I was given the deference of royalty. If anyone could have been treated royally in a place like that, I would have been. It was genuine. They were proud and excited that I was there with them.

None of us slept much that night. We were wet and cold and had neither dry clothes nor bedding. We slept until the chill soaked in, and then we stood by the fire until we were warm enough to doze off again. It was a long night, and as stoic as they were, I saw that they were as vulnerable to the cold as I. We were miserable.

With the first sign of approaching daylight, we were on our way again. This time we were less methodical about the hunt. We cruised the edges of the bush and shot from the boat at whatever we saw, and it proved to be equally as successful as surrounding high ground. With game heaped to the gunnels stem to stern, we headed home.

There was some debate as to how to get back to the river. Eddie wanted to go back through the creek.

"Is too far, Eddie." Abanil insisted. Others agreed. "We can haul over here." Abanil pointed toward some undefined hole in the bush.

"This not little dori." Eddie pointed out. "Not easy for haul over."

"But the water is high. Maybe we float over."

Eddie was out-voted. We went toward the bush. The water was high, and in fact there was a current running toward what was promised to be the river just a few short yards away. But we never got there. The current was running through the branches of trees, and we were soon swept broadside into the crotch of a big mahogany.

We had hardly come to a stop when machetes began clanging and men began pushing us along. I heard a scream and looked up to see Narcisso, and then Abanil, waving madly at the air and screaming. We had hit a hornets' nest. Someone had swung a machete right through it, and the air was becoming black with them.

"Jump!" I shouted. "Get into the water!" I dove in, and they all followed.

Under water, I rubbed and swatted at the stings. The hornets held on, stinging. I came up for air, and in the instant it took to take a breath, I saw Abanil standing stone still, chest deep in water, with hornets covering and stinging his face. It made me come up for a better look.

"Abanil! Get under water!" And then I saw it. A foot in front of his face was the head of a fer-de-lance, coiled in the branch of a tree, ready to strike.

I had no time to waste. If he even blinked, the snake would strike. If he didn't move, the hornets would kill him. I lunged for the boat and pulled out my rifle, swatting and slapping as I did. No one else moved. I waded quickly to a nearby tree, laid the rifle across a branch, sighted in on the eye of the snake, and squeezed. It was the loudest shot I've ever heard. The bullet passed just inches from Abanil's ear to get to the snake.

At the sound of the shot, Abanil's reflexes took him swooshing backward in the water. The recoil took my eyes off the target. For a moment, I did not know the outcome. I first looked at Abanil, half expecting to see a snake attached to his face. Then I saw the writhing, nearly headless body gushing blood into the water.

In the next instant, I became aware of the hornets again. I ducked under. When I came up, the boat was moving. Eddie had taken the anchor rode out away from the nest and was pulling the boat away. We followed. By the time I got into the boat, I was on fire, and my nose and eyes were swollen shut. I knew Abanil had to be worse than I.

"Haps to go fast now, Eddie." Ferlan said. I heard fear in his voice, and I knew there were tears on his face, hiding in the rain drops.

"Aieee," came from every voice, not at all in unison. The stings hurt, and they burned, and all of us were in danger.

"Eddie? Can you see?"

"I see fine. I not bit up much. Not like poor Abanil and you."

"Umpira yang." I attempted a joke. (Poor me.)

"Man umpira." Abanil answered, pleased with my Miskito. (Poor you.)

"Let's go, then," Ferlan ordered. We laughed through the burning pain, Eddie pulled the starter rope, and we were off. The rain felt good against the burning. There was no one there to notice our passing, as if we could have been seen. Sometimes the world is no larger than a boat.

Abanil and I sat together, each of us unable to see, each of us burning with uncountable hornet stings. I could feel my skin stretched tight with swelling. I touched my face and felt a balloon. My arms and fingers would scarcely bend. Every rain drop felt like a needle. I bent into the rain and shielded my face with the bill of my cap. I could still breathe, but the swelling in my neck worried me.

"This like the time I lost," I heard Abanil say.

I chuckled. "Got story? You're going to talk story at a time like this?"

He laughed, too, and I was happy to hear it. "Yessar, Mr. Bet. I always got story."

"Okay, Abanil, let's hear it."

"One day I was to the bush searching new ground for plantation. I walk all about all day, and I don't know, but look like I got lated. Night catch me far from Karawala. I find a gamba and make a fire, but rain come and wet the match and put out the fire. Then I know I was in trouble. The smoke keep the mosquito fly gone, but when no smoke, them fella come right to me. I slap and slap and slap all night, and I could hardly breathe, I tell you. When morning come, I see nothing but blood of my own on everything.

"People say when the mosquito fly drink all the blood from a man, can walk the bush for one week time and never see not even one-one. I know I haps to reach Karawala, but look like I gone wrong way. Night catch me again in the bush. From that, I don't remember. Them say they find me on the fip day, running through the bush, screaming like I mad. Clothes all torn off. Skin all cut up from the bush like I got no skin. Them say I run right past, like I never see them, but I don't remember. Must be I running from the fly, them.

"For one month time, I crazy. I got grisi siknis. All I know is fire, like I burning. Like now. From that month, I know I was home, but I don't see nothing but mosquito fly. I don't see no person. My wife and children them was all around, but I never see. I guess I lucky to be live."

"Damn, Abanil, how could you get lost like that? You've lived here all your life."

"Sure is truth, Mr. Bet, but is easy. If you get off the road, the bush is same-same. Can't see the sky. Can't see more than couple feet. Not so hard. Plenty people get lost. Always haps to carry blade and flame. Can live there then."

"You had a flame," I offered, but he said nothing in return. He had been careless. It had cost him his sanity, and it had nearly cost him his life. I tried to imagine a night in the bush with hordes of mosquitoes so thick one could not breathe without sucking them into the nose or mouth. What a horror.

"Well, I'm glad you made it."

"Right now, I not so sure," he laughed, and I laughed with him. We were not too far from anaphylactic shock, but we could laugh.

SUNK

Chapter Twenty-three

Yawanaiska Pura Yumhpa

I'm telling you he's not afraid of anything. If Satan walked in and sat down in front of him, he would be intensely curious, but he would not be afraid – not of death and not of eternal damnation. He said it's fear that kills most people – fear of pain and fear of death. Fear makes you weak and vulnerable.

Halley Stone

They had to lead me up the steps and into bed, and there I stayed for two days before I could open my eyes. At times I was delirious - neither sleeping nor awake, but in a nightmare world of fire. There was a fiesta in Karawala. I could hear it, but I knew that none of the hunters were there to celebrate. We were all in bed. Jane and Miss Pete brought me food and sat with me through the worst of it. As with all ailments, Miss Pete thought a bowl of limes and a medio of Flor de Caña would cure me. I sipped the rum, ate what I could and listened to Jane singing softly while the rain fell.

On the third day, I came out of it none for the worse. I was still puffy, but I could open my eyes, and I had a world class hunger. There must have been some hunger in my eyes when I sat up. Jane looked startled, dug her chin into her breast, blushed deeply and said, "I go now."

She got up and left rather abruptly. I could only wonder what I had done to embarrass her. I stood up and watched her wade away through the rain.

Two more months of nothing but rain, wet clothes and clammy skin might get depressing, not to mention debilitating. I was beginning to understand what it meant to have one hundred eighty inches of rain per year. It was like understanding how many pennies are in a million dollars. They are both incomprehensible to all but those who have actually seen them. Farther south they get up to two hundred fifty inches per year.

Half of me wanted to stay; to see it through the rainy season, giving thanks and krismis. The other half knew I had business to take care of elsewhere. With any luck, I could be back soon.

"Baha'i going soon." Eddie answered my question about a boat to Bluefields. I knew Willy couldn't find Karawala in this soup, let alone land here.

"Baha'i?" I repeated. "There are Baha'i here? Where are they going?"

"Not them. Him. Is the only one. The captain."

"The boat's name is Baha'i?"

No, Mr. Bet. The captain name is Baha'i. Like Poi is Christain, I think, but Poi not Christian like church. Only his name is Christian. Baha'i going leave off soon-soon Thursday from The Bar.

So Thursday morning Eddie, Poi and Ferlan took me to La Barra to catch a boat for Bluefields. Baha'i was just pulling away from the bank when we caught him. I handed my saddlebags up and climbed aboard. There was just enough light in the sky for me to see that I had lots of company. The boat was loaded with cows, pigs and chickens bound for the market.

Bofu, with his red and blue leather cap, grinned at me from atop a cow. I nodded and grinned back. The clatter of the diesel made a better greeting impossible. He pointed the only unoccupied space on the boat: a patch of raised deck by the exhaust stack. I sat. Heat radiated from the stack, making the humidity worse, and diesel fumes poured out of the engine room. At least I was dry. The sides of the boat were open, but there was a roof over my head, and the breeze blew some of the heat and fumes away.

The bar was cross. Vexed. Downright nasty. The Rio Grande has a wide bar that sticks out into the sea a mile or more. In the rainy season the river cuts a channel through it, but it is narrow and shifting. Outside the channel, the water is shallow and the ground swells crush boats. Jumping the bar is tense even in good weather.

We got most of the way out before we lost the channel and crunched into the bottom. It wasn't a bad one, but it did spring a leak. Baha'i's sailors scurried below to stuff cotton into the cracks and bail the bilge. There were ten humans who let out a collective sigh of relief when they came back smiling.

"Is okay for now," sang Maggie La with a big toothless smile. He didn't say it, but we all knew it. The patch might not last.

We cleared the bar and turned south. The seas were close and confused. The chop hit from all sides and rocked the boat in every direction at once. With the heat, the fumes and the unnatural motion, I began to feel uneasy. It wasn't until the cook started breakfast that I got my first taste of seasickness.

Next to the head, at the stern, there was a brazier on the other end of my raised deck. The cook filled it with coal, poured diesel oil on the coal and began trying to light his cook fire. It took most of his damp matches to get it lit. Before the diesel had burned off, he ladled gallo pinto into a pot and sat the pot on the coals. I watched in disbelief, and every time the wind brought the conglomerated smell to me, my stomach rolled.

When the mess was hot, he spooned a pile of it onto a plate, slapped a cold roll on it, and with great pride in his accomplishment, offered the first plate to me. I was gracious. I accepted it and thanked him for the honor. In their turn, my fellow passengers accepted their breakfast and set to it hungrily. I ate, but each bite went down like fevered meat. It was the first and only time I have ever wanted to puke my guts out at sea, but I didn't. I was gracious.

We chugged along at an unbearably slow pace. The wind came up from out of the south and slowed us to a crawl. It took forever to lay Tasbapauni, and as we did, the boat started leaking more. The sailors were kept busy bailing water and stuffing whatever they could into the cracks. It did not look good.

We were not the only ones having trouble. Through the wind and rain and diesel clatter, we heard LaNica's old DC3 fly by just above our exhaust stack. And as it passed, an old suitcase splashed into the water a few yards off our beam. We looked out and saw others falling from the air behind us. We passed more as we went. They were trying to gain altitude by lightening their load.

They were going to crash; we were going to sink. Aside from crowding into the center of the boat to get out of the rain and spray, my fellow passengers seemed unconcerned. Children tried to play, and their mother tried to make them sit still. She had been to see her sister up the river at La Cruz. Everyone else had come from La Cruz. Most of them had something to sell in Bluefields, and this was just part of a day's work.

Bofu remained downright cheerful. The big woman with the children let her brow furrow when an occasional wave broke over the bow and flowed out the scuppers aft. Those were a welcome cleansing of the decks of the dung and urine of the livestock until they became unnervingly frequent.

The wind strengthened and the seas began to build. No longer confused, as is the trademark of shallow seas, they became more like the waves of the open ocean, and instead of being pounded, we began to rise and fall with ever greater amplitude. By the time we laid Set Net Point, the wind was blowing the rain horizontally. To me, it ceased being a question of if - it was when. When she broke apart, would I be able to swim to shore? I took off my boots and shoved them into my saddlebags.

We were holding on to anything that looked solid. The line between the sea and the air was gone. The water just got a little less dense with altitude. We were awash with every wave, and the entire boat shuddered with every collision. Beyond Set Net lay thirty miles of deep water without the protection of reefs. The shoreline dropped away to the west, but we stayed to the south. The wind howled and the rain stung like buckshot. One by one, the cows and pigs and chickens disappeared over the low rail. We surrounded the two children and pressed them into the bulkhead of the pilot house. I braced my head against a post.

Shouting from below, almost unheard, announced the inevitable. A plank, cracked at the bar, had come out. Water gushed into the bilge. As long as we could keep her afloat, the boat was our best bet. I grabbed Bofu and pulled him with me into the engine room, where we each grabbed a bucket and began the futile effort of emptying the bilge of water.

"You could have been born a banker, Bofu," I yelled above the engine noise.

He stopped and looked at me with disbelief. He said something, but I didn't hear it. He shook his head and heaved another bucket up through the hatch.

Between buckets, I yelled. I yelled in anger, in desperation and in defiance.

"You might never have known hunger. You might never have been cold or hot."

I looked at my hands. "You might never have had blisters on your hands."

If anyone heard me, they did not reveal it.

"You could have taken years to die a miserable, lonely decaying death."

"This better?" Bofu asked, stopped for the instant of the question. His voice was strangely loud, as if everything else had been muffled. The sailors stopped to hear the answer.

"Bail!" I yelled. They turned to their buckets, and I answered, "Take my word for it. This is better. If I have to die today, this is a good way to go."

It was dark in the engine room. As the boat pitched and rolled, we banged into each other and everything around us. My hands began to bleed, my body ached, and the salt burned my eyes. We fell to bailing silently, rhythmically swinging the bucket into the water and up through the hatch.

The leak was no longer a geyser. Maggie La had jammed enough rags and cotton into the cracks to hold the plank in place under the weight of his foot. The water began to recede. We laughed and slapped each other on the back. The storm abated, quite suddenly, and we laughed and slapped each other on the back again.

Through the open hatch, we could see the colors of a sunset we couldn't watch. Slowly we bailed, but we could not stop. We heard Baha'i counting his passengers and bemoaning the loss of his cargo. Miraculously, everyone was safe, but only one cow remained on deck, legs wedged under the rail, drowned dead. We rose and fell, but no longer slammed.

The old Lister kept chugging. At midnight, we saw the lighthouse at El Bluff. By one o'clock we tied up at the wharf, stepped off onto solid ground, and watched the boat sink slowly to the bottom of Bluefields Bay.

There was nothing anyone could say or do. We were too tired to bail another bucket of water, and there was no hope for help until the first pangas brought workers from Bluefields in the morning. We staggered to the lee of the aduana building and slumped down to rest.

"Beth?" Bofu surprised me. He used my name.

"Yes?"

"My whole life, I want go to the States. I hear is heaven. Now I hear you say this better. I hongry. I wet. I cold. My bone, them hurt. I fraid to dead. How this better?"

I looked up at the sky. It was clear and moonless, and the stars shone with clarity and brightness unknown in the grungy skies of the industrial world.

"Look up, Bofu. Look at the stars. If you leave here, you have to give up the stars. If you leave here, you have to give up the experience of life for a little bit of comfort. They are trading life for comfort. They are killing the world so they may never be tired or cold or hungry." I looked around me. Their eyes were open. "You would like the safety and comfort. You might even think it was heaven, but it would make me sad to see you go there."

My eyes were heavy. I think I dozed for a moment, until I heard a child moaning.

"They have no life. Everything they have is an illusion, but they are safe, and if something unpleasant happens, they can always blame someone else."

"But you go back."

JORDAN

Chapter Twenty-four

Yawanaiska Pura Walhwal

He feels pain, but not like ordinary people. To him, it's just another sensation. It might be intense, but other sensations are intense - like an orgasm. Pain doesn't have to hurt. It can't hurt unless you fear it. Without fear, it has no power.

Uca Pugila

I had seen him before, walking the streets of Bluefields in his white suit and Panama hat. He seemed old and frail, which he was, and although dressed in white, he was unkempt, and his suit was not quite clean, as if he had no one to care for him. He carried a cane, which sometimes hung from his arm and sometimes steadied him as he walked up steps.

He was intriguing. His dress was unique to the coast, even for the more affluent. Although he seemed not to be engaged in any enterprise or positioned in leadership, he was paid great respect.

I was having breakfast at the Del Queto when he came in. He nodded in my direction and started toward his table. I asked him if he cared to join me, and he accepted with the eagerness of a lonely man.

We introduced ourselves with the customary formalities of Spanish speaking people, and although I could fake the accent of the area fairly well, his next words were in English. "I have been awaiting the pleasure of this meeting for quite some time."

"Oh? Am I a curiosity here?"

"We are all curiosities. A man's life is like a fingerprint; there is no other like it."

I looked into his eyes. The pure white given to us at birth was gone. In its stead were red lines crossing a background of browns and yellows - the colors of fatigue and pain and heady pleasures. In the center, there was a clear black pupil.

"But of course you are a curiosity. White men do not do the things you do. White men go about with armies of other white men to protect them. They do not have the courage to stand alone with us, and to a man, they think of us as savages.

"You, however, walk amongst us without pride, and you think of us as equals. That makes you more than a curiosity. It makes you a hero. You have more protection here than all the armies in the world could offer."

I was embarrassed. I am not a hero, and I told him so.

"Oh, yes, you are. And you are because it is not your ambition. You are because you could have power, but you do not accept it. You are because you could exploit us, but you have not. You are because you are not like every other white man who ever cracked a whip over our heads. You do not feed on our fear."

"How do you know?"

"Everyone knows. Everything you do is known from Puerto Cabezas to Greytown the minute you do it. Everyone knows your name: McBeth Johnson, but it is never spoken. You are Mr. Bet, and children are being named for you in all of the Miskito Kingdom."

"Mr. Jordan, this isn't fair. You know a great deal about me, but I know nothing about you."

"Hah!" He laughed. "My glory was being the highest paid nigger who ever worked on the Panama Canal. I was almost treated like a human being. All I had to do was keep all the other niggers in line and see to the burial of those who died.

After a pause, he added, "I was a traitor."

"Who do you think you betrayed?"

"All the other niggers. We had to stop work on the canal to bury the ones who died of malaria and yellow fever. Thousands of people died, and instead of telling them to run for their lives, I told them to work harder and ignore the fever. It was murder, and I was part of it."

"I'm sorry, Mr. Jordan, but you can't blame yourself. The Americans did it."

"Oh? I hear about the thing they call the Holocaust. They say following orders is no excuse, and they are still hunting the executioners. I have dreams about being caught. In my dreams I am in a Nazi Uniform, and there is a gas chamber in the Darien, and an American is telling me to lead my people into the chamber. I do, and they die, and I must dig a grave for each of them. And when the canal is complete, and I have buried the last nigger, they come for me, and I am thrown into the chamber, the last to die."

I needed to crawl inside myself and join the faceless voices. My ancestors were the executioners. This old, frail black man having breakfast with me had just informed me that we are all Nazis. Scrape away the veneer, and the core was the same. I felt sick.

"There is no difference between the guilt you feel and the guilt I must accept for what we did to you."

"No, Mr. Johnson, you had nothing to do with it. You are not the same."

I started to object, but he stopped me.

"The same thing happened here in Bluefields with bananas and lumber, and the same thing has happened everywhere the Americans have come. That is why you are our hope. That is why the King is watching you."

"The King?"

"You are in the Miskito Kingdom. On the map, it says we are Nicaragua, but we still have a King, and we are a Kingdom, and no Spaniard can take it away from us."

"But you are not Miskito. Why do you say, 'we'?"

"Because this is the land of my birth, and I will never be a Nicaraguan. I have a King. We all have a King, and one day, somehow, the map will be changed."

"Who is the King? Where is he?"

"If Somoza's people knew, they would kill him. When the time is right, you will know."

"Why are you telling me this? Why is the King watching me?"

"Because you are McBeth Johnson, and you are not like anyone else. Because tigers and snakes cannot kill you. Because you have been to Hill Pauni. Because you sleep in Orinoco. Because you stand alone, drink casusa and play baseball."

He stood. "Somoza is watching, too." And he walked away.

*

I finished my work, and in the evening, instead of seeking the company and enticements of Sunshine Down, I sought A. L. Jordan. He was sitting alone, in the empty dining room of the Del Queto, in the dim twilight, sipping a glass of Flor de Caña and sucking on a lime. He smiled and motioned me to sit across from him.

"I was hoping you would come."

"I was hoping to find you here."

He poured a healthy shot for me and slid the glass across the table. "Let's take these up to my house," and he stood.

Sr. Queto was coming in to turn on the lights as we were leaving. "No need," Mr. Jordan said with a nod.

On the street, we turned west, toward the last hint of orange in the sky, and walked up the hill past the old colonial mansions that were the homes of the banana and lumber barons. They still stood, but they were bare of paint, the columns were split, and planks turned up ski-like on the wide verandas. At the last one, he stopped at the walk and faced it.

"Is mine."

I looked. The light was too dim. All I could see was the outline of a once grand facade. I couldn't think of anything to say.

"I told you I was paid well. There was nothing to spend it on, so I brought it all back here. Tons of it. Sometimes I think I left myself there and brought back nothing but money. Come in, please."

Inside, he lit a kerosene lamp, and we sat in cushioned couches and set our drinks on an old mahogany table: all furniture from a distant past. The yellow glow lit old tapestries on the walls of a large, high-ceilinged room. We sat and sipped in silence, drawn to the flame in the lamp, like moths. Ceiling fans hung motionless, like propellers on airplanes that couldn't fly.

"Do you live here alone?"

"Yes, alone, like you. We are born alone, and we die alone, but I was lucky once."

"How so?"

"I wed the most beautiful person on earth."

"And when was that?"

"Before Panama. When she died, I could not bear to be here. Everything I saw reminded me of her. Everything we shared struck my heart like a lightning ball. I had to leave. I heard they needed men in Panama." He leaned forward, cupped his hand over the lamp, and blew it out. We were in total darkness, perhaps to hide the tears.

"I'm sorry. How long were you married?"

"One year. The only good year in my life."

"How did she die?" He seemed not to mind to talk about it.

"Malaria and childbirth. I lost them both. I have never seen or felt more pain in all my life. Not even in the thousands I buried in Panama.

"But I had that year with her. We were one person, and that was greater wealth even than Somoza has. It made my life worth living, and it makes my death trivial."

"I hope I can find that.

"Oh, Mr. Johnson," he said, "You have never been married?"

"No, Mr. Jordan, I have not."

"I envy you that," he said. "You have something ahead of you that makes my old age a sadness."

"Why?" I asked.

"Because it is a part of life I can never have again, and it is perhaps the greatest thing that can happen to a man."

I could hardly see him in the darkness, but I could feel him. I wanted to hear what his ninety years had to say.

"I've been in love before," I said.

"Yes, I'm sure you have. And you will be again. Perhaps the next time will be it; perhaps not. But some day you will have it."

"Have what?"

"The greatest, most beautiful thing a man can find. That is the thing I regret about being so old. I look at the young folk, and I see them look at each other the way only young folk can, and that is the only thing I regret. I don't even regret the coming of death.

"There is a paradise here on earth, and we walk through it every day, but until we have two pair of eyes to see it with, we are blind to it. And when we have the two pair of eyes, and we see what has been there all along, we lay claim to a great kingdom.

"That is the glory. When you find the only one who could ever be for you, and you swallow your fear of her and begin to court her, and she responds, then you will know my sadness. But you will be so high up in the clouds that you will not feel it; you will only know it. What you will feel is the real earth and the real being, and it will be as if you had never been alive before."

He fell silent, and I thought. We sat for a long while, and although my eyes were open, I saw nothing. It was too dark. I drifted off so far I forgot where I was or who I was with. When he spoke again, it startled me.

"You have much of life yet to discover. I have only death."

I hadn't thought of Hanover Stone or the CIA or revolution since Halley took off with Papa Kilo, but when I stepped out of the Del Queto the next morning, there was an American Marine waiting for me on the veranda. The hair stood up on the back of my neck.

He sneered and said, "Good morning, Mr. Johnson, or should I call you Mr. Bet?" His disposition was openly hostile.

"Sir will do." I had met him in Managua, after the earthquake, but he was innocuous then. Now he was more than a man in a uniform. He was a hunter, and I was his prey. If this attack had been serious, we wouldn't be standing in broad daylight.

"Other way around, asshole."

"Your name, please."

"Northrup."

"Well, Captain Northrup, deliver your message, and then get out of my way."

"You're consorting with the enemy."

"Enemy?!" I looked around. "What are you talking about?"

"Jordan. He's a revolutionary, and you know it."

I shook my head. He must be playing out a farce. "You're afraid of a tiny, frail, ninety year old man? Are there boogey men under your bed? Does your mummy tuck you in at night and chase away the ghosts?"

"Don't push your luck, asshole. I'll tear you apart."

"You won't do shit, Northrup. You'll send someone else to do it for you."

"What did Jordan say?"

"He said all the men he ever buried were better men than you."

"Have it your way, Johnson. I asked. That's all I was sent to do."

"Whoever sent you broke the rules."

"Stone's rules? Stone does as he's told and keeps his mouth shut. He can't help you." He turned and walked toward the Guardia station.

Who do you believe? No one. The best I could hope for was to stay out of their way. I saw no evidence of revolution. I knew of no enemy. How could it be that I could live alone in the middle of the jungle and fear nothing but American soldiers? What has gone wrong?

Why was a Marine Captain in Bluefields? What was he doing at the Guardia station? I should never have known or cared, but he forced it on me. I resented him for involving me in his sordid little game. He was a large boy playing army, and he was dangerous. I threw it off. I went to the airport and climbed into LaNica's old DC3.

SNOOK CREEK

Chapter Twenty-five

Yawanaiska Pura Matsip

I couldn't see them at first. He would show me where a snook was, but I couldn't see them. That's because I was looking for a fish. He told me to watch the water. He said everything changes its medium as it moves. Fish change the water. You can tell what kind of fish it is and how big it is by the way it changes the water. I can see it now. I'm no longer a rookie.

Halley Stone

Dusty got off the plane with a big grin on his face, came stomping up to me, grabbed a handful of my hair with each hand and demanded, "Are we going to catch fish?"

"More than you imagined," I answered, "and if you had any hair at all, I'd jerk it out. Let go."

Dusty was no spring chicken, and neither were Mack and Harry, but they were bouncing around like kids. Rob was young enough to bounce if his weight had let him. It was time to fish. It was time to get shed of the weight of business and the nightly news.

For Mack, it was time to get shed of the weight of his shoes. He looked at my feet. They were bare. He grinned and kicked his shoes off, looked around for a pair of feet like his and handed them to a man in the crowd. It was a gift that made two men happy.

"The river looks muddy, Beth," Dusty worried.

"It's sometimes muddy in September, but we're not going to fish in the river."

"Oh? Where, then?

"Snook Creek. Karas Laya. The surf at the bar."

When I had first sold them on coming to Karawala, it was the river I had told them about. They wanted snook and only snook, and the muddy river was disappointing. They feared a busted trip, but I knew better.

It was raining when we set out. The sun was still below the horizon, and my party was wet, cold and grumpy. They sat hunched over in their slickers with their backs to the rain. When they looked up, it was to scowl. The rain stopped and the sky broke as the bow began to rise and fall with the low rollers at the bar. We came out of our slickers and looked to the dawn.

There were deep blues and purples where the heavy clouds lay, and there was pure gold and flaming pink lining patches of infinite turquoise. If there is anyone on earth who can scowl at a show like that, he should be weighted and sent to the abyss with a corn cob up his ass. No one spoke, and no one looked away. It makes no difference how many dawns one has seen; they are all reason enough to get out early.

Eddy turned her north along the beach. There were no breakers: no white in the surf. The splashes of feeding fish were everywhere. Spanish mackerel schooled and fed just yards from the beach. A little farther out were acres of little tunny and blackfin tuna churning the water. Among them all were yet bigger and bigger fish, and all were eating and being eaten. The grumpies were forgotten.

Children lined the beach and waved as we passed Sandy Bay. We made a wide circle around men standing in dories and straining at heavy cast nets.

"What are they catching?" Mack asked.

"Chacalin," Eddie answered. And at the puzzled response, "Camarones. Shrimps. We catch coming back."

Snook creek is about ten miles north of the Rio Grande Bar. It is a narrow, shallow inlet patrolled by sharks on the outside and mined with logs half buried in the sand on the bar. One has to ride the crest of a wave to get in. Our passengers grew visibly nervous when they saw what we were up to. Rob was the least confident. "If we get in, we'll never get out. At least if we don't drown, we can walk home."

"You're not in danger. We might take a hit, but we'll make it." I wanted to tell them Karas Laya was worse, but I stuffed it.

We made it without incident. When the surf is up, it is dangerous, and we get excited, but the surf is never up in September, and this was easy. September is the month without wind, with the exception of the screaming squalls called *corre coyote*. They come out of the east without warning and are gone as fast. When they hit, they turn the sea into a stampede of white horses. But they are unusual, and they can be dealt with. One simply puts up with a few minutes of drenching, blinding pandemonium.

Eddie has an uncanny sense of timing, and he can read nuances in the water that few can see. We hung out until the right wave came along. We caught it and rode it in.

Running an unprotected bar is a sport unto itself and is not unlike surfing. This little bar offered little challenge, but I came to enjoy the adrenaline rush, the speed and the power of being at the helm on the Rio Grande Bar. That is life on the edge.

Once inside, we pulled the boat up on the sand and got out. The snook, I explained, might be stacked up on the outside, waiting to come in, or they could be inside, lined up against the current, feeding on whatever the tide swept in. We split up. Rob and Harry waded into the surf on the outside; the rest of us waded upstream.

The first casts produced nothing. The week before, when Eddie and Ferlan and I had first fished the creek, red and white Mirro Lures and Wiggle Divers had caught fish. They had worked so well we didn't try anything else. They had worked so well we went home when the snook were still feeding. But this time, after thirty minutes, we still hadn't caught a fish. No one had even gotten a strike. I thought about changing baits. I

327

wondered if the week before had been a fluke.

I was a hundred yards up the creek in waist deep water, pressed against the mangroves. I couldn't wade any farther. Dusty and Mack were not far behind. Cast after cast, no one asked, "When are they going to bite?" There were no accusing sidelong glances. They understood, but still I fretted.

What if? I depend on fish. I depend on the weather. If either of them fails me, even though I am not held at fault, I have lost those at hand and all they talk to. If I am indifferent to both, it is because I live here. They are here for only a week, and each day is opportunity fulfilled or lost. They have no time for indifference. They have no time to lose, and I have only time. I cannot lose it, I cannot squander it, and I cannot understand why anyone would choose to be bound by it. There is plenty to go around.

I saw the water change near the far bank, and I heaved a Wiggle Diver at it. As I took the slack out, the water boiled and a snook lunged for the open sea with my hook in his mouth. A minute later we had three snook on, and we were waving and shouting at Rob and Harry to join us.

Men are awkward waders. They cannot hop into the air and take flight like a heron. Their feet do not slip easily through the water, even as do those of hippopotami, and if they are in a hurry, what little gracefulness that can be ascribed to humankind is lost in comedy. Seeing three rods bent, the two charged for the beach, each grasping a rod in one hand and thrashing in waist deep water, looking for all the world like two giant coils coming unwound and churning out of control in our direction.

We turned to our fish and soon had them landed, unhooked and released. The bite was on. An unheard voice had declared that it was time to eat, and all creatures obeyed. On land, in the air and in the sea, all obeyed. The hunters were hunting.

If it is the time of day, the time is always changing. If it is the tide, the only thing we know is that it is usually not the slack tide. It is not always the flood, it is not always the ebb, and it is not always the strongest current, but it is almost never the slack. There are those who claim to know, but if they did, their tables would lead us to fish but an hour or two a day. If I knew, the fishermen of this earth would pay me handsomely for my knowledge.

We do not know why. We only know that a switch is flipped and fish that can be seen but not caught suddenly become voracious. Fish that will move out of the way of a lure in one hour will not let it pass in the next. Many times in many places I have thought, *there are no fish here*, when in fact the place was full of fish, and all it took to catch them was the right hour of day.

For years, I kept records of the moon and tides and time of day, but in all I found, I never found the key. I found only that what I thought I knew was only a hunch, and the fish swam through my hunches as through my dreams. If anything at all held up to probability, it is that there will probably be an hour or two in the first half of the day and an hour or two in the second when the fish will eat anything that hits the water.

This was one of them. Eddie and Ferlan kept busy unhooking fish and rigging lines. Some of them couldn't be stopped in their charge up the river or out to sea, and we were left with our arms trembling and limp, our mouths agape and a bewilderment and wonder at the size of fish it must have taken to do such a thing. Some of them we saw when they came out of the water; some of them we heard when their tails sucked air into the creek. They were thirty, forty and fifty pound snook, and with casting tackle and twenty pound test line, all we could do was watch the spool shrink until something broke.

Most of those we caught were under twenty-five pounds. The smallest were about five pounds. There were few casts that didn't draw a strike.

The fish began to move slowly upstream. As the downstream edge of the school played out, we waded up. A few yards at a time, we moved. I was on the upstream edge, where the water deepened and the mangroves crowded the bank. As the fish moved, I was forced into deeper water by the mangroves. But I was not to be stopped by chest deep water. There looked to be an opening just a few yards farther upstream, where I could stand and cast. I made for it.

As I rounded the mangrove and looked into the opening, I found myself face to face with a startled young soldier. We both gasped, and my heart tried to get out through my throat. I saw two of his comrades running away toward the beach. The boy's eyes were blue. He must have been Cuban, and they must have been a reconnaissance squad. He carried a pistol at his side; I was unarmed, but before the thought of danger came to me, he turned and fled after his friends.

Why were they there, and what was I going to do about it? Nothing, obviously. I would not even tell my party. Why concern them? If they meant harm, we would already have been harmed. I watched them go, but even as they disappeared, the malevolence of arms lingered and contaminated my peace. Whoever they were, wherever they came from, they were the agents of war, and they troubled me. No good could come of this.

I felt anger. The ugliest and most horrible of all man's inventions had intruded on the indefensible. My anger fell to a sense of helplessness, and it to bewilderment. What stood here that could prompt an invasion? Was this wilderness and its people to be destroyed simply because they were here? The irrational can't make sense.

I took a deep breath and heaved a Wiggle Diver across the river.

"There you are," Dusty called. "We thought you'd fallen into a hole."

"Just taking a breather," I answered. I couldn't see them, but above the hiss of the surf, I could hear the whir of the reels when they cast, I could hear the fish churn the surface and rattle their gills, and I could hear their excitement. I knew where they were, and I knew what they were doing. I knew that they were into the best snook fishing of their lives.

I remained uneasy and watched the path of retreat as closely as I watched the river. But even as the threat hung over me, I smiled. Just as they had their fish hooked, I had them hooked. Tomorrow, I thought. Tomorrow is Karas Laya.

I felt the heat before I heard the thunder. As a warning, the temperature rose and the air turned prickly. I turned and saw a black wall out to sea. Corre coyote. Run like hell, coyote. By the time you see one of these squalls, it is almost upon you. I waded back around the mangroves. Eddie was already piling things into the boat.

"Get back to the boat," I commanded. "We've got to get to shelter."

Mack continued fighting a big snook. As I passed him, I pulled a knife and cut his line. "No time for that," I said. "Get to the boat."

He wasn't happy about it, but he did as he was told. We motored up the creek until we found a thick clump of palms hanging over the water. We pulled the boat under them and waited, lodged between the bank and the overhanging fronds.

The storm was quick upon us. First the wind began bending the trees and whipping the water. Nuts, small and large, pounded the leaves above us. Leaves blew away without falling to the ground; branches fell crashing around us. We struggled into rain suits as the rain began falling.

It came like bullets, but most of it was deflected by the palms. The sound was furious. The wind howled, the thunder boomed and debris hurled down all around us. A coconut crashed through the palms and into the boat. All we could do was hold to the branches and keep our backs to the rain. A storm surge lifted the water of the little creek, and our boat was shoved up into the palms, forcing us to lay flat in the boat. It was not comfortable, but unless one of us took a direct hit, it was not dangerous. There was even a little joking going on.

"One helluva guide you are, Beth."

"Yeah, leave it to a guide to put you into the wind, into the sun or into a storm."

"At least we caught fish."

"Damn straight. Now all we have to do is get out alive."

"Do the fish bite in this shit? Can we doodle-sock in here?"

"Try it. Drop a bait off the stern."

There was a little open water there, so Rob squirmed his way aft with a rod and dropped a 72M11 into the water. He jigged it twice, and it was taken. Cheers went up, but they were short lived. Whatever it was took him into the roots and cut him off.

"Rig me up, Ferlan," he laughed. "I'm not done catching."

Ferlan was a bit nonplussed. "You going fish more? Can't catch in here."

"Damn straight. Rig me up."

Ferlan did as instructed, this time with a big Boone Tout. "Sink faster," he said as he dropped it in the water.

The storm still raged, but our attention was on Rob and the little patch of open water off the stern. Again, the bait was in the water but a few moments before it was hit.

"I'll be a ring tail tooter," Dusty proclaimed. "Gimme a rod. I didn't come down here to watch some fat kid catch fish while I cower down from a storm."

Eddie whacked some of the low fronds with a machete and soon there was room for all of them to fish, and the fish were hungry. I could feel the thunder against my skin. The lightning was blinding. The wind rocked us against the bank, the roots and the fronds, and these guys were fishing. It made my heart warm.

They didn't catch anything. Every fish broke off on something, but they had fun trying, and it kept them from bellyaching about the storm. My secret hope was that the soldiers had taken to the sea and were drowned by now. And then my stomach churned. I had wished death on some mother's son, when he was nothing but a servant.

Thirty minutes seemed like forever, but that's all it took for the squall to move inland. As suddenly as it began, it was gone, and we were left with dead calm and a pewter sky. We pulled ourselves out of the palms and returned to the mouth.

We were all a bit bedraggled, but we went back to fishing. No luck. The switch was flipped off. We tried upstream. We tried trolling to find fish, but they had quit, and there was no way of knowing when they would start again.

The stream had fallen again to normal level. "Maybe they went out with the surge," Mack suggested. Harry concurred. We tried the surf. Same result. No fish.

"Time for lunch," I suggested. "Let's head back."

"Fine by me," all agreed.

We had enough fish. We had kept only those that would have died from the hook or the stress. I looked into the fish wells and saw enough snook to feed the village. They were no more than ten percent of those we landed. The keep was bragging size for a lifetime, both in size and in numbers. The feed would put smiles on many faces.

The surf that had pounded the beach during the storm was now placid. We motored out without a hitch and headed south. No one spoke. We were tired, and the tired was catching up with us.

The fishermen at Sandy Bay had gone ashore before the storm and had not returned. Children lined the beach to wave, but the men were busy drying nets and heading shrimp.

"We going stop?" Eddie asked.

"Might as well," I answered. "Catch some chacalin."

We moved in close to the beach. Eddie killed the motor and went to the bow with a cast net. Ferlan picked up a paddle. We drifted. Sometimes the shrimp make it easy. One can see clouds of sandy water where they dig into the bottom, one can see them flipping on the surface, or one can see fish charging through them. Everywhere we looked, the water was sandy and shrimp were scratching the surface.

Eddie threw the net, and it splashed down in a perfect circle.

It sank slowly, and when he was sure it was on the bottom, he began to tuck it with short tugs until the net was closed. And then he began to lift. The line tightened, and Eddie strained against it, but he couldn't lift it. The bone and top half of the net were out of the water. We could see shrimp at the surface. The rest of the net was full of shrimp. It was too heavy to lift.

Eddie looked at me and laughed nervously. "Can't lift."

I grinned. What a predicament. "I guess you'll have to let some out."

'Letting some out' was tantamount to throwing money into the sea. It was something that would be next to impossible for anyone on this coast. I thought immediately of a monkey grasping a banana inside a bottle. The only way to get the hand out of the bottle is to let go of the banana, but the monkey can't let go. The difference is that we are human. We think. We await a solution.

He wasn't going to give up easily. "Ferlan, come help."

Ferlan went to the bow, and both of them heaved. "You're going to tear the net, Eddie." I warned.

Our fishermen were watching intently. Mack got up and went to the bow. "Let an old shrimper help. I gotta see this thing spilled in the bottom of this boat."

Then there were three, and three couldn't lift it. It was a twelve foot net, and I guessed it might have had more than two hundred pounds of shrimp in it. Three men should be able to lift two hundred pounds, but they were standing on the deck of a boat that was rising and falling in a gentle surf, and they were trying to haul that load up against the side of the boat with a quarter inch rope. It wasn't going to happen.

But we were not alone. Children from Sandy Bay had seen us and were gathering on the beach by the boat. They laughed and cheered and shouted encouragement and suggestions, all in Miskito. Others had seen, too. Men. Men who knew the importance of a full net. As Eddie, Ferlan and Mack held to the net and wondered what to do, I saw men running toward us, and they were carrying planks.

"Gangplanks?" Rob asked. "Are they going to board us? How many people do they think can hold on to a quarter inch rope?"

"I don't think those are gangplanks," I offered. "I think we're going to get those shrimp into the boat."

I moved to the stern and took the helm. "Hang on, Eddie. I'm going to move her in to the beach."

Slowly, we moved the great ball of shrimp toward the beach and the waiting men with the planks. When we were close to waist deep water, they waded in. They brought the planks under the net and settled the weight on three of them.

"All right, now. We going do it." And with a great heave from above and below, the net and all its shrimp and the boards and the men all spilled into the *Mupi Tara* at once. Oh, what a load it was. Cheers went up all around, from the beach and the boat, we cheered the landing of the net with arms raised. Having done what they came to do, the men with the planks, smiling broadly, waded to the beach, waved and walked away.

Drifting with the current, we looked at our catch. Shrimp and small fish covered the decks. They were the big brown shrimp that sell as *camarones gigantes*. Maybe six count or better. Sprat, snook fry, drum and all sorts of other small fish flipped about in the shrimp. It was a mixture of wonder. The longer we looked, the more we found, and like children, we sorted through the catch until we were satisfied that we had seen everything that came up in the net. There were seahorses and nudibranchs in the sargassum. A little flounder no bigger than an elm leaf came from the bottom. There were crabs and green shrimp and white shrimp and shrimp with little red spots.

And there were seven hungry men in the boat. Our sense of wonder satisfied for the moment, we made our way to Karawala. There was enough seafood in the bottom of the boat now to feed everyone in the village for days. Ferlan began heading the shrimp as we got under way. He quickly found that it took two hands to head one shrimp, they were so big, and every time he uncovered something new, he held it up for us to see.

Miss Pete greeted us with a smile as great as her girth. "I knew you was catching. I knew from how you was not here at mid-day. What you catch?"

"Mupi, mupi, mupi. And chacalin. Everyone is going to eat today."

We plopped down into the wooden rockers in the big house and Jane brought us all a cold Victoria. We were hot, grimy and caked with salt, but thirst had priority over a shower.

Word passed quickly that we had brought snook and shrimp, and children raced each other to be first in line at the wharf when Eddie and Ferlan started giving it out. They shrieked and laughed as they ran down the field, past the big house and down the path to the river. Men and women followed with buckets and big calabash bowls and anything else that might hold a few pounds of shrimp, and they all returned with all they could carry.

*

Karas Laya. Alligator Creek. The mouth is as far south of the bar as Snook Creek is north. But Karas Laya is a narrow creek through a tunnel in the mangrove swamp that winds a mile or so to its lagoon. We jumped the Rio Grande bar at first light, and the sun was barely up in a cloudless blue sky when we rose with a ground swell and let it surf us across the narrow bar and into the creek.

Humans rarely go to Karas Laya. It is only open during the rainy season, when high water washes over the beach and erodes a cut, and even then it is too difficult to make the effort worthwhile. The animals rarely see people, and so their fear is diminished. They are still wary, but one can get almost close enough to the birds to touch them.

It is a perfect nursery for snook, tarpon and shrimp. When the cut opens, snook swim in to spawn. The tides carry larval shrimp and tarpon in clouds so thick as to make the water appear roiled. When the rains stop, wave action sands the cut closed, and the lagoon nurtures the fry until the rains come again and the current washes them out to sea.

An outboard is useless in the creek. We paddled and pulled our way through, chopping deadfalls as we went. Save an occasional curse for the mosquitoes and the breathless, humid heat, my guests were silent, enraptured by a pristine and ominously wild setting. Prop roots reached up and aerial roots hung down in an endless tangle amid the shiny wet boles. Tiger bitterns and night herons squawked warnings as we approached and took flight only at the last moment. The water ahead bulged as impossibly big fish moved grudgingly out of their lairs and away from our intrusion. In the swamp, we heard moaning sounds from unseen creatures, and when they asked, Eddie could only shrug his shoulders. "Must be ghost." We were not feared; we were resented.

In the few places where we could use the motor, the prop sucked the water from under the boat and the roots, making the creek shallower. Water poured out of the swamp in little waterfalls as we passed. When Eddie cut the motor again, the boat was lifted by a surge of returning water.

The creek widened and opened onto the lagoon. An oyster bar stretched in a crescent from shore to shore about fifty yards in front of us. On either side of the bar, with their fins out of the water, sawfish were digging up oysters with their long, flat, tooth-rimmed bills and crunching the shells between the bony plates that line the mouth. They rolled and dug, curled and jerked. Most were over ten feet long, and some were fifteen. They ignored us even as we came alongside them, as if we were just something else come for a meal.

As we began to cross, the keel scraped and then dug in.

"Haps to we going push," Ferlan said as he put on his rubber boots. He hopped out, with me and Eddie following.

Our guests did not offer to help, and I would not have

allowed it if they had. A sting ray the size of a poker table stirred up out of the mud and flapped away. We pushed and pulled, and the big mahogany boat scooted across the bar one yard at a time.

"What do we use in here, Beth?" Dusty asked.

"They're going to hit anything that moves," I replied. "If you want some fun, tie on a Spook and walk it across the surface. Or you can just jig off the side of the boat."

"Jig off the side of the boat!?" Came incredulous replies.

Rob stuck his rod tip into the water. "It's only three feet deep here."

I nodded. "They've already eaten everything in the lagoon. They're hungry."

"I don't believe it," he retorted, reaching for a Mirro Lure.

Mack stepped up on the bow deck and let fly a Spook. Boom! A big snook hit it, knocking it clear of the water. When it fell, another hit it, and another, until one of them got it stuck in his mouth. I saw it hit; it was a big one, between thirty and forty pounds, and it took off across the lagoon without turning or slowing.

"We've got to chase it!" Mack yelled. "God damn, this is a big fish! Crank up the motor!"

"Which one are we going to chase?" I asked nonchalantly, nodding at Rob. He had dropped his lure off the side of the boat, jigged it twice, and his snook was already fifty yards away and running.

I reached into a bag and pulled out two bulk spools of line. "We've only got about six thousand yards of line with us. You guys had better turn some fish," I grinned.

There was no on/off switch that day. The snook hit and fought until my fishermen sat down and quit, exhausted and burned by a scorching sun. Soaked with sweat and too weak to catch another fish, they leaned back and panted. Several of the snook were over fifty pounds, and they were no match for casting tackle. Broken lines and empty spools were all we could show for them. The biggest in the boat went thirty-five pounds.

"There are world record fish in here," Harry said in a quiet, matter of fact voice. "I had one on."

I nodded. "I tell people about it, but no one believes me."

"I wouldn't have, either." They all nodded.

"And no one will believe us when we get back," Dusty said. "They'll come into the store, sit in my office and ask how it went, but they won't believe it. Hand me the water."

"No more," Eddie said from the stern, where he sat paddling us toward the oysters. I saw fatigue in his eyes, too. We were done. We would rest all the way. He had more than a mile of paddling ahead of him and a twenty-mile stint at the helm.

"We're out of water?"

"All done. Sun sharp."

"We drank five gallons of water?" Rob asked. "And my mouth is dry?"

"Can drink here," Ferlan offered, waving a hand at the lagoon. "Sweet."

No one took him up on it, even though it was safe.

The sun and tide were high when we crossed the oysters. No need to drag the boat. Eddie held up a burlap sack and asked, half-heartedly, "Want oysters?"

It was two o'clock in the afternoon, and we were beat. No one wanted oysters.

"We're here, guys, and this is the only oyster bar. If you want fresh oysters tonight, now is the time."

No takers. The only thing anyone wanted was a cold shower and a nap. Once Ferlan had tasted horseradish sauce and oysters, he could eat a whole gunny sack by himself, but even he had no interest. It was one of the few times I had seen Ferlan dog-ass tired. I guess it was the sun.

*

Dinner that night was quiet. The jokes, the banter and the friendly pricks were absent. I had overdone it. I took them too far, too long, and I had defeated them with fish. There can be excess, even with catching fish, and my crew and my guests had seen excess. I worried. The table was set with a feast. There was fried snook, baked snook and fricasseed snook, mashed potatoes, squash, cabbage, plantain, cassava, and a lobster and heart of palm salad to die for. But even after a siesta, the batteries were run down. The wine was poured sparingly.

"We won't be getting up early tomorrow, Beth," Dusty announced. "In the last two days, we've caught more snook than a man should be allotted in a lifetime. I'm bushed. Don't wake us. And don't start that damn light plant at four in the morning."

They were burnt, their lips were crusted, and they were listless. I didn't argue. They had done it. They had three more days of fishing, but if they wanted a day to recover, it was fine by me.

"Whatever suits you just tickles me to death," I said as they filed out the door.

I knew it would not always be like that.

I sat up, nursing a rum and puro, while Miss Pete and the girls finished the dishes. It was my job to turn the light plant off each night. It was my pleasure to pull the master switch and bring about a profound darkness and to hear the diesel wind down in decompression until the silence rushed in to fill the void. Each night, I could not help but smile at the simple beauty of what I'd done. Kerosene lanterns, not strong enough to escape the cabins, glowed where tired fishermen might still be awake, and sometimes I could hear low voices but not the words that conveyed the thoughts.

"Look, now. Someone coming," Jane motioned toward a triplet of lights bobbing our way from the village. "Haps to you going protect we."

"Oh, Jane, if they meant harm, we wouldn't know they were coming. They wouldn't have torches." It is still an amazement that darkness generates fear so easily. If darkness can strike a chill, then can't I do the same with its cover? I think so. I think we all can if we use it.

If there were bumps in the night while the girls were still there, it was always at that point that I would have to take out the Hi-power and chamber a round. It kept them from panic and perhaps from mutiny. They were certain that there was no terror I could not dispatch with ease. I was perfect safety.

Ferlan called from a safe distance. "Oh, boss, is me, Ferlan."

"Come in, Ferlan, and tell me what brings your tired bones to me at this late hour."

"What that?" Came his reply.

"Nothing, Ferlan. Just the rum. Come in."

With him were Narcisso and Abanil. They were clearly worried. Ferlan looked at the floor and shuffled his feet. Narcisso's smile was gone. "Boss?" Narcisso spoke for them. "We were to the bight today, at the haulover. You know the place. To Ralph place."

"Yes, I know it."

"There is Cubians there, boss. We came up to them close. They got blue eyes and guns. Them is Cubians, not Guardia. Guardia never come this side."

I nodded. Kukra Hill was the last post.

"What happened? Was anyone hurt? Did they say anything?"

"Notin, notin. They just turn and go. But, boss, why? Why Cubians here?"

"I don't know, Narcisso. How many were there?"

"Not so much. Mebbe eight."

"Soldiers?"

"Yessir. Is trute. Them was soldiers. Military man."

Two squads in the same day. And for every squad seen, how many more? Why were they here?

"Boss? We hear the Sandinistas going kill Somoza. They say the Cubians going help. They say they going kill us, too."

"Oh, Narcisso, I don't think they can do that. Jimmy Carter won't let that happen. No way is he going to turn this country over to Castro or communists."

"Sandinistas say they going take our land."

"Where did you hear this?"

"Is on the radio. They got, how you say it? Radio contrabando."

"Where?"

"Can't say. Always moving. Haps to they hide."

I didn't say anything about the squad I'd seen, and I did my best to appear casual about it, but in truth, my emotions were playing hell with me.

"What else do they say? The Sandinistas?"

"They going take all from Somoza and give it to the people. Only we they going kill."

"But why? That doesn't make sense."

"They say we all Somocistas. We friends to Somoza."

"Is that right?"

"He doesn't bother we. I guess so."

Abanil hadn't said anything. I looked at him.

"That right, Mr. Bet. We always like Somoza because he leave us be. We only want we alone, and he give us that. He don't give us nothing else, but he give us that, and he never take from we. Is a good thing, that. We don't want no Spaniards here."

"No, sir," Narcisso agreed. "Them is cross. Mannish. Always vexed. Better they stay next side."

And, I thought, disrespectful, discourteous, denigrating and contemptuous of the people here. I had seen it. If the Sandinistas routed Somoza, they would rape, pillage and plunder this entire coast. My belly knotted.

The people who fought for the Sandinistas had no ideology other than desperation. If someone convinced them that Somoza was the reason for their poverty and their oppression, then they would hate Somoza. If they were promised riches when he was gone, then they would fight. But as I saw in the eyes of the soldier on the beach, the fear of death doesn't take sides.

I sat up late into the night trying to make some sense of it, but always came back to the irrational. America has poured money into Nicaragua for more than a century. In all we spent, and in all the blood we let, we did nothing but enrich the puppets and a few Americans. We grew fruit, harvested timber and mined gold. We gave Vanderbilt a safe place to make a dollar.

Nothing about it makes sense. Why should we tax all Americans to make a handful of Americans obscenely wealthy? Why would our government spend more in this little republic than a handful of wealthy Americans could reap from it?

I took my rum and my puro to the porch. I sat on a tread and looked up to the stars. "This is inviolate," I said aloud. There was no answer other than the chorus of frogs behind me. A goatsucker began its ascendancy and climaxed in relief. I was the only living creature who had a fix on the desolation and madness that hovered above the trees, and my fix was mostly suspicion. Beyond this village, there was nothing I could trust. Beyond this village lay nothing trustworthy, unless it is void of human life.

In all I thought, I always returned to one conclusion: there is nothing here to attack. It makes no sense. Why not attack an ocean? Why not attack a rock? But I knew. I couldn't let it in, but I knew. Oceans and rocks don't die. They had to attack something they could kill, and what better to kill than a people with no defense? No risk. Life is life. Kill them all. Women and children first.

I went to my bed to sleep, but I was too troubled. Human history is the story of continuous worldwide war. Our achievements are our perfections in the machines of death. It is the twisted nightmare of our reality. We strive to perfect the methods of murder. What can be said of an intelligence whose history is war, whose economy is war and whose warlords govern? We are only slightly more advanced than a pack of snarling dogs. Our refinements serve only as camouflage. We are the species. Ours is not to protect ourselves from them; it is to control the planet and reap its fruits.

And in all, the most baffling consideration was the succession of minds so choked with greed that conquest by blood was the only thing they could come up with. It is a succession of the least of all the minds. All the world has allowed them to dominate. All the world has slaughtered and been slaughtered in their bidding. Those we deem a threat to society are locked up. All but the warlords, who we place in power and revere as leaders.

How long would it be, I wondered, before the sounds of the bush were replaced by the sounds of the guns? When would I have to flee, and to where?

BYRDIE

Chapter Twenty-six

Yawanaiska Pura Matlalkanbi

I knew him before he came here. He's never been so gaga over a woman in his life. The others were comfortable places to rest his eyes and sensuous flesh to stoke his fires, but he could do without them. Not so this one. Without her, he would founder.

Uca Pugila

"Yankee November One Papa Kilo, this is Yankee November Four Hotel Whiskey. Hello, Willy. Over."

"Yankee November Four Hotel Whiskey, this is Yankee November One Papa Kilo. Good evening, Beth. How are things in Karawala? Over."

"Couldn't be better, Willy. Fishing is as good as it's ever been. The lower river is full of big snook from Jamaima Key to Butku Dakara, and you can walk on the backs of tarpon from Sani Warban all the way to Tulu Warban. We've jumped several tarpon this week that were more than twelve feet long and pushing three hundred pounds. Over."

"I guess I have to believe you. I've seen them. When are you going to have room for your pilot? Over."

"Not this week, Willy. Every bed is full. Over."

"You're going to need another bed. I got a call from Texas today. They're bringing one more. Over."

This is YN4HW with YN1PK. No they're not. I've got ten beds and ten fishermen. If I had another bed, there's no place to put it. Out of the question. Call them back and give them my regrets. Over."

"I'll tell him, but he didn't ask me if he could bring one more. He told me he was bringing one more. I told him you didn't have room, but that didn't seem to bother him. Over."

"Just tell him I said no. Over."

"Will do. I'll be on again tomorrow. Same time. Anything else? Over"

"Nothing else. We'll have room for you the week after. Over."

"And then you'll say, 'You shoulda been here last week.' Over."

"I think not. Even if half of these fish swim away, there will still be more than you can catch. Over."

"I'll be ready. This is Yankee November One Papa Kilo signing off. Good night, Beth."

"Good night, Willy. This is Yankee November Four Hotel Whiskey signing off."

Ham operators around the world had been standing by patiently, waiting for a chance for a DX contact in Nicaragua to add to their QSL collection, but I was tired. I listened for a moment while hundreds of callers tried to get their call signs heard, and then I turned it off. I still had work to do before the morrow's fishing. I went about it thinking I had things settled.

Up in the morning at four. Start the light plant. Bang on a salvaged piece of rail from the old launching ways to wake up the fishermen. Knock down a cup of coffee and a bowl of fruit. Greet the guides. Prep the boats. Go fishing.

Every day I took two fishermen out on the river. Every day it was two different fishermen. There were ten fishermen per week, with five days of fishing per week. I was a guide, and I was a teacher. I taught fishing, Miskito history and natural history. And I loved every minute of it. There were tough customers, but there were no bad days. I knew, and they knew, that I had the best job on earth.

But I wasn't prepared for Byrdie. I signed on again the next evening.

"Yankee November One Papa Kilo, this is Yankee November Four Hotel Whiskey. Hello, Willy. Over."

"Yankee November Four Hotel Whiskey, this is Yankee November One Papa Kilo. Good evening, Beth. How are things in Karawala? Over."

"Fine here, Willy. How are things in Managua? Over."

"You've got three days to build another rondell and put a bed in it. She's coming. Over."

"She? What are you talking about? Over."

"The eleventh fisherman. This guy says he's bringing eleven people, and he doesn't care what it takes. He has no idea what *no* means. Over."

"I can demonstrate *no* when he gets here. I can spread a blanket on the ground and hand him a can of bug spray. Who is *she*, anyway? Over."

"His daughter. Over."

I guess at that point there were thousands of hams listening in and wondering how I would respond to that.

"Absolutely not. No children. This is not a place for little girls. Tell him if he brings her, you can't put her on the plane. Over."

"This is YN1PK with YN4HW. Full grown woman, Beth. Over."

Several choice comments went through my mind, but you can't say things like that and keep your license. I was in a can't-win situation with interesting possibilities. But it was still impossible. There was not an eleventh bed. Why was that so difficult to accept?

"Papa Kilo, tell him you have cargo for me, and you're going to be grossed out and maxed out. Weight and balance won't allow another ounce, even if there was space. Over."

"What kind of cargo? Over."

"A new outboard. Over."

"And when he gets here and there is no outboard? Over."

"It got hung up in aduana. Over."

347

"I'll tell him, Beth, but I think I'll be meeting eleven fishermen on the tarmac in Managua. I repeat: he's not asking. He's telling. Over."

"And he probably thinks he can stop the tides. Over."

"I get the impression it's the daughter who can stop the tides. Over."

Full grown woman. Stops the tides. Either she's on the far side of big and butt-ugly, or she's a knock-down drag-out answered prayer. Flip a coin. I'm not that lucky. When heads wins, I get tails. Nothing I am and nothing I have came by luck.

"If you don't mind, give it a try. If it doesn't work, I'll figure something out. Half of my life is improvisation. Over."

"Will do. Same grocery list? Over."

"Same list. We usually have more than enough. Over."

"Anything else? Over."

"I guess that does it. Good night, Willy, and good luck. Over."

"This is Yankee November One Papa Kilo signing off. Good night, Beth."

"This is Yankee November Four Hotel Whiskey signing off."

It was in Willy's hands. He didn't sign on for this job, but it was his business to fly, and that meant coordination and dispatch. He would make the call.

*

"The plane! The plane!" I swear it. Not one of them had ever seen *Fantasy Island*, but every time a plane came, that was the call. The moment the first faint sound of the engines was heard, they started clearing the runway of cattle, horses, pigs, dogs and children. It was harder to herd the children, by far.

I stood at the edge of the runway with a red bandana on my head and a parrot on my shoulder. The Navaho was first, crossing west to east for a visual on the runway, then disappearing until we saw him come out of the north on his downwind. He landed and unloaded passengers and baggage as quickly as possible. I greeted my guests and introduced myself as the Navaho taxied back to the end of the runway. As it lifted off, Willy appeared in the Aztec and went through the same landing procedure.

There were six people standing with me on the runway. Five more came out of the Aztec with Willy. All he could do was shrug his shoulders. Roll with the punches. The customer is not always right, but he usually gets what he wants.

With a cheerful smile on my face, I began assigning cabins and sending baggage off to the appropriate places. Three couples in three cabins, two old salts in another and the teenage boys in the last. That took care of the expected guests. Having no idea what to do next, I turned and started toward the big house.

"Wait!" she demanded. I turned. "Which one am I in?"

"There isn't another. Who are you with?"

"My parents and my brothers."

"I can have one of the girls make a pallet on the floor in one of their cabins. Who would you rather bunk with?"

"I don't think so," she informed me. "Which one are you in?"

I pointed. "But there's only one bed, and it isn't big enough for both of us."

"You wish. What's that over there?" She pointed at the boat shed.

"The boat shed."

"Do you have a hammock?"

"Several."

"Good. You need one." She turned, and I watched in disbelief as she took the path to my house, walked in and shut the door. "Send my bags."

"At least she's not on the far side of big and butt-ugly," I muttered, and I didn't care who heard me.

Hammocks are not for sleeping. They are good for naps and for reading and for sipping a cold beer on a hot afternoon, but they are not for sleeping. For one thing, you wake up looking like a waffle. And in the bush, the mosquitoes can attack front and back, top and bottom and both sides. I slung my hammock in the boat shed and resigned myself to one of the most miserable weeks in memory.

Byrdie's mother was in the big house when I walked in.

"That was so sweet of you to give her your house. We're all so happy you could make room for her."

I couldn't say what was on my mind. I was stuck, and the only thing I could do about it was to make the best of it.

"It's my pleasure, Ma'am. I'm happy you could bring her."

I used more bug spray that night than my entire combined consumption of a lifetime. It ranked among the most miserable experiences I have ever endured. I counted myself fortunate that I had enough blood in my veins to roll out of my hammock and stand upright without passing out.

Up in the morning at four. Start the light plant. Bang on an old piece of rail to wake up the fishermen. Knock down a cup of coffee and a bowl of fruit. Greet the guides. Prep the boats. Go fishing.

She didn't get up with the others, so I couldn't change clothes or brush my teeth. I considered walking in as if I owned the place, getting some of my things and leaving without saying a word. I considered a gentle knock on the door and a request for permission to enter. I considered drowning her in the river. I went fishing without clean clothes. I went with moss on my teeth.

At noon, I managed a foray into my house to collect a few necessities. Beyond that, I was a servant manipulated by guests who were completely at my mercy for their survival. The contradiction was lost on them. I was a servant in charge of their survival and of their entertainment. The possibility that I could lose interest in their survival was beyond consideration. Hadn't my interest been purchased?

She slept the first two days. If she ventured out onto the

river, she slept in the boat, and I never saw her, even though we were often on the same water. She came to table to eat, ate and left. She was there, unseen, like an infection at the edge of intolerance for the duration of its virulence. She was there until she left, and the certainty of her departure, like all others, offered a certain peace and the assurance that when all was said and done, only I would remain.

But she would undo even that.

Tuesday night the twins decided they wanted to go to the keys to catch a shark. Byrdie and her mother decided they wanted to go, too, and snorkel on the reef. Grateful for anything that would shorten my nightly ordeal in the hammock, I stayed up late into the night preparing shark rigs and snorkel gear, puffing on a puro and tugging on a medio by the light of a kerosene lamp. It seemed that I had only just closed my eyes when Eddie whispered, "Mr. Bet?"

"Okay, Eddie. Crank it up." Eddie went off to start the light plant, and I rolled out of the hammock and planted my feet in the dirt. Three more nights, and I would regain my house.

We put the boys in Eddie's boat and the girls in mine. Eddie would go blasting through the bar and off to King's Key without regard for the seas. Teenage boys could take that sort of beating, and it might have been just deserts for Byrdie, but her mother, in my care, would get the gentlest ride my seamanship could provide.

We didn't jump the bar. We eased through it in first light without a single pounding wave crashing over the bow. A mile from the beach we were clear of the combined effect of an outgoing tide meeting ground swells head on, and my passengers were none the wiser that we were not on a pond. I set a course that would find the sun come rising golden out of the water off our port bow. King's Key lay between us and the sun.

Byrdie was obviously enjoying the dawn on the open ocean. She moved to my side and asked, "Can I steer?"

The soft colors of water and sky in the early light

complimented her smile and the sparkle in her eyes, and I was disarmed. "Do you know how?" As if it would have mattered.

"I am a direct descendant of Admiral Byrd. Of course I can."

I stepped aside and let her take the wheel. I wanted her to take the wheel so I could watch her as she watched the sea. My resentment fell away in the wake. I tried to catch it, to bring it back, but it would not come. I almost called after it, as if it could hear.

A sailor cannot afford to be confused at sea. The ship and all hands depend on the command of one person to see them to safe harbor, and my attention had been suddenly and inexplicably diverted to a sea nymph in a gimme cap. I saw nothing else. I saw neither the horizon nor the fetch of the waves nor the fly of the scuds and certainly not the ball of fire rising from the sea that gave color once again where there had only been black and white. My mind and gaze were affixed to her as if welded by a sculptor. She was the dawn and the sea and the sky, and every color ever seen by all the sailors ever sailed.

I was putty. I was an absolute bowl of mush. I think back on it now, and I wonder what my other charges must have thought as I stood there with my jaw on the deck and my foot on my tongue.

I have no idea how long that lasted. It might have been moments, and it might have been hours. No matter how long, we made no forward progress in the interim. She had no idea which way we were going, and her course took us to the four points in random order. We were going nowhere.

A grin spread across my face as wide as light spreads across the horizon with the promise of day. "Bearing one-ten. You're a wee bit off."

"What?"

"You need to turn around. You're a little bit off course." At that time, she was headed back to the river.

"How am I supposed to know which way to go?"

"Are you watching the compass?"

"What compass?"

I pointed. "That compass."

"Well, no. If I didn't know there was a compass, I wouldn't be watching it, would I?"

"I guess not. Are you watching the waves?"

"Why would I be watching the waves?"

My jaw was still on the deck, but I was not standing on my tongue. "They are not going to change direction today. Head into them."

"How am I supposed to know which way they are going?"

I couldn't help it. I laughed.

"You're making fun of me." I think she looked for something with which to pound my skull, but came up empty.

"No, no, no, dear. I'm just trying to help."

"Then tell me which way to go."

"Okay. See that big red ball rising out of the ocean?"

"Of course."

"That's east. Keep it about twenty degrees off the port bow. King's Key will rise up dead on. Or you can give her to me, and I'll see us to the cove."

She thought for a moment and stepped aside. I wanted to wrap my arm around her and pull her to me as I took the wheel, but there was a large degree of separation between the proprietor and the guests. I could be many things, but personal was not one of them. I could be many things, but I was just a guide. Of all the things I ever was, there was a big black line between me and them. They could no more cross to my side than I could to theirs. I could look, but I could no more navigate her water than she could mine. I set the heading to equal the bearing and did my job. Pity. I saw the horizon, the fetch of the waves and the fly of the scuds. There was a ball of fire in my belly that might boil away the seven seas before it died.

She wrapped her arm around my waist and pulled me close. I didn't know whether to abandon ship or turn to stone. I tried to look casual, but I think my expression was more like the glee of a boy who had just caught his first fish. If it was never more than this, then this was enough.

King's Key was first a speck on the horizon no one else saw, and then the trees popped up out of the water and began to grow. If arriving meant the moment would evaporate, I didn't want to get there. The water changed from deep blue to blindingly bright blue, and we began to see the first coral. I took my time feeling my way through the reefs and across the flats to the little cove that was our harbor. Schools of barracuda and yellowtail parted as we entered the reef. On the flats, black-tip sharks eased out to deep water, and as we neared the cove, a big grouper bolted from the shallows and pushed a hump of water all the way past the reef. The boat came to a soft stop in the sand. We stepped out and waded to the beach.

Eddie and the twins were fishing for bait on the flats, and all three rods were bent. Jacks, I guessed, and by their lack of progress, they were too big to let these boys use them for bait. I did not want them to get locked into an everlasting battle with a fish big enough to eat the boat. A few six-footers would be exciting enough. Eddie knew what I wanted.

We unloaded the boat, spread beach mats, opened a cooler of fruit, and still they fought the fish. The jacks circled, and we watched amused as they stepped over and crossed under the lines to keep from tying themselves in knots, shouting at the fish and at each other all the while.

They caught the three jacks, and then they got into a school of yellowtail the perfect size for bait. Bait caught, they churned the water getting back to the boat, faces bright with excitement.

As they pushed off, I teased, "If you hook a tiger, stay in the middle of the boat," and I turned my attention to the snorkel gear.

"What?" They said in unison.

Eddie answered, laughing, "Tiger shark like eat people."

Moms and sisters do not like to hear things like that, especially in unfamiliar territory. In an instant, they were wagging fingers and tongues at me, and I was set straight about what I might or might not let happen to those boys. Before I could respond, it occurred to each of them that I was preparing to lead them into the very water that was certain to have sharks to catch.

All I could do was stand there and grin. "If sharks were dangerous, the beaches of the world would be deserted. Better you be afraid of driving."

"They are so dangerous. They bite people all the time."

"No, dear, people die in automobiles all the time. Sharks rarely attack humans, and when they do, it's usually because it looked like something else. Poor visibility has more to do with it than a hunger for humans." It did not help my case that *Jaws* was a recent sensation. Hollywood plays on the American propensity for absolute gullibility. Deceived by our own conceit, screen writers and directors have us carrying images that have nothing to do with the real world. Sharks do not growl.

They were visibly nervous. "Every time someone gets into salt water, there is a shark nearby, and it knows there is a human there. If sharks looked at humans as food, we would have learned long ago to stay out of the water. We're going to go snorkeling in a minute, and there will be sharks with us. We'll be safe."

We spent the day snorkeling through canyons of coral with carpets of white sand on the bottom below. I was as entranced by the bright colors and forms of the fish as were my guests, who were seeing them for the first time. We swam through schools of small fish, and we dove to the bottom to peer under the coral at lobster and an occasional moray. And always, beyond the reef in open water, there were the ghostly shapes of barracuda and sharks.

We were sitting on the beach enjoying the soft flesh of young coconuts when the boys returned. They were shirtless, and we could see from a distance that they had sunburns they would not soon forget. But for the moment their excitement overruled the burn. They were all smiles as they jumped out of the boat and ran to tell us about the fishing.

They had found sharks, and each had caught several. And each had hooked a monster that had taken every inch of the four hundred yards on the reels before breaking off. For boys who had never caught anything bigger than a bass, it was a heady experience. We were obliged to go to the boat to see the ones they had kept for the village.

Then the burn and fatigue began demanding attention, and we were soon on our way back to camp. Everyone had had enough. The heat and exertion are exhausting, and they are compounded for tourists unaccustomed to exposure. They sat and said little on the way in.

We showered and napped before dinner. I lay in my hammock and swatted short-jackets and dozed between bites.

Byrdie was a different person. She came to the big house well before dinner and was as animated as her sunburned brothers were not. Her smile was infectious and her non-stop commentary soon had everyone as lively as she. We had a little wine and a primitive dinner of fresh-shucked oysters from Karas Laya dipped in horseradish sauce, followed by heaping platters of spiny lobster drenched in lime and butter. There were bowls of rice and beans, too, but they remained untouched.

After dinner, out of the blue, she laughed and said, "Go ahead and admit it. You're in love with me."

First there was dead silence, and I'm sure I looked like a deer caught in the headlights. Then there was raucous laughter, and I still didn't know what to do. I knew exactly what I wanted to do. I could feel the pulse in my fingers, toes and scalp, and I'm sure I radiated enough heat to raise the temperature inside the big house by several degrees, but there was a gang inside that held me back.

Saturday morning, with everyone standing by their baggage at the edge of the runway, Byrdie's mother looked at her and asked, "Where are your bags, dear?"

"I'm staying here," she answered, and maybe there was a hint of a boyish grin on my face.

BYRDIE'S TARPON

Chapter Twenty-seven

Yawanaiska Pura Matlalkanbi Pura Kum

I have no recent memory of fear. I do know that when they talk about the taste of fear, it is not a figurative sense. I know the taste. Once tasted, it cannot be forgotten, but fear can be overcome. Now I am afraid. I am afraid she will disappear. It is worse than the fear of death.

From the Journals of McBeth Johnson

The water beneath the keel was one hundred feet deep, and the shore was closer than the bottom. A howler monkey sat in an ibo tree at the river's edge, roaring at the dawn between bites of the tree's soft nuts, watching us with a wary eye. Across the river he was answered by another howler, the bellicose reply echoing off the impenetrable green of the jungle that rose like the walls of a canyon along the banks.

"They get up grouchy around here, don't they?" It was Byrdie's voice. She was smiling and excited. When her family left with Willy, we watched until the plane was just a speck in the sky, and then we ran, holding hands and laughing, straight to what was now called *our* house. Now she wanted to catch a tarpon, and big tarpon were feeding all around the boat.

"Baboon bawling for rain," Ferlan said. "Must be going rain today."

Ferlan was newly promoted to deck hand on my boat. I watched as he hooked a mullet through the lips and set it in the water. The tide took it and pulled it out behind the anchored boat, where it swam in the current near the surface.

"What do I do when I get a strike?" she asked.

Ribbonfish were snaking up out of the water, trying to escape, only to fall back into an explosion. Occasionally there was a heavy swirl where a tarpon had lunged at a baitfish near the surface. When big tarpon are feeding like that, the strike can be strong enough to yank the rod right out of your hands.

"Just hold on to that rod," I answered. "He'll set the hook himself. We're going to catch fish. Get ready for a hard strike."

It only took a few minutes of moving the mullet around in the current before a tarpon slammed into it, very nearly pulling the her out of the boat. Before she had time to regain her balance, it jumped and threw the hook.

"What did I do wrong?" she asked, shaking visibly.

"Notin, notin," Ferlan said. He was smiling, reaching for another mullet.

Ferlan's English was sometimes hard to understand, even for me. I repeated his answer for her and elaborated. "Nothing," I said. "You didn't do anything wrong. That's just part of tarpon fishing. The inside of a tarpon's mouth is all bone. There is precious little that you can set a hook in. Experienced tarpon fishermen lose about nine out of ten."

"Was he big?" she asked. "I didn't even get to see him jump."

I assured her that it was big. All the tarpon we had seen were over a hundred pounds, which was typical of Sani Warban, and they had been feeding continuously ever since we dropped anchor.

Barring an extremely bad run of luck, she was going to catch her fish on the first morning out. Even Ferlan and I were excited about it. There were always big tarpon in that hole, but they were not always actively feeding. Sometimes you could sit there for hours without getting a strike, just watching them roll their backs out of the water.

The heavy mono leader was roughened some by the fine, sandpaper teeth, so we clipped some off and retied the hook. I checked the point by dragging it across my thumbnail. It dug in, still sharp.

"When the next one jumps, bow to it." I offered.

She looked at me like I was crazy. "Bow? Like the Asians bow to each other? Like a man bows to a king?"

"Sort of. Bend toward the fish and point the rod at it so the line won't be so tight. Give him a little slack so he doesn't throw the hook or snap the line.

The second strike came as soon as she put the reel back in gear. Several big tarpon rolled up behind the boat as she was letting out line, and they must have seen the mullet at the same time. They all charged it.

We saw several silver flashes, and the rod was jerked over by a hard strike. This time she was ready. She was braced, and the strike didn't budge her. The jump, though, shook her like a sack of dry bones. He came up thrashing, close to the boat, and she kept a tight line. Every gill-rattling shake of that huge head was transmitted through the line to the rod, jerking hard, pulling her arms and body forward and snapping her head back and forth.

She got shaken up a bit, but the hook stayed stuck, and the line didn't break. We saw a monster tarpon come thrashing up out of the river not thirty feet from the transom. In another instant, he jumped again, fifty yards away, and then again, a hundred yards away.

The line went limp, and she slumped with a frown on her face. But the fish had only turned toward the boat, and as he swam, the rod began to bend again.

Ferlan hauled the anchor up, and I started the motor. If we let him get too far away, water drag alone could break the line. But after that first run, the fish was sulking, leaning heavily on the rod, neither taking nor giving. Byrdie was having to work hard to hold her own, and I knew that before it was over, she would be exhausted.

"If you can keep that much pressure on him, you might boat him within an hour," I said, trying to sound casual. I hoped she could do it, but I knew that both she and her tackle were too light for anything but a marathon fight.

"An hour!" she answered. "I'm just barely doing it now. I don't think I can keep it up another five minutes, let alone an hour." She spoke through clenched teeth, straining against the heavy, steady pull.

After fifteen minutes, she was soaked in a very unladylike sweat and was repeating in very unladylike terms that she had more tarpon there than she wanted. It's amazing what a hard fight will bring out in a proper person.

I was guessing the fish's weight at about one hundred sixty pounds. There was no doubt that there was enough fish there to pop a bead of sweat on a strong man's face, and she was a small woman. It would take some coaxing to get her to fight it all the way.

She was using twenty pound class tackle, and with her limited experience, her size and the size of that fish, twenty pound class tackle was ultralight. The leader was slowly being abraded. The hook was gouging an ever-larger hole in the fish's mouth. The knots were under constant strain, and the line was exposed to anything that might nick or scratch it. If she rested, the fish rested, and that added to the length of the fight. The odds of catching it were diminishing.

"You've got to fight him for me for a minute," she complained. "I've got to rest my arms. I can't hold on for another minute."

"That's against the rules, lady," I chided, and I laughed. "You wanted to catch a big tarpon, and now that you've got him, you're going to quit? Give up?"

I teased her, and it seemed to work. She gritted her teeth and leaned back on the rod. The fish jumped again, cleared the water, and disappeared.

"That's your fish out there, not mine, and you're not even close to being tired yet."

Twenty-five minutes into the fight, she brought the fish within fifty feet of the boat. I had been coaxing and teasing and scolding all the way; she had been moaning and complaining all the way about how hard I was making her work. It was good natured, and I think it kept her from giving up.

I could see that she hurt from the strain, but she was beginning to enjoy the battle. She was looking out at the fish with respect, and she was beginning to learn something about herself. She would learn a lot more before it was over.

"I wish my brothers were here to watch this," she said. "They thought I'd just sit here with a pole in my hands while everyone else caught fish. They'll never believe this: not in a million years.

"If you put him in the boat, they'll have to believe it. Quit resting and put some pressure on him."

At her renewed effort, the fish jumped again, twice, and peeled off the hundred yards of line she had fought so hard to get.

"Oh, damn!" she yelled. "I thought he was getting tired."

"He did exactly what we wanted him to do," I told her. "You've got to put enough pressure on him to make him jump and run, or you'll never tire him out. He'll just sit out there and sulk until you give up and go home. Work him in again. His next run won't be as long as the last."

"Well, if I put too much pressure on him, something will break: most likely me. Then what will you say?"

"You can't put too much pressure on him. Whenever you get to eight pounds of pull, the drag will slip."

"Eight pounds!" she exclaimed. You can't be serious. More like eight hundred."

"Not kidding," I said. "Unless you increase the drag, you can't put more than eight pounds of pressure on that fish."

"Then why am I so exhausted? I feel like I've been trying to pull a truck out of the mud."

She wasn't exhausted. Not yet. She was just tired enough to make polite conversation about being tired. She had been

362

fighting the fish for a little over half an hour, and he was showing no signs of tiring. Her shirt was soaked and plastered to her body, and her wet hair hung in strings across her face, which was beginning to flush in the heat. Little blisters were showing on her hands, but she had a long way to go before she could say she was tired.

"Because you're holding a lever on the short side of the fulcrum," I answered. "When you pull hard enough to make the drag slip, you put eight pounds of pressure on the fish, but he's putting about fifty pounds of pressure on you. He's got all the mechanical advantage on his end of the rod."

Her tarpon was swimming with the tide, pulling the big mahogany boat, and us, toward the mouth of the river. Now and then it jumped or made a short run, but mostly it just swam steadily about fifty yards from the boat. It wasn't long before she was too tired to talk, other than to ask for a drink of water.

We came to a point where the river split around an island. At the point there was an Indian standing in a dugout canoe with a harpoon raised above his head, waiting for a snook or some other fish to swim near enough to spear.

It was a hand-made harpoon with a tip forged and filed from scrap iron salvaged from the old mill. I have seen them stand for hours, harpoon raised, waiting for something to swim within range.

When he saw that we were fighting a fish, he lowered his spear and began speaking in Miskito to Ferlan. Byrdie hadn't said anything for a long time, but when she heard the excited voice from the point, she looked at him and asked Ferlan what he was saying.

"He want strike the tapom for you," he said. The Indians of the area had never gotten used to the idea of fishing for fun. The man was offering to kill the fish for the lady, and for him it was a gallant gesture, not at all unlike offering to change a tire for a stranded motorist. He was completely unprepared for her response.

"You son of a bitch, you stay away from my fish," she screamed. "Tell him, Ferlan. Tell him to stay away from my fish."

She watched anxiously as Ferlan explained that Byrdie did not want him to harpoon the fish. When she was satisfied that he understood, she turned back to the fish, her head bowed a little, quiet again.

The man with the harpoon said quietly, "Woman cross!" It was a personal exclamation, but it came across the calm river like he had whispered in our ears.

She struggled more with herself than with the tarpon. She trembled as she strained to pump in each yard of line, and she came close to tears each time he robbed her of her efforts. To cool her off, I dumped buckets of water over her head. I had to wipe her brow constantly to keep the salt out of her eyes.

The sun climbed the sky, and she began to burn. I rubbed sunscreen on her face, arms and legs. She winced when the crusted salt scraped her burnt skin, but she said nothing. She was beyond acknowledging my presence. All that existed for her was the tarpon, the sun and the pain.

The blisters on her hands began to break, and the rod grips became slippery. I tore my shirt into strips and wrapped her hands with it. She whimpered and shut her eyes against the pain, but still she gripped the rod and leaned back against the fish. And still she said nothing.

We passed by a little shelter on the bank, and a bare-breasted woman stepped out to greet us. I waved, but Byrdie just stared ahead blankly at her fish. I was beginning to doubt that she could win the fight. If she had wanted to quit, I wouldn't have objected. She was near collapse, but I never said it, and neither did she.

We had been pulled almost four miles down the river, past rice fields and stands of bananas, past brightly colored birds and sweet scented orchids, and she had seen nothing but the patch of water where her fish swam.

Now and then she shook her head, as if to clear it, and flexed her cramped, raw hands. Several times I peeled the rags off her hands and replaced them with fresh ones. She cried out in pain each time. There was no more teasing; no more coaxing; no more scolding. I felt sorry for her, and I felt guilty about the pain she felt, but there was nothing I could do about it.

Sharks travel as much as one hundred miles up the Rio Grande de Matagalpa, so I wasn't surprised when one showed up. She had been fighting the fish for more than three hours, and all the time I had been watching for sharks. Ferlan saw it before I did and started yelling at it. Byrdie either didn't care or didn't know what it meant. When I told her what the ruckus was about, she just nodded her head.

The shark swam slowly, deliberately, unlike one pursuing prey. I felt great relief when it passed near the tarpon and swam away. But the mere presence of a shark was enough to send the tarpon into a frenzied effort to escape. He jumped and ran and peeled off another hundred yards of line.

It was more than she could take. She began to cry. Great heaving sobs wracked her chest, and her face distorted in pain and frustration. She tried to talk but couldn't. All she could do was bang her bandaged fists on the gunnel and cry.

Finally, through the sobs, she said, "He's...never...going...to...give...up...is he?"

I wanted to do something to comfort her, but I could think of nothing. I just sat there like a spectator.

Perhaps I should have taken the rod from her long ago, but I hadn't, and still I couldn't. She was badly burned, and there was blood smeared all over her where she had tried to wipe her hands and eyes. She looked, literally, like she might have been beaten.

The line was hanging limply from the rod tip. I looked up and saw her tarpon on the surface, a long way from the boat. "You've got him beat now," I whispered. "Don't give up now."

As gently as I could, I lifted her up and pointed at the fish. "All you've got to do now is reel him in."

Slowly, painfully she began pumping him in. A few times he righted himself and tried to swim against her, but mostly he just let himself be pulled to the boat. Finally, after almost four hours, she had her fish. The big tarpon lay on its side by the boat with his mouth open. The leader was wrapped around my hand; we were ready for the gaff.

She dropped the rod and slumped into her seat, limp and breathing hard. She looked up at me and smiled, and in a course whisper, said, "Turn him loose."

"If he's not a record, he's real close," I prompted. "Sure you don't want to take him in and weigh him?"

The official IGFA record for women's twenty pound class tarpon was only one hundred fifty-two pounds, and her tarpon had to have that beat. He was about seven feet long and very fat. It wouldn't be easy to let a record slip away, but it would be much harder to go against her after all she'd been through.

"Turn him loose," she repeated, a little more forcefully.

I understood. No explanation was necessary. I knew exactly why she wanted it released. I felt for the hook and found it. It slipped out, almost fell out, without any effort. She came to the gunnel to watch her fish swim away, and she stayed there, her knees on the deck, her chin on the cap rail, gazing down into the water long after her fish was gone, her heart still beating hard.

A gentle rain began to fall, drumming lightly on the jungle roof, and maybe the first drop to touch the water was a tear. Somewhere a howler monkey roared his approval. Ferlan sighed and said, "She got fish. He got rain. Let's go home."

*

Two days later I put her on the plane with Willy and watched them clear the pines in the savanna, bank west and disappear. I felt an emptiness I had never known and knew that something very precious had slipped out of my life. She said she'd come back in a month, but the distance was long and inconvenient. I looked around. What did I have to offer? I had known great happiness for two short weeks, and she had stories for the rest of her life.

GLORIA

Chapter Twenty-eight

Yawanaiska Pura Matlalkanbi Pura Wal

Don't let him kid you. He'll tell you not to worry about the tiger until you can see its eyes, but that's because he always knows where everything is. He's as wary as a deer and alert even when he sleeps. He's got eyes in the back of his head. Don't ever think you're putting one over on him.

Uca Pugila

"I was there the night Sandino was murdered." Doña Gloria looked old enough to have been a young lady in 1934. Her brother, her son, her nephew and their wives sat at my table. The night was dead calm, the generator was off, and the soft glow of kerosene lamps helped the faces conceal themselves.

She got my attention. Everyone talked about the Sandino of old and the Sandinistas of late, and most thought of themselves as experts, but I had never met anyone this close to the story. "Where were you, Doña Gloria? And how did you come to be there?

"I am President Sacasa's daughter. I was escorted there by a young military officer, and I was chaperoned by my father."

Miss Pete and the girls stopped cleaning up the dinner dishes and stood behind the counter listening to Doña Gloria. I think even the tree frogs stopped their chorus.

She didn't know what to make of me. On the one hand, I was just an innkeeper, but on the other, I entertained some high profile Americans, and she knew there was a connection in some way to Somoza. I wasn't offering, and she wasn't asking.

Again I asked, "But where?"

"There was a dinner that night to celebrate the peace." She spoke slowly and looked more at the center of the table than at those around her, but when she wanted to drive home a point, she looked into my eyes. "At the Palacio Nacional. It was not a big affair. Not more than two dozen people there, I think, but all very important. They told me that Sandino had come to Managua to make peace, and I think my father believed that, but it turned out that Somoza had lured him to Managua with promises that the U.S. Marines would leave Nicaragua and Sandino could live in peace.

"Your Marine Colonel Stimson was there that night. He had been trying to catch Sandino for almost eight years. I think that was the first war your country ever lost." She laughed, reminiscing. "The United States Marines versus Augusto Cesar Sandino, the man who invented guerrilla warfare."

I thought that might be stretching things a bit, but I didn't say so. No doubt he contributed to its perfection.

I nodded in agreement. "The Marines couldn't defeat Sandino, but neither did Sandino defeat the Marines. They left in frustration. But Sandino died in 1934. Didn't the Marines leave in 1933?""

"They left because Anastasio Somoza Garcia was in charge of the Guardia Nacional, and they thought he would keep the Liberals at bay. But there were still Marines on our soil, and Sandino knew it.

"They took a photo of Sandino with his arm over the shoulder of Somoza just before they shot him." I started to speak, but she gestured with her hand to stop me, took a sip of wine and continued. Looking out into the night, she said, "So sad. This is such a beautiful place. Our people are too poor to have to suffer war again." She spoke as if it were a foregone conclusion.

"The people loved Sandino, and now he is being brought back to liberate us again. He fought the tyranny of the

Conservatives and he fought the imperialism of the Marines, and if Somoza hadn't murdered him, he could have done great things for our country. He started as a worker in the mines, you know, in San Albino" and added, as if it were an accusation, "Mines owned by yanquis."

"That was after he returned from exile," I said. I had recently read his biography. Doña Gloria apparently knew Sandino as a folk hero.

"Yes, he was accused of trying to murder someone. I forget whom, and if he hadn't fled, he would have died in jail. But that's beside the point. He saw what the mining company was doing to his people, and his anger led him to revolution. From then on, he was a soldier fighting for the liberation of our people from tyranny and exploitation."

"Was he a communist?"

"Oh, yes. That is why they had to kill him. But he was also a nationalist, and he believed in the glory of personal heritage and liberty. He once said that the independence and liberty of a people are not to be discussed, but defended with weapons in hand. That sounds to me like it could have been spoken by one of *your* founding fathers."

I nodded my agreement.

"He was always an eloquent speaker and writer. Somoza knew that Sandino's ideas could spread to all the people, and if they did, Sandino would become president. So they killed him."

"And the Sandinistas? Are they communists?"

"Many of them. But we are all united in the overthrow of Somoza. He is a bloody tyrant."

I was shocked. Her family was shocked. Declaring oneself a Sandinista was dangerous. It occurred to me that her slip might be dangerous to me. Some of the Sandinistas were more vicious than they claimed Somoza to be. Would someone think I knew too much?

"What Doña Gloria meant to say," interrupted her son, "is that she is sympathetic to the plight of the people. She herself has no animosity toward our president."

"In that case," I said to him, "we probably think much alike. But it would make my heart sad to see this country in a civil war. So much death and destruction." I knew what she had said, and so did he, but now we could both lie about it.

"Nicaragua has always been in civil war. As soon as one is over, another begins. It is nothing new," the brother said. "The people die because someone says they must fight. Fight to defend or fight to overthrow. They are both the same. Nothing ever changes here. New governments are always as bad as the old. The ideology is money and power."

His sister shot him a glance of reproach. I thought his remark fit all government everywhere.

Speaking to me again, she said, "He was going to start a commune, you know. That was the only reason he came to Managua. They promised him land if he would stop fighting. We toasted the commune many times that night, and *you were not there*," she jabbed a finger at her brother. "He was going to call it Light and Truth. They gave him everything he wanted. Position, money and land. Had I only known it was because they were going to kill him."

"I was not there, and you were a little girl enamored of an icon of revolution. It was our father's sympathy to that icon that ended him."

Suddenly infuriated, she picked up my glass of rum and splashed it in his face. She was going for my cigar when I picked it up and leaned back in my chair. Such is civil war, but there is nothing civil about it. They were obviously at bitter odds about Sandino and the Sandinistas. I did my best to look composed while I prodded my wit to get me out of a tense scene. I stuck the cigar in my mouth and did my best to puff thoughtfully.

Doña Gloria was no less surprised than anyone else by what she'd done, but within moments, it had become a spill, and everyone was busy with wiping and cleaning and blotting. She and I were the only ones who sat in observant composure. The brother, the son, the nephew and the wives made great fuss about cleaning up the mess, but no one looked at Doña Gloria.

As Petrona carried away the towels, I asked, "Where did they kill him? Surely not in the Palacio Nacional?"

"Oh, no. They took him to the airport. They said they were going to fly him back to his commune on the Rio Coco. But they were not going to take him anywhere. The whole thing was pretense. They only went through with the dinner to appease my father. His death was a certainty the moment he entered Managua. The airport was just a convenient place to pull the trigger. There could be no witnesses there. In those days the airport was far out of town. It was dark and mostly abandoned at night. The only people there were a few of Somoza's Guardia."

"Was Stimson there? When they shot him?"

She poured a little wine for herself, took a sip and let it roll down her tongue as if the taste was the memory of a larger day. "Sandino was a Mason, you know, and a yoga master." She turned slowly to look at me, as if looking for surprise in my eyes.

"I've heard that, yes, and I've heard some other things, too."

She must have guessed that I knew more than she liked. "Do you have many snakes here?"

I gave her the out. "Of course we do. Sometimes the place is dripping with snakes. But I doubt that you'll see one."

"And why is that? If there are so many, I would think I could see one."

"Snakes stay under cover. Under cover of night or under cover of camouflage. They are easy prey in the open. Everyone wants to kill a snake. The only live snake is a hidden snake."

"They say the only good snake is a dead snake."

"There are no bad snakes."

"Sandino was good at hiding."

"Was he a snake?"

"Maybe. You said there are no bad snakes."

*

When Willy came to take out Doña Gloria's party, he told me to pack an overnight bag. "Ride with me in the Aztec. We'll get a steak tonight at Los Ranchos."

The churrasco at Los Ranchos is the best beef I've ever eaten, and their margaritas are made with fresh limes. He didn't have to twist my arm. Ten minutes later the Aztec and the Two-Ten were loaded, and we were on our way.

A twenty-four hour R & R in Managua was a bittersweet proposition. The devastation of the earthquake was still obvious everywhere one went. There were piles of rubble that would remain for decades. The reminders were depressing. Those who saw them every day were oblivious to them, but I wasn't.

The sweetness was a night in the best hotel in Managua and a meal in her best restaurant.

To my surprise, we flew into Las Mercedes International, instead of the smaller Los Brasiles, and taxied right up to the terminal. To my puzzled look, he said, "Some people get special treatment," referring to Doña Gloria. "Go up top and see who gets off this plane." He motioned at a Pan Am Clipper just touching down. "I'll pick you up in front of the terminal."

The roof is where everyone went to watch the passengers walk from the plane to the terminal. They could call out to friends and family before they disappeared into customs. I was more interested in why Willy wanted me up there than in who might be on the plane, but it never paid to ask questions. He wouldn't have told me. So I watched, assuming I would know it when I saw it.

All of a sudden the crowd hushed. It went from shouting and cheering to complete silence as everyone watched one person walk down the gangway. After a few moments of silence, an older woman in the crowd proclaimed, "She is a movie star!" Other voices echoed the exclamation.

I smiled, and the smile got bigger and bigger until I was laughing, not at the crowd, but in great happiness. Some were sure they had seen her movies, and they were trying to remember her name. Others remarked that she was more beautiful in real life than in the movies. I knew her name, and I boomed it out. "Her name is Byrdie, and she's mine."

They either didn't hear or thought I was a nut. The moment she went through the door into the terminal, the crowd moved en masse down the stairs to await her emergence. Friends and relatives were no longer important. A movie star was momentous.

I was afraid she would be mobbed by the crowd, but when she came out of customs, the nearest picked up her bags and the crowd parted, silent, in awe. There were oohs and aahs when we embraced. She took it in stride and nodded her appreciation to the crowd. Willy pulled up, we tossed her bags in the bed of the truck and hopped in.

"Surprised?" she asked as we drove away. I was grinning. She was here. She came back.

"He didn't have a clue," Willy laughed.

"Yes, I'm surprised. I'm elated. Ecstatic." I didn't say anything about tumescence, and if I didn't compose myself, it could be an embarrassment when I stood up.

She pushed me playfully and said, "Put a hold on it, big boy. We've got company."

"How long have you guys been hiding this from me?"

"I bought my ticket the day I got back," she answered. "I called Willy and told him it was a secret and he had better not take any other women over there."

"Well, he did what you asked. I saw him every Saturday and Sunday, taking clients out and bringing more in, and we talked on the radio almost every night, and not once did he so much as drop a hint. Like he said, I was clueless."

When we stopped at the hotel, Willy handed me a key. "You're already checked in. See you at eight. Los Ranchos."

THE SENATOR

Chapter Twenty-nine

Yawanaiska Pura Matlalkanbi Pura Yumhpa

A boy from Kara was bitten by a fer-de-lance this morning. His family came to me to ask for some gasoline so they could take him to a bush doctor to remove the tusks. They could not see the tusks, and the boy could not feel them, but they say the snake always leaves the tusks in the bite, and only the bush doctor can see them and remove them.

We are the same way.

From the Journals of McBeth Johnson

We were at the Aero Club the next morning with the Aztec and a Two-Ten, waiting on an inbound jet and our next guests. Willy wasn't as casual as he usually was. He always knows who is in his vicinity and what they are doing without appearing to be vigilant, but he was being obvious about it. When he began talking to someone on a hand-held radio, I knew there was more there than I had been told, and when Captain Northrup stepped out of the office, looked our way and nodded, I bristled.

"What's he doing here, Willy?"

"So much for incognito," Willy muttered. "He's not supposed to be here, and he's damn sure not supposed to be armed. The senator is going to be pissed."

"Senator? What senator?" I asked.

Willy nodded in the direction of the approach. "The one that's going to land here in about three minutes. The one that's going fishing with you this week."

"No one told me there was a senator coming. Not that it matters, but why the secrecy?"

"Because he doesn't want a swarm of sycophantic bureaucrats and politicos surrounding him. He'll want to know how Northrup knew about it."

"And he's not worried about going over there without protection?"

"He's a lot like you," Willy answered. "The tiger's not important until you can look it in the eye. You're his protection."

"That's my line," I shrugged. "No need to worry about something that hasn't shown up. If it suits him, it suits me."

Byrdie took my arm. "This sounds exciting. What's his name?"

"Boyd Bentley," Willy answered. "Your United States senator from Texas."

*

By the time we landed in Karawala, Byrdie had completely charmed and disarmed the senator. Much to the dismay of the aide traveling with him, he insisted on dropping formalities.

"Please, call me Boyd." It wasn't a patronizing request. He was asking us to accept him without all the crap that comes with his office. In Karawala, he wanted to be no one but Boyd, the fisherman.

I couldn't have been formal anyway. Karawala was no more the place for titles and formalities than it was for suits and ties. There have been those few who maintained their self-importance and air of condescension for the duration, and it was always easy to picture them on the bow in a clown suit, holding a casting rod.

But if that had been Boyd's way, Byrdie would have deferred to him. She would avoid awkward situations and keep her opinions to herself. She would do it cheerfully and with ease, whereas I might reveal resentment.

When we unloaded, Mudi picked up her bags, but instead of taking them to my cabin, he went behind the big house toward the boat shed.

"Wait a minute," Byrdie requested. "Where are you going with my bags? Who are you?"

"I am Mudi," he beamed. "Mr. Bet is my boss man. You have new utla. New house. Come look, now."

When the house came into view, Miss Pete, Jane and Teresa were standing on Byrdie's porch, waiting to greet her. She stopped when she saw it, and everyone laughed and clapped their hands.

By Karawala standards, it was big – a rectangle sixty feet long and forty feet deep. The ridge of the thatched roof was forty feet off the ground. A shaded veranda ran full length. It was unpainted hand sawn lumber - no less rustic than anything else in the area.

I walked up beside her. "You like it?"

She laughed. "Did you build this for me?"

I had been planning it for quite some time. The possibility that she might return had put it on the fast track. "Of course I did. I couldn't expect you to stay in a little cabin, could I?"

Poi walked out of the house with a door plane in his hand and a big grin on his face. "Is done!" he declared. "Now for three fingers. We must celebrate!"

Everyone laughed. Poi never missed a chance to celebrate. He would walk all the way from Mundo's at the end of the day just to get his three fingers and turn around and walk back.

Everyone waited for Byrdie's reaction. They were so proud of her new house they were about to burst, and they were thrilled by her surprise return. They had talked about little else ever since she left.

Byrdie threw her arms around me and exclaimed, "I love it!"

The girls rushed inside and returned with glasses, ice and a bottle of Flor de Caña. Miss Pete poured three fingers into each glass, and we toasted the new house. The rum disappeared from every glass but Byrdie's. After one tiny sip, she made a face and said it tastes like gasoline.

"Make I take it, then." Poi was more than happy to relieve her of such an unpleasant experience.

Byrdie went into the house with the girls, and I turned to my duties as a host. She hadn't said how long she was staying, but I knew that today was sweet.

*

"Somoza is no more important to The United States than a small town mayor. Why would I want to see him?"

The question was rhetorical. I don't think my opinion would have mattered to him any more than Somoza did. I had just ended my nightly contact with the world. The amateur radio frequencies were crowded, and I had managed little more than a brief word with Willy before the DXers bombarded us with QSL requests. Somoza had heard there was a U. S. senator at my camp, and he wanted a meeting with him. The senator was not happy about it.

"How did he find out I was here? No one was supposed to know."

"Somoza's pilot flew you over here. He was the second pilot, in the Two-Ten. Somoza probably knew you were here before you left Managua."

"That Brit is Somoza's pilot?"

"Yep."

"I really do not want to do this, but I suppose there's no way out of it."

"He asked for an hour. At the airport, before you leave."

"Everyone wants an hour, and he's the last person I need to see."

"He's the president of a country that might be headed for revolution."

"That damn sure doesn't make him special. A revolution in Nicaragua will have about as much impact on us as a fart in a hurricane."

"What do you suppose he wants?"

"Hell, I don't suppose anything. I know what he wants. Money. That's all any of them want."

"I heard he put most of the earthquake relief money in his own pocket."

The senator chuckled. "The money went exactly where we intended it to go."

"So I heard wrong."

"Absolutely not. Foreign aid goes where it does the most good. If it was spread out among millions of people, damn few of them would know where it came from and fewer would care. It would be wasted. No, son, the money goes straight to the people at the top. We keep them in power and they protect American business. It is a perfect relationship. We make a few of them rich, and they make a few of us rich. Everything Somoza owns was paid for with Yankee dollars."

For some reason, that made me think of Halley. It made me wonder where he was.

He smiled and tipped his glass. "It works. It works here, and it works all over the world. You can count on greed to get a man to sell out his people."

"And that's the way the greatest country on earth operates."

"By far the greatest, and that is how we are going to keep it that way."

"Why are you telling me this?"

"Why not? Do you think anyone would believe you if you repeated it? Even if they believed you, they wouldn't care. And if anyone at all cared, there is nothing they could do about it. Everything would be denied, and you would be discredited. We are very good at what we do."

I suppose my disappointment showed. He leaned forward, cupped his hands and said, "Look, when I went to Washington,

I really believed that I was going to be working with people who cared. I was correct in a way. They all care about money, and it didn't take long to learn that if I wanted to stay, I would do everything I could to keep the money flowing.

He shrugged his shoulders, and for an instant he was betrayed by fatigue of the spirit. "I wanted to stay."

"What do you think will happen here?"

"We'll make sure this little fire gets stomped out," and he smiled. "I'll do my best. I like it here, and you, son, will be the beneficiary of our foreign policy."

"And how will we do that?"

"We killed Sandino once. We'll kill him again."

"It might not be as easy to kill a ghost as it is to kill flesh and blood."

THE QUEEN'S PAPER
Chapter Thirty
Yawanaiska Pura Matawalsip

There will always be those who are helpless and defenseless. It is our part to acknowledge them, turn our backs and get back to counting our money. There will always be those who argue that they got themselves into the mess they are in. I would agree only that we got ourselves into a fine mess. Where will we get help?

From the Journals of McBeth Johnson

When Senator Bentley's planes lifted off, Byrdie declared it was time to go shopping.

I looked at her like she'd slipped a cog. "You're going to walk down to Mundo's? What do you need? We'll send someone."

"I need a boat. We're going to Kara," she answered. "There are no eggs here. Miss Pete says we can buy eggs in Kara."

I don't think she needed eggs. They were an excuse to take the girls on a boat ride. "Do you know where Kara is?"

"Well, no, but Miss Pete does. Miss Pete? Where is Kara?"

"Is up the river."

"How far?"

"Can't say," she said, not looking up from what she was doing. "Never been."

She looked at Teresa, then Jane. Both shrugged. "Me neither."

"None of you have ever been to Kara?" I was as surprised as Byrdie.

"Have you been to The Bar?"

"No, Ma'am."

"Miss Pete's been to The Bar. And Costa Rica and Bluefields and Managua. She's a traveler," I said.

"I walk Sandy Bay one time," Teresa said. "Is pretty there. Have ocean."

That did it. I tossed the keys to my boat to Byrdie. "Go west when you get out of the creek. There's a long S bend in the river. When you get out of the S, Kara is on the south bank. You can't miss it."

The girls hurried their cleaning. They had never been in a motorized vehicle of any kind. They were excited.

"Sherman?"

"Right here, boss."

"Get my boat ready, please. Fill it with gas, put in an anchor, two paddles and a torch."

"Yessir, boss. I going."

"Byrdie, I can send Sherman with you if you want."

"Thanks, but this is a girls-only trip."

And so off they went, and every Saturday after, off they went with all the passengers the boat would carry. With Byrdie at the helm, they explored the river from The Bar to Mairin Laya. The rides with Byrdie might have been the happiest those girls had ever been. For one afternoon each week, they were free of toil. They had the wind in their hair, and no man could tell them what to do; no child could claim their attention.

*

It was nine A.M. on a Sunday morning. I was in the big house taking care of routine maintenance when I looked up to see a group of men approaching. They were dressed in their Sunday best. White shirt, blue pants. I saw Leopoldo, Narcisso and Abanil. Leopoldo carried a package.

I invited them in and sat them at the dining table. Leopoldo spoke. "Mr. Bet, we fright about what we hear about the

Sandinista, them. They say they going kill we. They say they going take the coast." He began to open the package very carefully, as if it held something more precious than a material object.

"This the paper from the Queen," he said as he pushed it my way. It was a document about two feet square. They were quiet while I studied it, and when I finally realized what it was, I looked up.

"This is a treaty between the Queen of England and Nicaragua. It's the original. It ends the British Protectorate, but it gives you the land and autonomy forever."

They looked at each other and nodded. "You see? He study it good."

Leopoldo looked at me and said, "You got strong brain, Mr. Bet, and you is one of us. Only kum-kum Miskito know the paper is here in Karawala. Only three of us know where is hide. We alone and the King know it here."

I was awed. I sat and looked at the Treaty. I felt honored by their confidence. "Why? Why do you want me to see it? I am happy that you trust me, but why do you want me to see it?"

"You see the paper. Can the Sandinistas take the coast? Can they kill we?"

They wanted me to tell them that the Treaty would protect them. They came to hear me say they were safe, that someone would intervene and save them from the Sandinistas. I could lie to them, and if the Sandinistas were defeated, the lie might never be known. Or I could crush them with the truth.

I kept my eyes on the paper. "Treaties are only good if both sides want to keep them. If the Sandinistas win the war, they will make good on their threats." As soon as I said it, I wished I hadn't. But a lie can go in more directions and take more forms than the truth. It might make them feel safe for awhile, but it might also hasten their destruction.

"Our only hope is that Jimmy Carter makes sure the revolution never comes to Karawala. They are fighting on the

West side. My country is supporting Somoza, but there are those who want to see the Sandinistas win."

"Why that?" Narcisso asked in indignation. "You got communists in your government?"

"Probably," I answered, "But they don't come out and say so. They might not even know they fit the definition. They might not know they are communists. They have strong voices, and they think the Sandinistas would be better for Nicaragua than Somoza."

"Humph! They think we better off dead."

"They don't know about the threats. They don't know much about anything here. The only thing they know is what the reporters write."

"What is reporter?"

"News man. Prensa."

"What they know?"

"Not much. Whatever the Sandinistas tell them. There was one here once, in the election. Not much of what he wrote was true. The story here wasn't good enough , so he made one up."

"Was lie?"

"Was lie. He made up a story and said I told him so."

"Why?"

"For money. They pay him for good stories. If he doesn't have a good story, he might not keep his job. They paid him to come here to write a story about the elections. If he didn't write what they wanted to hear, they would send someone else next time."

They thought about that for awhile. I waited while they wrestled with it.

Abanil spoke. "Mr. Bet, is bad thing?"

"For me it is. Somoza would not like what he said I said."

"What that?"

"That the election was rigged."

"What that?"

I did not know the words. "That Somoza had it fixed up so only he could win."

"Is truth?"

"I don't know, Abanil. I only know he won."

Leopoldo looked at the treaty, and I could feel his thoughts on my skin like lightning in a bad storm. "This paper no good."

They all looked at him, and the reality sank in. Somoza was not an ally. Jimmy Carter was not an ally. They were looking at their only ally, and I was but one person against an army sworn to kill them. Where did I fit in all this? I was beginning to think I might fit best in Texas.

They were downcast when they left. Their movements were slower than when they arrived, as if they had shouldered a burden in my house.

THE MINISTER

Chapter Thirty-one

Yawanaiska Pura Matawalsip Pura Kum

*I didn't understand what A. L. Jordan meant when he
told me that some day I would have the greatest, most
beautiful thing a man can find.*
Now I look at Byrdie, and I know.

From the Journals of McBeth Johnson

There is a little one-room schoolhouse in Karawala, and
occasionally I passed it on my way from Mundo's or the village
wharf while walking to the camp. To the teacher, I was always
an unwelcome disturbance. As soon as I was spotted, the
children surged to the windows and waved and laughed at the
faces I made as I passed.

On this particular morning, they ignored me. Someone
within, who kept them clapping, laughing and cheering gleefully,
had captured their attention.

"Hey!" I shouted, but no one turned to look. It couldn't have
been the teacher. I had never even seen them smile at him. I had
to have a look. I walked toward the school.

There at the head of the class, not so surprisingly, was
Byrdie, teaching them hand games, and beside her was the
teacher, laughing and playing as enthusiastically as the children.
I laughed with them.

Carlos walked up behind me. "She is good with children,
yes?"

I nodded. "Yes, she is."

He put a hand on my shoulder. "You are a very lucky man."

Again, I nodded. "Yes, I am."

*

"This thing will be over within the month. The Sandinistas are on the run."

The Minister of Agriculture in the Somoza Cabinet was a friend who enjoyed frequent trips to Karawala. He first came in response to my plea for help when a commercial fishing company from Bluefields invaded the river with gill nets. I went out one morning to find hundreds of tarpon carcasses floating belly up. It would have been the death of my business.

When Carlos told me the gill net company was owned by the President, my heart sank, but the day after he returned to Managua, the nets came out of the water and the boats went home to Bluefields. Carlos came as often as he could, with an open invitation.

"Did you enjoy Doña Gloria's visit?" We had our feet propped up, a puro in one hand and a glass of Grand Marnier in the other, the latter brought by Carlos as a gift. The yellow glow of a kerosene lamp put out just enough light to see each other's eyes amid dancing shadows. The village was asleep.

"You knew she was here?" It didn't surprise me. The surprise was that he would mention it so casually.

"I always know who is here. It is my business to know who is here, and after all, we are competitors, you and I. Did she feed you that folk hero crap about Sandino?"

"You know her well?"

"Everyone knows Doña Gloria. She is also a folk hero of sorts for the people who believe the legend. She believes what she wants and ignores the rest."

"Like all of us. What else is there?"

"Sandino thought he was the incarnation of God, and his wife, Blanca, was Mary, mother of Jesus."

I laughed. "We have politicians in Washington like that."

"Maybe so, but they don't announce it to the world."

"Not in so many words. What else?"

"The man was a megalomaniac. He was born a bastard named Augusto Nicolas Calderon Sandino. It wasn't until he had a band of peasants behind him that he changed his name to Augusto César Sandino. He called his fighters *The Army in Defense of the National Sovereignty of Nicaragua*.

"He came up with his own history of Nicaragua and invented a new calendar that started on October 4, 1912 with Benjamín Zeledon's resistance to the American troops. All the rest of our history was erased. Nothing happened in the Western Hemisphere before that day."

"Makes as much sense as seven days and seven nights," I offered.

He shrugged. "Then he came up with his *Manifesto of Light and Truth*. He announced the coming of the end of the world and proclaimed Nicaragua the seat of the judgement against the unjust."

He was impressing me. I knew that he was well educated, but I had thought him little more than a pleasant bureaucrat. "You are quite the historian, Carlos."

"I've just been trying to make some sense of all this hero worship, but the more I dig up, the farther I get from anything that makes sense. How did he become a national hero? The man was delusional."

"Sounds like world history to me. Was there a war ever started by a rational man?"

"Oh? What about your American Revolution?"

"We didn't start it. We declared our independence, and they came to conquer us. We defended ourselves against invaders," I replied. "Just like the Viet Cong defended themselves against us. There was nothing rational about that."

"You changed the subject. You didn't have to fight the British, but you did."

I shook my head. "How can we have a rational argument about an irrational subject? Did Sandino seek relief from oppression?"

"Isn't that obvious?"

"So it seems to the Sandinistas. But was it nothing less than a transfer of wealth and power from their hands to his? Perhaps then as now? Doña Gloria's brother thinks so."

"That's just the thing, I think, that makes him so popular. It wasn't money. The people who followed him truly believed that he wanted only what was best for them. Delusions aside, any power he sought for himself was no more than what he had to have to implement his plans.

"She has never said a word about Sandino's claim that he communicated with a voice at the peak of Monte El Chipote."

I laughed. "It's one thing to talk to voices. It's a big leap to admit it. I suppose it was God."

"Implied, but he never went that far. I suppose that if one could separate the man from what he wanted to do, some of it made sense."

"Like talking to voices?"

"Not quite. He wanted to unify Central America. He announced the formation of the Union of the Central American Republics, gave each country a portfolio of ministries and set up rules for the election of a president. Then he turns around and appoints himself the Supreme Commander of the Autonomist Army of Central America and the Supreme Moral Authority of Central America."

"Was anyone listening to him?"

"In government? They might have heard him, but they didn't listen. They only heard the threat. He had just enough popular following that they had to silence him."

"And the Sandinistas? What do they want?"

"There is no secret there. They want to kill Somoza and his Guardia and distribute his wealth to the people."

"If they kill Somoza, will they do that? Will they distribute the wealth?"

"Of course not. Daniel Ortega and Tomás Borge will stuff it all into their pockets. The power and wealth will go from one hand to another, and nothing else will change. The people will have then what they have now. Nothing ever changes here."

I thought about Doña Gloria and her brother. "I have heard that before. This country is a history of one revolution after another, but nothing but the faces ever change. It's a game of king-on-the-mountain. It's the same everywhere. We have elections. The power and wealth go from one hand to another, and nothing but the faces change."

Carlos looked toward the village and took a deep breath. "Do you like it here?"

"I wouldn't be here if I didn't"

"The Sandinistas have promised to kill all the Miskitu and take this coast. They say they are stupid and lazy and do not deserve this land."

"Well, then, I can only hope that Somoza puts a quick end to this revolution. He is respected here, if only because he leaves them alone; the Sandinistas are not."

"It could go the other way. Not likely, but it could," Carlos said. "I think you should send Byrdie home. Let me fly her back to Managua and put her on a plane."

I didn't answer. I thought. Things could get difficult. I could never forgive myself if anything happened to her. I didn't even want her to be afraid. I was not concerned about myself. Even if I had to hide in the bush, I would come out of it none the worse, but I could not put her through that. Not for a minute. It hurt to think about it.

I nodded my agreement. I stood and said, "I'll go tell her."

DAVIS COMING
Chapter Thirty-two
Yawanaiska Pura Matawalsip Pura Wal

Son of a bitch scared the ever-lovin shit out of me. When we got to the bar, he caught a wave and surfed that damn boat all the way inside, screaming yee-haa like a madman all the way. I knew we were going to pitch-pole and the last thing I would ever see would be that boat coming down on me up-side down. That Johnson could have killed us all.

An entry in the guest book.

"Mr. Bet, they say Davis coming."

"I have nothing to say to Davis," I replied.

"He been talking."

"About what?"

"He say he going kill you."

I took a moment to answer. "When?"

"Tonight."

"Thank you, Abanil."

"Is nothing, Mr. Bet."

"Abanil?"

"Mr. Bet?"

"Do you think he'll try?"

"He will try, but can't kill."

"Why not?"

He shrugged his shoulders. "Tiger can't."

I sat there long after he had gone. Everyone must have known, because no one came to pasear. I had no visitors. Davis wouldn't come during the day, and he wouldn't face me. It would be an ambush. He would wait until I was asleep.

I found two pieces of bamboo large enough that my fists fit inside, and I began to whittle. I carved the septa into a crossbar I could grasp. At the end, I carved claws. As I worked, I thanked Davis for announcing his intentions. He had given me the opportunity to prepare. I thanked him, and I cursed him for what he was forcing me to do.

It was good that Byrdie had gone home. I missed her more than I wanted to admit, but her presence would have made this thing very difficult. There was no place to run, and there was no help. If I ran, it would be forever. Seeking help was as bad as running. Davis would always have another night. If he came, it had to be finished. One way or another, it had to be finished. I looked at my work. I had a fine pair of gauntlets.

I spent the remainder of the afternoon and evening trying to look as if nothing was out of the ordinary. At dusk, I sat on the porch with a puro and Flor, and then, under cover of darkness, I set the trap.

I thought for awhile he wasn't coming. It was late, and the lights had long been out when I first heard, then saw a shadow moving stealthily up the path from the river. I had guessed correctly. He wouldn't want to be seen coming or going. I watched him stand by the porch, waiting. Perhaps he was listening for sleep breathing. I hadn't thought of that. The silence might make him suspicious.

He began to back away, and I thought he was going to leave, but a short distance from the steps, eerily like the tiger, he stopped. He seemed to gather himself up, and then he charged. The door gave way to his shoulder. I heard the machete clang against the junk I had placed in the bed, and I turned and walked down the path. There was a tree with a limb that hung over the trail at just the right height.

I hadn't long to wait on that limb. In near total darkness, there was enough starlight on the runway that his silhouette was clear. There was no light where I perched. Now he knew. He looked side to side as he came, perhaps hunting me and perhaps fearing me. It didn't matter, and I would never know.

I dropped. I heard the air rush by as I fell. I felt and heard the gauntlets strike his collarbones even before my feet hit the ground, and I heard bones break with a dull crack. Two quick slaps with the claws slashed his face, and he screamed. He was helpless. He was blinded, and with broken collarbones, he couldn't raise his arms to defend himself. The scream was like the sound an animal makes when it knows it is going to die. As he screamed, the claws went deep into his belly, and I slashed down from the ribs to the groin. It was done in less than three seconds. The thing was finished. Davis Morales lay on the ground, gutted. I stood over him for a moment, thinking nothing and seeing only a vaguely human shape. I couldn't see the wounds, but I could smell blood and the distinct, indelible smell of mammalian entrails. Few but hunters and warriors know it. I stepped away. Everything in the bush would smell the same things I did, and some would come for their share. I walked home with my heart pounding so hard I was sure it could be heard in every house in Karawala.

The gauntlets went into the fire, and I went into the shower with a medio. I showered with my clothes on until I was sure there could be no blood left, and then I showered for myself, but I could still feel the blood, and my heart would not stop pounding. Waves of nausea were followed by sorrow. Davis was no longer a threat, but at what cost?

I was still awake when the light began to grow. Davis had done such a job on the sheets that they had followed the gauntlets into the fire. I could only imagine his fury after the first blow had told him I wasn't there. I did not want to think about what he felt as he died.

It wasn't long after daylight before the commotion started, and shortly after that, I heard Eddie's voice.

"Mr. Bet?"

"Hello, Eddie."

"Can come out?"

"Sure. Give me a minute."

I opened the door. Abanil was with him, smiling. "You never fret about Davis again," he said.

"Oh, Abanil, I don't fret much about him."

"He dead."

"What?"

"He dead. Tiger did catch him on the road."

I feigned surprise. "What are you talking about?"

"Must be he was coming here, like I said, but he never reach. Tiger did catch him. Come look see."

I did not want to look, and I wasn't going to. "How do you know it was a tiger?"

"We see it before. We know the sign. Is tiger, sure. Come, now. Look. Soon they going wrap him up and back him off."

"Thank you, Abanil, but I'll take your word for it. I've seen all I want to see of Davis, even if he's been eaten by a tiger."

"No, not eat. Claw. That tiger bad fella. Kill and not eat."

Eddie didn't have anything to say, but I could tell he wasn't convinced about the tiger. He had never looked at me so directly or without a trace of self-consciousness.

Someone called, and they turned. "Okay, then. We going."

"Okay, Abanil. Okay, Eddie."

I stepped back into my house and stood watching. People ran to and from the path. Children came to see the corpse, laughing as they came and silent as they left. Others came, but everyone was silent as they left. Finally, I saw four men carrying Davis Morales, wrapped in a sheet, to the village. The last of the curious followed.

The next time I walked that path, there would be no trace of the blood. The ants would carry every bloodstained grain of sand down into the earth, and it would not take long to do it. I would not even look. I would let Eddie or Ferlan tell me where it happened, and only then would I look at the ground where he fell. I don't know what they would have thought if I had told them I had done the deed. They might have said I had no choice. They might have said he deserved it. But I would never know, because a tiger killed him, and that's exactly how it should have been.

Davis would be in the ground as quickly as they could build a box and dig a hole. Bodies are not embalmed in the bush, and bodies that have been ripped open tend to become offensive more aggressively than mourning should allow. Word would reach Orinoco long after burial.

Even before they could dig a hole, the rumor started. It took days to get to me, but it started when they carried Davis from the path, and before the sun set, everyone in Karawala knew it. Everyone but me. The tiger couldn't kill me, so now the tigers protect me. Davis had come to kill, but a tiger had stopped him, and a tiger would stop anyone who came to harm me. Davis had come to kill, but instead had increased my security along with my fondness for mythical tigers.

The people of Karawala believed with absolute faith in their myths. They could not distinguish myth from reality. One can hold a lightning ball in the hand as well as one can hold a rock. I had murdered the man who came to murder me. I set an ambush for him, and in the dark of night, I took his life. And the next day, the people of Karawala added to my mythology. It made me more vulnerable than I had been before. Believe as they did, the tigers would not protect me, and believe as they did, the people of Karawala wouldn't either. The only people who could help if I needed saving were likely to watch me die because they thought I was protected.

There was no end to the way things bent back around themselves. The rainy season was upon us, and I felt the need to feel West Texas limestone under my bare feet. I wanted to trade, if only briefly, this place where the absolute could not always be contained, for the places I knew absolutely. I needed the desert. I needed to go from wet to dry. The sharpness and clarity of

Karawala was beginning to blur. At times I thought the things I saw might be less real than their appearance, as if I could touch, but not hold them. As if the people could speak without voices. As if I was disappearing. The tigers were there. They were real, and they really were protecting me, if only by discouraging other threats. But there was something else, somewhere in the distance, that could kill all the tigers.

I wasn't in a hurry. I wanted to see their reaction to the death of Davis Morales. I wanted to see it in Karawala, and I wanted to see it in myself. If I be honest, there was becoming less Karawala and more me. Part of the blur was the probability that everything I saw in Karawala was of my own creation. Was it not at all what I saw? Had I really killed Davis Morales? I listened less to the sounds of the night than to the voices inside, and although not frightening, they were distracting.

I lay on my back and asked the night why I wanted to leave. The territory here had suddenly become unfamiliar, and things were boiling up from the unknown to bring to life every shade of hell ever imagined. Always at the end of every thread, I led myself back to the inexorable certainty that my imagination was capable of all creation. My adventurous spirit kept itself entertained by creating a world that kept my heart pounding and my mind intrigued by the line between imagination and reality. The line was thin and nearly invisible. Every time I thought I had it, the damned thing would move.

They put Davis in the ground, and everyone went right back to whatever they were doing before they found him. Death strikes as deeply into the heart of the Miskitu as it does the more sophisticated. The difference is that they know how to mourn. They can mourn so profoundly that they can get it over with before it is time to go out and get another day's subsistence.

But I did not hear mourning throughout the night. I did not hear long, heart-rending wails of grief and sorrow pierce the dark silence. They did not go to a grieving place and cover themselves with bedclothes so that their sorrow could be expressed to each other in anonymity. The bell in the Moravian church did not toll. Karawala would have mourned more for a lost dog, and try as I did to convince myself that I should feel guilt, I did not. I knew that something of myself should have been buried with Davis, but I felt no loss. There was nothing missing. I was intact and alive. Davis had made a fatal mistake. If anything, I was entitled to resent him for involving me in his death.

A few days later, as I packed, Leopoldo and Abanil came calling. The word was out. I was going to Texas, and everyone in Karawala would want me to bring something for them.

"Mr. Bet, you leaving off soon?" Leopoldo asked.

"Yes, I am," I answered. "I'll be going to Bluefields tomorrow, and then Managua, and then Texas."

"Plane coming?"

"Not this time. Eddie will be taking me."

"We can catch a pass with you?"

"Leopoldo, if I took everyone who wanted to go with me, the boat would sink before we left the wharf. There will be a pass soon enough."

They were disappointed, but there would be many more before the day was out. "Haps to we going report on Davis to the Guardia."

Official business. It might be true, and it might just be a ploy. The local Guardia had a telegraph. The report was probably filed the day they found him.

"Okay, Leopoldo, Abanil. But Eddie is going to come back the same day. If you can't take care of your business quickly, he'll have to come back without you."

Big gap-tooth grins spread across their faces, and they turned and left.

NORTHRUP

Chapter Thirty-three

Yawanaiska Pura Matawalsip Pura Yumhpa

I continue to be amazed by those who are enslaved by their intolerance and bigotry. Because such an affliction could not be willful, I must wonder whether it is like a grotesque birth defect by which one is born without the part of the spirit that would make him human. It is as sorrowful as being born without eyes.

From the Journals of McBeth Johnson

Sunny was not in town. It takes most of a day to go by boat from Karawala to Bluefields, and it isn't worth it unless Sunny is going to be at the other end. Most of it is nothing but blistering sun and salt spray down eighty choppy miles of Laguna Perlas and some rivers. One arrives with burnt skin encrusted with salt, chapped lips and blurred vision. A rest stop in Orinoco was out of the question. They knew why Davis went to Karawala, and they knew he was buried there. I was through with Orinoco.

And for this trip, I was through with Bluefields. Instead of a night at Sunny's with good food and wine, there was a single bed in a cramped room at the Del Queto. I shouldered my saddlebags and walked up the hill.

Cold beer, shower, cold beer, nap, dinner. The dining room was dark when I walked in. At first glance, it looked empty, but as I moved toward a table, I heard, "Good evening, Mr. Johnson."

It was Mr. Jordan, sitting in the gloom by himself. I smiled and joined him. "Mr. Jordan, it is very good to see you." He was wearing a white suit, and I wondered if he had anything else.

"And I am happy to see you. This business with Davis Morales has made me very curious."

"Mr. Jordan, you surprise me. What do you know about Davis Morales, and how do you hear about something so far away?"

"I know that Davis did not like you."

"Then you know he is dead."

"Yes. They say a tiger killed him in Karawala. They say he was on his way to see you."

"That is what they say."

"Did a tiger kill him?"

"They are sure of it."

"That is not what I asked."

"I didn't see him. I couldn't say."

"Very well," he smiled. "I only hope for time, so you will tell me how you did it."

I started to protest, but he dismissed it with a wave. "As for how I know, I know by the voices that talk to me."

"Word of mouth is nothing but rumor. If I tell you something, and you tell someone else, the third person will not hear what I said."

He smiled. "I, myself, might not hear what you say. I have seen many men speak whose words had nothing to do with their meaning."

"Then you might agree that what you have heard about Davis Morales could be unreliable."

"Yes. From all from whom I have heard." He nodded at me, as if to assure me that I was included in the set of the unreliable. "It is possible that my own eyes and ears are unreliable, but I do not think that is the case. I am old, but I am a good observer, and sometimes a story is too implausible not to be true."

I was on notice that he thought I had killed Davis. And if he thought so, so did the person who told him, and so did, I assumed, most others. But why? It could be nothing but an assumption based on a mythology created by a people who craved something of mythical proportion to replace a wretched condition. It could not be both that the tigers protected me and that I killed Davis unless in their minds the two could exist together without exclusivity.

Our dinners arrived. Once again I was reminded that there can be a place on earth with an abundance of fresh seafood and a complete absence of those who know how to prepare it. I sighed.

"Yes, I know. But I am accustomed to it. If we can't have it prepared properly, at least we know we have the best. We can have the worst cooks and the best seafood and still have the best seafood. Like having two stories and both be true."

"Mr. Jordan, you are an amazing person."

"Thank you. Eat. And accept my apology for being far too serious. No one has tears for Davis Morales, and, I fear, no one will have tears for me."

"You are correct in the first place, but I hope I have time to prove you wrong in the second."

"Some who are here tonight will never see the sun again."

We did not talk about much, but it was enough to make me stare at the ceiling far into the night. To look at him, one could only see an old, frail man, but to talk to him, one heard a lithe and nimble mind. Like having two stories and both be true.

A carpenter began making lobster pots outside my window when the dawn gave him enough light to see what he was doing. Roosters crowed and dogs barked. If I was ever again to sleep during daylight hours, it would have to be in a cave.

The place was crawling with Guardia when I walked into the Lobby. A sheet covered what had to be a corpse on the floor.

I skirted the wall until I came face to face with a young soldier. I had no choice but to engage him. "Quien es?"

"Sr. del Queto."

"Como?"

"Una bala a la cabeza." He was nonchalant, as if a man had no more value than a beef, and his manner of death was not important. A bullet to the head was a casual event.

He let me pass, and I walked out onto the veranda gasping for air as I cleared the entry. I grasped the rail and drooled nauseously into the foliage in the garden. It wasn't that he was dead, but that I knew why, and knowing why, I turned and looked up the street toward Mr. Jordan's house. More Guardia on both sides of the street, and from the house, soldiers carried another body wrapped in white. It was A. L. Jordan.

"You beginning to think this is getting rough?"

My gut hardened involuntarily, and my expression turned into a snarl even before my eyes snapped to the source. Northrup stood at the end of the walk with a contemptuous sneer on his face.

"What kind of chicken-shit coward would murder a feeble old man?" I meant it as an accusation, and he couldn't have taken it any other way. I was enraged, and it took all of my control to hide it. I wanted with every ounce of my being to close the distance between us and take him to the ground, but I was outnumbered, and I could not yield to the urge. There were too many guns on the street.

"I don't like you, Johnson, and I don't know why. Maybe it's because I think you think I'm an asshole. Maybe it's just because Stone likes you and he makes me puke. But just because you're an American, I'm going to tell you that you should get out of here before we carry you out. The tigers can't protect you."

"Why did you kill them?"

"Like I told you before. They are the enemy. They don't have to be a threat to be a target. They just have to be on the other side. It's the same for women and children. Remember 'Nam?"

"What side were they on? What makes you think they were the enemy?"

"Believe me. They were Sandinistas. Communists. You would have been the first they killed."

"Horse shit."

"Get out or join Morales with the maggots." He turned and walked up the hill toward the Guardia station. I was left with a searing hot pain in my belly.

I detested the notion that he might think my departure was his doing. I was on my way out by my own volition, but now it would look like he chased me out. I could hardly think for the hate I felt for Northrup and the sorrow I felt for his victims. I had no particular fondness for del Queto, but I genuinely liked A. L. Jordan, and I think he liked me as well. There was a rancid smell in my nostrils and the taste of bile in my mouth.

The fumes from the engines of the old DC-3 did nothing to help, and when Northrup got on and took the seat behind me, I came unglued. I was standing over him before he knew I'd moved.

"Things change in the beat of a heart, Northrup. Now you don't dare move, because the slightest twitch will end you. There are no tigers. There is only me. Reach for your weapon, and you will die as you touch it. Lunge at me and you will never leave that seat."

He was silent and still. I let my words soak in before I spoke again. "The only safe place for me is across the isle from you, and that's where I'm going to sit, and you are going to be quiet all the way to Managua. All the way, you're going to think about how fast things can change. The doubt in your mind about yourself and about me will keep me safe. And as we sit here together, ask yourself how it is that I can live alone in the bush when you have to surround yourself with hired guns."

I sat. He stared at the seat back in front of him and didn't speak. He was not afraid, but he was not a threat, either. For the moment, neither of us was a threat to the other. My question was the echo of others. It was a bluff, but it made him think.

Why is it that violence is so sharply focused and the transcendent so diffused? The clarity of the moment was as sharp as broken glass. Does shared hatred make a bond? My resentment for Davis was waning, but in its place grew a greater resentment for Northrup and a dark foreboding of everything he represented.

Somewhere north of Rama, where the tops of the trees look like an unbroken field of broccoli, he leaned into the isle and spoke above the noise of the old rotary engines. His voice was calm and lacking in the venom I was accustomed to expect from him. "You could help us. You could help your country."

"I could help you murder my friends? Would you have me pull a wagon loaded with body bags?"

"Your friend was up to his nose in revolution. Without his influence, there would be no hope for rebellion on this coast. They don't like the Sandinistas here, but they crave independence. The only way to keep Somoza in power is to keep the Miskito Kingdom from using the Sandinista revolution as a way to declare independence. I tried to convince him to wait. I begged him to back off."

I didn't respond. I sat and thought about what he was trying to tell me. Was it a con?

"You're telling me there is going to be a revolution, and you don't know which way it's going to go."

"I didn't say that."

"You used different words, but that is what you said."

"You can be sure that there is a very strong movement in this country to get rid of Somoza. You can also be sure that the United States government, for the moment, wants to keep Somoza in power."

"That's where you come in."

"That's where I come in," he agreed.

"And it doesn't much matter how you do it."

"I am not a diplomat."

"What do you mean, 'for the moment'?"

"The bleeding hearts and the reporters are pushing the notion that Somoza is an iron-fisted dictator and the Sandinistas are poor, mistreated nationalists. They have Jimmy Carter's ear."

I laughed. "They have the first part half right and the second part all wrong. Somoza isn't the good guy, but he's a long sight better than Ortega and Borge. If those dogs gain power here, this country is gone, and so am I."

"If Carter pulls the rug out from under Somoza, he will lose."

I didn't answer, and Northrup seemed content to sit in silence. Grudgingly, I gave him the respect due someone who was open about his intent. He might have been a killer, but he wasn't a liar, and that was worth something. It wasn't enough to make me like him, and it was a little like admiring the fangs in a rattlesnake, but it was something. I knew where he stood.

Nothing else was said until we touched down in Managua and taxied to the LaNica pad. "Where you going?" he asked as we started down the ramp.

"I have no need to tell you. Stay where they need you and forget about me."

"We have ways," he said.

"I know you do, and so do I. I'll make a deal with you. You take care of me in your territory, and I'll take care of you in mine. You live and I live. Win – win situation."

"I'll think about it."

"That means no deal." I walked away. He didn't speak again, and I didn't turn to see what he was doing. He wouldn't shoot me on the tarmac with all those witnesses. I hadn't thrown down the gauntlet, but there was more than a suggestion that he should keep his distance. He couldn't be sure that the tigers were not real. I knew, and I knew that there wasn't always a warning. I knew that if there was no warning, one could go to sleep and never wake up. Knowing that the gene pool requires survival, why would anyone be the first to declare his hand?

There are no butterflies in Managua. There is only dust and trash and all manner of life in various stages of starvation. The stench from the earthquake was gone, but the devastation lingered. Children with distended bellies were oblivious to the flies on their faces. Their eyes were vacant. Their mothers and fathers were gone. The Sandinistas would not change that, and neither would Somoza. Their guns were more important. For the Sandinistas, it was the fervor of revolution and the conquest of Somoza. For the Somocistas, it was the defense of the government. The children were on the street, and because they could be of no help to either side, they were as stray dogs to both.

I took a taxi out to Willy's place to have a beer and find out what he thought of all the talk about revolution.

"Oh, there is already a revolution," he said as he handed me a beer. "It just hasn't gotten to us yet. But it will come. It will be in Managua, and it will be in Karawala. We'd better start thinking about how we're going to get out of here."

"You think it's going to get bad."

"Somoza either won't or can't control his lieutenants. Amorette gets more murderous every day. It's like he's posturing for the reporters."

I remembered what Northrup had said. 'The reporters are pushing the notion that Somoza is an iron-fisted dictator. They have Jimmy Carter's ear.'

"Amorette is cutting his own throat. If that's what he's going to show them, then that's all they are going to want to see. It proves their point." I felt a sinking feeling. Coronel Amorette was giving Carter a bona fide reason to end our support of the Somoza regime. He was being shown only half the picture, and by the time he saw Castro and Brezhnev standing behind Ortega and the Sandinistas, it would be too late.

"You think Carter is going to pull out?" I asked.

"I think he's been wanting to for quite awhile. This is his excuse."

"How could he think it won't fall to the communists?"

"He knows it will fall to the communists. You think he listens to reporters? He's not that stupid. He doesn't listen to those jackals in the embassy, either. They know less than the reporters." He smiled and chuckled. "We've got one bunch that never leaves the embassy compound, and they are sending information to Washington, and we've got another bunch that never leaves the hotel bar except to follow Pepe Amorette around, and they are telling all America what's going on down here. It couldn't get any worse."

"So how do they get reliable information?"

"Guys like you and me," he said with a wink.

"What do you mean, 'like you and me'?"

"Come on, Beth, everyone knows you're a spook."

"Dammit, Willy, we've been through this before. I am not a spook."

Willy has the bushiest eyebrows I have ever seen. He looked at me from under them and said, "Sure you're not. Right. And you don't have any rank, either. That's why everyone here is afraid of you."

"This is ridiculous. The people in Karawala think I'm protected by tigers and the people in Managua think I'm a spook. I'm neither. Cut me and I bleed just like everyone else."

"So do we all. But no one knows anything about you, and Washington keeps telling everyone you are what you say you are. That's impossible. No one here is what they say they are. You've got deep cover. You live alone in the bush and answer to no one. That's fearful."

"Northrup isn't afraid of me."

He threw his head back and laughed heartily. "Northrup is a loose cannon. He thinks he's the best there ever was. If the press really wanted something juicy, they'd follow him around instead of Amorette."

"What's he doing here?"

"He's an advisor."

"What are you doing here?"

"I'm your pilot."

A car pulled up. The engine stopped, a door shut, and there came the sound of footsteps crunching gravel. Both of us sat up. This was unexpected. I went to a window, and Willy went to the door, not out of fear, but as a practical matter of caution.

"Stone," he sighed. The door opened before there was a knock.

"Hello, Willy."

"Come in, Halley. Say hello to Beth."

"Hello, Beth. What brings you to this side?"

"R and R. My buttons are rusting."

"Everyone else goes to Karawala for R and R. You didn't come to the asshole of Central America for R and R. Where are you going?"

Recent events were beginning to close in on me. I felt as if I was talking to myself when I answered. "To the very opposite of Karawala. To a place so dry that rain can't fall all the way to the ground. To a place without trees, where the birds run along the ground hunting snakes and lizards. To a place where life is sacred."

"Uh-huh. You're going home to Texas," Halley said. "I was there once. Rocks, sand, thorns, gila monsters and sidewinders. You're damn sure not going to a party. I'd tag along, but I've got three more months to serve here before they let me out."

Willy handed us another round. "You're out of here in three months?"

"Not just out of here. Out of this fucking uniform forever, if Northrup doesn't kill me first."

"What's Northrup got to do with it? Just lay low for three months."

"I'm one of Northrup's tools. Either someone told him to use me up or he came by it all by himself, because he never lets me rest."

"Let me tell you a little about Northrup," I interrupted, "Something you might not have seen on this side. I just came from Bluefields. I had to step over bodies to get out of the hotel. Northrup's work. He killed two old men last night. Said they were the enemy."

How do you know it was Northrup?" Willy asked.

"He was there. He all but claimed the kills."

"I've known him for years," Willy mused. "I knew he was a hard-ass, but I thought he was an All-American hard-ass. I guess I'm going to have to find out about this guy."

"What's an All-American hard-ass?" Stone asked.

"I don't know. I guess it's someone with all the right motives. Someone who fights hard for principles."

"Not a blood-thirsty bully who thrives on conflict?" Stone asked.

"We have to have war," I said. "We can't let peace break out. We have to have the real thing to test our weapons, and we have to train our soldiers in live fire. If we have to have war, we have to foment war. That's Northrup."

"What are you talking about?" Willy asked.

"The absurdity of this thing. We're guiding this country into civil war when we could just as easily prevent it and improve the country at the same time. But for some unfathomable reason, we are going to allow and abet conditions that will plunge this country into misery. And the greatest tragedy is that we are going to inflict war on a people who have never seen it before. We're going to take it to Karawala."

"But we're not going to test weapons here or put soldiers here."

"No? Who does Northrup work for?"

"He's not here to fight."

"He's here to kill."

Willy didn't like what I was saying. I decided he wasn't too deep into our business deals. He was more farmer and pilot.

"I think we've lost control here, Willy. As long as we had control, it was in our interest to keep things running smoothly. We're losing control everywhere, and wherever we lose control, we dynamite the bridges. This revolution is just our way to dynamite the bridges here, and we don't care who the bridges fall on."

"I gotta get out of here," Stone said. "I don't have three months."

THIEF

Chapter Thirty-four

Yawanaiska Pura Matawalsip Pura Walhwal

All that I am and all that I have are transient parts of the whole. Steal what I have, and I will get more, even if you take it all. But none can take what I am. Take my life, but you will not have what I am. That is mine, even though a thief might become part of it. It cannot be taken. What does the thief leave that diminishes him so?

From the Journals of McBeth Johnson

I could not move. I was completely paralyzed. I was awake, yet still asleep, and I knew that if I could not move, the thing that was trying to turn me inside out was going to win, and I was going to die. I struggled, but consciousness would not respond. The icy hands of a wraith come to steal my spirit had its claws around my heart, and I could not even open my eyes.

The thing had done something to me to prevent my resistance. It had taken everything but my will to live and was dragging it out into the night to gnaw the last sinew of my existence. From somewhere deep within me came my roaring refusal to go. I have never heard such a sound come from a human being. It came as if from deep within the earth, with all the power of the age of the earth and everything that had ever lived on it. It was as if life on earth had refused to go.

My eyes opened, and my muscles responded. I sat upright in bed, the sounds of my challenge still reverberating against the trees. The light of day made me blink and rub my eyes. Only moments before, it had been the dark of night. Sounds to the east caught my attention, and even before I could turn to look, my gut tightened and the hair on my neck stiffened. And when my eyes finally found the source of sound, my heart sank, and I wished that I had let the wraith take me.

The swamp had been cleared and paved, and there before me was a used car lot. Harvey Friedman waved and smiled and offered me a great deal if I would take him snook fishing. He turned back to his cars and sang, "Daisy, Daisy, give me your answer do. I'm half crazy all for the love of you."

"Mr. Bet?"

"Ferlan?"

"Yessir, Mr. Bet. Have coffee."

The piam-piam were just beginning to cry. It was neither night nor day, but that time between each when neither reigned, when all life knew what was coming. It was dawn, and Karawala was as it had been the day before. The dreams seemed as real as life as I slept, but my waking self knew them to be ephemeral. So I hoped. There was always the chance that the wakeful world was no more real than the dream world. We just remember more of one than the other.

I walked to the big house and noticed that where there had been a stack of new mahogany lumber the day before, there was now nothing.

"Ferlan?"

"Right here, Mr. Bet."

"Where is the lumber I bought yesterday?"

"Can't say. Is gone?"

"I don't see it anywhere. Did someone move it?"

"Don't think so." He looked out where the lumber had been. "Sure is gone."

I poured a cup of coffee. "Take a walk through town, Ferlan, and see if you can find out anything."

"Haps to I going church first."

I had forgotten it was Sunday. "Okay. Go to church first. Someone knows where that lumber is."

Someone had come in the night and stolen my lumber. At first it was hard to believe, and I wanted to think it had only been moved, but that was nothing but a naïve hope.

Ferlan was gone a long time. I had plenty of time to sit and think, and my thoughts went to all the things I had lost and could not find. There came creeping into consciousness a suspicion I did not want to think about.

In a white shirt and blue pants, Ferlan came striding up to me and announced, "That lumber to Eddie house. It have your mark. Same count."

Eddie's house? Why was it at Eddie's house? I was slow to consider the possibility that he had stolen it. Not Eddie. "Thank you, Ferlan. If you see Eddie, tell him to come here."

I sat on the steps with my coffee, staring blankly at the bare ground where the lumber had been, and looked back. How many times had I thought I had more gasoline than was in the storage tank? When I asked Eddie, he always said, "No, Mr. Bet, we use that up."

I knew how much fuel the boats burned each day, and I knew how much should be in the tank, but it never occurred to me that I should verify what Eddie told me. I had always shrugged my shoulders and bought more gasoline. It was the same with hooks, lures and line. People would come to me and tell me Eddie was selling my things, but I always assumed he was selling things the fishermen had given him. I had complete trust and faith in Eddie, but at the moment I was feeling a bit uneasy at the prospect of betrayal. If it was true, it had been going on for years.

I was like a father to him. He had told me so. Who steals from a father figure? Eddie had the best job in the area. The work was hard during the season, but his income was immeasurably more than it was before I arrived. The people of Karawala were so envious of him, and everyone else who worked for me, that there was a continuous stream of schemes to dethrone him. Many of them involved his dishonesty in one form or another, and I disregarded all of them as nothing but jealousy.

I was sitting there in a stew of emotions when Narcisso Simong appeared from around the big house.

"Good morning, Narcisso," I said as he edged along the house. It was obvious that he didn't want to be seen here. "How is it?"

"Right here, boss." He looked nervous. "They send me tell you Eddie thief you lumber last night. They say now you know good he thief you all time." As suddenly as he appeared, he turned and left, taking a route that shielded him from view in the village. He had risked a feud with Eddie's family by coming.

My body ached; I felt ill. My mind rebelled against the treason but could not deny the obvious. I had been wrong about everything I had ever thought about him.

I was sitting at the long dining table when Eddie arrived. "You call for me?"

"Yes, Eddie, I did. Sit down." I motioned to the chair across from me. He sat. He seemed defiant, as if he knew why I had called him.

I wasn't going to mince words. "You took my lumber last night."

"No, Mr. Bet. That my lumber. I did buy it."

"That lumber has my mark on it. You took it last night while I slept. You will bring it back today." My voice sounded tired and distant, and in the brief silence, I wondered if I had said it or thought it.

"I not going do that," he said. It was as if he was taking a stand against me; challenging my authority and my ability to protect what is mine, and it was entirely uncharacteristic. Eddie is more meek than bold; more apologetic than defiant. But as he sat slouched in the chair before me, his demeanor was smug. It was a declaration that everything I thought about him was contrived deception. He was, after so many years, nothing but a thief and a liar. He was as perfect in his duplicity as I was in my self-deception.

We were the same as we had been the day before and the year before. He had stopped pretending, and I had stopped denying.

"Do you remember that lawyer in Bluefields? Santamaria?" I didn't need a response. "He told me this would happen. He told me to send a message when it did so they could pick you up and take you to Bluefields, where they could punish you properly, I believe is the way he put it. I guess I need to take a little walk to see the Guardia."

The people of Karawala might not be idyllic and free of vice and avarice, but they are simple. They don't think even one move ahead, let alone three, five or seven. The mention of the Guardia was a little jolt, and it was one he hadn't considered. He had trusted my denial – my self-deception. The possibility of a response or confrontation was not a consideration.

He winced. He was trapped, and so was I by what he had done. He knew he was caught. I had a gaff through his jaw, and I was hauling him in over the gunnel. Too many knew, and too many would be eager witnesses. He began to squirm at the thought of the Bluefields dungeon.

I have never hated a moment more. I sat across the table from a man who had been with me every day since my arrival in Karawala – going on seven years. I had taught him the arts of angling and guiding. They were his way to the only affluence he would ever know.

I thought there had been a bond. I honestly believed that he liked me as much as I liked him. When he told me he loved me as a father, I believed him. He was sincere when he thanked me for all I had done for him. I never claimed to love him as a son, but my fondness for him was genuine, and I rewarded him well for everything he did for me.

The Guardia was too great a threat. It presented the possibility of imprisonment in a place that horrified all who contemplated it. The stories of Spaniards torturing Indians were more than most would care to endure for any end. Eddie capitulated.

"All right, then. I going. I bring the lumber."

"I think that's a good decision, Eddie. When you have it stacked where it was yesterday, we'll have another talk."

I watched him walk away toward the village and his house. The only thing I could think about was what he had destroyed. The lumber was nothing. I can buy more lumber. He had taken something far more valuable, and he could never bring it back.

I watched Eddie and his cohorts bring the lumber, board by board, until it was all stacked as it had been. With each trip they made, a little of the numbness wore off and a little anger replaced it. Then it was done, and the four stood before me.

"Georgie, Larry, Louie. Go from here and do not ever come again. I want nothing to do with you. Eddie, come inside."

I turned and went in. At the table, I turned. Eddie was still outside. "Come in, Eddie. You know what I'm going to say, but you have to hear it."

He came in and sat down. None of his defiance had been replaced by contrition. "I don't get it, Eddie. You have the best job on this coast. You have more money than anyone else. You make more in one week than most do in one year, and you have to supplement your income by stealing from me. Tell me why."

Nonchalantly, he answered, "What you give me not enough."

"Not enough? Not enough for what? By Karawala standards, you are wealthy beyond imagination. And what you get in tips...." I raised my arms in exasperation. "Tell me about the gasoline."

"I have to sell that to buy things for my family."

"And the hooks, the line and the lures."

"That, too."

"How long has this been going on?"

"All along."

"You fucking idiot. You don't work here any more. You're

415

fired. Get out and stay out." I pointed at the door.

He had not expected that. I can't imagine what he expected, but it wasn't being fired. Chagrined, he said, "Look to all the things are yours. Something gone, you get more. You never miss."

"Oh, Eddie, that's not it. You took my security and my trust, maybe all I had. Where will I go to get more of those?"

"I never take all. Only one-one."

"And you think your thievery is inoffensive because I have plenty."

"Not me alone."

"Not you alone? There are others?"

"All of we take some. Miss Pete, Teresa, Ferlan, Nelson...sure you must know."

"No, I didn't, and I can't believe you, because a thief is also a liar. How many times have I told you a thief is the scum of the earth? Did you think I was talking about someone else?"

"I don't study that."

"All this time, they've been telling me you are a thief, and all this time, I've been defending you, thinking they were liars. Get out. Do not come here again."

"You can never find anyone here to do my work. No one here know it."

"And where did you learn it? From me. If I can train you, I can train others. Last call. Get out or I'll throw you out."

I think he considered a challenge, but thought better of it. Slowly he rose and went out the door.

I watched him leave, as if he moved in a dream. When he was on the field, I went to the porch, and everything in me yearned to call him back. A fire burned between us, and a bridge crumbled. As he walked away, his affluence diminished with every step. Before me and after me became the same.

"Eddie!"

He stopped and turned.

"I did love you."

He stood and looked at me. I was not supposed to say that. It was not something one man said to another. He had no answer. Across that little gulf, we looked at each other. I said nothing more. He turned and resumed his walk home.

*

The match sparked and fizzled, and a tiny flame hung to the waxed-paper stick. I cupped it against any puff of air that might end it and willed the flame to grow. In a moment, I moved a tiny flame into the little pile of dry kindling I hoped would ignite the damp twigs piled around it. The kindling caught, and flames licked the twigs. Steam rose, and I put larger stems around the twigs. Within minutes, I was putting logs on a blazing fire.

The sun was gone. I sat by the little stove we had made in my first week at Karawala. It was the same stove that had made countless pots of coffee in the darkness before fishing. It was the same stove we had sat around countless nights with rum or casusa, telling stories. This night, in all the universe, there was nothing but me and a fire, and I was mesmerized by it. My purpose in life was to feed it. Its purpose was to consume itself and die.

I could not hear the sounds of the night, though they demanded attention as ever before. If death had stood behind me, I would not have felt it.

In the coals, I saw a pair of eyes glowering at me. "What do you see?" I asked. "I am not what you think. Believe as you may, but nothing is ever as it seems. What you think you see does not exist. You trust me to feed you, but I may rise up at any moment and douse you with water."

"Don't be absurd," said a voice inside. "Eddie's only fault was not obeying."

"You could not control him," said another.

Yet another said, "He was free of your rules - even your rules for freedom."

The beast in the fire was unimpressed. "The only absurdity is death," it whispered.

What I judged to be true was unimportant. My perception has nothing to do with what is real. Trust and betrayal are illusions. I blinked. For fear they were not there, I could not look up at the stars. I put another log on the fire.

*

I was sitting at the fire when the piam-piam began warning the night of the approaching sun. The birds knew the day was about to begin. I had not slept, but neither had I thought. I had only met the gaze of the beast. The stub of the puro was still in my fingers; an empty medio lay at my feet. The pile of logs beside the stove was gone, as would be the beast when the light began to grow. I felt as if something within me had been consumed by the fire, but it could not be identified. I was not myself. Eddie Wilson was dead, and Karawala was not where I thought it was.

I heard the day beginning in the big house. Miss Pete, Jane, Teresa and Ferlan were all there making coffee and watching my back for some sign of my disposition. With the first clatter, the beast vanished, and I was back in the world I had tried to leave, but it had followed me, and it had caught up with me, and it had proven to me that I could not have what I wanted. No matter what I wanted, I could not have it. There had been no magic in the night. I stood up and walked off to get my coffee.

"Is Eddie dead?"

"No, sar. He plenty live," Jane answered. "He planning ways to get you."

"You sit out all night?" Miss Pete asked.

"Look so," I answered.

"You not fright?"

"It did not occur to me that I should be afraid." I looked at each of them. There was nothing revealed in their expressions.

"Why should I be afraid?"

"The animal, them," Teresa answered. "And plenty bad people here."

No one had ever said anything about bad people before. "Mankind is the only animal I will ever worry about. How does Eddie think he is going to get me?"

Miss Pete put a cup off coffee and a bowl of fruit on the table in front of me. "He only talking big. Nothing he can do. All Karawala know he thiefing you."

"All Karawala. That means all of you, too. All of you knew, but none of you told me. Not even when I asked. Why is that, Miss Pete?"

"Oh, Beth, not my place. We can't make enemy here. Plenty people tell you."

"Yes, plenty of people told me. I would have believed you. And if you were loyal to me, you would have told me." I took a sip of coffee and wondered, again, why one could not get a decent cup of coffee in a country that claimed coffee as a major agricultural product. Maybe it was because I hadn't brushed my teeth. Maybe my entire sour disposition was owed to the fact that I hadn't brushed my teeth in the past twenty-four hours.

"Why no guesses here, Beth? No plane yesterday," Miss Pete wanted to know.

"There will be no guests this week, Miss Pete. All the talk about revolution has made some people think Nicaragua is too dangerous. The group that was coming this week has cancelled. You all have the week off."

"No danger here," Jane said, quizzical about why anyone would think so.

"I know that. Everyone here knows that. But the people in the States are watching television, and the only purpose of the news is to make people afraid."

"I don't study that, Mr. Bet."

"I know you don't, Jane, and I'm glad you don't have to. But if there's nothing to be afraid of here, why did you ask me if I was afraid in the night?"

"That different."

"That plenty different. You must go inside at night." The girls always had an escort with flashlights when they left after dark. They were fearful of the night to the point of hysteria. They would not budge from the big house without their escorts.

I changed the subject back to something I could get worked up over. "What does Eddie say he's going to do?" The one thing I love about mankind is that they make so much noise on their way to get you that you have plenty of time to get out of the way.

"Him say he going to the law," Teresa said

I laughed. If I'd had coffee in my mouth, it would have been sprayed all over the big house. "What!? The law? What's he going to do, give them a list of all the things he stole from me?"

"No, sar. Him say you owe him vacation pay for all these years."

It was too early for rum and cigars, but I considered it. It would not be long before it was too hot to sleep, but I decided it was worth a try. I told the girls and Ferlan to go home and enjoy the day. I lay on my back and stared at the thatch through the gauze of the bar. Vacation pay. I made a mantra of it. I heard it in my mind like echoing voices in a monastery. It became a Gregorian chant in a cavernous cathedral.

If Eddie Wilson could get vacation pay, then Harvey Friedman could have his used car lot.

GILL NETS

Chapter Thirty-five

Yawanaiska Pura Matawalsip Pura Matsip

There has never been a civilization on earth. Throughout history, there have been civilized individuals, but there has never been a civilization. Who can imagine a planet full of civilized beings that have not realized that we should not pollute our well?

From the Journals of McBeth Johnson

I awoke the next morning with a need to be out on the river. Brushing my teeth had not helped. Nothing had made any difference in the way I felt. Karawala had changed in the blink of an eye, and I had changed with it. My mistrust of people now extended to all people. I had believed that everyone was deserving of trust until there was a reason to withdraw it. It seemed now that trust would always be betrayed. No one could be trusted.

I walked the path to the river in darkness. As I neared the dock, I called to the night watchman. He responded by shining a light in my eyes. The only thing I had in mind was being away from Karawala for a few hours, but I put a fly rod in the boat just in case. I motored slowly down the Rio Karawala, past the village wharf and on to the Rio Grande. I hardly made a wake. I heard the sound of the motor more from the echo off the trees than from the motor itself. The air was still, and the water was a black mirror with the constellations sparkling in it. I closed my eyes and breathed the sweet essence of flowers. I watched fishing bats fly at the surface of the water.

It was getting light when I got to the big river, and I pushed the throttle forward. Just as I did, the prop hit something. It was a sound I had never heard before. It was not the bottom, and it was not a log. It sounded soft. I turned to look, but the light was still dim, and I could not see anything. I pushed the throttle again, and again, there was the same thud. And then I saw.

The prop had struck a tarpon - a dead tarpon floating belly-up. In front of me the growing light revealed the bellies of tarpon as far up-river as I could see. I shook my head as if that might change the scene, but daylight only clarified it. I headed west, upstream, toward Sani Warban. There was no wind. The river was smooth enough that every dead fish showed its belly, and I saw bellies as far as I could see. There were enough carcasses that my eyes and nostrils began to burn. Vultures had begun circling, and one had found a landing on a large fish.

I could not imagine what catastrophe had caused such a massive kill. I ran through the possibilities and discounted everything I thought of. Not chemical. No one on the river could afford pesticides or fertilizers, and if anyone had them, they were far too dear to risk a spill. Not an algal bloom. Not bacterial or viral. The system was too well balanced.

I looked closely at one of the tarpon. There was a deep gash in its head. Puzzled even more, I wondered what could have made it. On the next fish, I saw the answer. It wore a necklace of gill net. My questions were all answered in one moment of realization. Somewhere up the river, there was a boat, or boats, from Bluefields. They had brought gill nets with them, and they were giving them to the Indians, and they were buying snook from them. The tarpon, and everything not food fish, were pests.

Gill nets are entirely indiscriminate. They kill everything. The sensory systems of fish, as perfectly adapted as they are for a life in water, cannot detect a gill net. Stretched across a river from bank to bank, everything that swims becomes entangled and dies. If the purpose of the net is to catch snook, then all the other fishes are a nuisance, and the way to reduce the nuisance is to kill it.

As members of this human race, one of our moment to moment activities is categorizing everything we witness into right and wrong. I tried to convince myself that what I saw was wrong and perhaps even evil, but something stopped that thought and brought me back to the present. What I saw in the river was neither right nor wrong nor good nor evil, but was now.

I had missed the point. All this time in Karawala, I had glorified the notion of living in the now. I had watched a people that had lived not for the past or the future, but for and in the present. I had admired them for that. It had not occurred to me that they would occlude the future by taking everything the day could offer without leaving anything for tomorrow. It was all about taking everything that could be had in the energy of one day. The only way they could have a past was to use everything up and look back to a better time.

I sat in the boat and drifted. The tide was flooding. The boat and the carcasses were moving inland. I did not think about what this event meant to me. There were greater issues about, but this was one that could change the lives of all that lived by way of water on the Rio Grande. This was a moment in the annihilation of the future. Tomorrow, the fish will be gone.

My mouth was dry. My future was floating belly-up with the tarpon. No one will pay to fish where people are so openly contemptuous of life. No one will fish among dead fish, even if the fishing is good. The looming revolution hardly mattered in the face of the destruction of the fishery. These were not vandals who had pillaged in the night. They were commercial fishermen who had found a river full of snook. They would stay, and more would come.

I drifted past Sani Tingni. Crabs were finding the carcasses, but the armor of a tarpon denies them and most other carrion animals the pleasure of a meal. These fish would ebb and flow with the tide until they were flushed from the river, and then they would come to rest, washed up on the beach. Maggots and the bacteria of decay would stake the only claim on them. Tomorrow's dawn, and every dawn thereafter, would see fresh corpses until every snook in the Rio Grande had been frozen and shipped off to Florida.

I chuckled and shook my head. This is what I thought I had escaped. I thought I had left the voracious appetite of the United States behind me, but it dominates the globe. It reaches with its dollars into every faraway hideout on earth. There is no place too remote, too inhospitable or too inaccessible for the dollar, and there is no resource safe from plunder. We stop only when we have harvested the last one.

I could not be certain about what I saw floating belly-up in the river. Whose greed was it? How could I blame anyone? The fish were going to Florida and from Florida to all the other states. Those who ate these fish in Iowa would have no idea where they came from or what died to get them. Those who caught the fish were ecstatic to have the money they earned. The commercial fishermen were in the Rio Grande because they had caught all the snook near Bluefields, Pearl Lagoon and Puerto Cabezas. When there are no more snook in the Rio Grande, the commercial fishermen will move. When there are no more snook anywhere, the people in Iowa will eat some other kind of fish from somewhere else, and they won't ask where they came from. The people in Karawala will have no fish, and they will go hungry.

ALMOST THE END

Chapter Thirty-six

Yawanaiska Pura Matawalsip Pura Matlalkanbi

There is nothing permanent in Karawala. Not houses, not people, not river. I was the least permanent.

From the Journals of McBeth Johnson

"Yankee November One Papa Kilo, this is Yankee November Four Hotel Whiskey. Hello, Willy. Over."

"Yankee November Four Hotel Whiskey, this is Yankee November One Papa Kilo. Good evening, Beth. How are things in Karawala? Over."

"Gone to hell, Willy. The gill net boats are in the Rio Grande. Over."

There was a pause before he spoke. "We've got bigger problems, Beth. Over."

"If we've got bigger problems, I might not want to hear about it. No matter what happens, I'm through here. I have to cancel the rest of the season. There probably won't be a next season. What could be worse? Over."

"Jimmy Carter jerked the rug from under Somoza. No more money. No more bullets. It hasn't hit the news yet, but when it does, the Sandinistas are going to take the offensive. Over."

It was my turn for a long pause. That meant one and only one thing. The Sandinistas were going to win this thing. The nets didn't matter. "Okay, Willy. Come get me. Tell Byrdie I'm on my way home. Over."

"Uh, Beth, that's another problem. I'm grounded. General aviation is grounded. I can't fly, and the order might not be lifted. Somoza is shooting down everything that moves. I can't even get myself out. This place is exploding. Over."

Doors were slamming shut all around me. If I couldn't get to Managua, I was trapped. When the Sandinistas won, they would come up the coast from Bluefields, down the coast from Puerto Cabezas and down the river from Matagalpa, converging on Karawala. "Are the roads safe? Over."

"If I can't talk them into letting me go get you, you're stuck. I'm working on it, but so far I don't think they'll budge. Don't try to get to a road. Don't even try to take your boat to Bluefields. They'll blow you out of the water. Over."

"Sounds like I'm in a fix. Over."

"You'll find a way out. Gotta go, but listen for me. Same time. I'll call if I have something to say. This is Yankee November One Papa Kilo, signing off."

"Yankee November Four Hotel Whiskey signing off and clear."

Things can change in the blink of an eye. I was beginning to dislike blinking. South, west and north, I was surrounded, either by the Sandinistas or the Guardia Nacional, both of which would likely be shooting when they saw me. Only to the east, by sea, was there a possibility of escape. Still listening to local chatter on the 80 meter band, I got out my charts.

If I loaded too much fuel, I would be lugged down to hull speed; no better than six knots, and I would burn too much fuel doing that. But if I was light enough to bring her up on a plane, I wouldn't have much range. Where would I go, and how long would it take to get there? Key West was my first thought, but it was quickly discarded. It would take too many stops, several tons of fuel and a long passage too close to Cuba.

By a process of elimination, I settled on San Andrés, just 125 miles offshore, heading 100 degrees. Weather permitting, I could get there in nine hours or less from castoff at my dock, and 100 gallons of fuel would give me plenty to spare. The Mupi Tara could make thirty knots with a light load and smooth water, but at sea and full of fuel, she did good to make twenty. I used fifteen in my calculations.

If I went south to Costa Rica, I had to pass too close to Corn Island. The Guardia probably wouldn't be patrolling the area, but I didn't want to chance it. I would not have satisfactory answers to their questions. Going north, the Miskito Keys were treacherous and unfamiliar, and I would be navigating by less than dead reckoning. That, and Honduras might not give me a warm welcome.

My chronometer was an old railroad pocket watch, which was not as accurate as the path of the sun, moon and stars. My compass was good, but I could only guess at my speed. But in all that, I had more than the ancient mariners had. I knew where my lay was, my heading, and how long it should take to get there. Others have gone off without knowing any of that, convinced that the world is not flat and hoping they would not fall off. Radios and loran were last minute inventions and were unavailable to me. With luck, there would be clouds hanging above the island like a halo, as if there was a sign saying *STOP HERE*.

This is not the way I wanted this to end. I wanted to hire a manager for the camp and spend most of my time in Texas, raising a family and tending to Silas Johnson's spread west of Fort Worth. Now I was planning my escape, and it made bile rush into my throat. Jimmy Carter hadn't pulled the rug from under Somoza; he jerked it out from under me. He broke the dam that allowed the Sandinistas to flood my life. That son of a bitch!

I awoke in the middle of the night with my head on the table, radio still on. I turned it off and went to bed.

There are few things in my world that are dependable. The sun will come up and go down, the stars will wheel across the sky, and Miss Pete, Jane, Teresa and Ferlan, laughing and chattering as if the day would be the best they ever had, will always be waiting in the big house when I get up in the morning.

Teeth brushed and bladder empty, I walked in to get a cup of coffee.

Stirring sweetened condensed milk into instant coffee, I turned to Ferlan. "Ferlan?"

"Right here, boss."

"I might be taking the Mupi Tara out. Get Sherman. Mix two drums of gas and put them in the boat."

"You going far." It wasn't a question.

"If I go, I'll go far. Miss Pete?"

"Yes, Beth."

"I'll need some bread, soda cake, fruit and water. Enough for two days. Get it ready, please, but keep it here until I know I'm going."

"Where you going?" All of them watched me.

"Can't say yet. Maybe nowhere. But if I need to go, I want to be ready. Ferlan?"

"I going." He walked out the door and headed for Sherman's house. Miss Pete and Jane busied themselves in the kitchen.

I went back to my radio loft to think about what else I might need to put in the boat. It couldn't be much. Passport, clothes. Things I might take for a little vacation. I thought about guns, but they could only be trouble. If there was an encounter, there would be many against me, with nowhere to run, and a gun would make my end quick. It would be time to smile and deal.

When would I be safe? My course would put me over King's Key. The tiger is not a threat until you see its eye. So if it is not a threat, why worry? Once I cast off, it's nothing but a little cruise.

By sundown, I had everything ready to go. I got a medio and a puro and sat on the steps of the big house. I poured three fingers, lit the cigar and watched the colors begin to change. How many more times would I get to see this? Having left, would I ever be back? My future was as uncertain at that moment as it has ever been. I wasn't even sure I could make it to San Andrés.

When night fell, I started the light plant, went to the loft and turned on my radio. Willy had told me to listen. As much as I wanted to send out my call sign, I left the mike alone and listened. The night was full of chatter, but it was distant and dim. Anything in Nicaragua would be loud and clear. When it came, it was unsettling. From somewhere up the river, someone was warning that Sandinista soldiers had left Matagalpa, on their way to La Cruz. The message was brief, and then he was silent.

There isn't anything between La Cruz and Karawala but river. Alamikamba and Makantaca are on the way, but they might not slow down a military expedition if its intent was to capture a runway. Maybe the Guardia would stop them at La Cruz. There was sure to be a fight that would, at the least, slow them down a few days.

My sleep was uneasy. I was glad when the piam-piam began to cry, warning the world of approaching day. I had water on to boil for coffee before Miss Pete and Jane arrived. Not far behind them were Leopoldo, Abanil and Alonzo Knight. Alonzo was one of those who always managed to avoid work, yet always had more than most. He was a local politician, the Alcalde of the Community of Karawala. As I watched them approach, sipping my coffee, I knew why they were coming.

After pleasantries and the offer of coffee, Alonzo got right to the point. "We hear you leaving off."

"It appears that you would be correct, Alonzo. I had to cancel the rest of the fishing season." I leaned closer to him and looked him in the eye. "Someone gave the gill net boats permission to net the river. How much did they pay you, Alonzo?"

Leopoldo and Abanil snapped their attention to Alonzo. "What this is?" they demanded.

"We not here for that," Alonzo countered, trying to change the subject.

Abanil stood up, his anger obvious. "You take money from the captain, them, for you alone. You not going tell we?"

I had only guessed that Alonzo had taken something under the table, but it struck home. He was a cornered rat.

Leopoldo spoke. "You not have permission for that. You going take it back and send them off to Bluefields."

"No!" He was defiant, and at that, they broke into verbal abuses in Ulwa, a language reserved only for the Sumo. I didn't have to know the language to see that Alonzo was in hot water. Neither Miskito nor Ulwa has a word for gill net, but I heard it said in nearly every sentence. He had done something that would ruin my business, and along with it, every job in the area. The list of things they would lose was long. And he had sold the rights to something he didn't own. Everyone in Karawala was going to be pissed about both. Leopoldo sent him packing.

Mudi came in as Alonzo left. "I hear too much shout," he said.

Abanil laughed. "Mihtan ba taski."

I understood that one. It was in Miskito. "His hands are dirty."

They filled him in. "Hoopah," he said. "Karawala going be vexed." He looked at me. "Is truth, Mr. Bet? You going leave off?"

"I think so, Mudi. You know I always leave off after the fishing season. With the nets in the water, the season is over." I wasn't ready to talk about the revolution.

"You not fret about the Sandinista, them?"

I nodded. "I hear they could be a problem." Ready or not, there it was, and I suspected that was why they had come. Every time I left, whether for R and R in Costa Rica, business in Managua, or home to Texas, they feared that something would happen to me, and I would not return. The revolution wasn't a possibility; it was fact, and we were all at risk. If the war went well for the Sandinistas, it meant calamity for Karawala and for me. This time, I might not return.

"Where you going?" Abanil asked. "Too much gas for Bluefields."

"Like I said, the Sandinistas could be a problem, and if not them, then the Guardia. I'm going to avoid both of them, but I haven't decided where to go. Maybe Puerto Limon in Costa Rica." I lied, but I didn't want anyone to know. If they don't know, they can't tell.

"You alone?"

"Me alone."

"You know the pass?" Leopoldo asked, a bit doubtful.

"Oh, Leopoldo, it's an easy pass right down the coast." And it was. The border was one hundred forty miles south. In better times, a sailor would not have to lose sight of land. But I don't think they were worried about me.

They were worried about themselves, and the worry was becoming fear. They could not leave. They knew things were changing fast, and whichever way it went, it was going to go hard on them. My pending departure verified their apprehensions. I could blame the gill nets, but this was too sudden. It was an escape, and they knew it.

"Mr. Bet? Karawala going dead out?" It was Mudi. "Sandinista going kill we?"

A question came into my mind. *Could I help them if I stayed?* It was a serious question. Would leaving be a betrayal? No. Staying would be suicide. I would be their primary target.

"Mr. Bet?"

"Sorry, Mudi. I don't know what is going to happen. Maybe nothing at all. I've always thought the revolution would stay on the Managua side and that it wouldn't last long. Maybe that's true. But maybe it will overwhelm the entire country and drag on for many years. I can't say. I don't know. But it looks like the Sandinistas are gaining strength."

Depression and confusion were gripping them with such force as to be palpable. They were trapped, and though they were free to come and go as they pleased, there was no escape. They were as far removed from the machinations of despot and state as they could get, but those who would rule will rule all. If the revolution came to them, they had no defense. Their only option would be to flee to the bush and live with the animals until the soldiers were gone. They were like prisoners awaiting execution.

Being inconsolable in my own plight, I could not console them. We talked, and I tried, but they could see that I was not convinced. My own sense of doom amplified theirs until it became crushing. They left without knowing where to go.

That night I dreamt of an entirely defenseless village being slaughtered by opposing armies. The soldiers had no interest in killing each other, but were intent on killing every man, woman and child in Karawala. They encircled the village and set fire to the houses. Killing the men first, they drove them from one battle line to the other, gleefully gunning them down. The sounds of the guns, the crackling of the fires and the screams of pain and anguish were the torturous cacophony of madness. There was no other sound. When the women and children had watched the last man die, wretched with the pain of loss, the soldiers began raping them, and as they raped, their phalli turned to swords, and they gored their victims, ripping their wombs and piercing their hearts with every thrust. Blood gushed from the wombs and covered the soldiers, and the sight and smell and taste of blood aroused them ever more. Their eyes grew wild with lustful excitement. There was no silence until the last mother's breast was pierced by a bullet. The soldiers looked at their work and saw that it was good. And still tumescent, they began killing each other. Standing on the bodies of the dead, they slashed throats and lopped off limbs until none were left alive. Smoke rose from the smoldering embers of the village. Blood drenched the earth. The light grew dim and vanished.

I woke in a cold, clammy sweat and fled the bed as if it was full of corpses. I showered in the dark, and the cold water washed away the sweat, but it could not cleanse me of the dream. It remained vivid, not fading and then forgotten like dreams are supposed to do.

I stayed in my house most of the day. Byrdie's new house.

They knew not to bother me there. There was a vacant feeling, as if I had come to a place with no direction. I was alone in the void, and even the air seemed reluctant to fill my lungs. Sitting and waiting was not the answer. There was an urgent need to get away and an equal need to wait for Willy. I did not want to go to San Andrés. I would be a sitting duck out there. I wanted to fly to Managua, walk into the terminal, buy a ticket and board a plane. I didn't even care where it went.

But I couldn't stay. I decided that if Willy didn't make contact that night, I would slip out of Karawala under cover of darkness. That resolved, I sat on the couch and tried to read, but I turned the pages without seeing the words. I could not tear my mind away from the moment. Nor could I nap. I could only sit and look outside at the circle of cabins that had been my life for seven years. My plans were forever gone. With one decision, someone far away had changed my life forever. Is that why they call him the most powerful person in the world? That by changing his mind, he can change the world?

He is no more important than I. I got up and went to the big house. The girls were gone, but they left lunch in the fridge. I smiled. Green sea turtle. There is no finer meat in the world, and in all likelihood, I would never taste it again. They had been very thoughtful.

I looked up from an empty plate and saw Buldóser coming toward the house, an axe over his shoulder. He had worked for me when I built the camp and from time to time after that. He got stung by a tmisri once, and his arm had swollen so much that it stuck out from his shoulder, useless, but he had refused to stop working. He was afraid he would lose his job. Short, thick and powerful, he could work like a bulldozer.

I met him at the steps. In a bloody hand, he held a white rag, and in the rag were five toes. I looked down. The end of his boot was gone. I didn't have to ask. He had chopped his toes off with the axe and had walked in from the savannah to find me.

Holding his palm up, showing me the toes, he asked,

pleading, "Can fix?"

He must have been in pain, but it was not in his expression. He must have felt anguish, but the only thing in his eyes was the hope that I could repair the damage.

I put a hand on his shoulder and said, "Come inside, Buldóser. Sit down and take your boot off. I can help, but I can't put your toes back on."

He came in and sat, clearly disappointed. "But you fix Ferlan lip."

Ferlan had come to me one Sunday morning after a Saturday night of way too much rum and a bad run-in with a machete. His upper lip was split clear through in a long diagonal gash. I had sewn him up.

"Yes, Buldóser, I fixed Ferlan's lip, and the scar isn't all that bad, but toes are not easy. I can't do that."

"You fix Louie arm, and he bawling so."

"Louie's shoulder was dislocated. All I had to do was pull on it just so, and it popped back into place."

"But you the doctor here."

"I'm not a doctor, Buldóser. I have some medicine and just enough knowledge to be dangerous. All I can do is clean and bandage your foot."

He watched quietly, without a wince, as I did what I could. I asked a passerby to send Buldóser's family to help him home. By the time I was through, they had come. I gave him some antibiotics, aspirin and money for a doctor and told him to go to Bluefields.

"You can take?" his wife asked. "You always take."

"Not this time. The Guardia are looking for boats. Sandinista boats. I can't risk it." I looked at Buldóser. "Keep it clean and dry."

He nodded. They turned and left. I went inside to clean up the mess. He didn't know what I meant by *clean and dry*, and he wouldn't go to Bluefields. He was in for a hard time.

Miss Pete, Jane and Teresa came to fix my evening meal,

and when it was time for them to leave, they cried. I gave them each a hug and told them not to worry, but I couldn't have been very convincing. We all knew the end was coming. We just didn't know how it was going to end. Never again could we depend on tomorrow to be like today. It was a complete unknown, and the odds favored a bad day, and every day thence a little bit worse until the horror arrived. I did not say goodbye, but they knew it was. They knew that I would be gone when the piam-piam cried on the morrow.

I climbed to my loft and turned on the radio long before the appointed time. I could not afford to miss a message, regardless of who it came from. I sat and listened, but local traffic was silent. I heard nothing but casual conversations from other lands. And then it came.

"Do not use call signs. Are you there?"

It was Willy's voice. "I'm here."

"Look for a bird in the morning. Be quick. Do not key your mike again." And he was gone.

That was urgent. No pleasantries; no goodbyes. It was so quick I couldn't be certain it was Willy. When I answered, I was sure, but then it was over, and I wondered if I had answered a call for someone else. What if I stayed and no one came. What if a war bird gunned me down as I stood waiting on the runway.

I forced myself to believe it was Willy. I was packed and ready, and if not relieved, I was hopeful. I went outside and fired three rounds into the air. Silently, I apologized for the fright I must have given Karawala. In a silent world, a pistol shot is as thunderous as a bomb. Ferlan knew it as his call. When he arrived, I asked him to gather the ball players and have the field cleared by dawn.

"Plane going pitch?"

"I hope so, Ferlan."

For the first time ever, he looked into my eyes, but he had nothing to say. He looked, and I looked, but nothing could be said. I saw tears welling up in his eyes. He turned abruptly, and in leaving said, "Safe pass, boss."

From a boy to a man, I had seen him grow. House boy, deck hand, guide, first mate. Not a day had gone by without him by my side. He disappeared into the darkness. I stood for a moment, turned full circle, and whispered, "Goodbye, Ferlan. Goodbye, Karawala." I turned and went inside, crushed by a brutality I could no more understand than he.

I woke before the piam-piam, and when I stood, I saw lamps glowing in the big house. They would all be there waiting to see me off. All the guides, helpers and the girls were waiting. I had already said goodbye. I had said it to each of them, but they would cling to me until the Aztec disappeared. I threw my saddlebags over my shoulder and walked to the big house.

I opened the door and said, "Naksa," trying to sound cheerful. They answered, but it was a half-hearted reply. I had coffee and fruit while they talked about the smell on the river. Going to plantation was getting difficult. No one wanted to paddle up the Rio Grande through the stench, but, "Haps to, we going to." If they didn't go, they couldn't eat. Some of their plantations were close, and they could walk. Others were as much as forty miles up the river, at Wanka Laya. If they wanted fish, their major source of protein, they would have to go beyond the gill nets.

As if it was an afterthought, Ferlan said, "Eddie bawling all night."

"Where is he?"

"To home."

I let it pass. Eddie was the past. Most of it was a fond past, but the end was revolting. I could never come to terms with his deceit.

Just as it was getting light enough to see, we heard it. Everyone caught their breath, looked to the west and listened, until Ferlan announced, "The plane! The plane!"

With great relief, I said, "Time to go," and grabbed my saddlebags. Without a word, I stepped out onto the porch and searched the sky. There, where he was expected, was a light twin, not yet close enough to be identified. The sound had come to us long before the sight.

As always, he flew directly over the camp, banked to the north and disappeared. When he reappeared, he was on his downwind and the wheels were down. He banked again and started his final. Still nervous and looking for trouble, I walked across the runway. I was ready to be quick. The instant he came to a stop, I was in the door and buckled up.

"Mornin, Willy."

Without looking at me, he pushed the throttles forward to taxi downwind, his expression intense. As we approached the end of the runway, I saw a lone, sleepy soldier approaching. It was the radio operator. He would want our papers, and he would want to sign off on our flight plan, but before he did, he would want us to give him a little something for his trouble.

Willy saw him, too, and said, "We don't have time for him."

"He's got a rifle."

"He won't use it. He'll turn around and run back to his radio." With that, he spun the tail around, and without a preflight, started to roll.

Everyone in Karawala had come out to watch me leave. They lined the runway on both sides. Some smiled and waved; others looked forlorn. Willy swore at the pitcher's mound when we bounced over it. Abeam of the camp, the wheels left the earth, and I was separated from Karawala. I suffered a moment of anguish for all that might have been and all that was sure to come, and then Karawala was behind me. The sun had not yet risen, but the earth was awash in its light. I would be in Managua in time to catch a flight out.

When the gear was up and we were on course, Willy spoke. "Some Senator called Somoza and told him to get you out of here. He gave me three hours."

That explained the urgency. It was an hour and a half each way. But it didn't explain the Senator.

"Who contacted the Senator?"

"That's what Somoza wanted to know. I thought you must have gotten a phone patch through."

There it was again. He thought I could just snap my fingers and get a United States Senator on the line.

"It wasn't me. Which Senator?"

"How would I know? Probably your fishing buddy."

That made me laugh. I had never met the man before and hadn't seen him since, but everyone in Nicaragua thought I was chummy with a Senator. I chuckled all the way to Managua. How else could it look to people who assumed too much and were suspicious of everything? There was a spook behind every tree.

From the western slope of the mountains to the Pacific Ocean and as far north and south as one could see, there lay a thick, acrid grunge of smoke from slash and burn agriculture. It was on the Caribbean side, too, but not so thick that we could not see through it. Their only fertilizer came from a fire, but most of it went up in smoke. It was time to plant; if the winds did not blow it to the far corners of the earth, the rains would soon cleanse the air.

When we cleared the mountains, we lit up the radar at the airport. We also had line-of-sight for the radio. Willy called the tower to identify himself, but that didn't stop them from scrambling a jet. I got nervous when I saw that it was heading straight for us. What were his orders? Were we about to become a notch in some trigger-happy pilot's gun?

Willy changed frequency and casually bid someone a good morning. The jet was on us, turned and pulled up on Willy's wing before I had time to wonder what it was like to free fall to the earth, perhaps in a fireball. They saluted; they knew each other. I relaxed. We had an escort.

We landed and taxied to the Aero Club on the far east end of the airport. I would much rather have been let off at the terminal, but bureaucrats will have their way with you, not because they should, but because they can. They always want some of your money and as much of your time as they can extort, and the officers of the Guardia Nacional are as good as they come. There was a Pan Am Clipper on the apron, and I wanted to be on it when it left. Closing our flight plan shouldn't have taken more than a minute. In less troubled times, it would have been done over the radio while inbound. The lieutenant behind the desk made it a sport to process us as slowly as humanly possible.

In spite of that, I did get to the ticket counter on time, but the flight was full, and the standby list was long. I bought a ticket for the next day and rented a car. An overnight stay at the Intercontinental and a churrasco dinner at Los Ranchos would not be a great hardship.

I took the Bypass, a newly constructed divided thoroughfare laid with the ubiquitous pavement bricks made by one of Somoza's factories. It was lined with ramshackle buildings on bare earth, built by those dispossessed and displaced by the earthquake. It was a third world poverty that had always made me resentful. Human beings should not have to scrounge like scavengers to stay alive, and if we were human beings, no one would starve to death. But we're not, and they do. If Somoza was, indeed, one of the richest men in the world, thanks to the largess of our foreign aid, then the United States of America created this poverty, and our people maintain it by pretending it's not our fault. 'Mihtan ba taski.' I thought. My hands are dirty, and my outrage reverberates in a void.

The Sandinistas will distrubute Somoza's wealth to the people, they said, but I didn't believe it. Daniel Ortega, Tomás Borge and cronies would divvy it up amongst themselves, and the people would have nothing but battle scars and unmarked graves to show for it. For these people, it made not one whit of difference who won.

I turned onto Carretera Masaya and within a hundred yards heard the popping sound of fireworks on both sides. Then I heard a *kathunk* as a bullet went through the rear door and out the other side of my little rent car. Then there were more *kathunks* as bullets from both sides of the street riddled the car. I was caught in a crossfire, with the Guardia on one side and Sandinistas on the other. I jammed the accelerator to the floor and ducked, and I didn't slow down until I couldn't hear the popping sounds any more.

My neck was stinging. I reached back and felt it. It was wet. I looked at my hand. It was bloody. A bullet had creased my neck. I had been just one inch ahead of death. It was almost the end. I stopped the car and got out. First I looked for more wounds. Finding none, I looked at the bullet holes and wondered how I was still alive. The car was a mess. I should have been trembling, but the thought of returning it in this condition made me laugh. It wasn't even noon yet, and already my day was full.

Somoza's bunker was just past the east end of the Intercontinental. The bunker and the hotel were heavily guarded. I was safe, if only for the night. I parked the car and checked in. That night, when the rent-a-car agent was gone, I dropped the keys on his desk.

AISABÉ, KARAWALA

Chapter Thirty-seven

Yawanaiska Pura Matawalsip Pura Matlalkanbi Pura Kum

He would have left, anyway. You could tell it was eating at him, with her being there most of the time and he being here. Sometimes you could talk to him half the night and he wouldn't hear a word you said, and then he'd turn and say something that was completely off the wall. If there hadn't been a revolution, he'd have sold the place or hired a manager. He would have found a way to go to her.

Halley Stone

I watched the revolution on TV with Byrdie, in the safety and comfort of our living room in Texas. What they showed us had little connection with what was actually happening. The news media gave ideology to looting bands of thugs whose only notion of government was a mirror of organized crime. They were not fighting for anything more than the spoils of the victor, but to hear the reporters tell it, they were one and all making the ultimate sacrifice for freedom and democracy, and the glory of their struggle was nothing less than our own revolution against the oppression of England.

It was as far from the truth as you could get, but Jimmy Carter must have fallen for it. He jerked the rug out from under Somoza, and down he went. No sooner had Somoza fled to Miami than the wolves flung off their lamb's cloak and declared their allegiance to Marx. We had fallen for a decoy.

I was flabbergasted. It seemed impossible that any of those reporters actually believed the things they were telling the

American people. If they did, they were very naïve and gullible innocents who should have been covering a cake sale at a hometown church. They damn sure hadn't ventured beyond the bar at the Intercontinental to collect their "news".

There were no good guys in that revolution. Somosa's Guardia Nacional and Sandinistas alike took barbarity to the extreme. Rape, murder, pillage and plunder were the only motives; nowhere was there any vestige of civilization, and the notion that ideology of any kind existed on either side was laughably absurd. They were a people gone mad. Children were torn from the arms of their mothers and beheaded. Suspected sympathizers of both sides were dragged outside and gutted alive while friends and family watched in horror. The revolution, like all wars, was conducted by sub-humans against humanity.

It extended even to Karawala, where the people wanted nothing but to be left alone. The threats of the Sandinistas rang in my mind. "We will take your land and send you away." And what a familiar ring it was. The conquering of the new world was nothing less than the same refrain. The Stars and Stripes waved in the background, but never did they mention that we were there.

Night after night I sat at my radio trying to find just one voice from the network of Americans in Nicaragua. Siuna, Alamikamba, Ocotal, Rivas...all silent...perhaps forever. Or perhaps like me, waiting for just one voice to give the "all clear" signal.

I wanted to go back. I did not presume to think that I could resume business there. The cloud of war would hang over the country for years to come. I wanted to see Karawala. I wanted to see that they were safe: that the war had not come to them. And I wanted to know what, if anything, remained of my life there. I could not leave all those loose ends dangling.

I called the Central American desk at the State Department. I knew better. I knew they were no smarter than the reporters, but I had to talk to someone.

They told me what I wanted to hear. They said the new government would welcome me back. They said our capital and our trade would be necessary to rebuild the country. They said moderates were in control, but the names of Borge and Ortega, the most radical Marxists of the revolution, were among those in the new Junta. Only Eden Pastora, Comandante Zero, was truly a nationalist and a moderate. Not one of them had any love for the United States.

My need to return was greater than my distrust of my government. I boarded a plane for Managua.

The changes hit me like a heel driven well into the solar plexus. Managua was a captured city. Sandinista soldiers were everywhere. They were young boys and girls in fatigues with machine guns and hand grenades. They were children who had killed only recently, and now they were the police.

Before we rolled to a stop, I could see it, and a ball of molten lead rolled into my gut. I thought for a moment about staying on the plane and going on to Costa Rica, but that would not have answered my questions about Karawala. With great trepidation, I walked down the stairs to the hot tarmac, where soldiers glared at each passenger as he deplaned.

The crowds were gone from the airport roof. No one had come to celebrate the arrival of friends and relatives. The terminal was empty of civilians. There were only the scowling, suspecting eyes of the soldiers who occupied every office and every position. There were no smiles, no laughing voices and no children selling Chicle.

I had brought very little, but Aduana fussed over everything I had. The knife and matches were suspicious and very nearly confiscated. I had guessed well. The knife was old, rusted and dull. A good one would have been taken. I sharpened it that night.

Allowed entry, I found a cab and went to the Intercontinental. I knew I would be relatively safe there, and that I would find Americans there. It was late afternoon. The doors of the hotel closed behind me, and I found myself in a bubble without soldiers. It was the only place in Managua that seemed normal. I went straight to the bar, and without surprise, found it full of reporters.

Never have I gotten so much free advice. When it became known who I was and where I was going, everyone in the bar had to tell me what to do. None of them were very enthusiastic about my chances of getting to Karawala, and fewer about my chances of getting back.

Acting on advice I thought was reasonable, the next day I visited the Minister of Defense, for permission to fly to Karawala, and the Minister of Tourism for permission to resume my business. My Cedula de Residencia was not enough; I had to start over again with new documents that would allow me to live and conduct business in Nicaragua.

The offices were in the same places, but the faces were all new and not in the least cooperative. The new bureaucrats at the desks of the outer offices were people with accusing faces. The ubiquitous Russian AK-47, weapon of the Revolución, was within reach of each of them, as if bloodshed could resume at any moment. They were Sandinistas, and they made no pretense about welcoming an American. Only recently it had been their duty and pleasure to seek out and kill us. The new ministers had a smile, but it was their official duty to be pleasant. At both offices I received letters of safe conduct, permission to go and do as I pleased and a welcome that was not quite as enthusiastic as I had hoped.

Riding on the streets of Managua, it became evident that most of the American homes and businesses had been gutted and burned. At the bank, I was told that the Revolución needed my money more than I did. My account had been expropriated. I did not feel safe. It was obvious that I was not on friendly ground.

Most general aviation pilots were grounded. I could find only one that wasn't, and he didn't want to cross the mountains.

Before he agreed to fly, I had to double his hourly rate and assure him that I could navigate. Just great, I thought. My pilot was afraid to fly. No wonder he wasn't grounded; he didn't know how to get home.

It took most of the morning to file a flight plan and get clearance. Again and again, I explained why I wanted to go to Karawala, produced my papers and watched them huddle to read them. They took sport in slowing things down. If I had shown impatience or frustration, it could have taken days.

When we finally took off, I had the small satisfaction of having spoiled their game. I had been pleasant and cooperative, and I hadn't offered a bribe. Nicaragua had become a strange land. I was very careful not to offend or to break a law, lest I become the victim of zealous revolutionaries.

I remained stiff and uneasy until well after we crossed the divide. It looked peaceful enough. The canopy was still an unbroken field of broccoli with slivers of rivers running through it like mirrored veins. There was comfort in it, and I relaxed.

We left Wawasang to starboard, the last lone sentinel of mountain rising fifteen hundred feet above the trees. We crossed the Kurinwas, and I was in familiar territory. We crossed the Rio Grande, and the heat returned to my belly. My heart picked up its beat.

Our first pass took us over the wharf and the camp. There was nothing left at the wharf. The boat shed, the dock and the boats were all gone. There was no livestock on the runway, and on our third pass around, there was still not a person in sight.

My pilot asked if I wanted to land. I nodded and pointed down.

No one came to greet us. No happy faces; no children looking for candy; no, "So happy to see you, Mr. Bet." I saw faces in windows in the village, and I waved to them. They quickly disappeared.

I turned to the camp. The screen was torn from the houses. I climbed the steps of the big house and stood in the open door.

Everything was gone. The kitchen equipment, the tackle and the furniture were all gone. They had converted it into a school. I walked to the work shop. Empty. I took a deep breath and walked to my house. It had been cleaned out. Not one thing remained of all I had in Karawala. Not even a fish hook. The silence was louder than ever before.

I don't know how long I stood there looking at the emptiness. Time seemed to have stopped. I had not expected this. I had not expected anything, really, but this scenario was out of the question. It numbed me. The loss was absolute.

A sound caught my attention, and I muttered, "I suppose I'm next."

I turned and walked back to the plane, where I was quickly surrounded by soldiers. Seven machine guns pointed me toward the big house. Inside, I was ordered to stand while they sat surrounding me. Two of them sat at a table. I turned to face them.

They were all very young and seemed uncertain as to what to do with me. They had assumed I would never return, and having returned, I was an uninvited problem. I stood patiently while they conferred in whispers. If not for the guns, I would have taken on all seven of the little bastards at once. They had come to terrorize this village, and now they were looking for an excuse to execute me.

They demanded my papers. I gave them my passport, Cedula and the letters of safe conduct. The boy who took them couldn't read and had to ask his friends if any of them could. Two could, but it took them several minutes, lips moving over every word, to read two short letters. After a short discussion, their leader wadded them up, tossed them over his shoulder and said, "Those are no good."

A boy about sixteen years old said, "We will have to decide what to do with you." He was light in complexion and color. I wondered where he had come from. Only one of them was from Karawala. He was older, and he had never hidden the fact that he hated me. Now he was dressed as a soldier and held a gun. I had to force myself to appear calm, when what I wanted to do was vent my rage against these punks who had ruined every life for miles around.

"You have exploited the people of this place," the leader said. "You are C.I.A. You are the enemy. You must pay for your crimes."

He meant that I should die. My life expectancy was being compromised, but instead of fear, I felt an absolute clarity of purpose. It was not my day to die.

"Isn't it enough that you have destroyed everything I had here? Where are my boats? What happened to the cattle, hogs and horses that were here? Why are the people all afraid?"

"We earned what we took," he answered in anger. "We fought and died for it. We buried our brothers and sisters for it, and now it is ours. Everything that was Somoza's is now ours."

"Oh? Where is it? Where is your share? Somoza had nothing here."

I was going in the wrong direction. This was just making them angrier. I tried another tack.

"I could help, you know. There is plenty of room here for more camps. The Americans spend lots of money when they come. I could build a camp for each of you and put you in charge."

It piqued their interest. The Texas mystique was illuminating their greed. Not for a minute did they question my ability to come through. Perhaps there were spoils here for them after all.

"I could make you wealthy," I said to boys who had rarely had enough to eat.

I sighed and looked out toward the plane. A small group of Indians had gathered, their subdued appearance conspicuous. I knew them all, and I knew that they should have been laughing and talking, not standing cowed and silent.

I jutted my chin in their direction and said, "Those are my friends. Ask them if they were exploited."

After a few whispered words, the soldiers started calling them one by one into the big house to be witnesses at my trial. I was stunned, hardly believing what was happening. I stood amid the ruins of my life. The empty shells of my buildings were the only remaining evidence that I had ever been there. I was on trial, and my witnesses were terrified of my judges.

Each one met my eyes for only an instant coming and going. Otherwise, their heads were bowed and their eyes were on the floor. This could backfire, I thought. They could tell my captors what they wanted to hear instead of defending me.

Eddie was not in the crowd, but Ferlan and Mudi were there, and I saw Sherman, Dexter, Teresa and Jane. They tried to call people who didn't work for me, but at one time or another, nearly everyone in Karawala had been on my payroll.

To the disappointment of the court, I heard repeated, "No, sar, he help we."

The last one to enter was the parson, and he was not afraid. He spoke very carefully. "This man is not my friend. I do not like him. But he has made this a much better place. He gives us food when we are hungry. He gives medicine when we are ill, and he heals our wounds. He calls for the plane when we need a hospital. Many people you see here would be dead if not for him. And he does not ask for pay; he pays us for our work."

He looked at me and smiled. I nodded, returned the smile and said, "Thank you, parson."

The soldiers had tired of holding their weapons, and one by one had put them down. One had leaned his against the table within my reach, but I avoided the temptation to snatch it up until it began to slide. I reached out, reflexively, and took it. Before they could react, I was outside their circle and had an automatic rifle aimed at them. I had waited for a mistake, and this was it.

Their relaxation could have been terminal. I was the only one in the room with a weapon in his hand, and before they could move, I had them covered. But I could not pull the trigger. Nor could I trust them to let me go.

"Now I must decide what to do with you," I said with a smile. "I am going to leave, but I am not going to give you the chance to stop me."

Those gathered outside saw what was happening. I heard excitement grow in their voices. Sensing their willingness to help, I ordered the soldiers away from their weapons, with their hands up, and called to my friends to come get the guns.

That done, the boys were no longer soldiers. I ordered them outside, behind the big house, and told them to strip naked and get into the bush. They could find their clothes after dark where they lived.

Back at the plane, I found a group of smiling friends and one petrified pilot. I didn't have time to talk. I handed my weapon to Ferlan, who said, "We hide some things in the bush. Not good here now."

"I know, Ferlan. Don't let them frighten you. Throw the guns in the river."

There was some laughter and some crying. I looked at my pilot and shook my head. He would not get back in his plane, and I was not going to let anything impede my escape. If he was too frightened to fly, I would do it myself.

I met the eyes of each of my friends in turn, for the last time, and said, "Aisabe', Karawala." Each look was a death: a rending of souls torn forever apart. There was nothing to say. Everyone knew it was the end.

In unison, they responded. With a heavy heart and a lump in my throat, I climbed in, shut the door, flipped on the mags and hit the switch. The takeoff might be a little sloppy, but I knew I could get her into the air. I taxied, turned, ran it up and let her roll. For the last time, I saw Karawala men lining the field to keep the animals away, only this time there were no animals. As

I passed, I saw men cry who had never cried before, and tears ran down my cheeks.

It was easy. I lifted off long before I ran out of runway and cleared the trumpet tree by a hundred feet. In the air, I screamed. I cried like an infant child torn from his mother's breast and thrown into the fire. I cried not for what I had lost or for what Karawala had lost, but for the loss of their future; for the hell that would be inflicted upon them. I cried against the pain to come.

Without hesitation, I headed east, out over the Caribbean, and set a course for San Andrés. Any other course would have kept me in Nicaraguan airspace, and I wanted out of there as fast as I could go.

In my mind, I tortured and killed Sandinistas for what they were going to do to the Miskitu and Sumu. And I tortured Jimmy Carter for giving them victory in their revolution. But I had to admit that government is government, no matter where it is, and the similarities of them all eclipse the differences. This one was little different than the one before, or the one before it, and ours differs little from all the others.

Why is it so difficult to imagine a world of cooperation?

In sight of San Andrés, with a glide path that would put me close to the beach, I killed the engine, called Mayday, and ditched.

Made in the USA
Lexington, KY
11 June 2012